ALSO BY KYELL GOLD

Argaea Universe
Volle
Pendant of Fortune
The Prisoner's Release and Other Stories
Shadow of the Father
Weasel Presents

Forester Universe
Waterways
Bridges*
Science Friction*
Winter Games*
The Mysterious Affair of Giles*

Dev and Lee Series
Out of Position
Isolation Play
Divisions
Uncovered

Dangerous Spirits Series
Green Fairy
Red Devil
Black Angel (2015)

Other Books
In the Doghouse of Justice
The Silver Circle*
X (editor)

*Published by FurPlanet Productions

UNCOVERED

by Kyell Gold

This is a work of fiction. All characters and events portrayed within are fictitious.

UNCOVERED

Published by Sofawolf Press, Inc.
St. Paul, Minnesota
www.sofawolf.com

ISBN 978-1-936689-39-2
Printed in the United States of America
First trade paperback edition: July 2014
Third Printing: November 2019

Cover and interior art by Blotch

For BlackTeagan and Kenket
with affection and gratitude
for the life you bring to these stories

CONTENTS

Part IV

Part V

LEE'S GUIDE TO FOOTBALL

When I was seven, I had a bunch of classmates ask me whether I wanted the Devils or the Firebirds to win the championship. I didn't know what they were talking about. My dad liked football, but I liked stories, and I may have said a couple things I shouldn't have about people who liked to watch thugs run around on a field and hit each other. So while my mom was combing the playground sand out of my face and chest and tail, my dad started to explain football to me.

Even though I was still at that age where I wanted to be like my dad, I didn't have much interest in football. But with the championship coming up, he thought it was the perfect time to get me started. Whatever else he's done in his life—and I've run through the list more than once—he got me into football. So if you're one of those kids who likes chess and books, listen up, because reading this story you're in the middle of is like growing up in Nicholas Dempsey Middle School. You don't have to like football to get through it, as my dad told me, but it helps.

See, what I always hated about football was that I was bad at it. I'd only played one football game up to then, at camp. I didn't understand the rules. To me, it was just a stupid excuse for big kids to beat up little kids. What my dad told me is that football is actually like a chess game.

Hang on. Stay with me. Imagine you've got these eleven guys. Each one can move in a certain way. You want to advance your position (symbolized by the football) up the field, either by giving it to a piece and having him carry it forward, or by passing it to a piece down the field. The guys who line up right at the boundary are the offensive line—like a bulwark. Behind them stands the quarterback, and behind him the halfback (or running back) and fullback. They're the ones who will carry the ball if you choose to run it. Out to the edges are the speedy guys whose job is to run down the field and be ready if you choose to throw the ball: the wide receivers and tight end.

Your quarterback is like a queen (and believe me, more of them are than you'd think). He's the most powerful piece and he directs the offense. Wolves and lions make good quarterbacks, because they have this inbred pack mentality. The offensive line is like pawns: they only move a very short distance, and their job is to protect the queen. You get big, aggressive guys in there, like bears and boars, because they also have to move the defenders in such a way as to leave room for the running back to run through. This is harder than it sounds, but I'm not going to get into it. The tight end (yes, we've all heard the jokes) either helps block or runs a short way down the field to act as a receiver. Then you've got the running back and fullback, wolverines and horses most often, who are like the bishops: they have to move through the spaces cleared by the pawns. The knights would be the tight end and the slot receiver, who can either help defend or jump short distances down the field. And wide receivers are rooks, who take advantage of long open columns to run down the field. For all those last ones, you get deer, cheetahs, and foxes. And what you have to do with these pieces is design a strategy that will help you gain ground, program a series of moves in advance, and watch them go. Meanwhile, our opponent has his own eleven guys, and he's trying to figure out what your guys are going to do so he can stop them.

If you're defending, your aim is to stop the progress of the other team. This is the part of football I hated, by the way, because I could never tackle, and they could flatten me with one arm. The QB starts out with the ball, so you go after him. You look at the situation on the field, you look at the way the pieces are set up, and you set up your guys to hopefully disrupt what the offense is doing. Your defensive line, setting up across from the offensive line, is actually attacking, which is why the best ones tend to be large, fast predators, like big cats. Then you have a bunch of guys that stay behind the defensive line to mess with the wide receivers and tight end if they get back into that territory. The best ones there are medium-weight predators, like coyotes, bigger foxes, and cheetahs. And because it's such a big field, you have to decide things like do you assign one defender to each specific offensive player, or do the defenders just cover sections of the field, and so on.

And then, not to make things more complicated, but there's everything else, which is called "special teams." If a team doesn't move the ball well enough on offense, they end up kicking it, either to the other team (a punt) or through the goal, if they're close enough. Horses and rabbits, of course, usually do the kicking. On the other side, you need someone quick and slick to catch the kick and try to run it back, and while you get a couple rabbits who are good at this, the best ones have always been weasels and otters.

The thing that makes football more interesting than chess is that the pieces can actually think (well, some of them) and make decisions on the field. They know what they're supposed to do, but if they see something that'll block them, they can make an adjustment and change it. Sometimes they do really stupid things, which is fun, and sometimes they do amazing things, which is even more fun.

Also, I mean, it's guys in tight clothes. There are closeup shots of the quarterback sticking his paws under the center's tail (with some definite touching). There's muscles galore, occasional tail-grabbing, and after the plays, there's butt-patting. What's not to like?

Quick reference guide

This is an example of how the players might line up on the field.

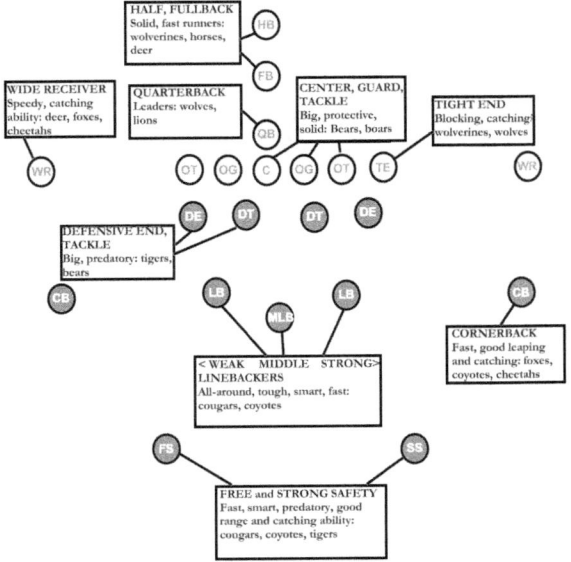

Dev's Game-Day Briefing

Okay, with Lee telling you what all the players are supposed to do, I can walk you through how an actual game goes. The teams flip a coin at the beginning of the game. Winner gets to pick whether they want to kick off or receive. To receive means you start on offense and have the first chance to score. But sometimes teams want to kick off, because if you start the first half on defense, you start the second half on offense. Also if you stop the other team right away on the first drive, it gives you a lot of energy going into your offense. The coaches all figure this out. I just know I liked being first on the field.

When a team gets the ball, they line up like Lee described. They get four chances to move the ball ten yards; those are "downs." So there's first down, second down, third down, fourth down. I don't know why they're called that, they just are. Anyway, on first down usually you try to run the ball. That means the QB hands it to the RB and he tries to get ten yards up the field. Actually, if he gets four or five, that's pretty good, and then on second down you might try to run it again. If you can get three or four yards every time you run the ball, you can just run it all day long.

The thing is, though, if you don't get your ten yards in four tries, the other team gets the ball. So most of the time you only take three tries, and if you don't get ten yards, you punt. Punting is where the punter kicks the ball down the field and the other team gets to catch it and try to run back with it. Basically you do that so that they don't get the ball at the spot where you didn't get your ten yards. This is called "field position," as in having good field position (near the other team's goal) or bad field position (near your own).

The other thing you can do on fourth down, if you have good field position, is kick a field goal. If you've gotten close to the other team's goal, but not actually into it, you have your kicker try to kick the ball through the goalposts (the uprights, we call the arms on either side), and you get three points if he makes it.

Once you get your ten yards, you get a whole new set of downs. This keeps up until you punt, or get a field goal, or score a touchdown by getting into the other team's goal. Or—this is where I come in—until one of your players loses the ball and the other team gets it. It has to be a "live" ball, which is complicated and there are lots of rules around it but essentially it means that the play isn't over yet. So if your running back drops the ball and I pick it up, or your quarterback is a crappy passer and I get the pass before his receiver does, then that's a "change of possession" and the ball belongs to us. We can run it back as far as we can on that play, then our offense takes over on the next one.

That's why I love playing defense. We get to be in on the big plays, the game-changing ones that "turn the tide," "shift the momentum," whatever you want to call it. There's nothing like the feeling you get when you get your paws on the ball as a defender. Nothing.

Not to say there's nothing better. Just nothing like it.

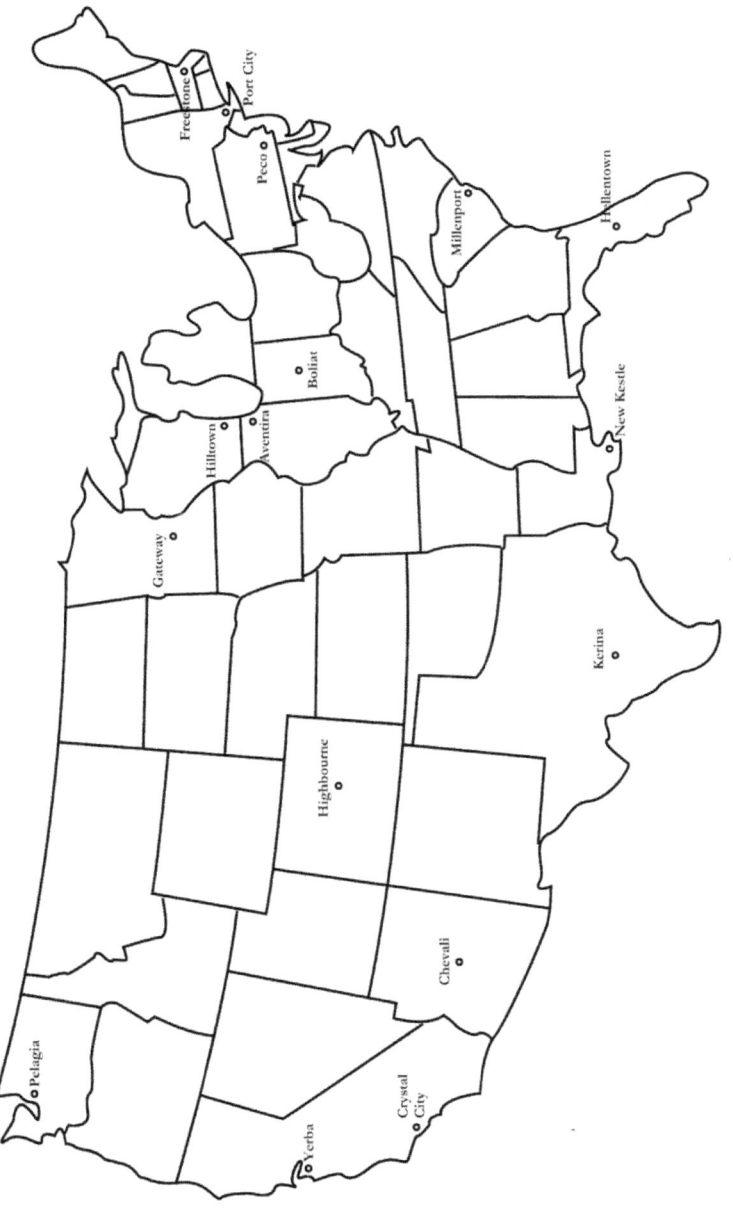

Freestone
Port City
Peco
Millenport
Hullentown
Boliat
New Kesle
Hilltown
Aventura
Gateway
Kerina
Highbourne
Chevali
Pelagia
Crystal City
Yerba

I'm not saying the Forester Universe cities are in the United States. But if they were, this is where they'd be.

PART I

Chapter 1 – Role Play (Dev)

As nice as it is to get a private plane to go to Crystal City to film a commercial for Strongwell beer, part of me wishes I was on the other plane, the team plane flying out to Hellentown. Here on my own, I keep replaying the scenes from the previous day's loss in my head—the fox, number 83, snarling "faggot" at me; the tackles we missed; passes going a whisker's breadth past my claws—and I know that on the team plane, the coaches will have the guys pumped up for the week of practice and the first game of the playoffs. Sure, we lost, but thanks to the quirks of scheduling, we get another chance at the same team, back in their home stadium this time, where we beat them earlier in the year. And this game, the first time a Chevali team has been in the playoffs in over a decade, will be more important than the last by a factor of like a zillion. We lost last week and we're still playing. Lose this week and our season is over. Win three more games and we'll be champions of the UFL.

Even though I try to imagine Coach Samuelson's inspirational speech as we're taking off, I still can't replace the camaraderie that's sure to be on that plane, the sense of optimism as we take off. I'd be sitting next to Charm, the big stallion I room with on the road, maybe near my linebacking partners Gerrard and Carson, and we'd be buzzing with ideas about how to beat the guys who just beat us. I'd be part of a team, an important part, with people relying on my skills to help us all win.

Instead, I'm in a tiny chartered jet with our recently-added receiver Lightning Strike, a cheetah who has lived up to his name in the three games he's been with us. He's dyed his fur blue and gold—the Strongwell beer colors—and in close quarters, the dye smells pretty strongly. He sits right across the aisle from me because it's just me and him on the plane, and during takeoff he goes into some kind of meditative zone. Once we hit cruising altitude, he turns to me with, "Okay, here's what you need to know about being in a commercial."

Thank God Strongwell has a rep on the plane to give me actually useful information. Charisse, a kangaroo rat in a sharp blue business suit with a gold lapel pin, greeted us when we came on board with a cheery, "Congratulations on making the playoffs." She's seated facing Strike, and she interrupts the cheetah before he gets to tell me any of his amazing advice (which if it's anything like his "only eat organic plant material" advice or "don't have sex during the season" advice, I am happier not knowing).

"Let's just get the release forms out of the way," she says, "and I'll go over what's going to happen when we touch down." She glances at Strike, then at me, and says to me, "You're the gay one, right?"

Before I can reply, Strike leans forward. "That's right," he says. "He's gay. I'm straight."

He says it with a smile that I would think was flirty, if he hadn't spent all that time telling me how sex detracts from his energy level or something—I was really only half-listening. Also, I'm not thinking about that because I'm now "the gay one." If Strike were to flirt, the girl might be interested, but I'm sitting apart from both of them now. I'm the other, the stranger, the weirdo.

"We're both football players," I say.

They give me almost the same odd look. "Yes," Charisse says. "I just wanted to make sure I didn't mix you up."

She hands me the forms just the same as she does to him, and gives us both the same smile. Maybe I'm just thinking too much now about Lee and that Equality Now meeting he wants me to go to with the senators up in Potomac. If I feel this awkward now, how would I feel in a room full of suit-and-tie politicians talking about how gay I am? I told Lee I wouldn't do it, and he hasn't mentioned it in a couple days, so I'm hoping he's dropped it. If not, it'll be another argument. Which isn't the end of the world, and making up afterwards is good, but lately my fox has been broody and our arguments a little sharper. I hope to God he gets that job in Yerba. I'd rather see him once a week and have him busy and happy than have him moping around every day, even if I do get to take him to bed every night.

The forms, standard publicity releases, take about five minutes to skim and sign. Strike says his agent's vetted them, which for my money is better than having my useless ferret agent look at them. Ogleby's equally likely to let something sketchy through as to hold up something harmless. Between putting me on the hook for more Ultimate Fit commercials and calling the press conference that forced me to address being gay, he's got two strikes and about one frayed wire left of my patience. Lee would call that a mixed metaphor. I call it being honest. Anyway, it's such a relief to sign papers and not worry about what I'm signing that I'm done before the experienced Strike is.

Charisse collects them and puts them into her folder. "Great," she says. "When we land, a limo's going to take us to the studio. We have half the day for filming, then lunch, and then if we need to pick up any shots, we have another two hours reserved after lunch. You'll be back at the airport at five p.m. sharp to fly to Hellentown, getting in around midnight, I'm afraid."

"There's no curfew until Friday," I say. "So that's fine."

"Great!" She smiles winningly.

Strike gives her a bright smile back. "Could we hire you to fly out to Hellentown with us?"

"Oh, I'm afraid not." She pats her Blackberry. "I have appointments all day tomorrow. But you've got my full attention today."

"Lovely." Strike leans forward, almost purring.

"Don't get the wrong idea," she says. "I'm a Sabertooths fan. I think this is our year."

"You grew up in Crystal City?" Strike asks.

"Actually over on Fox Beach, by the ocean." Her attractive, pointed muzzle turns toward me with a smile. "Now, I know him, of course, and I've read about you. You're a defensive player, right? Linebacker?"

It's a relief to be addressed as a football player and not "that gay football player." So I nod. "Outside linebacker."

"Well." She grins. "Our coyote linebacker can kick the shit out of your coyote linebacker."

Crystal City has a pair of coyote linebackers, in fact, but I assume she means Polecki, who wears the same number #55 as Gerrard and plays his position, middle linebacker. I just grin back at her. "Maybe we'll see."

"You know," Strike says, "if we end up in the Championship against the Sabretooths, I might be able to get you tickets."

When we land and get to the limo, he sits alongside her facing me. It's an amusing contrast; he's huge, and has to sit either with his knees almost at chest level or his feet resting on the seat beside me. Charisse keeps a professional but amiable demeanor, and Strike just keeps edging closer to her, once picking up her tail to move it gently out of the way. The continuing flirtation sets me on edge. But Charisse takes it in stride, even returning it, and it's none of my business anyway. I'm the gay one. So I don't say anything, I just sit back and watch the crowded streets of Crystal City go by.

I never thought of myself as a country boy. Hell, I went to school in Hilltown, and I live in downtown Chevali, and those are both respectable cities. But Crystal City isn't a city. It's an unending landscape of concrete and glass and people. It's like someone took Chevali and squeezed it down so you could fit it onto the Forester U. campus, and then put a hundred of those campuses all right next to each other. Where Chevali is low and spread out, every building in Crystal City is at least three stories, and usually four or five, and there are several clusters of skyscrapers on the horizon that look like any of them could be the downtown area. About the only thing similar to Chevali is the warm sun in winter and the range of mountains you can see to the east. We pass strip mall after strip mall, crowded with more kinds of people than I can count, gold fur and red fur and brown fur, long tails and short tails and fluffy tails, dye jobs that make Strike look restrained. I even see one species I don't think I've ever seen before, a woman with a long narrow muzzle, but she's past the window before I can look twice.

When we finally make the turn into the studio lot, I think at first that it's another strip mall. Then we drive past building-sized posters of some TV shows I recognize, and it occurs to me that I should've called my actress friend Caroll while I was out here. I take out my phone, but we're already pulling up in front of a large beige building and Charisse ushers us out of the car almost before the car's stopped.

"Right in here," she says, holding open a door, and I step through into another world.

It couldn't be more different from the Ultimate Fit setup. There's a small village inside, clusters of chairs and people walking about, constantly moving, all centered around a small stage on which approximately eight hundred lights are trained. When Charisse closes the door, no noise from outside penetrates, all the movement echoes, and my whiskers twitch with the air currents bouncing off the walls. Scents flit by me here and there: people, the sizzle of high-powered lights, and…food.

As I turn, stomach rumbling, Strike nudges me and lifts his nose toward a table stacked with edibles. Busy people run over to it, grab things, and run away again, while others just stand by it eating. "That's the catering table," he says. "Just help yourself if you're hungry."

"Is that our lunch?" A lot of the stuff on the table looks good, but it's mostly snack food: energy bars, fruit, cookies, juice, soft drinks. There is a stack of Strongwell beer cans at one end, artfully arranged into a pyramid that makes it obvious that nobody's taken one yet.

"Oh, no!" Charisse, standing next to us, laughs. "We're taking you to DeLoup's for lunch."

Clearly, the name is supposed to mean something to me, so I nod and say, "Thanks."

"They do this terrific goat cheese and toasted pepita salad," Strike says.

"Do they do burgers?" I say it partly to be funny, and Strike and Charisse both laugh, but they don't actually answer the question.

"All right," Charisse says. "You two will be there." She points to the stage. "We'll call you when we're ready for you, which should be in just a couple minutes."

"Can I make a phone call?" I ask.

"Of course, but when they call for 'quiet,' you'll have to turn the phone off, I'm afraid." She smiles. "Otherwise it can cost us a lot of money in lost time."

"He has a boyfriend he needs to talk to all the time," Strike says.

Charisse's smile doesn't waver. "Oh, that's sweet," she says. "My boyfriend never calls me unless I call him first."

"What does he do?" Strike asks.

"Excuse me." I move off to the side to call Caroll. But it's either too early or she's busy, because I get her voicemail. I tell her I'm in town filming a commercial but that I'm leaving at the end of the day and wouldn't probably have time to see her anyway unless she was on this same studio lot.

Then I call Lee, and just listening to his voice makes me feel better. I don't mention the meeting in Potomac; I just tell him what's been happening with the commercial so far. Even though I warn him I'll probably have to go any minute when they're ready for filming, he's the one who ends up having to leave to get to lunch with Hal. "Tell him hi for me," I say, and look around as I hang up. Nobody seems to be any nearer ready for us than they were before. Strike is still chatting up Charisse, and when she walks off to tend to something else, I join him.

"Hey," I said, "she has a boyfriend, and I thought you weren't interested in girls anyway."

"I'm interested in girls," he says, "just not sex during the season."

He says that louder than I would have, but nobody even perks an ear nearby. I guess they hear weirder things like that in Crystal City all the time. "Anyway," Strike goes on, "it's always good to make people feel appreciated."

"I guess." I fold my arms and stand watching the spectacle. I try to figure out what any one of the people running around is doing, but they seem to be tinkering with mechanisms, checking something, then tinkering again. None of the people standing over by the catering table seems particularly concerned or in a hurry either.

Charisse reappears leading a busty female leopard with a light robe hanging open over a two-piece bikini, and a slender black wolf wearing a light robe over—well, I assume he's wearing shorts, but the robe is cinched at the waist and I can't really tell. "Hi, guys!" Charisse says. "This is Iva and Keith. They're going to be in the commercial with you. Iva and Keith, I'm sure you know Lightning Strike and Devlin Miski."

"Sure." The wolf shakes my paw, looking up at me. "Pleasure to meet you."

"You're going to be putting your arms around them at the end of the commercial," Charisse goes on, "so the director wants you to get used to some physical contact. Just put your arms around each other while you're talking, then it'll look more natural when we're filming. Okay? Sound good? I have to go talk to the director, but I'll be right back. Do you two need anything? Something to drink?"

She looks at me and Strike, and we both shake our heads. So she bustles off in the way everyone in this building seems to when they have to move, and we're left with the two scantily-clad...actors? Models? I'm not sure.

"You ever done this before?" Keith says to me. Iva is already cozying up to Strike, standing next to him, arms around each other. He's so much taller than her that when he looks down at her face, her cleavage is just naturally in his view too.

"Uh..." Keith's standing close now. When Lee's this close, his tail always brushes mine. "I mean, I've hugged my boyfriend, of course..."

The wolf laughs. "A commercial, I mean."

"Oh. Just once. The Ultimate Fit one."

He shakes his head. "Sorry, haven't seen it. I don't really watch sports that much. I mean, I know who you guys are. You were in the news all last month, and him..." He gestures at Strike. "He was on *Colleen* a while back."

I'm not sure what to say to that. "So you've done a lot of commercials?"

"Sure." He smiles, bright white teeth perfectly aligned. "You ever see the Sparkle Clean Shampoo ad?"

I frown. "I don't watch a whole lot of TV..."

"Oh, well, that's me in the shower." He rubs his muzzle. "Or the Floral Times ad? I'm the husband who comes in with the load of dead fish?"

I shake my head. "Sorry."

"Ah, it's okay." His ears go down for a bit, then come up. "Beer ad, though. Whole new market."

"Right." I glance over to where it looks like Strike has his paws inside the leopard girl's robe.

Keith follows my look. "Yeah," he says, and comes over to stand next to me. "You okay with this?"

"I guess I have to be." I force a grin and stop my tail from lashing. "What should I do?"

"Well, you've put your arm around your boyfriend, right?"

"Um." I don't know if I want to be having Lee-thoughts when I'm in a commercial.

Keith's patient. "Okay. You hug other guys on the team?"

"Sure."

"So just think of me as a teammate."

I try, but he's really slender for a football player, and a little short. I wait for him to make a move, but he's just standing there, so I drape an arm over his shoulder. Immediately he slides his paw around my lower back and holds me against him.

It's a weird feeling, because yeah, I hug my teammates, but I don't *hold* the hugs. I hold hugs with family members, but as this one goes on, it surpasses any family hug and lands firmly in the territory of hugs I've only shared in the last few years with Lee.

And Keith is close to Lee's build; he's slender, if not quite *that* slender. His tail is naturally shorter and a little better managed (I would never in a million years tell Lee that), and he definitely smells different and talks less. He does feel sort of similar against me, or if not similar in a physical way, similar in the casual ease of his embrace. Because he's comfortable, I relax until I wonder what it means that I'm feeling comfortable hugging another guy. Does this mean I could just get close to anyone who's willing to get close to me? The Firebirds t-shirt I'm wearing feels warm where he's pressed against it, and even where he's not.

"Devlin? Do you go by Devlin?"

He's got blue eyes that remind me of Lee at first, but as I look more closely, I see that they have a green cast that Lee's don't have. The difference calms me a little. "Uh, yeah. That's fine."

"Okay, Devlin, you're a little tense here. Let me just try this." And he takes the paw I have resting on his shoulder and moves it down, below his arm, curled around his chest. He's got some muscles, and I find myself thinking that maybe Lee ought to work out more. Then I dismiss that. Lee's fine the way he is, and I love him.

The weirdness of having my arm around another guy doesn't go away, but I do get used to it over the next fifteen minutes. And Keith helps a lot. "I'm a part-time masseur," he says, and puts his paws on my shoulders and then my hips, telling me where to relax. At first, that doesn't help, but when he takes his paws away and I can focus on the spots and not his touch, I am able to relax a little more. It reduces the weirdness I felt about being "the gay guy." While it's not as reassuring as being with Lee, it's better than being alone.

"Hey," Strike says. He and Iva look like they've been going out for years. His head's almost resting on hers, his left paw's firm around her back, and his right paw rests on her stomach. "You having fun over there?"

I still feel awkward, but I grin. "Sure." I wish they'd just put us on stage and get it over with.

"Okay," Keith says. "Now let's work on your smile."

"You're not a director," Iva informs him.

"I don't see Hemmler over here, so I'm going to help him work on his smile, if that's all right with you."

She sniffs and turns back to Strike. Keith lowers his voice. "Bitch," he says. "Now try to imagine something you're happy about, if you don't like putting your arm around me."

"It's not that I don't like it," I say.

"I know, I know. It's awkward. We just met. So imagine I'm your boyfriend. What is he?"

"Fox."

"Oh, good, so that isn't too far off. Just imagine bigger ears and a longer tail." He flicks his ears with a grin. "You don't have to imagine anything else."

Lee's much more than just ears and tail, but I don't say that. I don't want to think about Lee while I'm holding Keith, so the first thing I imagine to make myself smile is intercepting the ball against Hellentown, preferably right in front of that fox, Eighty-Three. I see it in front of me, my paws closing around it, hear his angry grunt as he swipes at me. I see my teammates swarming around me, feel that glow in my chest from knowing I can do something well, knowing that in that moment I'm better than anyone else on the field. Then of course, I imagine Lee watching, jumping up and down in the stands, and from there, it's not a big jump to Lee watching this commercial, getting excited about a major (well, fairly major) beer company asking me to be gay on national TV, putting their money behind an athlete hugging another guy. I imagine that kid he was so worried about maybe watching the ad and thinking that gay guys can get beer commercials and be successful too. I think about Lee coming up to me after the commercial and saying that I can wait until the off-season to do those other gay rights spots, that this is actually enough, and it's something I got paid for. I imagine cashing that check for however much it's going to be after Ogleby's cut.

Thinking about Ogleby reminds me of the two extra Ultimate Fit commercials I have to do because he screwed up the contract, which endangers my smile, so I focus back on this commercial. I've got my arm around Keith and his body is warm and close and he does kind of remind me of Lee. That seems to work pretty well, because after a few minutes Keith says, "Great, that's great. It really looks like you're happy to be with me here."

"I am," I say, "It's just…"

He holds up a paw. "You're not an actor. I know. It's okay. Didn't that other commercial have you do anything?"

"Just run around in tight clothes."

"Oh." He nods. "One of those."

My stomach rumbles a little; I haven't eaten since before the plane flight. It's not loud, but Keith feels it and grins. "You want something to eat?"

"No, I'm good…"

"Come on." His arm slips away from my waist; I follow him over to the catering table. Strike and Iva trail behind us, which I think is going to be great because Strike's not going to find anything to eat here, but to my surprise, the table has mini-veggie wraps and skewers of roasted vegetables in addition to cold sandwiches, energy bars, apples, bananas, and cookies. Strike grabs a veggie wrap; I take an energy bar, partly just to tweak him. But he doesn't seem to notice, just starts talking to Iva about his diet and how his body is a temple and so on and so forth.

Keith, meanwhile, takes one of the energy bars too. I look toward the stage, which to me looks exactly like it did when I walked in. "So I thought it was only going to be another ten minutes," I say.

He laughs. "It's always 'another ten minutes,' until it's 'right now!'" He eyes the crew and then checks his phone to see that it's almost eleven. "We're supposed to wrap by one, so I'd say probably they'll need to get going by quarter after."

"Oh, okay." I look at a pair of raccoons farther down the table, idly chatting while they eat cookies, and a weasel rushing back and forth between the stage and the director. It's so different from football practices, where everyone knows where he has to be and everyone except the kickers is always doing something. "So, you have a boyfriend?"

Keith grins that perfect smile at me again. "Oh, I'm not gay," he says.

I stare at him. "But…" Those paws that were just on my hips, wrapped so securely around me…

He shakes his head. "I'm an actor." The smile gets wider. "I'll take it as a compliment that I was able to convince you that I'm gay. I guess the TV audiences won't be able to tell either."

Just like that, I'm back to being the only gay one. "Aren't you…aren't you worried about people thinking you're gay when you show up on TV?"

His head tilts back with a musical laugh. "I wish! You know what kind of parts a guy who's willing to play gay roles will get? Like every year there's a Best Actor nominee from a 'thoughtful gay movie.' And if it's a straight guy playing the role, then people are even more impressed. Because there's going to be gay love scenes, you know, so if I can act well in those…" He holds up a paw with crossed fingers. "Course, I have to get smaller roles first. Get the attention of some good directors. I dunno." He laughs. "I guess it's the same with you, right? You don't just start out like, Devlin Miski, superstar."

"He's more the superstar." I jerk a thumb over toward Strike.

Keith gives the cheetah a thoughtful look. "Well, he knows a lot about keeping his image up, right? I mean, for me to hear about him, he's got to be getting his name out into non-sports places. That's one of the things about acting: you have to just take a bunch of different jobs. The more things you do, the more chance you have of being seen."

"Football is a lot more focused. Well, I mean, I started out on special teams—that's the guys who only play on kicks and returns, field goals, things like that—and I got a starting spot when the guy ahead of me got injured."

"Then you proved you could handle it, right? What happened to the guy who got injured? Still hurt?"

I shake my head. "We traded him for that guy." Again, I jerk my thumb toward Strike.

"Huh." Keith grins. "Well, there's so many different jobs for actors that I guess it can be kind of the same thing, but it's more like if I happen to be available one day when, say, Bennie Rays is doing another project, I might get that spot. Then if I do well, people will notice. But if I screw up, the phone might not ring for months."

"Yeah." I think about how quickly Corey was traded after his asshole stunt breaking that deer's leg. "Same thing kinda goes with us."

Charisse comes running back over. "They're ready for you," she says to me and Keith, and I think, *finally*. I give her my iPhone and ask if she can take some pictures of me during makeup and the commercial to show Lee. When she's done admiring the phone, she reminds me that the contract I signed means I can't talk about the commercial or distribute pictures of it until after it airs, and that she isn't even sure she's allowed to take pictures, so she has to go talk to the director while I head for the stage, not wanting to hold them up if they're ready.

But "ready for you" turns out to mean that they want me to sit in a chair for twenty minutes while they brush out my fur, examine it under lights, apply tint to it, get some of the tint in my eye, apologize, make me take off my Firebirds t-shirt, bring out three Firebirds polo shirts for me to choose from while I'm sitting there shirtless, apologize for the tint in my eye again, dress me in the shirt, and then take the shirt off when the director comes over and says, "Get that off him."

All the while, the makeup people are oohing and aahing over Strike's fur, asking him where he gets it done, and he's preening in the attention. He doesn't get his shirt taken off, so I guess whatever he was wearing was fine, and meanwhile I'm sitting patiently in the chair while they decide between the remaining two polo shirts, and the head of makeup, a female raccoon, keeps saying things like, "the shorter sleeves on this one will really accent his muscles" and "we really want his chest to show."

Keith says, "Why not have him do it shirtless?" and that leads to Iva sniping at him again.

"Jesus Dog, people," the director, a grey wolf who reminds me of Coach Samuelson, says when he comes back over and I'm still shirtless. "What the hell is going on? No, not that shirt either," as the raccoon brandishes a shirt at his muzzle. "We don't have permission to use the logo."

"I…" The raccoon stares at the shirt in her paw. "I thought…Kevin told me…"

The wolf clutches his cheekruffs. "Kevin was reassigned. You're killing me. *Killing me!* What's that one?"

He points to my discarded t-shirt. I hold it up to show him the Firebirds logo, and his ears flatten. "Shirtless," he says. "In two."

He stalks off, while Keith murmurs in my ear, "You look better that way anyway."

"I thought you weren't gay," I mutter back as the makeup team descends on me again, brushing out my chest fur, applying finishing touches to my muzzle, apologizing one last time for the tint in my eye.

"Hey," Strike says. "If he's shirtless, I want to be, too." So we wait another five minutes while he takes his shirt off and they touch up his fur.

After all that, the filming of the actual commercial takes only about thirty-five minutes. It goes something like this: Strike says, "A football team is made up of offense," and then I say, "and defense." And then Strike says, "But no matter what side of the ball you're on, you work up a big thirst."

Then I hold up the beer bottle, which just has water in it, and I say, "On defense, we drink Strongwell." And I look at Strike, and he says, "Hey, we drink that on offense, too."

I have to say, Strike is a lot more natural than I am. He gets most of his lines in three takes, whereas it takes me that many just to get one that sounds natural to *me*, and then four or five more of the director saying, "That was great, Dev, just great, it was perfect, let's have one more and try to keep your ears up this time."

When we're finally done with our lines, Keith and Iva come in from either side (without their robes, and yes, Keith is wearing shorts underneath, and they're in the Firebirds colors, no less) and we put our arms around them and I do my best to look natural. It's funny, standing there for about fifteen minutes with my arm around Keith as we try various poses that make us look "casual but intimate," as the director says, or "like we're totally going to fuck later," as Keith whispers to get me to laugh. I spent the last two years worrying about what would happen if I just hugged Lee in public, and here I am, shirtless, holding a half-naked guy close against me with all sorts of lights and cameras on us, and his fingers are buried in my short stomach fur and everyone is just acting like it's normal.

Even so, I'm acutely aware that he's straight, and they're all professionals. And it's not "normal," because the whole point is that it's a guy and not a girl. But it's still a strangely warm, reassuring feeling. By the end of the shoot, it barely seems weird to me, although I can't quite forget that I'm only in this commercial because I have a boyfriend. Keith's in this commercial because he can act gay, pretending to be like me, and not in the same way as my football fans who want to run like me, or tackle like me, or pick off passes like me. Maybe there are fans who want to be like me in the way that I love Lee, and that feels very personal and strange if I think about it too much. So I don't.

The director says they'll add a lot of voiceover later, and he's going to review the footage and see if we need to do any pickups ("pickups," Keith tells me, are re-takes of shots that didn't come out quite right). Meanwhile, Charisse comes back and hands me my phone with about a dozen pictures on it, of me in makeup and me during the filming, and one of me looking lost as the director is telling me to do it again.

"You did great," she says with a perky smile. "Ready for lunch?"

I kind of expect Keith and Iva to come along, but as we're getting ready to go, Keith shakes my paw and says he's enjoyed meeting me. Iva just disappears.

DeLoup's does do a burger, it turns out, with avocado and bean sprouts and heirloom tomatoes on it and some kind of garlicky spread that is terrific with the rich beef. Charisse prompts us to talk about football history, and Strike and I are happy to discuss championship teams we all grew up watching. I'm especially happy because it takes me out of thinking about my sexuality for once. She and Strike are closer to each other in age than either of them is to me; Strike's 29 and she's 31. I would've thought that would lead naturally to more flirting, but Strike holds back over lunch. Maybe he really loves football enough that when he discusses it, he's not thinking about anything else.

Even though I don't specifically remember a few of the teams they're talking about, I've watched enough of the old UFL Films shows to be able to chat about them. Charisse says her boyfriend thinks this year's Sabretooths are among the great teams, and Strike and I say that's just hometown rooting going on. Strike says that now the Firebirds are good enough to win a championship, and Charisse kind of nods with a long smile, her tail twitching, and says that of course we will. "Just not this year."

She picks up the tab and takes us back to the studio, where the director says thanks for coming back but he's got everything he needs, and then we're on our way to the airport in the limo. I want to call Lee and tell him about the shoot, but I don't want to do it in front of Charisse and Strike. So I wait until we're at the airport and then I tell them I need to go to the bathroom, and I slip into one of the phone cubicles there.

"It was weird," I say when he asks about it. "I had to have my arm around this black wolf."

"Was he cute?"

"Yeah, he was. But he's straight."

Lee laughs. "Good. Was it a good commercial?"

I think about that. "Yeah. I mean, they went with me on defense, him on offense, and, like, 'no matter what side of the ball you're on, drink Strongwell' was how it ends."

He laughs harder. "Oh my goodness. I can't believe they're really going to air it. That's amazing. So did you have your paw on his butt?"

"No, just around his waist. We were kinda close, but just hugging." I clear my throat. "And shirtless."

"Both of you?"

"Yeah."

He chuckles. "Can't wait to see it."

"I took pictures for you."

"Cool. And Strike has a girl? Were they shirtless?"

"He was. She wore a bikini. And he was hitting on her all morning." I lower my voice to a whisper for that.

"I guess maybe even his tantric meditation has limits." Lee snorts. "Well, sounds like you survived it. So back to football now."

"Yeah. I've got the playbook with me to study on the flight and about six hours of tunes." I try to frame what I was thinking about during the prep and during the commercial. "It was kind of cool, you know. That I'll be up there in a beer commercial with my arm around another guy and that, you know, kids and sports fans will see it."

"It's a good first step," he says.

16   *Uncovered*

I sigh. Of course that wouldn't be enough for him. "It's all I've got time for," I say.

After that, he gets kind of quiet. When I push, he says he has a call scheduled with David Rodriguez for later in the week, so at least he's still considering doing community outreach with the Firebirds. I don't ask him whether he's already told his ex-friend Brian that I'm not going to be doing the gay rights spots for Equality Now.

I hang up thinking that not much has really changed with him moving in. We see each other a little more, but it doesn't feel like that much more, especially since I just got done talking to him on the phone like I used to every week. I'm traveling most of the time, and he could come with me, but I've also got my team, which is like my other family, and he can't be a part of that. But we just have to get through to the off-season. A couple months of solid time together (or less, depending on how the playoffs go) before I have to go back to training camp in March will help reaffirm our relationship. Last year we took a short vacation because of his job; maybe this year, if he doesn't have anything lined up right away, we could take a longer trip somewhere. And as much as I resist all of his equality stuff, I have to admit that it feels good to know that we wouldn't have to worry about being seen together in public anymore. Especially after this whole day, which was cool but also weird: "You're gay, so we want to take pictures of you." Being treated differently and well is still being treated differently, which I think is part of what Lee wants me to understand, but it's a lot easier to just push that aside than to think about it.

Thinking about Lee is a lot more pleasant, especially if I imagine sitting on the couch with my arm around him when the beer commercial comes on, and seeing his expression when I have my arm around Keith, and what I might have to do to reassure him. I do that for the first half hour on the plane, then open up the team playbook, going through my responsibilities for that week, and I'm a football player again. Strike and I sit across a small table from each other, but while I open the playbook on the table, he just listens to his music, eyes closed, fingers tapping on the table surface. It's a little irritating, but not too bad.

The flight attendant, a short bobcat, serves us what I guess is dinner at seven o'clock West Coast time, ten o'clock Hellentown time, and that's when Strike turns off his music and starts talking. He asks how I liked the commercial shoot and I said it seemed really complicated for as simple as it turned out to be.

He gestures at the playbook I set on the seat beside me and says, "Everything's like that. It just depends on your field."

"Guess so."

"So that wolf was pretty good-looking." He spears pieces of lettuce on his fork. "Did you get his number?"

"Who, what? Keith?" I look up from the lobster pasta, which is not too bad. "No. Why? I thought you weren't into…"

"Not for *me*." He waves his phone. "I got Iva's number. She said to ring her up next time I'm in town. I come out there pretty often, you know. My agent's trying to get me a movie deal in the off-season."

"I don't think my agent has anyone's number in Crystal City." I half-laugh, but in the middle of the laugh it occurs to me that it's not such a funny joke, so I just take another bite of the pasta.

"Okay, well." Strike sets his phone down and takes another bite himself. "Guess he wasn't your type?"

"Keith?" I set down my fork. "You met Lee, right? You know I have a boyfriend?"

He gives me a mild glance. "Isn't it part of the deal with being gay that you get to just sleep with any gay guy you want? I mean, it's nice you've got a guy who'll wait at home for you, but if you get the chance…it's not like you have to be careful about it. You're not married or anything. No unexpected cubs."

Annoyance is blossoming into full-on anger. "Okay, first of all, Keith's not gay."

Strike grins at me. "When did he tell you that?"

"What?" His self-confidence derails my anger. "I don't know. We were at the catering table and I was asking whether he had a boyfriend, I think?"

"Right. Probably after he'd come on to you and you hadn't responded. Or you mentioned your boyfriend or something. Classic move. He anticipated you rejecting him so he rejected you first by saying he wasn't gay."

I feel like I'm getting coached in a bizarre sport by a lunatic. "No, I'm pretty sure he's straight."

He laughs. "When you've been around those movie types a little longer, you'll start to learn that nothing they tell you is true. Come on, he volunteered to be hugged by a gay football player in a commercial. Probably fought for that part. I'm telling you, he's queer all the way through. Did he seem at all nervous about having a guy touch his hips?"

"No, but—"

"Did he try to get you to rest a paw on his butt?"

"Um." I don't think he did, but there were a couple times—no. "No. He's straight. He wanted this part because all the good awards are going to gay roles. Something like that. He's a masseur when he's not an actor, that's why he was comfortable with the touching."

"Oh, he's an actor all right, if he was acting straight."

I take in a breath. "Okay, listen. You can't possibly know what he is. Hell, most of the team thought I was straight until I came out."

He raises an eyebrow. "Well, I wasn't on the team then."

"You think you woulda been able to tell?"

He shrugs and crams another bite of salad into his mouth, chews, takes his time. "I got a sense of these things."

"Okay, then." I lean back. "Is anyone else on the team gay?"

"This team?" He glances down at the playbook. "I haven't met everyone, but nah."

"Port City? Hellentown?"

He holds up two fingers. "Two guys on Port City. One at Hellentown."

I lean forward. "Who?"

He gives me a skeptical look. "Would you have wanted me telling people you were gay before you came out? Have a little bit of respect for individual privacy."

"You're full of shit," I say.

"Look, don't get worked up over nothing. That wolf was gay, you didn't want to hook up with him, it's cool. It's not a thing." He takes another bite of his salad and looks at my pasta. "Probably it's that heavy cream sauce affecting you. Just sits like a weight in your stomach, doesn't it?"

The bobcat, coming back in to refill our wine, looks alarmed. "Is there something wrong with the pasta, sir?"

"The pasta's fine," I snap, and take a big bite of it, glaring at Strike. The cheetah just shakes his blue-and-gold dyed head and eats more weeds.

As soon as dinner's over, I take out my iPod and put in the earphones. I look back at the playbook, focus on being a football player, and I don't talk for the rest of the flight.

Chapter 2 – Standing Out (Dev)

Hellentown is even warmer than Chevali and so humid that the first day of practice we end up panting, sweating, and uncomfortable. The second day we're more used to it, and by the third day it only feels mildly disturbing. Still, happy December, huh? I feel like we're back at the beginning of the season, because this would be a cool late summer day in Hilltown, but of course I'm a lot more beat up than I would be in September. Also, I didn't get to bed until about two a.m. local time and we were up at seven, so I'm dragging.

The other thing flashing me back to the beginning of the season is that Fisher's back in practice. Pike returns gracefully to his backup role—good team player—but they keep him working with the first team. He'll take some of the plays until they're sure Fisher's leg is going to hold up. I watch Fisher's practice when I can, hoping for the best. There are no new plays for this week; of course, he's missed half the season, so there are a bunch of plays that are new to him, and he looks like he's struggling.

I go over on a five-minute break because I haven't seen him since Christmas. As I walk over, the defensive line is practicing a strong-side running play, and Fisher misses his assignment and runs into Brick. He shakes his head, the coach talks to him, and then they take their break. "Hey! Good to see another set of stripes back on the field," I call, walking up to him.

"Yeah, same here," he says, tail lashing. "Where the hell you been?"

My ears fold back. "Filming a commercial. I told you at the dinner."

He blinks and looks past me. "Right. Right."

He's helped me so much this season that I want to give a little back. "That running play—they changed it a few weeks ago. You have to—"

"No shit," he growls. "I got it."

He's not looking at me, just staring at the coach, paws on his hips, panting. "Okay," I say. "Um, is your leg…"

"It's fine," he snaps. "Lion Christ, the doc cleared me, okay? Do I need a fucking sign? Let's just play."

And he sure seems to be fine. He can cut and get a good push on the second-team offense when they're out, and after that morning, I don't see him look lost on a play. After the first day I stop worrying so much about him. Physically, at least.

In the locker room, he's not quite the same. He still jokes with the guys, but the jokes are forced, as though he's trying to prove he still belongs. I try to chalk it up to being gone for three months, and maybe that's all it is. But he's also not the leader he used to be. There's an awkward moment when Fisher suggests we all go to dinner Tuesday night for New Year's Eve, and the guys look at Gerrard for confirmation. Fisher pretends not to notice, but on our way out he scowls and says under his breath to me, "Like I don't know how to get a team out to dinner anymore."

"It's the playoffs," I say. "Just tell the guys what to expect. Most of us haven't been here before."

"You nervous?" He gives me a sideways glance.

"No." I exhale and then take a breath. The evening is dark overhead, but Hellentown is full of artificial light, neon and incandescent, and it's still seventy and humid, like I'm standing in the shower room. "Yeah. A little."

"Good." He grins. "Nervous is good. Means you're feeling the pressure. I'm not going to give you some bullshit speech about the field being the same dimensions. You know all that. I'm going to say that you're a professional, and this is the same game you've always played. You know it inside and out."

"I was in the playoffs in college."

He nods. "Same deal, kind of." His whiskers slide back as he grins. "But more. Lots more. Crowd's going to be a factor, loud and pumped up. You need to be able to shut them out and focus on the game. Once you get into the game, it gets easier, more familiar."

"And hey, you'll be out on the field."

He flexes his paws and growls deep in his chest. "Finally."

We walk past our hotel, getting some attention from the locals there. A pair of armadillos, wearing party hats with "2009" written on them, yell, "Get ready to get your tails handed to you!" Other people yell less polite variations along our two-block walk to the restaurant opposite the strip mall.

In the steakhouse, the staff are very polite, even after they find out who we are. "I promise not to spit in the beer," the raccoon waiter says with an exaggerated drawl and a grin. He's wearing a Pilots pin on his vest, and when Vonni asks if that's part of the uniform, he says, "This week it is."

I encourage Fisher to tell us stories about playoff games. He needs little encouragement before launching into the time he had a case of nerves once and threw up on the sideline, then going on about what it's like once you get into the groove of things, about how good it feels to be standing up on that podium, touching the championship trophy. About how for a week after the championship—both times he won—he barely slept, just lay in bed staring at the ceiling and reminding himself that it was real.

About how those memories fade and they're like drugs, how the most important thing in your life becomes getting back there.

My phone rings in the middle of that, and it's Dad, so I let him leave a message for later. The call makes me think of family, and combined with Fisher talking about championships like they're the best thing in the world…I wonder how Fisher feels about Gena and the boys. If I asked him whether he'd leave his family if it meant he could have one more year playing at a high level, what would he say?

The waiter catches part of Fisher's speech and says that even for fans, the championship is a pretty big deal. "I'm looking forward to our victory parade," he says.

"Sure you'll still be alive when that happens?" Pace says, and the waiter laughs.

At midnight, we watch the ball drop on the bar TVs and get a champagne toast, inviting the waiter to join us. Lee calls me at five 'til, and I keep him on the phone so I can hear him say, "Happy New Year!" I tell him I'll call him later, since I'm the only one with a phone to my ear and I don't want to be rude.

The waiter brings us another round of champagne on the house, but we can't stay much past 12:30. No curfew tonight, but practice at 9 am, and we all need to get sleep. We do leave a pretty big tip when we go. Got to appreciate fans, even if they're not yours.

At quarter to one, as I'm walking through the hotel lobby, my parents call to wish me Happy New Year. Mom is in good spirits and even Dad is a little tipsy. I tell them about the commercial and Mom says, "Oh, Gregory will be so jealous," and she laughs. Privately, I think she's right, and that it's not funny, but I don't know what to say about that. Thank God Gregory isn't actually there for them to insist he talk to me. I'm just buzzed enough that if he started mouthing off about Lee, I'd probably start needling him about his shitty law practice.

I call Lee from the hotel room, since Charm's out still, probably at that topless bar he loves. My fox is kind of quiet, listening to me talk about practice. He offers a few tips, but doesn't talk about what he's been doing. "How're you spending your New Years?" I finally say. If he mentions his mom, I'm ready to listen.

"Watching college bowl games."

His voice is just a little slurred, a little off. I presume he's been drinking, but hey, so have I. "Any of your players do well?"

"Some. Some had bad games. I'd change the ratings on them."

"I think you should get out more. Maybe Hal wants to watch some of the games with you?"

"I'm seeing him tomorrow." In the background, I hear the TV going. Sounds like a sports news show.

And then I ask about Equality Now, because they wanted a decision by January first and that's tomorrow. And it's all tangled up because the guy he's talking to is Brian, and there's so much history there—the end of their friendship back at the college we all went to, Brian coming on to him (and Lee giving in, but that was just once and it's in the past and I've forgiven him), Brian more or less outing me, threatening me with pictures, then pressuring Lee to get me to do more gay rights activism—that it's impossible to be objective about it. So I do the next best thing and just stay quiet, and wait for him to tell me.

"I told him you're not going to do it," he says finally.

A lot of tension drains from me. I lean back against the headboard, stretch my legs out on the bed, and exhale across the phone. I wish I could hug him right there. "Thanks, fox."

"Well, you weren't. It wasn't like I could lie to him." Of course, because he's Lee, he has to be a little foxy-snippy about it.

I try to not mind, to not snipe back. I don't quite succeed. "No, but... you could've kept bugging me about it."

"I know better than that. You were right. I told you to focus on football and that's what you should do. No matter whether there's people out there who need to be recognized. That's their problem."

He's definitely a little drunk. I say, "Doc," and he apologizes, and I try to talk sexy with him, and it sort of works. At least, it gets me missing him, and that gets us through to the countdown. There's a brief hiccup where he won't tell me what he wants to do with my playoff check, some forty grand. I don't care; I've already put it out of my mind. He wants to give it to Equality Now, great. I just want to start this new year fresh.

I kiss him through the phone when it hits midnight, and he kisses me back.

"New year," I say.

"Playoffs," he says. "You ready?"

"I'm ready."

"Good." He takes a breath. "Love you. I'll see you Friday. Practice hard."

"I always do."

And I do, every day of the brand new year. The coaches do their best to make the week feel like a normal practice, but there are more and more media around every day, and it's impossible to escape the feeling of having your every move scrutinized. The week kicks off another round of "The UFL's First Gay Player" articles, which means reporters keep me busy for hours after practice every day while my fellow linebackers are relaxing in a spa or getting a massage.

I don't watch TV or read the media much, so I don't know when these articles actually come out. Without Lee to tell me about the things being written and said, the first indication I have of it is during Thursday practice when Colin starts being a dick again. Well, that fox never really stops being a dick, but Thursday he starts doing it louder. "Chevali Flaming-Birds, they're calling us now," he snaps while we're eating. It's to a bunch of his buddies, not to me, but as I look up, he's looking my way, clearly hoping I heard. "Heck with that," he goes on. "Look, I told my agent to make sure anyone who calls him knows that there's only one on this team."

He's holding a phone, but I don't know if he was reading something someone sent him, or talking to his agent or what. Zillo, next to me, folds his big coyote ears down as I look past him at Colin. He mumbles, "He's not a bad guy."

"You've said that," I say. "But he keeps acting like one."

Zillo is Colin's roommate, like I'm Charm's, and they used to be close. He looks over at the fox now, but Colin turns back to his friends, a few special-teamers. "Yeah," the coyote says, "I mean, put yourself in his place. What if, like…suddenly everyone wasn't cool with you being gay?"

"You mean like my entire life before three months ago?"

I didn't think his ears could go down farther, but they do. "Yeah, but— no. I mean…"

"It's not the same." I feel Lee talking through me. I allow him a little leeway. "For one thing, I'm not telling him how to live his life."

"I know." Zillo doesn't look at me.

"I just want to have *him* not tell *me* how to live *my* life."

"I know! Jesus—" He stops, and we look at each other, and then we both just start laughing.

"Jesus, all right," I say. "Look, I know it's got nothing to do with you."

"Yeah," he says. "I'm Christian too, you know. Not all of us are judgmental, ah…" He trails off, maybe unwilling to say "assholes" about his former buddy and still-roommate.

It isn't until that night, when I talk to Lee, that I find out that not only did the sports reporters write their articles, but three different websites— two gay rights ones and one "lifestyle" one—and one TV show I've never heard of recycled old stories about "the first openly gay player." I tell him that none of them talked to me and he isn't surprised. He says it looks like they just dusted off quotes from a few months ago and added a bit about me going to the playoffs. "If you win—when you win—"

"Damn right," I growl.

"—then there'll be more interviews and stuff. Probably. But you can just put it off, too. The important thing is winning."

He doesn't sound sarcastic when he says it, so I take it at face value. I'm glad. I don't want to immediately start fighting when I see him in person tomorrow.

Friday is a full-pads practice, everybody going all out, so I don't have a lot of energy to spare to think about Lee coming in that night. I do anyway, a little, while we're stretching afterwards. I take a long shower and opt for the massage rather than the trainer, where a lot of my teammates are going for treatments. It's not that I don't hurt; it's that I don't hurt that much. Nothing I can't walk off. The ribs from a month ago are pretty much healed, and I'm banged up by the game, but that's football.

Only when I'm dressed do I pick up my phone. There's three messages from Ogleby asking how the commercial went—he should upgrade his calendar—and telling me about the articles Thursday and how he's getting more endorsement opportunities. I call back and ask him if any groups have been asking me to do equality PSAs and he says yeah, but he's not responding to those because they're free.

"Schedule them for after the playoffs," I say. "Along with the commercials. No more commercials, no more anything until after the playoffs are over."

"Okay, but Dev, I gotta tell you, some of these guys are really hot to go."

I'm not the only one on a phone as guys get dressed and take off, but Gerrard is looking at me and Zillo's right nearby too. I don't want to talk about commitments to my time with Gerrard around. "I said no more until after the playoffs."

The drawback of this iPhone is you can't snap it shut with a satisfying clack. So I just turn it off and shove it in my pocket.

"Those guys'll take as much of you as you're willing to give," Gerrard says. "You gotta make sure you keep enough of yourself to do your job."

The confidence he has in me is great. I hold it to myself, and I remember Gerrard's words in case Lee brings up any more requests for me to do gay rights work while I'm trying to win a championship. I'm excited to see Lee, of course, but I've also learned with my fox to be prepared for anything.

I stop by my hotel room to drop off the playbook and put on a nicer shirt. Excitement has won out over worry about what he might say as I slip down the service elevator and out the side entrance they've set aside for us. I'm bouncing on my feet, and then I stop, because the area around the side parking lot where my cab is waiting isn't empty, like it has been all week.

They're hanging out in two groups: a deer, a weasel, and a cacomistle, all female, the weasel puffing on a cigarette. On the other side are a female wolf and a male fox wearing a colorful filmy scarf. I know the females by their type: their glittering jewelry catches the light of the afternoon sun and most of them have more bare fur showing than clothed. They all have the same predatory, desperate looks on, and one or two of them start toward me before others pull them back. If they don't recognize me specifically as a guy not interested in females, I know how to get by without making eye contact, and they usually don't press.

The male, the fox, I know by name: Argonne. His scarf is a pastel, pale yellow, and he stands with his head tilted and his muzzle up, like he's looking down on me. I get almost out to the street before he calls out behind me, "So long, sister."

He's definitely not talking to any of the ladies; his voice is too loud. I hesitate just for a second, and then ignore him and keep going. He's got dedication, I'll say that for him. And I'm glad that there's someone else on the team he can hook up with, so he's not just after me. Curiosity stings again, making me think I could just hang out, see who catches his eye... though they don't do it that publicly, or I would've heard of it. Then why does he hang out here in public like this?

I remember Strike asking, "Would you have wanted me to out you while you were still closeted?" My feet keep walking, taking me to the cab, and I get in without looking back.

Chapter 3 – Hidden Messes (Lee)

Without Dev at the apartment, it's hard to keep my mind from going back to my mother. Especially when I walk around looking at my clothes, my pictures, my computer, and all the other things reminding me that Chevali is my home now, I don't think of my apartment in Hilltown. I think of my bedroom, sealed behind a lock at the top of the stairs in my mother's house. I think of my pride jacket, burned with all the things that might remind my mother that I grew up. I know none of those things are me; I'm still the fox I am whether my jacket is denim or ash. But lying in Dev's bed—our bed—alone at night, I feel so isolated that I have to resist the urge to call my tiger.

I do call Father and talk to him on Wednesday the first, when for some reason turning the calendars over brings back lots of memories. He gives me some generic advice about remembering that I'm loved by a lot of people and then some specific advice to remember that my mother is not only that person we ran into on December 28th; she's also the mother who loved me and raised me. I point out that I'm not the cub she raised anymore, that she and I have grown into these people we are now, that I am perfectly willing to talk to her, only *she* doesn't seem to want that. After a pause, Father goes on to talk about my job possibilities, how the guys in Yerba will probably call me now that the season's over (*their* season is over, anyway) to finalize whether they want me to take the scouting position, how the guy at the Firebirds was going to talk to me about doing community outreach there, how I could just do none of those things and live off Dev's money and be an activist.

It's hard to articulate to him why that last one won't work, but I give it a shot. Dev feels all this pressure to be part of the activist stuff I do, which admittedly is partly my fault, but it's not something I can put back in the bottle now. He knows how I feel; if I don't talk about it, then he'll think I'm hiding it specifically to spare his feelings and he'll feel guilty anyway. "If you talk about it," Father suggests, and yes, I think over a year or two we could work it out, which is what he's getting at: our relationship is not contained in these few months.

"But I want to do the scouting, too," I remind him, and he laughs.

"At least you know what you want. You're lucky."

What I want seems like it should be so simple: I want a tiger to love and curl up with at night, and I want people to think I'm smart about football, and I want gay people to be treated like everyone else. Is that so much to ask?

On Thursday, I talk to Rodriguez, the Firebirds' General Manager, about the community outreach job. I've prepared a few ideas, standard LGBT awareness tactics for community involvement, and I toss them out just to see what his reaction will be. He sounds interested but not excited, and launches into what sounds like a lot of stuff he threw together at the last minute out of a marketing brochure: "Increase awareness, build excitement," stuff like that. He doesn't really react to anything I say, but says he wrote it down and he'll discuss it with his team. I tell him I have to think about things too and that I'll touch base this coming week.

I still want to know if Dev was the one who set up that job. But again, that'll wait. I keep going back and forth on how important it is. He probably thought he was doing something nice. Or was he just trying to keep me away from the Equality people and Brian? I just haven't had a chance to talk to him about it and I don't want to distract him from this game.

Getting on the plane to go to Hellentown reminds me of the last time I boarded a plane, in Hilltown, still so angry from the shock of the visit to Mother's house that I picked at the fabric of the armrest all the way home without realizing it. This time, I make sure my paws just lie on the armrests, claws quiescent, and I remind myself that I'm flying out to visit Dev, that I'm going on vacation for a weekend. Also I order a rum and Coke and I listen to angry punk music all the way there. The drink relaxes me and the music draws my anger out so that when I shut it off for landing, I feel much more calm.

And then I get my luggage and walk outside, and my purring tiger's there in the purring cab. I toss my bags in the trunk and settle into the back beside him, and we do the awkward half-hug-in-the-car-seat thing. I want to kiss him, but not in a public taxi, not here in Hellentown.

"I'll walk you to your hotel room," he says, "then I gotta go to this team thing we're doing. Order yourself some dinner at room service or just go out. There's some fast food near the hotel. I'll be back late."

"What's the team thing?" I ask. "Gena said she was coming out to Hellentown this week. Is she going to be there?"

"I don't know." He shrugs. "It's just a dinner, but, you know, it's the guys."

"Okay." Room service dinner doesn't sound bad after the long day of flying anyway. Plus I need time to pick up a Hellentown t-shirt before

Saturday night, to re-enact what we did the night before the Kerina game. I didn't have a chance to get one last week, what with coming back from Mother's place and all. I kind of wanted to spend an evening with Dev just relaxing from the flight, but hopefully a change in scenery will be calming enough for me to get some rest and get in a better mood to spend tomorrow with him.

He does at least walk me up to the hotel room, where he puts his arms around me and kisses me, and that puts some wag in my tail. "Mmm," he says as we break apart. "Tempted just to blow off the team dinner."

I know he's tempted; I can feel it. I am too. If I say, "Stay with me," he probably would, but of course I shouldn't, and he shouldn't, and we both know it. "I'll still be here when it's over," I say. "Go."

"Mmm." He grins and kisses me again, a shorter peck on the nose this time, and leaves.

My phone rings over dinner, but it's not Dev's number, it's Hal. Just seeing that lifts my spirits, and so I finish chewing the bite of steak and take a sip of wine, and pick up the phone with a smile on my muzzle. "It's Friday night," I say. "Aren't you supposed to be going out with your girl?"

"In an hour," he says. "Time difference, remember, genius?"

"Yeah, yeah. Where you taking her?"

"Caravan. Upscale Middle Eastern."

"Nice. She likes the hummus, huh?"

"I'm hoping so. If not, there might not be a future for us."

"And after?"

"Dancing at the Spot."

"Never heard of it."

"It's a place guys take girls. I wouldn't expect you to've."

"Nice place?"

"Smelly. Good music."

Every place is smelly when you've got a six-inch nose. I prop my legs up on the bed, let my tail hang off the chair, and grab the dinner roll from the desk where I've put my meal, ignoring the rest of my dinner for the moment. "That's what dancing's all about. You feeling any better about her?"

"Yeah, I don't know. We'll see after tonight."

"Oh ho. So after the dancing, it's back to your place?"

"You kidding? Have you seen my place?"

I laugh. "No."

"There's a reason for that. No. Her place. Maybe."

"Maybe?" I lean back in the chair.

"We'll see how things go. How's Hellentown? How are you holding up with the thing with your mom?"

"Trying not to think about it too much."

"That's okay for a bit. Don't let it become a habit. Got to deal with it sooner or later, and sooner is easier."

"Yeah. I talked to my dad on New Year's, and I'll call him again. It's this whole Families United angle that's making it really hard, you know? Like she's deliberately trying to hurt me."

"I'm sure she's not," he says, and then, "Oh, hey. Got a note from that sheriff back east today. This'll interest you."

"Back east?"

"The King family. Seems the parents have retained an attorney and are filing a suit against Families United."

I jump and almost overbalance backwards, scrambling to my feet as the chair clatters to the floor. "A lawsuit? Criminal?"

"Civil. Says it was filed Thursday…" He gives me the name of the court while I run to get my laptop out of the travel bag.

"Hang on, hang on. I want to look up the court record."

"There's not much there. It's been filed but they haven't responded yet."

The laptop takes forever to power up. "This is amazing. This is so cool."

"I dunno about that. They must be pretty desperate if they're gonna drag this through the courts. Sheriff thinks someone's pushing them to do it. He called me 'cause I 'seemed genuinely interested' in the kid, not just the sensationalism of the case."

Finally I get to the startup screen. "So, this make it more interesting to you?"

"Maybe."

"Still just maybe?"

"I'm still working on this injury article. It's hard to do two big stories at once."

I open a browser and look up the court. "The injury thing is big, huh?"

"To the people I usually sell to. Hey, you know, if you go write up this case, I'll help you polish the article. Could sell it to a couple papers, I'm sure."

"I don't need extra incentive to look into this," I say. "There's the court case. Nothing more than the initial filing."

"That's my way of saying I'm interested too." Hal chuckles into the phone.

"You think this could become a big case?"

"Honestly? No. Ten to one they settle out of court—make that a hundred to one. Those groups have deep pockets and a good interest in keeping their dirty laundry out of the media. Couple papers picked up the kid's suicide, but it wasn't national news, and from what I saw, Families United wasn't mentioned in any of the articles."

That makes my teeth grind. "Can't you write something mentioning it?"

"What, now? A month and a half later?"

"In connection with the court filing."

"Enh." I hear the rustle of fabric; sounds like he's getting dressed. "I can't just write things and have 'em published, you know."

"You could start a blog."

"I haven't hit rock bottom yet, kid. You want me touching tails with your friend Brian?"

Brian would be interested in this, too. Course, he won't want to talk to me after our last dinner, after I sent him home with a bottle of wine and a "thirty pieces of silver" comment. "Maybe I'll write him. Anonymously."

"Told you things would go bad."

There's nothing more on the case. I save the link and close the computer, then stand and stare out the window. "You didn't, and even if you had, so what?"

He chuckles. "So how's Hellentown? You talk to your tiger about that job yet?"

The clouds outside glow softly with reflected city light. Hellentown is about as big as Chevali, but brighter, gaudy with neon and fluorescents, and the low cloud cover reflects the light back down. One of the buildings has a "GO PILOTS" sign hanging from it. I step back and sit at my laptop again. "The one in Yerba or the Chevali one?"

"Look at you, poor little rich fox with your two job offers. The Chevali one, of course. Why, do you think he was calling up the Yerba guys to get them to hire you, too?"

"He's in the playoffs, and it can wait." I search online for any other info on the case, but nothing comes up.

"The job offer might be off the table by the time their season's over."

"I know." I sigh. "But if I confront him about it and they lose…"

"He won't blame you. Not entirely."

"I'll blame myself." And I think about Dev claiming he was losing concentration for one key play in the last game. He'd blame me, even if he didn't say it out loud.

"So you just have to make the decision yourself."

"Yeah."

"Know what that'll be?"

"The only reason I'd take it would be to stay in Chevali with him. But what if I take the job and he gets traded? What if I take the job and Yerba pulls their offer because I worked for Chevali, and then the Chevali job runs out?" I sigh, my tail curling back and forth as I pace the room. "No, the Yerba job is what I want. If they offer it."

Hal chuckles. His voice sounds strained for a moment. "Let me get this tie on…"

"A tie? You own a tie?"

He wheezes and then comes back. "Har har. Anyway, look. You gotta chase the thing you love to do, first and foremost. Settle along the way if you have to, but never lose sight of that."

"Very inspirational."

"It's life. You haven't been around as long as I have—" I snort. "True story, *cub*."

"I figured things out pretty well on my own. I had to." I put the laptop aside and poke at the cooled dinner.

"Doesn't mean you should turn down advice when it's offered."

"All right, all right. I'll think about it."

"Write back to Emmanuel. Ask him if it'd affect his decision if you take a short-term position with Chevali."

"I will."

"Great. I gotta go. Have a good night."

"You too. Good luck."

"You're more likely t'get lucky than I am. But thanks."

I pick up a bite of steak and hold it near my muzzle. "Hey, just because you're old doesn't mean you can't get some action."

He laughs. "Take care."

The dinner's cool but not too cold to eat, so I finish it and then turn on the TV and lie back on the bed not watching it. I don't call Brian and I don't write Emmanuel. I manage to keep my thoughts away from Mother, away from my job situation, and mostly I think about the lawsuit and how that might change things. That's a good topic for my mind to wander on, as there is absolutely nothing I can do about it one way or the other, so I don't have to decide, I don't have to commit. I'm safe. I lie there and daydream and I don't do anything except wait for Dev.

"Hi," he says when he comes in.

I thump my tail against the bed and say, "Hi," but don't get up. I do turn off the TV, though.

He turns down the lights. My eyes adjust seconds later to the sight of him stepping out of his pants, pulling his shirt off. Wearing nothing but a tight pair of boxers, he drops on top of me, purring so hard I feel like I put a quarter in a Magic Fingers bed.

"You okay?" He pushes his big nose at my muzzle, his warm breath tickling my whiskers. "You're wearing lots more clothes than I would've thought."

"I'm good," I say, putting arms around him and rubbing fingers through his fur, over his muscles. "Just thinking."

He exhales and settles atop me with a comforting press. "About your Mom?"

I lick the side of his muzzle. I'm definitely not going to tell him about the court case, not after how he reacted the last time I brought up Vince King. "If it's all the same to you, I'd rather not talk about my parents while you're half-naked on top of me in bed."

"So…" He chuckles. "Should I put some clothes on?"

I tighten my paws around him. "Why don't you take mine off?"

Fingers slide under my shirt. "You sure? I know it's been days, but I can talk, too." The vibration of his voice shivers through my chest. "I could tell you about the commercial."

"What, about that sexy wolf you had to hug?" I slip my paws under his boxers on either side of his tail. "All that stuff will still be there after the game. It can wait."

He kisses me and stops arguing, and then he makes me forget everything else.

•

Saturday I go out walking. Hellentown is as humid as Chevali is dry, and my fur feels thick and unruly by noon. I spend lots of time in shops because they are climate-controlled, even if most of them have terrible plastic souvenirs of the local amusement park and its millions of associated characters: cartoon lizards and ducks and unicorns and dragons. The non-copyrighted souvenirs are worse, all swamps and gators, whether just plastic or actual gator meat, gator-skin leather, tacky stuff like that. Actually, I find a gator-skin tie that Hal might like, and buy it for him just in case.

In a sports store, I find the Hellentown Pilots shirt I want to wear that night, with the word "PILOTS" over their aviator logo, and then I find an air-conditioned coral-pink and sand-yellow food court where I can have lunch and call my father to tell him about the court case. "You think she knows about it?" I ask into his silence.

"I've no idea," he says, not needing to ask who I mean. "Are you thinking of calling her?"

"I wasn't going to." Well, I was thinking about it. I still might. I mean, what do I really have to lose?

"Didn't think so. But I wouldn't necessarily say it's a bad idea. I know—" He senses my interruption and stops it. "I know what she did. I'm not excusing that. It's been a week, and probably you need to give it a little more time. I was going to say, if you want to call to talk, to apologize for screaming at her—"

"I was thinking about just telling her about the court case." Two raccoons waddling past me stop, huge white shopping bags weighing them down, and glance at me before continuing on. "Apologize? Seriously?"

"*And.* And give her a chance to apologize in return."

"Right. Did you get a forecast for snow in hell today or something?"

"You might be surprised." He types on his keyboard. "She doesn't want to lose you."

"Of course not. She just wants to lose the gay part of me."

"Wiley…"

"Am I wrong?"

Silence. I remember that I'm in Hellentown, out in public, but nobody seems to have noticed my "gay" comment. I don't see any ears perked in my direction, no curious muzzles or grimaces.

Finally, my father says, "It's not that simple."

I rub my whiskers back. Outside, a slinky male weasel in a tight t-shirt and shorts struts past the window and then stops to peer inside. So gay, I think. "It never is. But I need to worry about me and Dev."

"You don't need to worry about the King family." I stay silent. He types some more. "As long as you're not just doing this to get back at your mother. It'll affect her, you know, but maybe not as much as you're thinking."

"I'm not," I say, and then I take a moment to think about it. Am I? No. No, I'm pretty sure I'm not. "No, it's really just to get at the people involved."

"All right." He types again, click-click on the keyboard.

The weasel has apparently decided the food court is acceptable. He comes in but walks toward a table as if he knows someone, then keeps going, vaguely in my direction. I check myself—I don't look that gay, do I? "Busy at work?"

"Very. There's a lot of really interesting things going on. Now, with the potential of having some clients from your team—thank you for that, by the way—it's likely to take even more of my time."

"It's not my team, not yet. And probably won't be."

He chuckles. "They're your team by association."

"Fair enough." I rub paws down my shirt and think about the oversized Firebirds polo I got from the owner's plane, and that makes me smile. "Did any of them actually call you?"

"Angela Marvell did. The others I think are waiting 'til the season's over."

"Dev is, I know."

"How's he doing? Relaxed, ready for the game?"

He was certainly pretty relaxed after climbing on top of me last night. I take a moment to savor the memory of his warmth, the muscular ripple of his chest against my shoulders, the hard warmth inside me, his whispered growls in my ear, the letting go of all our worries and concerns in our movement together. "Pretty relaxed, yeah."

"Good. I don't have any other teams to root for now, so they better win."

"Doing our best."

"You giving him football advice still?"

The weasel walks past me, one paw resting on his hip. I give him an appreciative smile and then turn back deliberately to my phone. He flips his tail and walks on past me. "Not a whole lot. He's getting good advice from Gerrard and the coaches and he's executing on it. He knows what he needs to do. Doesn't really need my advice any more."

"I'm sure he still wants it."

"Maybe. He hasn't really asked in a few weeks. I saw him miss an assignment and I told him, but he already knew. He's doing really well." I'm pretty damn proud of him, and I wish I could keep helping him.

"There's an article in SI about the Firebirds' defense. They mention him."

"Mostly talks about Gerrard, I guess."

"Of course. He's the big star. What's amazing is how he seems to keep getting better every year."

"Hope Dev does too. He's got lots of years ahead of him." The weasel completes her circuit of the food court without getting any attention. He lifts his head and pushes open the door, strutting back outside.

"Seeing him before the game, or is he not allowed?"

"He's allowed. Has to be back to the hotel by eleven, but that's plenty of time." I cough. "For dinner."

"Uh-huh. Have a good weekend, then. Go Firebirds."

"Go Firebirds," I echo, and hang up.

A ringtail teen coming back from Pizza Hole with two huge slices pauses near me. "Firebirds?" she laughs. "Those faggots are goin' down."

Oh, if only the weasel were still here. There'd be a fight for sure. Thinking of the last time I was in Hellentown for a game, I want to challenge her to wager some money. But there'd be no way for me to collect, and anyway, she's just a teen. "Don't bet on it," I say. "Word of advice."

"Hah." She shoots me a superior look and walks on.

I want to yell after her that the word is "homosexual" and there's only one—who's out—but the food court is moderately crowded and I don't want to attract that much attention. So I just grab my bag with the t-shirt and gatorskin tie and walk out.

For the rest of the afternoon, I wander into music stores and bookstores and look at titles I know I'm not going to buy while my imagination kicks into overdrive. I'm telling Mother about the court case, telling a national paper about the case, confronting the humiliated Families United people, listening to Mother tell me she can't believe she ever fell in with them—in other words, fantasizing. Eventually I give up and go back to the hotel, check e-mail, read all the articles on the playoffs, and wait for my tiger, trying to turn my fantasizing to a more pleasant subject.

Dev actually gets away to meet me for dinner, so we order room service again and sit next to each other at the desk. I push my laptop out of the way to make room for the food. While we eat, I ask, "How're you doing with the practices? You guys ready for the Pilots?"

He nods. "We know 'em so well now we could probably run their plays for 'em."

"Maybe you should. Confuse 'em a bit."

He grins. "We already got five formations to counter what they're doing. Coach wants us to get more aggressive on the defensive side."

"What's Steez think about that?"

Dev shakes his head. "Steez says we shouldn't take chances. But I dunno, Coach has been around a while."

"So has Steez."

"Yeah." He stares down at his plate. "But Gerrard says all that means is we keep doing what we're doing, and if we see an opportunity, we jump on it faster."

"Smart guy." I sip the house wine, which isn't all that bad considering where we are. "You're doing really well, by the way."

He tilts his head. "At…?"

"Football. I haven't really found that much to critique you on. You know your routes, you're working well with Gerrard and Carson, and you're kicking ass on the field."

"Okay. Thanks?" He smiles and puts an arm around me.

I lean into him. "Just wanted to say I'm proud of you. No matter what happens tomorrow."

"Aw, fox. We're gonna win tomorrow." He squeezes me.

I grin. "I know."

"All right. So how was your day?"

I rest a paw on his thigh, rubbing through the fabric to the thick muscle beneath. "Pretty good. Talked to my dad. He's handling Gerrard's money now, I guess. Angela got in touch with him."

"Cool." He curls his tail back over mine. "I'll set mine up with him as soon as the season's over."

"Lots of things can wait 'til the season's over."

He turns to look at me. "You knew that, though."

"Uh-huh." I lean against his shoulder and don't look up. "You just play the best you can. All this stuff will work itself out."

He puts a finger under my chin and lifts it until my eyes meet his. "It's part of my job, fox," he says.

"Yeah." I move forward and give him a kiss. "And I meant it. I'm proud of you and we'll have time to talk about the rest of it."

"Okay." He searches my eyes. "You still seem kinda down. Did you talk to your dad about your mom at all?"

"A little."

"You can talk to me about that if you need to, you know. I can't imagine how I'd feel if…" He sighs and lets my chin drop. "Did I tell you when I told Mom about it, she got all—all Mom—and she told me you'll always be welcome in our house?"

I shake my head and don't have to force my smile. "Thanks. Thank her for me, too." My chest tightens, and I wonder how I can feel that flash of love for Duscha and still be so angry at my own mother. "I'll be okay. Let's finish up."

"Mmm." He grins at me and lets me go, and for the rest of the dinner we just talk about the Pilots and the other game, Highbourne at Peco. It should be a good one; Highbourne's the better team, but Peco's at home and that's always a tough place to play. As the higher seed, Hellentown got to choose their game time and they chose afternoon, so Rocs-Fraters kicks off at noon, and then Firebirds-Pilots is at four.

"You ever hear from Seito?" I ask. The white wolf backs up the QB position for the Rocs, and played against Dev in the Division II playoffs their senior year.

He shakes his head. "He's busy same as I am. But it sounded like he wanted to get together after the season, so maybe I'll contact him."

After dinner, Dev cleans up while I go into the bathroom with my Hellentown t-shirt, put it on, and take off everything else. I try to leave all my unsexy thoughts in the pile of clothes on the bathroom floor, all the worries about the court case and Families United and Mother and Rodriguez and the Yerba job. It's just me and my tiger tonight. I watch myself in the mirror, black paw on my white sheath, the tip hidden under the edge of the shirt, and I think about Dev chasing me, grabbing me, holding me and pressing into me. A little squirt of lube under the tail and I'm ready.

When I walk out, Dev stares. I give him a saucy smile. "Come on, defense, tackle me."

He growls and leaps; I dodge around the bed and he comes across it, lightning-fast. I'm laughing now and also getting more aroused, and in my haste to get back to the other side of the bed, I stumble over one of the decorative pillows that got dropped on the floor. In a second, Dev's on me, arms wrapping me up tightly, bearing me down to the floor. "I'll show you defense," he growls.

"Eek!" I squeak, mostly theatrically. "Let's at least get on the bed!"

"Nuh-uh," he growls, keeping me pinned with his weight while he undoes his pants.

So we do it there on the floor. It's hard and a little uncomfortable, and maybe that's why some of those thoughts I tried to leave behind come back, like the sour thought that he doesn't mind being gay here in the hotel room, where he can fuck me on the floor and nobody has to see, but what about out in public?

I know with my head that those are silly, insecure thoughts, that I'm going through all this because of my family and my joblessness and insecurity about my own future. Dev can't just parade me around in front of the team, but he hasn't been ashamed to bring me to events, and the guys know me. And Dev loves me, I can tell by the passion with which he's holding me, rubbing against me, mouthing at my ears. When he gets himself all slick and ready, I tell my inner voice in no uncertain terms to shut the hell up. Eyes squeezed shut, I lose myself in the sensations, in the rocking and thrusting, in the weight and solidity on me, in his warm breath still smelling of the dinner we just finished, and in the love that underlies all of that. His paw reaches under me to finish me off and that carries us all the way to the yelping, moaning, growling end.

"We've made a mess on the carpet," I murmur, my stomach pressed down into it.

"Uh-huh." He kisses my ear. "Don't care."

If this hotel had a surcharge for foxes ("scent neutralization fee"), I wouldn't care either. But they don't, and I don't want to leave a dried, sticky carpet for the maid to clean, so I know I'll clean it up myself after Dev's gone. But I'll probably use the sticky Pilots shirt, and that makes me smile. "Me neither," I say.

CHAPTER 4 — GAME ONE (DEV)

We sit in the locker room stretching and doing light exercises while the Highbourne-Peco game is going on. The bets—friendly bets, of course, because betting in the locker room is illegal—are pretty evenly split between the teams. The guys who bet on the Rocs are remembering losing to them in Chevali; the guys betting on Peco are mostly betting the odds and hoping we don't have to face Highbourne again. If they win and we win, next week's game would be in their stadium, about a mile higher than ours.

Charm is all for that, because kicks travel farther where the air is thinner—"I'll kick it from seventy!"—but the rest of us who have to breathe it for an entire game hate the idea. We're hopeful early on, with the Rocs and Fraters trading scores to finish the first half tied, and then the Rocs' pounding running game breaks open the third quarter and they're up 28-17 at the end of three. "Get the oxygen tanks ready," someone says.

And then something funny happens. The Fraters tighten up their defense. The Rocs seem pretty happy to just run, run, run, chew up the clock, keep the lead. But they can't get a first down. The Fraters get the ball and go down the field for a score, showing patience. "Poise," Fisher says. He stands up and points to the screen after they score, and stays through a few half-hearted "siddown" calls. "Poise. No panicking. That's the mark of a champion. That's why they're gonna win this…" He pauses, and then goes on. "Game. And they're a threat to defend their title." Pretty bold for him to predict a win. I'm absorbed in the game, though, and I don't really pay much attention.

It turns out he looks pretty smart as the game goes on. Clinging to a four-point lead with the clock running down, now it's Highbourne that panics. They still can't get through the Fraters' line, so they start throwing, and as soon as they do that, Fisher turns away in disgust. "Getting away from what works," he says. "Game over. You guys who bet on Peco might as well collect your money now."

"Hang on there," Vonni says. "Rocs got a chance still. They got a Hall of Fame quarterback."

"Uh-huh. And who's he throwing to?" Ty puts his two cents in.

"A bunch of guys with more experience than you," our tight end snaps at him, but everyone else stays quiet, watching. Ty's not entirely wrong; the Rocs have a middling crew of wide receivers. Personally, I think we've got three that are more talented than their number one, but their quarterback is good enough to make middling receivers shine. He used to be, anyway, as recently as earlier this season, but here it's not working for him anymore. He gets them a first down with a short pass, but the run still isn't there on first, so he throws again on second down, or tries to. The rush overwhelms him, his receivers can't get open, and he goes down seven yards behind the line.

He comes out of the game then, limping slightly. The commentators say he can't put weight on his ankle, that he's trying to walk it off, and meanwhile there's Seito, white paws and tail in the white uni, trotting out to take the snap. It's third and long, so he drops back and scans the field. A moment before the defensive end hits him, he gets off a nice-looking pass, but he overthrows the receiver by about five yards, and he's lucky it's not picked off.

Head down, he trots back to the sideline. I make a mental note to call him later. Methodically, like clockwork, the Fraters drive down the field and score on a short run with thirty seconds to go. The stunned Rocs can't even muster a block attempt on the kick. It's 31-28 and the home crowd is crazy loud.

Lee calls me just then. "Phone off soon?"

"In a few. Once the game's over."

"The game's over," he says. "It was over when they started throwing."

"That's what Fisher said."

"Seito didn't get much of a chance. Anyway," he says, "I know you've gotta go. I just wanted to say that I know you can do this. You're really good. You're better than you were two months ago, and you're going to win this game."

I flush all warm and get a big smile on my muzzle as I look up and see the score go final. "Thanks. Any advice on running the plays?"

"Nah. You know it all. You don't need me."

"Hey." The TVs go off and money changes paws as the guys who were betting on the Rocs all remember money they had previously borrowed from the guys who bet on the Fraters. A few sit hunched over their iPods; some are just chatting, but most of us are getting dressed in earnest now. "I need you."

"Thanks," he says, "but not for the next few hours, you don't. I'm up in section 224—no owner's box this time."

"You're not even sitting with Gena?"

"No. Where's she?"

"She's with the player's wives in 109. Go down there, I'm sure they can find a spot for you."

"I'm good here. I just wanted to say—if that fox or any of them gets on your case again, you know what to do?"

"Ignore it."

"Or give it back to them. Tell him, 'Hey, if you want a date I'll see if I know a leather daddy who wants a little bitch.' "

I laugh. "Maybe I'll try that one. See, I do need you."

"Have a good game, tiger. I'll see you after. Love you."

I turn the phone off and toss it back in my locker, then pull my pads on and my jersey over it. It never really occurred to me to get Lee tickets with the other wives, but of course I should do that. For next week, I remind myself.

The locker room is getting more restless. Fisher goes around to the defense saying, "Poise! That's what makes a champion. Let's go out there and take care of business."

His energy makes me feel better about our chances. Even Pike, demoted to backup, seems excited and happy. Of course, when I asked him how he felt about Fisher coming back, he said, "Y'know, I think I played myself into a good position for a new contract." Part of it was the coaching staff changing things to fit him, but he also played his heart out, and people notice that.

Gerrard sits and watches with amusement. I edge over closer to him and say, "You miss being the veteran in the room?"

"Nah." He grins. "Saves me the energy of making people get up for the game. Fish does it better than I do anyway."

"Not true," I say, but I say it low because Fish comes over just then.

"You ready?" he asks me in particular and the three of us in general.

I nod, give him a fierce smile. "We know how to win in this stadium. Don't worry about that."

"Yeah." He rubs his leg and growls. "Wish I'd been here for that. Fucking boar."

"Happens," I say. "Part of the game."

"I never missed more than one game a season before." His tail's switching, and he flexes his claws in and out. "Just let me out there."

That's just when Coach comes in and sits us all down for the pre-game speech. He doesn't say anything at first, just paces back and forth in front of the room as we all watch him. "I'm not gonna tell you this is just like any other game," he says finally. "You'd all call bullshit on me. But I'm gonna tell you about a friend of mine, Captain Richards, was an F-18 pilot in the war back in '91. He and his squadron did drills until they were perfect. Top marks every time. Then they went to war, and they thought the drills weren't going to matter. But they did. What saved his life, he said, was remembering that he'd been taught those drills for a reason, that whether it was live warheads coming at him or a simulation, he had to remember that he'd been trained in what to do, and trust his training." He points out the door. "This is our war, yeah. We lose here, we go home. But that field is a hundred yards long. You're going to line up against the same eleven guys you did last week. The plays are the same. The ball's the same. There's pressure, yeah. Thrive on it. That's where champions are made. This is the reward for all the shit you go through, all those injuries and the defeats. You know how to play this game. And if you go out there and play the game the way you know how—the way I know you know how—we're going to Boliat next week."

"Yeah!" We scream it, echoes ringing through the locker room.

"On three," he says, and as a team we put our fists in and call out, "FIREBIRDS!"

Blue Yonder Stadium is one of those big, bright ones, built right before the craze of putting roofs on things even though Hellentown gets regular rain showers. Today, in fact, the clouds are threatening and it's already damp on the sidelines. Supposed to be rainy but not so much that it'll affect anything in our game.

Shows what the weather guys know. The rain starts right after the national anthem. I inhale the moisture and feel the dampness soaking into my tail. Some of the guys grumble, but it energizes me, takes me back to my days in Hilltown and Forester. Playing in a desert is nice for the warmth and all, but you get dehydrated easily if you aren't careful, and days like this remind me that I still haven't gotten completely used to it.

We win the toss and elect to receive. Zillo comes up to stand next to me as the game kicks off, and we cheer our offense as they run out. Again, the Pilots try double-covering Strike, and Aston responds by handing off to Jaws and dumping off short. Ty is targeted twice in the first five plays and hauls in both catches easily, including one that wasn't very well thrown.

We're excited and cheering as we get to midfield, and then I look at how the Pilots are lining up and I see the safety cheating toward the middle. "Safety," I say to Gerrard.

"I see it," he says. "Aston does, too."

I look toward the wolf under center. He's barking out an audible and then he hurries back to the shotgun position. Jaws listens to him and breaks out to the right, as if they're going for a screen pass. It draws the attention of the corner on that side, which is also Strike's side; the safety, who should cover when the corner switches assignments, doesn't see it.

At the snap, Aston fakes the short toss to Jaws and then looks down the field, not even bothering to conceal where he's going to throw. The safety sees it and sprints toward Strike's side, but the cheetah's already almost past him. Aston's throw arcs through the drizzling rain.

"Long," Zillo says, beside me. "Dammit."

It sure looks like it's going to fall two yards in front of Strike. But... "Wait," Gerrard says.

Strike glances up, sees the ball. And then, amazingly, he extends his stride, sprints faster—visibly faster, kicking in that extra gear. He reaches the ball and doesn't even have to dive for it, just raises one paw and snags the ball out of the air in stride and keeps going. The safety has no chance, already two yards behind him and losing ground, and by the time anyone else even gets to within ten yards of the cheetah, Strike is dancing in the end zone.

He's painted his fur with patriotic colors, red, white, and blue, and the red isn't the true red of the flag, but it's the red of our away jersey so it all goes together, even with his gold number. When he drops the ball in the end zone, he faces the flag hanging above it and holds a salute for a good five seconds, until Ty and Rodo get to the end zone and mob him. On the sidelines, we're jumping up and down and hugging each other, and Charm flashes us a smile as he goes out to kick the extra point and says, "Watch me," and sure enough, he knocks it clean and true between the uprights.

Then it's our turn to go out and keep that lead. The field squelches under our paws as we hurry to our positions. Brick comes up beside me and taps my arm. "Hey," he says, "that guy mouths off to you again, you want we should flatten him?"

I shake my head, spotting the fox in brown and gold, the big "83" on his chest. "I got him."

When we line up, the fox doesn't say anything at first, focusing on the snap count. So I yell across to him, because I'm up at the line to stop the run, "Hey, you get a boyfriend yet or are you gonna be hitting on me the whole game again?"

Fisher, next to me, laughs. The fox's ears flick toward me, but he doesn't react otherwise; still, when the ball's snapped, I think he's a little slow to get off the line. He doesn't block effectively and I get past him, teaming with Fisher to drop the running back for a loss.

As we're walking back to our line, the fox passes me and snaps, "Don't flatter yourself, homo."

"I wasn't," I say. "Just thought you looked lonely."

"Fuck you," he yells after us.

"That's how to get to him," Fisher says with a pat on my back. We huddle around Gerrard with the rest of the defense.

"Watch the short pass," he says, "but they could audible to a draw."

"I've got my eye on eighty-three," I say.

"I think he's straight," Brick says. "Just a guess."

"Yeah, well." I flex my paws. "I'm gonna stick closer to him than his girlfriend does."

"Don't let him in your head," Gerrard says. "Don't start anything if he doesn't."

Fisher pats my shoulder. "Dev's got that asshole," he says. "Don't you worry about him."

We line up, and I spare a glance for their QB, Andy Buck, a big lion who's starting to get "future Hall of Famer" attached to his name. I see his head turn toward eighty-three, but I'm as close to the fox as I promised, matching him every step, running the play just the way we drew it up. Buck tries to go long to one of the receivers in the middle of the field, and Vonni knocks the ball away.

On third, they throw long, and there's not much for me to do except help cover the middle. Fisher is a dynamo, a force of nature collapsing the line with his speed and strength, playing like he's ten years younger. He hurries the quarterback and the pass falls harmlessly incomplete. They punt it back to us.

By the second quarter, it feels like it's not even going to be a contest. We've marched for a field goal and they've only gotten past midfield once, and then only to the 45. We get another score in the second quarter, and even when they match us with a touchdown, we feel like we've got it under control. The fox receiver has shut up more or less completely, acting more tentative in the damp grass. I'm heavier, with firmer footing, and I knock into him plenty of times just off the line. When he tries to block for the run, I shoulder him aside and hit the gaps hard. He only catches the ball once.

Late in the second, the lion throws to eighty-three and I tackle him right as the ball gets to his paws. He clutches at it, but it's slick and it squirts away from him, off to my right. I see a flash of red, and turn to watch the ball drop neatly into a pair of tan paws. They cradle it to the big gold 55, and the next thing I see is Gerrard's tail as he takes off. I drop the fox to the ground and get up immediately to block for Gerrard down the field, knocking aside one of the speedy Pilots receivers who turned to chase him. We get into the end zone untouched, where he sets the ball down and folds his arms before I jump on him and yell, "No flags!" because the field is clear of yellow penalty markers and the touchdown is going to stand.

He laughs and then the rest of the defense catches up to us and all of them pile on and we don't even care that they block the point after, we're up 23-7 and we're *feeling* it.

They get another score before the half, but we block the extra point to keep it to 23-13, a two-score lead still. Coach has a hard time getting us to calm down in the locker room. "We're doing great," he says. "Keep it up. That's all I'm gonna tell you. They're going to make some adjustments, but you just keep doing what you're doing. It's working."

That said, he still huddles with the coaches and Steez comes over to us afterwards with a list of simple things to watch out for and two plays he wants us to focus on executing better. "You are all doing well," he says. "Heads in game. Very good."

We run out for the third quarter into harder, driving rain. Charm has gotten over the blocked extra point enough to tell me that this makes the Pilots' cheerleaders look even better. I say, "Why are you telling me?" and he says that just because I don't want to hit that don't mean I can't appreciate beauty in the world.

The Pilots come out as hard as the rain. They block ferociously, taking advantage of the slippery conditions when we can't get complete leverage. Play after play, we give up a couple extra yards because we can't hit the holes as hard, even when we dig in our claws. Twice we think we've got them beat, and then Buck makes an amazing short pass to pick up the yardage. He drives them down to our nineteen, and there we finally stop them, getting more pressure on the line so our corners can make plays on the passes.

On fourth down, they don't settle for a field goal, and we huddle up, tense. If they get a touchdown on this drive, then our big lead is down to three or four. What's more, they'll be confident, feeling in their element here in the rain and slop against the team from the desert. I think they're going to pass, but Gerrard looks at the formation and barks, "Up! Up!" which means he thinks it's a run. Sometimes when he does that, the QB changes the play to something else at the line—sometimes that's why Gerrard does it. But Buck just goes ahead with the snap, the Pilots charge forward, and we all charge against them, the line, linebackers and safeties. I'm pushing Fisher forward; Vonni piles in behind me, adding his weight to the scrum. We're forced backwards an inch and then we shift the momentum, pushing forward, and our strength wins the day. The running back lands a yard short. It's our ball.

After that, I look up toward Lee in the stands, and realize that this is the first time I've done that in the game, at least from the field. I hope guiltily that he didn't notice, but even if he did, I'm sure he understands. I'm just thinking about the game and doing the best I can. And anyway, after the last game when I was distracted thinking about him and his equality issues, maybe it's better I keep my mind on the field until I can get back to focusing on the things he's helped me with and done for me.

I look up his way again from the sidelines while the offense is marching down the field, just as the crowd collectively gasps and then groans. So I only see the big play on the JumboTron replay: Strike slips on the grass, and the cornerback covering him tries to change direction and skids and falls. Strike recovers his balance and takes off down the middle, and our offensive line has given Aston enough time to make a beautiful throw, a spiral that finds Strike right in the paws. Two seconds later, it's 29-13.

"That's what Strike does," Gerrard says as we prepare to go back out. "That's why he's worth all the trouble. He knocks a team down, makes them feel like the game is out of their reach. If he can get that touchdown at any time and they know it…that's hard, mentally. He got into their heads from the beginning."

"Also Fisher is kicking ass," I point out.

"He had half the season off." Pike comes up behind us.

Gerrard half-turns. "Don't worry. You'll get back in."

"Oh, I know." Pike laughs. "We're gonna have one more game at least."

After that, the fox, eighty-three, is completely silent, his tail wet and muddy, his ears splayed to the side. None of the Pilots play with the same energy they came out of the halftime break with, though they go through the motions and get another score. We control the ball as the fourth quarter winds down, up by a comfortable 38-23 margin, which has the defense standing on the sidelines and starting to celebrate once we get under a minute of game time left.

"Hey." Fisher elbows me. "Help me get the Bolt."

The clock's ticking down past twenty. A couple other players have the same idea, so we all grab the big tub of Bolt-Ade and come up behind Coach. The assistant coaches behind him grin and move out of the way, and we heft it and pour the whole thing over Coach's head.

He laughs and shakes himself, turning around to see our grinning muzzles. "First playoff win!" Fisher yells, and we pounce on Coach, hugging and congratulating him as the clock runs down to zero.

"I gotta go! I gotta go!" He wrestles free of us, laughing, his tail wagging, and runs out onto the field to shake the paw of the Pilots' coach. We all follow after him, squishing through the wet grass, our bedraggled tails showing our giddy highs even as we try to keep our features calm. We know what it's like to be on the other side, and as hard as it is to keep that in mind during our first playoff win, we remember last week only too well, so we don't rub it in.

The Hellentown linebackers come find us again, like they did last week, and compliment us. "You guys are tight," the wolf Kniss says. "Go kick the hell out of Boliat for the South, huh?"

"Do our best." I shake his paw, and Zillo, next to me, does too. "You guys played 'em this year, any tips?"

He shakes his head. "They got a hell of a tight end game. Carson's gonna have his paws full, so you might have to cheat over to help. We played 'em here, so I dunno, but I hear that stadium is insane."

"Fucking domes," I say, and we all look up into the rain and laugh.

"Wish I could be there," he says, and I see that longing in his eyes that Fisher was talking about. "Hey," he says, lowering his voice. "Now the season's over—for us—just wanted to say, good luck. There's a lot of us straight guys pulling for ya. My cousin's gay. Didn't know about it 'til a few weeks ago. He e-mailed me and asked what I thought about you and I said I didn't know, thought it was cool, and he told me he's gay too." His smile shows his canines. "I'd ask for an autograph for him, but not out here…"

"Yeah, send me an e-mail, I'll send him something," I say. "Not a problem."

"Cool, thanks."

The other wolf, Price, is talking to Gerrard about the Boxers. "That raccoon, Pietro, the tight end—keep tight to him. He'll block and then spin out to catch a screen. They run that fucking play at least once a series."

Carson nods. "But here's the thing," Price says. "You guys can take 'em. We kept the game close, just didn't come up with the ball at the end. You play like you did today and you'll have a chance." His eyes drift beyond us, to our sideline. "That fucking cheetah," he says, and shakes his head. "Gets to be too much, y'know, the off-the-field shit. He takes off, you say 'don't let the door hit your ass,' and you think you won't miss him. And then this… bet he couldn't fuckin' wait to come in here and stick it to us."

"Too bad we can't just play his former teams," Gerrard says, and they laugh. But the laughter is short, and their ears are flat with more than just the rain, and they don't talk much beyond that.

"That's what we don't want to feel," he tells me and Carson and Zillo as we trot back to the locker room. Zillo hangs back, and I drop back a bit with him.

"Do you get that a lot?" he asks.

"I dunno. Never won a playoff game before. But some of the guys on other teams are usually cool about upcoming opponents. We try to—"

"No, I mean." His ears flick, spraying water. "People who know people who are gay. That sort of thing."

"Oh. Yeah, well. More now than I used to." I grin at him. "Why? You know someone?"

He rubs his ear and takes a long time to answer. "I probably do, but nobody's talked to me about it."

"Okay…"

We had been jogging, but he slows to a walk. Vonni jogs up beside us and slaps Zillo on the shoulder with a rain-wet smack. "Come on, we can enjoy this in the locker room!" he says.

"We'll be in in a minute," I say.

"See yas there, then." He jogs on ahead.

"So what's up?" I ask Zillo when Vonni's out of earshot.

The coyote brushes rain from his whiskers. "I know I was kind of a dick to you," he says finally.

"That was a couple months ago."

"Yeah, but." He sighs. "I dunno, I'm probably just being stupid. I'm wondering if I'm just a dick in general. And, like, people don't want to come out to me because I'm a dick."

"Maybe. I hear gay guys like dicks, though."

He squints. "You makin' fun of me?"

"A little, maybe."

He shakes his head. "I know, I shouldn't even be worrying about it. I just don't wanna be an asshole."

I laugh and put an arm around his shoulder. "What made you all worked up about that?"

"Ah, it was just…the shit last week and this week, and you've been working with me, helping me out, and you're a good guy. Colin said you'd try to turn the rest of us gay, or put the moves on us or something, and hell, I didn't know any gay guys except from movies."

"Uh-huh."

"But you know, after that Gateway game, it was like, I realized you were tryin' as hard as you can, and that…I could trust you. And you weren't pushin' the gay thing on me or anything, you weren't trying to get in my pants or make me 'admit to my repressed gay fucking feelings' like Colin says a lot of those fag—those guys do."

I can't help thinking about how I met Lee. "Do you have repressed gay feelings?"

He half-twists away from me, and I drop my arm. "No." Then he looks at me and laughs. "Hell, I dunno. If I do, they're repressed pretty deep. But I wanna be a good guy."

"I think you are." We get to the tunnel. "You're talking to me now, anyway. Are you talking to Colin again?"

He shakes his head. "He asked Coach for a new roommate."

"Who's he hanging out with these days?"

"I dunno, really. Most of the guys I talk to on the team don't give a shit who you're sleeping with, to be honest. I'm glad you don't hold it against me. From when I was an asshole, I mean. I'm learning a lot working with you."

"Thanks. I'm learning a lot from Gerrard."

"Yeah, he's awesome. He's gonna be a coach as soon as he retires."

"If he wants to be. He's got a family to spend time with."

Zillo doesn't say anything, but his ears, which came up once we got indoors, are down again. I nudge him at the entrance to the locker room. There aren't any other guys in the tunnel, and I keep my voice low enough that even the big-eared foxes in the locker room shouldn't be able to hear it (one thing I have practice with, having a fox boyfriend). "You know something about Gerrard?"

He shrugs. "Not really. But you notice how Fisher's wife is out here, and Vonni's wife, and your boyfriend, and...where's Angela?"

I wipe my whiskers clean of water. "Watching the cubs?"

"Yeah, I guess. Ah, forget about it."

"I know he's got a couple flings on the side when he's on the road," I say, quietly. "But I just got here last year. You know more?"

Zillo hesitates. "More than just a couple flings," he says. "Look, if you really wanna know, I'll tell you later." He smiles, big and long and coyote-ish. "But maybe not. Maybe talking about it would make me an asshole, y'know? Let's go get some champagne."

"They won't have champagne," I say, but we open the door and I'm wrong. It's not popping and running all over everyone, but there are bottles all over the locker room and guys are hooting and whooping and drinking. Soon as I get in, someone presses a bottle into my paw and I drink through my mouthguard, then hand it off to someone else and run to my locker to get at least the helmet and my soaking wet jersey off. The whole place smells of champagne and wet fur and sweat and it's glorious.

"Great game," I say to Gerrard when I get to the locker, but it might as well be to any of the guys in the room, and it's Ty who responds with a whoop, shoving a bottle of champagne at me and spilling it on my uniform.

I laugh and take it, gulp some down, and pass it on to one of the defensive line guys nearby. The room is full of "you freak!" (in a good way, mind) and "remember that play" and "we did it," bursts of reminiscence replaying the game over and over, every moment a highlight, every one of us a star. This is the kind of moment I live for, just out of battle with another team, when we've imposed our will on them and proven ourselves better. With the Dragons, I had precious few wins to celebrate; only in Chevali did I contribute to the team winning, and never in a game with higher stakes than this one—until next week.

We're a little giddy—some of us more than a little—when Coach tries to calm us down. He keeps it short: we did great, we've got a tough game to prep for, enjoy ourselves tonight and we'll be on the plane tomorrow, practice Tuesday. He clears his throat, looks around, and says, "Thanks for the shower. No more until we win a championship, okay?"

"Yeah!" We laugh, and those closest to him hug him.

"Hey!" Steez and the other assistant coaches and coordinators have all gathered in a group, with the cougar speaking for them. "Maybe one more shower, yes?"

He steps aside to reveal the offensive coordinator with his thumb over the mouth of a bottle of champagne, which Coach only registers for a second before he's getting sprayed with the contents. He laughs and swipes at the bottle, but they keep it out of his reach. "First playoff win," Steez says. "Is worth celebrating!"

"All right, all right." Coach licks champagne from his dripping muzzle. "We've got the hotel ballroom reserved for tonight and we're ordering out from Jack's Steakburgers, so I'll see all you winners there."

He and the other coaches disappear back into their offices while the rest of us continue to gulp champagne and get undressed and showered and dressed again. Near me, Vonni's on the phone with Daria, his wife, telling her where to come for the dinner. I hadn't thought that spouses—partners—would be welcome, so when Vonni's off the phone, I ask if his wife's coming, just to confirm. He says, "Yeah," so I take out my phone to tell Lee to come over too. As soon as I turn it on, it comes to life with a dozen text messages, only a few of them from my fox. My parents left me a voicemail, and a couple of my teammates from the Dragons texted me congratulations. But Lee's are the ones I read first.

Great job!

Then, at the end of the game, *Yeah!!!*

And then: *So proud of you. Two more. :)*

I put the phone down, feeling the warmth in my chest that Lee always brings when he's like that. I resolve to do my damnedest to win our next two games—devote myself to practice, learn every assignment, watch hours of film, whatever it takes. This feeling echoes back to those games in college when he gave me a goal to play for, showed me how I could be great. I want to be the best for myself, for the guys around me, and maybe most of all for him.

Fisher's walking out of the training room when I look up. "You okay?" I say. "What got dinged?"

He puts a paw to his head and shakes it slowly, but he doesn't appear to be limping or anything. "Nothing much, just wanted to check out the injury, make sure I didn't make anything worse."

"So?"

"I'm good." He gives me a fierce smile.

I nod. "Okay. Gena's coming to the thing tonight, right?"

"Uh-huh." He sits by his locker, but doesn't move to get dressed right away.

"All right. I'll tell Lee he can come too." I call my fox and tell him he can come over to the hotel and that I'll see him there. He asks twice if it's okay and I assure him it's fine, the other wives will be there. He snorts and says he loves me, and I kinda lower my voice and say I love him too.

And when I hang up, Fisher's still just sitting there on the bench in front of his locker, stripes wrinkled on his forehead like he's trying to remember something. "You getting dressed?" I say. "Or just going to go in your Ultimate Fit underclothes?"

He blinks at me, and the stripes straighten out. "Quit fucking rushing me! I'm fine." And then he peels off his undershirt so violently that one of the seams rips, and he heads for the shower.

He doesn't seem quite right, but I don't want to ask him and maybe get him more agitated. And most of the other guys I would confide my worry in have already left. The only one nearby is Pike, with Kodi the brown bear trailing behind him like always, and as Fisher's backup I'm not sure Pike wouldn't go right back to the trainer and say there might be something wrong with Fish. He says he's okay being a backup again, but seriously, which one of us would be in this locker room if we didn't desperately want to start? Well, Kodi and a few other backups seem happy to ride the bench. But not Pike.

So I just go out to talk to the media as per usual. I'm amused that they've pretty much stopped asking me if the other team is targeting me because I'm gay now that a team was actually doing it. But I don't mind; I'd rather not talk about it. Mostly they don't want to talk to me anyway. They want to talk to Strike, who was voted player of the game with his two touchdowns, and they want to hear why this game was so different from last week's, and so I get away with a couple questions about containing their slot receiver, the fox, and that's it.

After the media session, I see Fisher again, laughing and joking with Gerrard. He looks fine now. So maybe the doc just gave him a painkiller and that was his initial reaction to it. I did notice he didn't drink any champagne that I could see, which we're told not to do if we get the extra-strength painkillers.

On the bus back to the hotel, he's just as jovial and happy as the rest of us, so I stop worrying about him. He's a football player. He'll be fine. We've switched to bottles of beer, being tossed around the bus and opened in a spray of foam, and I manage to get through one of those on the short trip, by which time I'm feeling definitely buzzed.

The hotel ballroom is set up with Firebirds flags and red and gold crepe paper, TVs in the corners tuned to ESPN, and several buffet tables that are empty as of right now. I'm still in a giddy good mood—the beer and champagne helping—and so are most of the guys. We stand around talking about the game and how hungry we are, so when the guys from Jack's Steakburger arrive, we hover over them as they're unpacking their stack of delivery boxes.

Lee calls me just then to ask me to come down and get him past hotel security, and I say, "They're delivering our food on a forklift. This is amazing!"

The Jack's guys are trying to arrange the burgers on the table, but we're not patient. I don't know who the first one is who just grabs a burger, but pretty soon we're all grabbing at them and the poor ferret just has to jump out of the way as this mob of football players descends on his food, ripping open the next delivery box when the ones he's unpacked run out. Then they run over to the 'roo setting up the fixings bar with lettuce and tomatoes and onions in huge bins. Well, some of them do. A bunch of us just cram the burgers into our muzzles without any condiments or toppings or anything.

"These are really good," Jaws mumbles through a mouthful.

The ferret edges away from the huge wolverine and back to the table. "Thanks," he says, and takes the next delivery box and starts setting up burgers on the table.

"Got any mustard?"

The ferret points over to the kangaroo who's setting up fixings and condiments. "Did they not feed you guys all day?"

"We just won our first playoff game!" someone shouts, and the whole room cheers and whoops and hollers.

"You a Pilots fan?" someone asks the ferret.

He puts his paws on his hips and looks around at all of us. "Not for the next couple hours."

We all laugh and slap him on the back. I grab another burger and head out to fetch Lee. Somehow when I meet him in the lobby and hold the burger out to him, it's already half-gone.

"Thanks," he says, looking at it, "but I already rummaged around in the garbage bin back at my hotel."

"Sorry." I take a few more bites from it. "I'll get you a fresh one. Meant to, just…I'm really hungry."

"It's no problem." He smiles. "Hold up, Gena came with me."

"Oh, okay." I finish the burger and look around the mostly-empty lobby. "No groupies this time?"

"I guess not." He follows my gaze. "Maybe it's still too early. They'll be around later, I'm sure. Phew. Have you been drinking beer and champagne?"

I flatten my ears. "Not at the same time."

He laughs. "Well, that's good, anyway." Gena walks out from the restroom and Lee says, "Okay, let's go on up."

By the time we get back up, more of the wives have shown up. I don't really think Lee needed me to get him through hotel security this time. We walk over to the buffet table to get burgers for Lee and Gena, and then stand a little ways away.

Fisher finds us quickly. "How're you feeling?" Gena asks.

"I'm fine," he snaps. "Never felt better." He rips a chunk out of his burger.

"You looked great," Lee says. "Like old times out there."

"Yeah." He chews and swallows. "Good as I ever was."

Gena looks worried but doesn't say anything. I'm not sure why she'd be worried. She should be happy that Fisher is back to his old self. Less for her to worry about around the house, I guess.

We talk about the game and about Boliat's team, which leaves Gena kind of out of the conversation, but Lee makes an effort to say things she can follow. I grab a third burger and a beer and am starting to come down a little off my buzz when a sharp voice interrupts us.

"Hey," I hear a yard away. I turn to see Colin standing there, a beer in one paw. Behind him are two guys I only vaguely recognize; I think we signed them to the practice squad a month ago. But Colin's staring at Lee. "I thought this was for players and wives. You a player or a wife?"

His breath reeks of beer. He points at Lee with the paw holding the bottle. Lee hunches inward for a moment and then stands up straighter. "I'm here with Dev," he says.

"I asked, are you a player or a wife?"

"Listen," Fisher says, "there's no problem here. Why don't you just go back—"

"Not talking to you, old-timer," Colin says. "I want to know why this little bitch is here at our playoff celebration eating our food."

Lee opens his mouth. I pre-empt him. "Hey," I say to Colin, "Just keep walking. We're having a nice chat here."

"Who the *fuck* are you calling old?" Fisher's voice rings out. Gena holds his arm, and I really think he might just clock Colin in the muzzle if she lets go. I don't move to help her.

Colin turns on me. "Wasn't talking to you, either," he says. "I know what you think."

"No, but you were talking to me." Fisher strains against Gena's hold, not as hard as he can, of course, but enough to make Colin take a step back. "You want to show a little respect, you pissant little snot?"

"I got plenty of respect for you," Colin says, "and any other guy who actually *plays* this game."

"Chill," I tell Fisher. I'm worried about Lee, but he's frozen, ears flat, eyes wide. I don't know what's up, but at least he's not causing more of a scene, and I'm more worried about Fisher right now.

"No." He yanks an arm free of Gena and pokes Colin in the chest so hard the fox stumbles backwards. "*This* motherfucker has to chill. You play on a team, you give everyone on that team your respect!"

His voice is so loud that silence spreads in ripples around us. Colin glares at Fisher, his ears down, and his fists are clenched, but I don't think he's going to try anything. I'm tense too, ready to go for him if he does.

Then Gena breaks the silence. "That's enough." She grabs Fisher's arm and drags him backwards. "Sorry. We're leaving."

Lee opens his muzzle again and though I try to edge in front of him, I can't think of anything to say to that, and Lee talks before I can get a word out, his voice low and quiet. "I'll go."

"No. Fuck that." I turn on Colin. "You don't like it, go stand in another part of the room. But he's here with me and he's gonna stay here."

I see Pike making his way toward me, Charm near him. Colin just stares at me and says, "I'm trying to do you a favor, asshole."

"Watch who you're calling asshole, dickweed," I say. "And if you call my boyfriend a bitch again, I will show you who's a little bitch."

Colin shakes his head and then looks between us, at Lee. "You people. Corrupting your immortal souls, throwing away God's gifts."

"My soul's prepared," Lee says. "How's yours?"

"Shut up!" He flinches forward, like he's going to start something, but I don't budge. "You want to do something for this team, you should just get out! Out of here, leave him alone…" And then Pike is near us, and Charm, and Kodi, and Zillo, and the coyote is the one who grabs Colin's arm.

"Hey, listen, Colin, just let it go. Let's all just enjoy this, 'kay?"

Colin shakes Zillo off violently. "I'm sick and freaking tired of everyone just pretending this is okay!" he yells.

"We're not pretending," Charm says. Pike and Kodi stand off to the side, behind Fisher. "Come on, there's lots of things to get upset about more than who Gramps wants to date. Like that Dijon mustard. What the fuck is up with that? My nose is burning."

"Joke all you want," Colin says. "This is a trave—a tragedy. No. A travesty. It's…"

Zillo grabs him by the arm again. "C'mon, let's get back to the room," he says. "Maybe you should lie down for a bit."

"I don't need to lie down!" Colin yells. "I need to be in a place where people respect the bond between a male and a female."

But he lets Zillo drag him off. And then we all stand around and look at each other, and Lee finishes the last of his burger. "Well," he says, ears flat, looking down at the floor. "Maybe I should get going."

"You don't have to." I put a paw on his shoulder. "Fuck that guy."

"It's okay," he says. "I'm tired. If you're not ready to go back, I'll just… see you later, I guess."

I'm disappointed, and angry at Colin for ruining the night. So I tell Lee, "Wait for me outside. I just want to go find Coach and tell him about this."

He nods, but his ears stay flat and his shoulders are slumped, and right now I want more than ever to go punch Colin in his smug little fox muzzle. But I walk Lee to the door, keeping my paw on his shoulder so everyone knows he's with me. And when he's out the door and it's closed behind him, I feel like shit.

Chapter 5 — Aftermaths (Lee)

I should've expected something like that to happen. I mean, alcohol— lots of alcohol— and emotions with all these people gathered together. Colin's probably not the only one who feels that way. He's just the one who's most comfortable expressing it.

I sit in the hallway, tail curled around my ankles, wondering how this team can offer me a role doing gay outreach when Colin can make that outburst at a team function and the most anyone can say to him is, "You're being rude." Shouldn't he be fined for it? Isn't that hate speech? Maybe not calling me a bitch, not in a football context. I guess he could argue that it's a common epithet.

It wasn't my place to say more, I tell myself. I'm not a team employee and might never be. The truth is, though, I flashed back to Mother yelling, to myself yelling, and that loss of control that scared me. The cross around his neck, his fox's muzzle, that species familiarity betrayed again—I wanted to open up my throat and scream, but at the same time all that rage terrified me, paralyzed me. Behind that, too, was the memory of my ill-advised attempt to get into the Firebirds' locker room in drag, when one of the players spotted my false chest and things got a little bit rough. Colin was there—not one of the guys pushing me around, but also not the guy who got things under control and escorted me firmly out. Both those guys are gone, cut before the first game of the season. Colin's still here.

Thank God he insulted Fisher, too; without that distraction I might have just run away, or called Colin a bigoted self-righteous asshole, and none of that would be helpful to Dev and his playoff run. I'm sure my movie quote wasn't helpful either, but it was the only way I could think to respond, challenging but half-jokey if he got it, and allowing me to feel superior if he didn't. Only of course it fell flat, because he didn't get it and it just pissed him off.

Running away doesn't feel good, no matter how much I tell myself it was better than the alternative. The hallway is empty and silent, so there's no judge but my own thoughts. Two confrontations in just over a week, and I didn't handle either one of them admirably. There's got to be a middle ground between yelling and running away, but damned if I can find it.

When the door to the ballroom opens, I look up, expecting to see tiger stripes. Instead, I see the heavier figure of a brown bear, and Kodi walks over to lean against the wall beside me. He doesn't look down, but he folds his arms and talks softly. "Dev's talking to Coach. I said I'd come out and keep you company."

He's tucked his paws into his arms, shakily, and his shoulders are hunched inward. He stares down at the floor and a moment later looks over at me. There's only a slight haze of alcohol on his scent; I don't think he's been drinking. Maybe it's a personal or a religious thing. Or maybe it's someone afraid of what he might reveal when drunk, what he might do without control of his desires. I can read body language well, and when he meets my eyes, he gives a guilty start. The suspicions I had at the Christmas party crystallize, and I decide to take a chance.

"I don't think you should 'come out'," I say softly. Recklessly, maybe, considering what just happened. If I'm wrong, I could get kicked or punched or worse. But I don't care.

And I'm not wrong.

He doesn't even ask how I know, doesn't act surprised. Maybe he figures coming out to be with me when we barely know each other is enough for a fox to figure out. Maybe he remembers our conversation at the Christmas party.

"It's easy for Dev." His voice is so soft, I need to perk my ears up all the way, and even then the whisper is ghostly in the empty hall. "He's a starter. He's important, he's special. He's got someone."

"You don't have a boyfriend?"

Kodi shakes his large head, slowly. "I—I never thought I could. I dated in college, but always broke it off. I'd go to clubs, dress down." He picks at his claws. "Nobody knew who I was."

"Does Pike know?"

The bear twists his paws together. I know that gesture; it's hard for me to stop myself from unconsciously imitating it. "We haven't talked about it. I don't know. Maybe?"

"Do you ever talk about your personal lives?"

He shakes his head, but hesitates. "I mean, I know he has girls. I try to talk about girls a bit, but it always feels wrong."

"Yeah, I know."

He looks down at me. "Were you always out? Not around Dev, I mean, but…you just seem so comfortable."

I laugh shortly. "It's been a long journey for me. And I'm not sure it's over. Scratch that: I'm sure it's not." After all, I was just yelling at my mother, then frozen nose to nose with this other guy I don't even know. Maybe my journey isn't about discovering how to be gay, but just about discovering how to be myself. You know, without pissing off everyone I care about. "But no, I wasn't always out. I was closeted when I worked for the Dragons. When my relationship with Dev was exposed there, I was let go. So that was my price for being outed."

"So you know," he says, and leans his head against the wall with his eyes closed. "Nobody'd miss a backup tackle. Nobody'd notice if I just…went away."

"It's a business," I say, looking up at him. His pose stirs a memory, but I can't place it right away. I rest a paw on my curled tail. "But you have friends who'd miss you."

"There's twenty guys who could do my job who aren't…" He slumps, then bobs his muzzle in the direction of the ballroom door. "And there'll always be moments like that, that make you feel…just worthless. It's easier if I keep quiet."

"I want to tell you that you don't have to," I say. "I'd like to tell you that you'd be making the world a better place by being honest. I think you would. But I think you're right. I don't know that the team would let you go, but…you know the situation better than I do."

"If I had the chance to start," he says. "I could become part of the team. Dev was lucky. They traded Mitchell! Beginning of the season, I never woulda thought…"

"Well. Korey did kind of dig his own grave. Hot-headed and reckless."

Kodi nods. "Don't think any of the line is going anywhere. Even Fisher came back and now Pike's a backup again."

"Next year, maybe. I mean, Pike might get a contract somewhere else and then…" I try to remember if Kodi is the primary backup. "There's always injuries, always a chance."

"I know. That's what I keep telling myself." He scratches the hotel wall with two claws, up and down. "Just another six years. Eight if I'm lucky. Then I can retire and it won't matter any more. I'm saving my money. I won't have to work."

I push myself to my feet. "If you need someone to talk to, you've got my number, right? You can always call me, even if you don't feel right coming out to Dev. I promise I'll keep your secret."

He turns to me, and I know I've only met him twice, but he gives me a smile, an actual smile, with something like hope behind it. "Thanks. It does feel good—"

The ballroom door opens again and Dev comes out, scanning the hallway and then stomping toward me when he sees me. Kodi jumps and says a quick, "See ya," and hurries down the stairs.

Dev barely spares him a glance. "I talked to Coach, and he's gonna talk to Colin, but he says people are under pressure and you can't expect everyone to like you all the time and I know he's not gonna do anything." He smacks a fist into his paw. "We can't even just fucking celebrate winning a goddamn playoff game. This fucking gay stuff has to…"

I flatten my ears. "I didn't have anything to do with it. Maybe it'd be better if I just didn't come."

To his credit, if there's even a split-second when he agrees with that (which I'd expected), I don't see it at all. He meets my eyes and loses the anger, and puts a paw on my shoulder. "I'm sorry."

"Not your fault," I say, and I feel a bit better. "But Colin's got some issues. More than just whatever he did in college with the illegal money, I mean."

"It's just religion," Dev says. "But I mean, I'm sorry I…y'know, sorry I didn't do more."

His ears are down and he's looking past my muzzle to my feet, whiskers drooping, paws limp at his sides. I'm glad he feels bad about it, but at the same time, I don't want him to feel bad. There are a bunch of things he could have done: he could have started a fight (bad), he could have insisted I stay (good), or he could have taken it up immediately with Coach (probably bad in the short term). My heart wants him to have done more, but my head tells me he did pretty much all he could while keeping the peace with the team. He can't take my side against them. So I reach out and squeeze his paw. "It's okay. I don't know what else you could've done. You stood up for me."

"Yeah." He looks at the door, swinging closed. "Was nice of Kodi to keep you company. He feels bad for taking off in the middle of the trip to Korsat, I think."

Kodi accompanied us to the café, coming along with Pike, but left before we all went to the gay club to dance. I hadn't thought much about it, but it slots in neatly to his confession now. I wish I could've done more for Kodi. I wish I could do more for a lot of people. "I told him not to worry about it."

That gets me a smile, maybe just relief, as Dev squeezes my paw back. "Look, you wanna get back to your hotel? I'll walk you back. I can stay the night with you, too."

I do want that, and so we walk on. But I think, too, that my moving to Chevali has exposed just how much I am still a stranger in his world. When I was only visiting every weekend or every other weekend, it was easy to say "well, they just don't know me," and "well, Dev just needs to get used to having me around." All of the courtesy they treated me with the two times I was at Gerrard's seems hollow now. Only Fisher and Gena seemed to genuinely like and accept me. Vonni, maybe, but he is a fox—though that didn't make much difference with Colin. Anyway, they all just stood there and didn't say a word to Colin.

Not that I'd expect them to. He's a teammate. They live and die with him on the field. I guess I'd been fooling myself into thinking that maybe there was more there—respect, if not friendship. After two months of living with Dev, it's harder to keep doing that.

All of that doesn't matter now, though. I just need to tell myself to relax and enjoy the night, and then enjoy the week leading up to the next game. I need to be supportive, because Dev has a chance to have the experience of a lifetime in the next month, and if I do anything to mess that up, I'd never forgive myself. I'm not sure if he would, either.

There are phone calls I can make this week, though. Planning for the future.

That night, Dev is sore from the game, and we've had sex the last two nights, so I suggest we could just sleep together—really sleep—and he thinks that's a great idea. He's affectionate, maybe a little more than usual, and I let his tongue wash over my whiskers and muzzle, his large paws rubbing behind my ears as I press my slender fingers into the fur over his hard chest, feeling the muscles shift ever so slightly with each of his movements. It's nice, just the warmth between us, and his scent and the custom of what we do in bed does get me a bit worked up, but I'm also tired and worn out from the evening, so sleep comes easily.

I'm still thinking about stuff in the morning, and Dev picks up on it. "You're not still worried about Colin, are you?" He wraps his arms around me. "I told you, I talked to Coach about it. He's not going to fine him or anything, but that shit shouldn't happen again."

"I'm not worried for me," I say, but I stay in his embrace because it feels good, warm and safe. I curl my tail around his legs and he curls his tail back around mine.

"I'm doing what I can, but you know, football comes first."

I can't help flicking my ears back. That just makes me think about that meeting Brian wanted Dev to go to for Equality Now, the one with the senators up in Potomac. Did Dev remember that was supposed to be tomorrow? Why did he have to say it like that? Is he just making sure I don't ask again? I try not to tense, to force myself to relax, because he's going to be gone in half an hour and anything I say is just going to linger throughout the week.

It was a lot easier to just shut up and not argue about the same things over and over again when we were apart. Our times together were more precious, arguments could happen over the phone and be resolved over the phone, muted by distance. I wonder if the muting of distance was a good thing, if perhaps the arguments we had were just surface issues, leaving the deeper rifts untouched.

This isn't the time for that. His body pressing against me is so nice, his arms around me feel so strong and warm, that I feel like a total ass. These are thoughts for later, when I'm alone on the plane flight back, for when I'm sitting alone in his apartment surrounded by the smell of him wondering what the hell is going to happen with my life.

So I turn my muzzle to the side and I kiss his arm, and he kisses between my ears again, and if he noticed the flicking of them, he doesn't say. I turn, lift my muzzle to his, and wrap my arms around the solidity of him. For the moment, I try to forget all my doubts.

As soon as he's gone, though, it's a different matter. I don't feel like talking to anyone, so I keep my phone put away, but I do wear a Firebirds shirt on the way to the airport in the hope of getting into a fight, or at least a snide argument (the kind of fight I'm most likely to be able to win). Sadly, the people of Hellentown, or at least the people coming back to or leaving it, are mostly well-mannered, and the worst I get is, "Hey, maybe I should send your luggage to Chesterfield," from the airline agent behind the counter.

"How about Boliat?" I counter snidely.

That just makes her check the ticket again. "Wait, I thought you were going back to Chevali."

I sigh. "Yes, I am."

"I was just being funny, sir."

"I know. I was trying to, too."

"Oh." She smiles at me, full-on fake smile, and hands me my boarding pass. "Have a nice flight."

I don't, not really. The plane is so full that even with the Neutra-Scent tissue I bring to my nose every so often, the scents of all the people crowd me, make me dizzy. I downloaded Dev's e-mail to go through on the plane—the volume jumped after they qualified for the playoffs and after yesterday's win, but I hadn't been really looking too closely at it. Reading through just the subject lines is hardly inspiring. The tone of the messages is mostly positive, but there are still some negative cranks mixed in to the lot. Anything with "fuck" in the subject line I delete immediately, but even in skimming the rest of them, I still get surprised once in a while. A letter with the subject "You're Going All The Way" begins "... To Hell" and just gets worse from there. At least that lets me turn some of my anger and frustration toward these letter writers. I write out responses to the nice letters and nasty ones both, and then delete the nasty responses right away.

Hours later, as we're landing in Chevali, I've gotten through most of the letters and there's nothing really worth spending much time over. Two kids just getting back into high school or college wrote to ask if he would answer some questions for an interview they wanted to do about famous gay people, and I compose responses to both of them saying that we'll answer their questions. At least I can do that one for him if it's just over e-mail.

When I land, I have two messages on my phone. The first voice that hits my ears is Brian's high, nasal whine. His words are slurred, so I don't even need to hear him explain, "This is some good wine. I toasted you after the game and had a little left over this afternoon. A lot left over maybe." He goes right from there into an almost-Shakespearean monologue. "Oh, Tip, fie upon me for a sentimental fool. I had thought my newfound fire for the crusade enough to win you back to the side of light. I have seen sparks in your eyes and the straight, proud rise of your ears, and I thought you could at least give some of yourself to this cause. Alas, alack, I prov'd insufficient to the cause, my earthbound delicate spirit no competition for the angelic and heavenly cock that fills you every night." He pauses there to chuckle, or perhaps to drink again. "But cry not, sweet prince of foxes. This is not farewell. We may not tread the same roads, but still our paths run parallel... no, damn...I'll run alongside you and you've but to look over and I'll be there. Hope has not yet fully left me, you see. Our journeys are not yet at an end. There is much we can yet do, together or apart, and by my troth, I'll see it done."

I look at the phone and then delete the message. I had hoped that leaving him with the snide remarks I did would bring our journeys to an end, but that was optimistic. Whatever Brian has in him will not be dismissed so easily. I thought he'd changed, too, I really had. I thought he'd found a direction and wasn't going to let personal issues dictate his life, thought he was going to let go of his little vendetta against me and Dev. I suppose that only lasted as long as he thought I was really going to join his group and he would have something in common with me.

The second message, from an unfamiliar number, is in a female voice. "Mister Farrel, this is Paula from Equality Now. I'm sorry to call you directly, but Mister Dallas gave me this number and said I should call you regarding Mister Miski's participation in our meeting tomorrow. I assume he can make his own flight arrangements, but I will need to provide him with the time and location, and I would like to talk to him for about an hour tonight to brief him, as well as for half an hour before the meeting tomorrow. Call me back at this number." She reads off the number that shows on my screen.

So Brian didn't pass along that Dev's declining the meeting. Thanks so much. I sigh, standing just outside the airport parking garage, deciding I really should call her back pretty soon, and now is probably the right time. I set my bag down, hit 'Call' on the display, and put the phone to my ear.

When she answers, I introduce myself and say, "I'm sorry. I tried to talk him into it, but he just doesn't want to miss practice during the playoff week. It's really important."

She says, "Right. Well, thank you for trying," in a tone that makes me wonder if her next call is to cancel Christmas in Narnia.

"Is there anything else—"

"I'm very busy," she says. "Good-bye, Mister Farrel."

The line goes dead. Well. It doesn't look like I'll be doing anything with Equality Now, not while Paula is still there. Not unless I can get Dev's attention in the off-season, and while that once seemed a sure thing, now I'm less confident about it.

At home, I grab a snack and sit down with the phone. I dial the number, get through to his secretary, and she says he's free. A moment later, I hear the familiar voice on the phone. "Peter Emmanuel."

"Hi, Mister Emmanuel. Wiley Farrel. Just calling back to check in and say hi."

"Farrel. Hello there. It's nice to talk to someone who's enjoying the playoffs."

"Sorry about your finish," I say. "You played well against us." It's one of the first times I've said "us" and didn't immediately think of the Dragons. I guess I'm getting over that breakup, however slowly.

"We caught some lucky breaks. At the end of the day the season was already pretty much blown." He's relaxed, casual, just about the opposite of Paula. "I guess you're calling about next steps on the position."

The paw not holding the phone plays with my tail, idly. "Right. I like where you're headed and I would like to know more about being a part of it."

"Sure," he says. "I want you to talk to some people, which might be tricky since some of them are taking off on vacation, but we can do it by phone if necessary. Your references came through pretty good, and there's just one guy you really need to talk to."

"Is that your boss?" I try to remember what I know of the Whalers' owner.

He laughs. "Nah. Jocko, director of scouting, he'd be your direct boss. He doesn't trust anyone who, ah, didn't play the game."

There's that little pause in there, that "ah," that makes me think it's not just non-football players Jocko doesn't trust. But I don't press it. "Okay. I'm free all week. This number's fine."

"Great. And I would like you to come up here to meet the staff before we finalize things. Everyone usually comes back here championship weekend, so if you're not traveling with your boyfriend... Hey, what does he think of you taking the job?"

I'm in our couch, Dev's scent all around me. I inhale. "He's supportive. We'd like to stay close, but we realize that with the careers we've chosen, that might not be possible. Football life is a lot of moving around. Even living with him here in Chevali, I don't see him all that much more than when I was living up north."

"True enough." He laughs. "Front office jobs are a little better, but the scouting always takes you all over the place. Glad he's supportive, though. I never had to deal with an employee's boyfriend before, but I've seen a lot of players' wives and girlfriends. They run the gamut from easy-going to controlling everything about the player's career."

"I've met some wives," I say, though the wife I'm thinking of is my father's ex. "I know what you mean."

He laughs. "Right? Okay, Wiley, thanks for calling. I'll have my secretary get back to you with a time as soon as I have enough info. Should be late this week. If you don't get a call, call back on Monday."

"Thanks, Mister Emmanuel."

"Call me Peter."

I hang up feeling vaguely positive, but also a little bit like I'm betraying Dev by not pursuing the Chevali job. So rather than going out to celebrate progress, I make myself a simple dinner with stuff we have lying around the apartment: a can of soup, a frozen burrito. And when Dev calls to tell me he got safely into Boliat, I don't tell him about the call with Yerba, or the calls from Brian or Paula. I just tell him I got back safely and the apartment is still in one piece and I miss him, all of which is true.

The next day, Hal asks me to lunch at a Sonoran taqueria I haven't been to yet. I've got a good parking spot a block from Dev's and I'm used to taking the bus around Chevali anyway, so I ride over to a sketchy area and walk through old, dirty smells before getting a whiff of delicious meats outside a small, grungy place.

Hal walks up a couple minutes later. "Got to show you all the cool dive spots," he says when I eye the place and hesitate before going in. "Not that you're living on a reporter's salary or anything, but still."

"I'm not living on anyone's salary," I say, following him inside. "But now I don't feel as bad about getting you this."

I hold out the alligator-skin tie. It was worth it just to see his expression. He reaches out and takes it between two fingers. "Okay," he says, "I honestly don't know if this is a gag gift or if it's actually fashionable."

"Anything's fashionable." I gesture to my t-shirt and jeans. "You just have to own it."

He still looks skeptical, so I relent. "It's mostly a gag. But I think it might look good on you with the right outfit."

He stuffs it in his pocket and turns with me to the counter, where we order two tacos each. On his recommendation, I get one with carnitas: crisp, juicy, shredded pork that is really delicious. The other has chicken, which is good enough chicken, but doesn't hold a candle to the carnitas. The salsa has good bite and the taco shells smell strongly of corn.

"Pretty good, all in all," I say, dabbing along my muzzle with a napkin, catching tomato and cilantro from the salsa.

"Used to come here two, three times a week back when Cim left." Hal is much more practiced with the tacos and doesn't have nearly as messy a napkin. "So what's with the mopes? Your team won and your ears ain't been up all the way even once."

"Ah, it's stupid." I tap my fingers along the table and don't look at him. I don't want to tell him about the incident with Colin, because it's not that important, really, and I'm still just a little bit wary of the line between 'friend' and 'reporter.' "It's just Dev and the Equality thing. And the job at Chevali, and the job at Yerba, and my dad and my mom and…everything."

"Tough time," he says, and takes a drink. "How you gonna get back on your feet?"

"I talked to Emmanuel at Yerba. Things are getting more firm. So I might be moving up there."

"Even though it's not a hundred percent what you want?"

I trail claws through the fur on the back of my paw, resting it on the table. "What I want is the way things used to be. I want…" I flex my paw. "Even some obstacle I can just charge forward at. A bigoted father, a turncoat ex-best friend."

"A nosy reporter?"

"Yeah." I grin at him. "I can't go after the Vince King thing until the trial moves forward. I can't yell at my mom any more than I already have.

I can't get Dev to do more for gay rights without screwing up his football career, I guess. And I don't have a job to fall back on."

"I told you I'd help you write up an article on the trial. Why don't you talk to the Equality people about reporting it?"

I flick one ear. "My ear still has frostbite from the last call with Paula there. And Brian drunk-called me after the game to monologue at me."

He chuckles. "I'll see if I can find some other outlets. But you do the legwork."

That perks me up a little. "Sure. I'll see what I can dig up." I lift my nose and look back at him. "So how about you? How was the date? Did you get some coyote love?"

His ears flick to the sides: embarrassment. I grin. "That good, huh? Didn't think about Cim?"

"Oh, I thought about her." He opens his muzzle and then stops. "I'm not sure I'm ready to get this personal with you."

"Come on. Gay best friend, remember? Did you think about her while you were in bed with...have you told me your coyote's name?"

"I don't know." He glares at me.

"You don't know if you've told me, or you don't know if you thought about Cim while you were in bed?"

"Her name's Polly. She likes to be called Pol."

"Nice." I grin at him. "So? She stayed over?"

"Yeah." He says it grudgingly, and his self-consciousness is pretty adorable. He has trouble looking me in the eyes.

So I tease him. "Come on, you didn't brag about your conquests in the newsroom?"

"Sure," he says. "Made up a lot of shit there, too. Never really just talked about it with a friend before."

"All right, well. This is how we do it." I lean forward. "How did you do? Did it feel natural?"

He takes a breath. "Felt pretty good. And I didn't think about Cim while we were doing it."

"Did she scream?"

He narrows his eyes. "Don't see how that's relevant."

I tap my temple. "I'm building a mental picture." He flattens his ears, and I hold up a paw. "All right, all right. So you're in bed and you're not thinking about Cim. But you did later?"

"Yeah. I felt like calling her—I didn't, don't worry," because he can no doubt see how close I am to telling him what a bad idea that would have been. "But I kinda wanted to rub her nose in it."

"I'm sure her nose is too deep in her boyfriend's crotch to care."

He winces. "Thanks."

"Look," I say. "She's fucking another guy. I thought you came to terms with that."

"Doesn't mean I like picturing it."

I shrug. "You're moving on, too. You seeing—what's her name? Paul?"

"Polly." He shakes his head. "I can tell from guys in dresses now. 'Specially when the dress comes off."

I grin. "You seeing her again?"

"Yeah. Friday." He finally grins back at me. "Sent her flowers yesterday."

"Nice. Are you supposed to do that the first time you sleep with someone?"

He raises his eyebrows. "With girls, yeah. I dunno what you guys do."

"Usually just say, 'That was fun, want to do it again sometime?'"

"How romantic. I can see why you want to get married."

"Hey," I say. "Just because we're not so fucking uptight about sex…well. Most of us aren't." I brush my whiskers. "Some of us."

He laughs then, and leans back. I see his tail uncurl. "I dunno. I liked marriage. It's a pain sometimes, but it feels that much better when you get it right. And I took your advice. I'm just thinking about the good times with Cim. I'm not thinking about her leaving. I mean, this situation is completely different."

"For one thing, you're not married to her."

"That's a big one. But also, she's not a fox. It's a little difference, but…"

"It's a pretty big difference."

"Yeah, yeah." He smirks. "I know how you red foxes feel about other species."

I just raise an eyebrow. "I mean, you're not going to be able to have a natural family with her."

His dusky-brown ears flick, and he nods. "I know." He lifts his eyes. "But you manage. Ever thought of having a family with Miski?"

I give that question a little less thought than it deserves. "Sometimes. Probably we'd adopt tiger cubs, kids big enough to play football."

"And raised by a fox, so smart enough not to."

"Maybe. Your injury thing again?"

He nods. "But anyway, thanks for the advice with Pol. She's a good gal."

"Not worried about her scheming? I mean, hello. Coyote."

He laughs and points to himself. "And I'm a fox. Nah, my biggest worry is that she might want a family one day. Then I might be visitin' some of those adoption centers."

"Maybe by that time we'll be figuring it out together." The thought intrigues me. Maybe having a cub to take care of would give me something to do. Like Gena, like Angela. I'm sure with Dev's money, we could get an adoption pretty quickly. If I wanted to commit to that career.

Hal laughs, echoing my thoughts. "I sure think you'd shake up the PTA meetings."

"Yeah." I grin. "Maybe I'll spare the other moms that trauma for now."

I wish him luck with his coyote girlfriend as we head off, and tell him that next time I want details, and that if we have to go stand by the water cooler in the lobby of the bank, we can do that. He snorts and suggests a coffee shop instead. "Why do you even want details?"

I pat his shoulder. "I'm interested in your well-being."

"Jesus Dog. Just go research that trial. That oughta give you somethin' to worry about besides my sex life."

"Yeah. Lawyers. Much more titillating."

He snorts. "Thought you didn't care about tits."

I point at him. "You're better than that pun, Mister Journalist."

He laughs. "Want a ride home?"

On the way back to Dev's, he gives me a few tips about researching the proceedings of a trial. When I get home, I open up the laptop and go through a little more of Dev's e-mail. The high schoolers wrote back with interview questions, so I write out answers for Dev and then file them away to read to him on the phone that night.

Hal's tips for researching the trial involve a lot of phone calling and identifying myself as a freelance journalist. He suggested not mentioning any affiliation with Equality Now, because lawyers tend to be less forthcoming when dealing with political organizations. Not that they can say much about their cases to journalists, but what little they can talk about, they'd keep to themselves if they think it's going to get a political spin.

Unless they're taking a *cause celebre* or something. Which this might be, or might turn into, depending on the prosecuting attorney. I find the case number easily enough, but to get records from the court I have to actually go there in person. So I call up the prosecuting attorney's office and talk to the secretary there, who stalls for a bit and finally puts me through to the attorney, a lady who sounds cervine over the phone. She tells me very politely that the family is not interested in having a great deal of media coverage over this case.

I don't have any illusions about deer being pushovers, and I don't approach her that way, but I try the best arguments I can think of: "What about the chances that it might save another young teen's life? What about putting pressure on them with public opinion?" She does say that she'll talk to the family and will give them my contact information in case they want to talk about their son, but she also says that this will likely not happen until the case is over.

So I thank her for her time and hang up. I wonder if there's anyone I know in that general area whom I could convince to go down to the courthouse for me. I wonder if it's healthy for me to get caught up in this again, when I was just about to let it go. There's no hope that this is actually going to end up like the final scene of a bad movie, with a judge in the courtroom decreeing that Families United is evil and forcing them to disband, but that makes for an entertaining daydream.

I'm still musing over that when Dev calls. "Practice today, practice tonight," he says. "Boliat's cold. Still looks the same as the last time we were here."

"I'm not staying in that flea-ridden motel this weekend."

He laughs. "I got you a room at the Intercontinental. You'll like it. It's three blocks from our hotel. Everything's really walkable downtown here. We could probably walk to the stadium."

"How's the town look?"

"Crazy. Boxers signs all over, blue and white flags flying out of cars. Strike painted himself all red for the flight."

"He's got a dye person in every city, huh?"

"Must be." He breathes into the phone. "Miss you."

"I miss you too."

"What've you been up to?"

I recap my day, briefly. Then I take a breath. "And just looking into this lawsuit over Vince King."

He pauses, but doesn't otherwise react to the name. "For Hal, or for you?"

"For me. But he's going to help with the article if I get enough info to write it." He doesn't say anything. I feel a prickling of worry. I thought I could talk about Vince King in this neutral context, that he wouldn't have that anger flare up again. It's not like I'm asking him to do anything, after all. But in his silence, I feel the tension rising, and I change the subject, like a skater avoiding the middle of a suspect lake in early winter. "In return, I might be helping him with adoption if he keeps scoring with his coyote gal."

That shakes him free of his silence. "Adoption? What do you know— have you been—wait, do you want a cub?"

He sounds strangled. I consider teasing him a bit more, then remember it's a playoff week. "Not for a while. But he figures it wouldn't hurt for us to know. If we ever did."

"If we had a cub, I'd want to be living in Lake Handerson so my folks could take care of it."

"Oh, you think we'd have a tiger cub, do you?"

"Not necessarily, but they wouldn't care. They'd love a fox or a tiger grandson."

I'm not so sure about that, but again, this isn't the time to argue. "Well, we can see in a couple years, I guess. How's practice?"

"Intense. Hard. Feels good, though."

"Good. What are you working on?"

He tells me about the plays and it all sounds good to me, but I haven't watched film of the Boliat team, so I don't know their tendencies beyond what I can read in the columns this week. So I make approving noises, and remind him to keep his footwork and timing crisp.

"Want me to book your ticket for Friday?" he asks, when the conversation lulls.

"I have your credit card," I say. "I can book it."

"Okay. Can't wait to see you. You going to get a Boxers shirt?"

"Of course." I grin, rub my paws down the Firebirds t-shirt I'm wearing. "It'll be a nice change to wear clothes. Right now I'm not wearing anything. Just lying here."

"Send a pic," he says. "You've got that new phone. Use it."

"Ooh. Okay, I will. You going to send me one back?"

He taps his claws on something. "Maybe. Depends if Charm goes out tonight."

"I'll be waiting."

So when I hang up, I do strip off my shirt and pants, work myself up nice and hard, and then spend ten minutes on the bed figuring out how to make the phone take a picture of me, by which time any arousal I had is long gone. But I get the picture, and then I have to take two more 'til I get one that looks good. Then it takes me another ten minutes to figure out how to send it to him.

I wrap an apron around my middle and make another quick dinner of chicken with lemons and capers, thinking about the day and how else I might get to the King lawsuit. Because it feels kind of daring and naughty, I leave just the apron on, sitting my bare butt on the chair to eat.

There is another way I might be able to get some info on the lawsuit, I realize, only my fur prickles when I think of it, and my ears flatten, and I have to put my fork down. It takes a moment for me to recover from the memory of the visit to Mother's place again, not because I'm having a nervous breakdown or anything, but because I keep running through all the things I wanted to say, all the brilliant, sharp, cutting remarks that would make her feel terrible for what she did. I press my fingers to my eyes and shake my head until I manage to sidetrack my thoughts.

I could call Mrs. Hedley, the otter, I guess. Pretend to be someone else—maybe a friend of one of her kids? She mentioned sons. But no, that's probably a bad idea, too. No, there's really only one person I can call, and so I put some pants on and call my father.

"This is becoming interestingly regular," he says when he picks up. "Not that I'm complaining."

"If you wanted to ask Mother a question about Families United," I say, and he interrupts.

"What you mean is that you want me to ask her something."

I fidget, curl my tail around my free paw. "I want to know what's in the case."

"Why, Wiley? What possible good will that do?"

"Do I really have to tell you about bringing things to light?"

"Do I need to remind you what happened last time?"

My left thumb, buried in my tail fur, twitches. "I got what I wanted."

"Eventually. Probably not the easiest way possible."

"All right, then." I settle back into the couch. "Tell me a better way to go about it. Should I just let this happen, let them go out and tell gay kids how broken they are, that their only chance in life is to give up part of what they are?"

His sigh comes from a long way away. "Maybe you should focus on the parts of the world that directly affect you and your life. If you're going to call your mother, you should call her to work out your differences, not use her to push your political agenda."

"I *am* trying to work out our differences. By showing her the things those friends of hers won't tell her." He starts to object, and I say, "What good is being an activist if I can't even convince my own family?"

"Is being right more important than being at peace with your mother?"

It takes me a while to sort that one out. I can't separate the two, is the thing. I went through years downplaying my sexuality, hiding it from my workplace, not discussing it with my family, and now that it's out, it's inconceivable that I could shove it back into its closet.

The thought occurs to me that that is exactly what Brian would tell me, and I squirm on the couch while I remind myself that people who support gay rights can also be assholes. "I can't choose between them," I say, because Father's still waiting on the line. "It was hard enough not sharing part of my life, but if she's actively working against it…"

"I understand that," Father says patiently. "But she's joined that organization for support. If she saw that she didn't need that support, if she thought you would talk reasonably to her and address her concerns…"

"Oh, what concerns?" I sit up and glare out the window. "That she's going to get gay fleas from my pride jacket, so she'd better burn it?"

"She has a lot to explain to you, too," he says. I am really amazed at his patience. I would've hung up on me by now.

"Maybe she can explain it to you and you can translate." I do bite back "from crazy bitch," which was sort of on the tip of my tongue, but also was giving me a real bad feeling while it was there, because I didn't want to say that. I swallow it down and it sits uneasily on top of my dinner, making my stomach churn and my chest tighten.

"I don't expect the two of you to talk right away," he says. "God knows that day was hard on all of us. At least you didn't call me in tears later."

"She called you in tears?" I think that should make me feel better than it does, that she regretted something that happened.

"Angry tears, I suppose you might say, but yes, after our visit she was quite upset."

"Good. So was I."

"Wiley, she does still love you."

"She loves who I used to be. Who she thought I used to be."

"Well, yes. But that's still you. So the other thing I would do is try to remember the cub you used to be and remind her that that's still you, that you haven't changed all that much just because of whom you want to date."

"That's an important part of me," I snap, but I'm thinking about it as I say it. There is more to me than just my boyfriend, although over the last few months, that's really dominated my life. When he started for the Firebirds, when he came out, when I was outed, when I tussled with his family…all of that was about our relationship. And maybe what's happening now, now that all of that has settled down, is that I am finding these other parts of myself that were neglected. That I like being useful, helping toward a goal, that I like the sport of football and miss it terribly now when I'm away from it, that I like having friends like Hal with whom I can have normal conversations.

"It is an important part," Father says, "and eventually that is something she's going to have to come to accept. I've talked to her a little bit about Christmas and what a warm and accepting community you've surrounded yourself with, how you are building a life that looks in many ways like the life we always wanted for you. The fact that you are building it with a male tiger rather than a female fox has remarkably little effect on how happy you are."

If I say anything, it'll be along the lines of "then why can't she see that?" and we'll just go round and round and I am tired of that. I might actually end up in angry tears if I do that many more times. So I switch topics. "I had a discussion with Hal about adopting cubs," I say. "He's dating a coyote."

"Seriously?"

"Is he dating seriously, or did I seriously have that discussion?"

He chuckles, and I feel the relief in his voice to be away from the topic of family as well. "Yes."

"The dating isn't all that serious as far as I know. But we did have the discussion. I'm not really looking to adopt any cubs yet, but it made me think. You know, Angela and Gena kept themselves occupied during their husbands' football years by taking care of a family. I'd bet Vonni and Daria are pregnant within a year, too. Seems to be one of the things football wives do."

"Feeling bored? How's the Yerba job look?"

I tell him briefly about the Firebirds job and my conversation with Emmanuel. "So there are things I can do. Just not right now. But Hal's helping me with—um, researching the…"

"The court thing. What have you found out?"

"The court docket just says 'negligent homicide and aggravated assault.'"

"Because the kid killed himself?"

"Yeah." I curl my tail back around my hips.

"Doesn't seem like much of a case."

"That's why I want to know more about it. What the basis is. The lawyer won't talk to me, and I can't even find out who the lawyer is on the other side."

"It's an interesting problem. I wouldn't be surprised if they're doing it more to get publicity than to actually win the case."

"The lawyer didn't seem all that interested in talking to a reporter."

He chuckles. "You're a reporter now?"

"I'm apprenticing with Hal. Well, he said he'd help me write out the story when I researched it. He's busy with some big article on sports injuries."

"Good luck, then. Hope it keeps you from going stir-crazy. When are you flying up to Boliat?"

Uncovered

"Friday. And then back here on Monday. Who knows, maybe I'll have a job by then."

"If you continue on as a reporter, you can go to Media Day if your tiger goes to the championship."

I laugh shortly. "I wouldn't dare. I'd ask some stupid question and be featured for years in news stories about the stupid questions people ask on Media Day."

"I don't think you'd ask a stupid question."

That makes me smile. "Thanks for the confidence."

"That doesn't mean I don't think you'd say something stupid if you talk to your mother."

"Thanks for the confidence," I say again, in a different tone.

He sighs. "And I'm not going to talk to her about the court case."

"Father…"

"No. It'll only cause more trouble. Maybe if you promise me that when things cool down a little, you'll try to talk to her, then *maybe* I'll help you bring it up."

"If you talk to her first—"

"Wiley."

Fuck, why is the right thing to do so hard sometimes? "Fine. When things cool down."

After we hang up, I pace around the apartment. In a way, I wish I could recall that anger, how pure and clean it felt, without all the underlying guilt. I wish I could just scream about how stupid she's being, that she can't see how obvious it is that being gay doesn't have to affect our relationship, that she's buying into the agendas of all these people who are uncomfortable with gay people because it challenges their concept of what love and life mean—or, if you believe studies, because they've beaten down their own gay urges and don't want anyone else to be happy.

But no, that's an easy way out. The truth, when you come right down to it, is that they hate us because we're different, and therefore we're scary. They bring up Bible verses, they invent social issues, they talk about their missing grandchildren. They make up stories about us and then use those stories to scare each other. They tell us we were better before we were gay, as though there was a time before we were gay. If only we could give it up, go back to that paradisical time of innocence of our lives, then we would be just fine. But they won't forgive us our sin, the one that's coded into our bodies, even though their Lord and Savior supposedly died to expiate our sins.

Thinking about religion doesn't help. I fume, standing by the window, putting paws up against the glass and then turning away to pace the small, empty apartment again. My tail, which I can normally control, flicks against the couch and the TV.

One of the things we dealt with a lot in college, talked about at the FLAG meetings, was that these hate groups want gays to feel like there's something wrong with us, like being gay is our fault, a defect in us that stops those close to us from loving and understanding us. I've had it hammered into my head that that's not true, but now that my family has exploded in my face, that worry feels like a hydra that keeps growing heads no matter how many times I cut them off.

We share the responsibility for our fractured relationship, Mother and I; I know that in my head. But aren't teenagers supposed to be rebellious? Isn't it a parent's job to understand that and weather the storm? Father adapted, he met me halfway, he opened his mind and accepted me. Why can't she do the same thing? Granted, I know I haven't been the easiest gay son to deal with.

If she can't accept my lifestyle, then that's fine. She'll never meet Dev (again), she'll never come down here to visit. I can live with that. But maybe I could be a little less in her face about it. Like maybe being a nationally known figure got her fur ruffled. I don't know what I can do about that, because I want to be more prominent, more well-known. I want to have a platform from which I can tell people to love their gay children.

Do I want her to accept me? Do I not care?

Do I want her to give up Families United so she can accept me? Or do I want it because it's embarrassing, like a dentist's kid with crooked teeth?

That's a long ways off, though, I fear. As bad as things are now, it'll be a good while before I'm able to talk to Mother at all, let alone the way I can talk to Father. And that should be fine. I didn't want to for most of the last three years. So why does my paw itch now with the desire to pick up the phone?

I sit down and play UFL 09 against the computer, to take my mind off it. I win, because the computer is lousy, and I wish Dev were here. Curling up against the couch pillows just isn't the same. At the end of the couch, I can still faintly smell the place where he jerked me off. It's one of those smells that just touches right at the back of the nose, something so faint it might not be there. Maybe it's just my imagination. I call my tiger anyway, to say goodnight, and I don't think he notices any extra urgency in my voice when I tell him I miss him.

But I lie there in our bed, looking up at the ceiling, tail limp between my legs. There's no tiger weight on me, no warmth in the empty bed, and I feel like I might float away in the night. I pull the blankets around me and turn onto my side, squashing one ear against the pillow. The apartment is silent, no breathing beside me. I close my eyes and inhale Dev's scent. Smells are memories; I tell myself it'll only be a couple days before he's there beside me again. But I wish I could talk to him about everything on my mind, not just the careful distraction-free edit of my life.

Wednesday morning, I get a call from David Rodriguez of the Firebirds. It's just before nine a.m. and I'm still lounging in bed, but I snap awake quick enough. "Is this a good time to talk?" he starts with.

"Sure." I rub sleep from my eyes and sit up, dismissing my dreams and the tempting brush of the soft sheets against my morning erection. "Thanks for calling back."

I don't have the phone quite against my ear, so his voice is a little distant. "I just wanted to talk to you a little about your thoughts on this outreach position. We haven't got a lot of the details worked out, so what we'll need is a self-starter who's really motivated to bring new out-of-the-box ideas to the table."

I'm glad he didn't talk like this when I saw him in person, because I would've either laughed or said something snide. "I wonder if you can tell me," I say, "why you're hiring for this position if you don't have a plan in place for it. Is there an urgent need right now for it?"

"Truth is," he says, "we don't really have anyone in-house who can create a good plan. This was an idea we've been kicking around ever since Devlin's press conference, and we saw this opportunity to bring someone on board who's more familiar with the world we're trying to reach. I'm going to tell you honestly that I don't know if this is a long-term position. What we want to do to start is a three-month contract and then see how things go from there."

"Three months. That's barely time to get a campaign organized and material out." And it's also, paradoxically, too much time; I would have to report to Yerba in the middle of that. If they hire me. But I'm arguing academically now. I rub my cheekfur on the right, which is matted down from sleep, and suppress a yawn. "How would you decide whether to continue the position?"

"Oh, three months is usually enough for us to get a sense of how someone's going to work out in a job."

"On the field," I say, before I can stop myself. "If you're judging publicity campaigns, it takes a lot longer to see how effective they are."

"Right. Well, like I say, after three months we'll see how it goes. Could you talk to me a little about your experience?"

So I tell him about my college days, and I make sure to insert in there that when I got the scouting job with the Dragons, my passion for football really took over and I let the activist stuff fall by the wayside. I don't mention that it's mostly because of the need for me to be closeted, first as Dev's boyfriend, and then as a Dragons employee and Dev's boyfriend.

"Sounds good, sounds good. So would you like to come in and meet a couple of our marketing people? We're all pretty busy, but I can set up something for tomorrow. I don't want to commit to next week, because…" He laughs.

"Right. Hopefully you're all going to be very busy next week."

"Fingers crossed."

"Let me think about it and give you a call back," I say. It's really hard for me to say no outright, even though I'm fairly sure I'm not going to want to take the position. Anyway, until I see how the interview with Jocko at Yerba goes, I shouldn't close off any doors.

I get out of bed, make coffee, and catch up on e-mail and the morning news. After that, there's nothing for me to do but wait. Wait for Emmanuel to call back, wait for Father to call back, wait for Dev to be done with practice. I go out for a walk and then to do some shopping for food and for clothes, because I feel like I need to wear something different and sharp to the playoff game in Boliat. Pants-wise, at least. There's no question I'm going to wear the over-large Firebirds polo I got from the owner's jet.

In the middle of the day, Brian calls. I ignore the call and don't listen to the voice mail. Half an hour later, Gena calls to ask about my flight up. She's going up with the other wives and says they're meeting Saturday night to have drinks before the game, and she tells me I'm sitting with them.

"All our tickets are in the same place?" I'm walking outside a shopping mall under a cloudy sky, swinging a bag in which I have a nice new pair of khaki-gold pants. Also a couple pairs of tight boxer briefs I found that I hope Dev likes on me.

"Devlin got you tickets with the wives," she says.

I laugh. "Well, all right, then. I'll join you for drinks after Dev has to go back to his hotel."

"And don't worry about Penny."

My ears flick back. "Penny who?"

"Oh. Colin's wife. Angela talked to Daria who kind of knows her and we made sure she knows that you're one of us. She doesn't have to like it, but she has to be polite about it."

Now my ears go back, and my fur prickles. "And she was okay with that?"

"She says she is." Gena pauses. "Or maybe she wasn't planning on having a drink with us anyway. There are a lot of wives, and I guess she has other friends."

"I don't want to cause any problems."

"You're not the one causing the problem," she says, and that makes me feel warm even though the clouds stubbornly refuse to let the sun through. "Anyway, we figured we'd leave the guys alone on their Saturday night. Whatever routine they have, it's got them this far, and we shouldn't mess it up. If there's a celebration, we'll be there Sunday for it."

I think of the routine Dev and I have and swish my tail a little more vigorously. "Is Angela coming?"

"With their boys, yes. Our boys are coming along as well. They're so excited."

"I can imagine." I smile broadly. "Closest I ever came to being this excited about an event my father was in was at a party his office threw for him at his ten-year anniversary."

She laughs. "They've gotten used to it. They went to all the games when we lived in Highbourne, but they got tired of being the big star's cubs when they got older and the team wasn't winning as much. Of course, now they're thrilled that their father's going to be in one more big game."

"Hopefully two."

"I would hate to go to Peco in the winter. I'm hoping it's Crystal City."

I laugh. "That's where I'd bet if I were you. The Sabretooths don't have a lot of weaknesses and they've stayed pretty healthy."

"So have we."

"And we had good backups step up to fill in when we did have injuries." We wrap up, and I walk on, back to the bus stop. But I'm thinking about the wives, and the stories of the guys, and Gena saying she wanted to leave them alone. Everyone has rituals, of course, but are those groupies I saw in the hotel lobby part of Gerrard's ritual? Fisher's? Anyone else's?

Not Dev's, I'm pretty sure. That one gay fox—Dev told me about him, but I forget his name—he's given up on Dev. And unless Dev is indulging the straight side of himself on the same nights he's indulging the very gay side of himself with me, I don't think I have anything to worry about. So the gossipy side of me wonders which of the other players are cheating on their wives, which ones would get a rude surprise if their wives interrupted their "lucky" Saturday night ritual.

In the evening, I call Dev. "Drills and drills," he groans. "Film in between. Study sessions after. They're killing us with these new plays."

"You need it. Is it cold there in the Midwest?"

"Not as bad as Hilltown. It's fine, I'm in the hotel most of the time, and we heat up pretty quick during practice."

"What plays are they putting in?"

He tells me a little about the plays, which I compare to what I know of Boliat's offense. "Sounds good. You're not going to rattle that quarterback."

"Nah. We're trying to hassle the receivers and stop the run. That's about all we can do."

"It's not all you can do. You can learn his reads."

"That's what this film session was about. Learning where he looks, everything like that. Argh."

"How's things with Strike?"

Dev snorts. "He comes over once in a while to show solidarity or something, but he's actually working pretty hard right now. He still calls out the offense, but just in private. Ty and Rodo grumble about him, but Ty says he's learning a lot from him too. And he doesn't bug the defense."

"That's not too bad, I guess. I mean, you know what you're gonna get with him."

"Wish he'd just shut up and do it instead of having to tell us about it all the time. If I have to hear one more time about his macro-veggie-otic diet, I'm going to choke him on his spinach."

"Don't do that. He's changing the game for you guys. I still think you should've gotten a better left tackle for Aston, but…"

"I'll mention that to Coach. Better yet, why don't you mention it to Rodriguez?"

"Maybe I will." I sigh and lean back into the corner of the couch, letting my tail uncurl along the seat where Dev should be. "I wish he wanted to hire me to do that."

"You'll get another scouting job," he says.

"Someday. Maybe." I lower my ears.

"And I'll see you Friday."

"Uh-huh."

He pauses. "That's where you're supposed to say that your next scouting job will be on Friday. When you get to scout me. Only you're supposed to say it better."

"Sorry." I smile, and that does lift my ears a little.

"What have you been up to? You're all quiet."

Change from the last call, I think, when he was the one who went quiet on me. I'm worrying about the Yerba job and if I have to interview with a homophobe, I wonder what's going on with the King family's lawsuit, and most of all I don't know what to do about Mother. But I don't want to dampen his feelings when he's in a good mood like this, and bringing up all my gay-related issues would do that for sure. "Talked to Father," I say. "Just dealing with Mother, you know?"

"Yeah," he says. "Sorry. You feeling any better?"

"A little. He thinks I should apologize to her." That just spills out.

"What?" The indignance sets warmth blooming in my heart, banishes my shadowy fears, and I want to kiss him and tell him I love him.

"I think maybe he has a point. I mean, I did yell at her. If I want her to apologize, I have to be willing to…" I sigh and adjust my position on the couch, leaning my head against the back and closing my eyes.

He doesn't say anything for a bit, waiting for me, but I don't know what else I can say. I'm dropped back into the tangle of memories of that day and what I said and should have said, and shouldn't have said. Perhaps sensing this, Dev changes the subject. "Coach took me aside today."

I wait. He doesn't go on. "And?"

"He said he talked to Colin. Said he told him if he doesn't like seeing you around team family functions, he doesn't have to attend them."

I wonder how Colin and Penny will react to being told in the same week that they have to put up with me. At the same time, it's tremendously heartening that both Coach Samuelson and Gena are supporting Dev and me. My tail wags against the couch. "How'd he take it?"

"Ah, Coach didn't say. I mean, it doesn't matter. Coach lays down the law."

"All right." I wish I could get him or Gena to call Mother. I search for something else to talk about. "Oh, did you get those e-mails with the interviews?"

"Yeah, looks good. Wish you could do all my interviews that way. They keep bugging me even though it's the playoffs."

"If I could, tiger."

"All right, I need to stretch and then sleep. I'll talk to you tomorrow?"

"And see me Friday."

"Love you."

"Love you too."

I hang up and lie back on the couch. I think about Colin and Mother and the lawsuit. In a fantasy, I tell Colin and Mother about the lawsuit at the same time and watch the two vulpine muzzles struggle to reconcile their beliefs with the reality of a dead kid. And then two images click together in my head, of Vince King slumped on the bench and Kodi slumped against the wall, victims of that poisonous painful rhetoric. If Colin could see the effect his words had on a teammate…

He wouldn't care. But I sit upright with another thought. If—if the lawyers in the court could see another example of Families United breaking up a family…if they could hear that the group regularly tries to turn mothers against sons, make sons feel worthless…

There's a thing called an *amicus curiae* that I've read about in some of the gay rights court cases, where people file testimony pertinent to the case, things that might not otherwise come to light. I'm a witness to some of the behavior Families United promotes: telling parents to discard and disown their cubs. Mrs. Hedley telling me her sons are dead. That's got to be relevant.

And if I can show Mother that, if I can tell her that her behavior is being used by the court to rule against that organization she's thrown herself in with, then she'll have to listen. I won't be a prick about it…

I stop rubbing my paws together. No, of course I won't be a prick about it. I'll…I'll talk to Father, figure out the best way to do it. But it's something concrete, something tangible, something I can do to help.

I get out the phone to call Hal, because I don't know shit about filing an *amicus curiae*, and when I turn it on, it reminds me that I have a voicemail to listen to. Right, the one from Brian. I sigh and put the phone to my ear. "Hi, Wiley," he says. "Just wanted to let you know that today makes five interviews your boyfriend has turned down from his local chapter of Equality Now. Maybe there's something you can do."

I turn the phone off and drop it to the floor, lying back on the couch. Here's one more thing I can't talk to Dev about. I lay an arm across my eyes and exhale. Brian's wrong. There's nothing I can do, not about Dev. But there might be something I can do about Mother.

Chapter 6 – Aggravated (Dev)

By the time Friday rolls around, I'm feeling better. We practice in full pads, hitting hard, but we all feel better that night than we have since Sunday—physically. Mentally we've been charged up all week, and Friday's no exception. It's even gotten to the point that we don't mind Strike all that much. At least, the defense doesn't. Whenever I'm hanging out with Ty and Strike's name comes up, the fox just says, "let's change the subject."

So I'm in a pretty good mood as I walk over to Lee's hotel. Boliat's cold in January, with a wind that knifes down between the buildings and whistles as it rounds the corners, but the lights are pretty and everyone I pass has cheerful smiles. Small flakes of snow sprinkle the air, settling on my jacket and collecting in the concrete corners of the buildings. It's a nice reminder of the Hilltown winters, though the air is drier and the sky clearer than I remember from my Januarys up north. Still, it feels familiar, friendly and close. I haven't been in Chevali all that long, but being back in a Midwestern city reminds me of the things I loved about Hilltown: the chill in the air, the feeling of camaraderie among all the people fighting the weather together, the warmth of coming in out of the cold to a hotel lobby.

The Intercontinental is pretty posh. My feet slide along the marble lobby floor, and I reflect that the hotels we meet in are all nicer than my apartment. I go up to the room number Lee texted me and find him in a small, comfortable hotel room looking out onto a large public square with a gilded statue of a white-tailed deer in the center. Founder of the city or one of its early mayors or something. They told us when we arrived, but I was thinking about the Boxers' receivers at the time.

Anyway, there's more important things to think about, like the fox in the pretty yellow polo shirt wagging his tail in front of the large white king bed. I step up and take him in my arms, feel his light frame warm against me, squeeze him close. My tail curls around his leg. "Missed you."

"Mmm. Me too." He nuzzles against my chest.

I kiss his ears. "You said you had news about your jobs?"

"Sort of." He slides his paws down my back to rest just above the base of my tail. "You want to hear it now, or after?"

I grin and take one of his ears in my teeth. "It's up to you."

"Oh, before, then." He squirms a little. "I'm going to have some calls next week for the Yerba interview, and they want me to come up there to meet more of the staff."

"Hey, that's great!" I squeeze him.

"Emman—Peter says a lot of the guys come back for championship weekend, so I might go up then. Up Saturday, then to watch you in the game Sunday."

My grin widens. "One more game to win. If we don't…"

"You will."

I nuzzle his ears and remember the Firebirds job. "So, the job doing community stuff for the Firebirds?"

He goes a little tense. "Yeah. I dunno. They're still talking to me, but I don't think it's going to work out."

"Why not?" I wonder if I need to make a call to our media person, the one who set up the job.

"It's just…we talked about what they wanted, and what I wanted, and it doesn't look like a great fit right now."

He's not meeting my eyes when I stare down at him. He can't know that I set that up. Unless Vince or someone told him. They wouldn't have, though. "But I thought…I thought it'd be perfect for you. You'd get to be around football again, and you could do your activist stuff too."

His nod is a slight motion against my chest. "Not everything's gonna work out even if it seems perfect at first." He sighs, warm breath through my shirt and fur. "It was a short, experimental thing, and I was worried it'd mess up my chances to get a scouting job later on. Also, it's only three months. Rodriguez was clear about that. If I get the job at Yerba, they'd likely want me starting within a few weeks after the championship, and honestly, the Yerba job is the one with more long-term potential."

Up close, his scent is a little different, a little subdued. Not fear, but maybe he's getting sick. "Isn't that giving up the activist stuff you want to do?"

"As a career. Peter says the job takes a lot of time and I know that, but I still think I can do things in my spare time. On planes to come see you."

"What if you could move into scouting with the Firebirds?" If he's in Yerba, I guess that's good too, but it moves us back to living apart, and I really like having him in the apartment with me.

"In what, three years? Their scouting department is pretty solid. I don't think there's much open there for a gay outreach person to cross over."

"Still. You'd have a lot of meetings with the front office…"

"It's okay," he says. "It didn't work out." He looks up at me, his blue eyes set.

"All right." I shrug, disguising my disappointment.

Not well enough. "I appreciate the thought behind it," he says. "I'm still trying to figure things out, and that just wasn't the right thing. Besides." He laughs, though it seems to me his laugh is a touch forced. "Then I'd have to be the one harassing you for interviews. Or harassing Ogleby, anyway."

"You could harass him anyway," I growl. "It'd save me the trouble. He still lets through a bunch. I had to talk to True Sports for twenty minutes today."

"Oh, so you are still doing interviews."

"Some of them." I slide paws down his shoulders. His ears are down, and he's not looking at me. "Ogleby sends me some and I do a few. The guys from SI, you know, it's good to stay on their good side."

"I'm all in favor of that," he says. "I like seeing positive coverage of you there. You could also get positive coverage in other places—" Now his ears go all the way flat. "Sorry."

I let him go and fold my arms. "You're mad at me for not going to Potomac."

"No. Well." He rubs his paws together. "Maybe a little. But they called you to talk about the discussions they'd had, just to get your views on marriage. And you wouldn't even talk to them for fifteen minutes."

"Um." I try to stop my tail from lashing. "You know, I'm not hosting a debate on marriage on Sunday. I'm playing a football game."

"So you stop being gay until the season's over?"

"There are a lot of gay people out there. Do they all have to have an opinion on everything?"

He folds his arms, mirroring my pose. "There aren't a lot of gay people featured on TV every Sunday."

I mention a flamboyant, jewel-encrusted preacher we both hate. He doesn't even smile. "Look." I cross to the bed and sit on the edge of it. He turns to face me, but doesn't move. "*You* are the one who told me I should focus on football. It's my job. I'm just starting out. There'll be plenty of time for me to become a gay marriage activist later."

"You don't have to be an activist, or even an advocate, to do a lot of good for—" I wait for him to say that bear's name, but he swallows it and skips past it. "It just...it seems like you'd be happy for the world to forget that you're gay."

"Maybe I would." My voice is rising. I control it. "At least for the next few days. Maybe—hopefully—the next two weeks."

"People have short memories," he says. "Once football season is over, how many people are going to care?"

"More if we win the championship, right?"

"Still not as many as during the season." He lowers his eyes. "You know, you're right. I'm sorry. I promised myself I wouldn't put this on you this week, and I just got caught up in it, and…it's not fair to you. You need to do what you need to do. Win a championship."

He comes to sit next to me, and I wait before putting an arm around him. I'm not sure if I've won this argument, or just delayed it, or some other alternative. And I'm trying to sort out what that little outburst sparked in me, because while I'm annoyed as shit that he's still trying to make me feel guilty, I'm also more excited than I've been in a few days about being with him because there was, for a bit, that passion in his eyes. When he sits on the bed, he slumps, and I want to put my arm around him and say, *Keep fighting! You can fight without me and I love seeing your passion and fire!*

But if I say that, he'll just keep trying to get me involved. And it's only another two weeks. I don't really think he wants me to lose on Sunday so I can start agitating for equal rights with him, but I don't even want to open that box again. So I just curl my tail back around against his hips and rest a paw on his shoulder, and I say, "I love you."

"Love you too," he murmurs, and when I pull him toward me, he doesn't resist.

•

Saturday is a semi-rest day, when we just do a lot of stretching, some cardio workouts, and film study and playbook review. Ty comes over and sits with me, Zillo, and Charm over lunch, as he's taken to doing since Strike started eating with the offense.

"Hey," Ty says into a lull, as though the thought had just occurred to him. "You think anyone else on the team is gay?"

The other three all look at me. "What?" I say.

"You're the one with some kinda, whatsit, gay-dar," Charm says, drawing out the word.

"Yeah." I take a long drink of Bolt-Ade. "You know what I wonder about when I'm around the team? Who's gonna come in to cover the slot if I break off to stop the run."

"Oh, come on," Charm says. "Don't say you ain't thought about it."

"Sure. But it's their private business."

"It's kinda funny," Zillo says. "I thought I'd be able to tell easy. When you…y'know." He ducks his long muzzle and avoids my eyes. "I thought about all these things like you not going to clubs, and being private, and stuff. And I thought I shoulda known. But after a while…" After the Gateway game, I'm sure he means, when he stopped thinking that a faggot couldn't be a tough football player. "I started seein' that there are a lot of guys who do things that seem the same, and y'know. Some of them are married."

"Doesn't mean they're not gay," Ty points out. "You see that movie about that guy who was married and having an affair with his doctor?"

Again, everybody looks at me. "What? No. I didn't see it. Did you?"

Ty shakes his head. "I'm just sayin', married guys could be gay. You had a girlfriend in college, right?"

I wonder how long they've wanted to ask these questions. "Could we talk about football?" I say.

Charm drops a hefty arm around my shoulders. "Had a girlfriend every night, he told me. Didn't you used to take 'em to the ice cream parlor, Gramps? Or was it the soda fountain?"

"I'm six months older than you," I remind him. He calls me "Gramps" because I spent all four years in college, unlike him, and he's been in the league two years longer than me.

"See?" Ty says to Zillo. "So maybe."

"Maybe." Zillo looks unconvinced, his ears half-down. "They don't sound like—I mean, they sound happy."

"Seriously, guys," I say. "Remember that game we play? There's kind of a big one tomorrow."

Ty laughs. "Get your fox to take us to another gay club," he says, whiskers twitching. His black ears stay perked up. "We'll see who wants to go."

"Or who doesn't wanna go," Charm says.

"It was cool anyway," Ty says. "I take my guys out to clubs, I end up a few grand in the hole. I go out with you guys and dance instead of drink, I got out for two hundred. Should teach that in those money management seminars: go to gay clubs, save your money."

"So," I say, leaning over to Zillo, "did you see what they like to run to the weak side on short-yardage downs?"

•

All through the afternoon, I do my best to put those thoughts out of my mind so I can focus on plays. But I remember Argonne saying he had another engagement. I remember Rodo and Pike and how much all the guys enjoyed the gay club, and I start analyzing my memory for clues about who might've enjoyed it more. But no matter how much I think about it, the one I think had the best time keeps coming up Vonni—the guy who ended the night with a girl.

According to him and Lee. But he wasn't cagey about it at all, wasn't ashamed or weird. When he told us about it, his body language was the same as Charm's when he comes back to the locker room after a night with a girl or three. And I don't think Vonni is gay. Just married. But that's another whole bag of fucking problems I don't want to open.

If I have gay-dar, it's a really poor model, because there's nobody on the team who seems even the least bit gay. The only one—maybe, though I'd never say it—is Carson, who hangs around Gerrard all the time and never says much. But Gerrard's married *and* he has at least two coyote mistresses on the road, and apparently something more that I'm not sure I want to know anything about.

I get my mind back on the film, and finish out the afternoon. The guys are going to dinner, but I promised Lee I'd take him somewhere nice so we could have dinner before our traditional pre-game sex. Fisher bails on the team dinner too, saying he doesn't feel like being in a big group, and suggests maybe he and Gena could join us. I check with Lee and he says it's fine.

The steakhouse is nice but not extra-fancy: white tablecloths and candles, dark oak trim and tuxedoed coyotes and bobcats waiting tables. The steaks are rare and juicy and the wine is smooth and fruity. The smell of the place is all sizzling fat, roasting potatoes, and contented customers.

We get a small table for four in the back. Lee's still quiet throughout the dinner, which is probably good because Fisher's growling about the coaches and the practices. "They're going soft on us," he says, and adds in some choice words for the line coach, about how the playoffs are different and they're treating it just like the regular season.

I take a break from worrying about Lee. "They're sticking with what got us here. That's what Coach said."

"Yeah, well, the regular season's totally different from playoff intensity. They're not getting us ready for it. Do we play the same in preseason as in regular season?"

"Preseason games don't count on the record."

"And regular season games don't count in the playoffs." He stabs his fork into the steak and attacks it with the knife.

It makes enough noise that other people in the steakhouse turn and look. Lee's ears flick down. Gena looks at Fisher and then across at me, then the movement of Lee's ears catches her eye and she turns. He raises his head to meet her eyes. "Well, he's right," he says. "But I've also heard of coaching staffs saying it helps to keep things the same."

"Oh, what the hell would you know?" Fisher growls.

"Hey," I say, but Gena cuts me off.

"You know, the town is really coming together for the playoffs. I haven't seen anything like this in Chevali. I had a cashier ask me what I was doing for the game." She laughs, forced at first and then easing. "I didn't dare tell him I was from out of town."

"Sorry," Fisher growls across the table at Lee. "Just that you don't really know unless you've played in the playoffs. That's why these coaches don't know, most of the players don't know. It's frustrating, is all."

Lee nods, and I step in. "It's something we're all working toward, and I know the coaches are doing the best they can."

"Samuelson doesn't know what he's doing. You can't just do the same things over and over when the situation's different. It's life or death in the playoffs." He cuts another piece of steak and stabs at it. "Might be my last chance. I don't want to waste it."

"It's really helped having you back," I say. "Not that Pike is bad, but he doesn't have that spark."

That gets Fisher to smile, a glint in his eye. "Damn right."

"Statistically, he's not as productive on the field," Lee says. "The coaches make up for it by drawing up plays that have other players covering for him, and Dev does a terrific job of that. But his numbers aren't as good as yours." He nods at Fisher. "And I don't even mean when you were his age. I mean three months ago."

Fisher eases up on his steak and even purrs a bit as he says, "Well, I keep in shape."

I chew my own steak and think about him coming out of the trainers' room, and I don't say anything.

Fisher picks up the check and we walk out of the restaurant lost in football talk about last year's playoffs, about our mindsets, and the defensive line. Behind us, Lee and Gena are talking in low voices I can't catch, but Lee's ears are down and Gena looks intense when I look back. She's talking and he's listening, nodding. I angle an ear back, but then Fisher says something else about Brick, and I have to pay attention again.

Gena's staying in the same hotel as Lee, so we all walk back together like that, and by the time we get to the Intercontinental's lobby, they've moved on to another conversation: Lee reluctantly telling Gena about his mother and the anti-gay group. The large tigress puts an arm around Lee as we get to the elevators. "It must be so hard on you," she says.

His tail is curled around his legs, but he smiles up at Gena. "Thanks. I'm dealing with it. Father helps a lot. So does Dev."

"Her own son." Gena clucks. "If Bradley or Junior were gay, we'd be supportive." There's a bit of an awkward silence, and then she says, "Well, at least we wouldn't burn their old things. I hope she comes around soon."

The elevator dings and the doors open. "I'm working on it. Thanks," Lee says again, and we all get in and go to our different floors after "good night" and "see you tomorrow."

"What were you guys talking about?" I ask as we walk out onto his floor.

He hesitates. "She asked me to do some research on some things, and to not talk about it with you yet." He glances back at me. "Sorry."

"Huh. Okay." I shove that back onto the pile of things I'm trying not to think too hard about. "Is it about us?"

He shakes his head. "Nah, just…a thing." He smiles up.

"At least she was nice about your mom." I fidget, not sure what to say next. I wish I had better advice to give him about his mom. I really think he should talk to her—calmly, not yelling. But I don't know how to say that, or what I could say that would make him do that. Part of me wonders if he was exaggerating how bad the fight was…but he wouldn't have lied about her burning his things. And how do you forgive that?

He's lost in thought too, so I go on. "What did you mean, you're working on it? You think she'll ever change?"

He walks over to the desk and stands near it, dropping his room key there and then his wallet and some coins from his pocket. "I don't know. In my dreams, yeah. But probably the best that I can hope for is we'll go back to calling on the holidays and acting like nothing's wrong."

I know there's not a lot he can do. I can sympathize with that helpless feeling, so I go stand next to him and pull him against me. "You'll be welcome at my house."

"Unless your brother's there."

"Yeah, well, fuck him."

He grins up. "I'm not even going to make a remark about that."

"Good." I lean down to nuzzle his ears. "We've got an hour and a half and I don't want to spend it talking about either of our families." I take a breath. "I kinda feel like I didn't do so great with the make-up sex last night. Give me another chance?"

He raises an eyebrow. "You think it was a real fight last night?"

"We were yelling at each other. Or at least, we were snapping."

"We had an argument." He unfastens his pants and slips them off. "It happens."

"It felt like a fight."

He gives me a look. "Do you want to spend your hour and a half talking about the difference between an argument and a fight?"

I glance down at his briefs, nice and tight and revealing, and then follow my look with a paw, holding the warmth of his sheath through the cloth, curling my fingers under his sac, rubbing there. "No," I say. "Not really. Are these new?"

His eyes widen, and then he presses into my paw, letting me get him warm and hard. "Uh-huh," he breathes, and for what seems like the first time that night, he really relaxes into me. "I didn't want to wear boxers here."

"I like them." I grin and tease a finger through the opening at the front so I can feel the warmth of his sheath right against my pad, and then the skin of the shaft above it.

He pants against my chest, his fingers working at removing my shirt. "Don't you want me to put on the shirt?" he says.

I get a second finger in beside the first, enough to curl around and stroke him. "In a minute," I say, and wrap my other arm around his back, just enjoying holding him without any game thoughts or social issues to distract me and ruin things.

After a good few minutes, when he's got my shirt open and his little teeth tugging at my left nipple, I'm panting pretty good myself. So I pull my fingers out of his underwear and grin. "Go put the shirt on," I say.

He flips his tail at me as he saunters back to the bed, and while he's got his back turned, I get my pants off. He turns around with the Boxers t-shirt on and grins at the sight of me standing there with a paw under my own erection. "Well, look at the big bad Firebird," he says, and turns his back on me, sliding his briefs down. He curls his tail over his naked rear. "Think you can get through this defense?"

I lift both paws and step forward. "Just watch me."

After a brief chase around the room, I have him pinned to the bed on his back, legs up against my chest. It still isn't as good as some of our make-up sex has been after fights, but it's as good as I've felt the night before a game in a long time. I let out a lot of tension, and from the way he squirms and thrusts back and gets into it, it feels like he's doing the same. Sure hope the Intercontinental has thick walls.

We lie on the bed, post-climax, me on top of his sticky Boxers shirt, his muzzle up against mine. I slide my arms under him and hold him. "Just two more weeks," I whisper into his ear.

He flicks it and murmurs, "Does that mean we only get to have pre-game sex one more time?"

"Depends how far before the game we can do it." I press my hips into his rear, making him squirm again. "And there's always next season."

"That's not too far off."

I think about who else on the team is having pre-game sex, and that leads my mind back to the conversation over lunch. "You think someone else on the team might be gay?"

He goes really still and his ears flatten. His eyes dip to my nose and then back up. "What makes you say that?"

"Oh, the guys were wondering at lunch. Ty says there's got to be someone else."

"Did he say if he thought anyone…" He trails off.

I nose between his ears. "Did one of them come on to you?" I play-growl.

"No." His tail flicks up against my legs. "No, but I think he's probably right."

"Your gaydar's better than mine, then." I exhale. "But Argonne said that he had been with someone else."

"Doesn't mean they're gay," he says. He reaches up to hold my shoulder. "Being gay is more than just letting a guy blow you. Or fucking a guy. It's about building a relationship with one."

"Mmm." I kiss his ears. "I'm glad I have you, fox."

"Me too," he says softly.

As much as I would like to lie there all night, I have to get back to the hotel for curfew. But I feel much better, very relaxed, all the way back to the hotel. When I get to my room, Charm is there already, wonder of wonders, playing with his new phone. He grumbles about how the clubs all close at eleven, and we actually have our lights out before they come to check.

Sunday morning starts with Charm throwing a pillow at me to wake me up, a hearty breakfast of oatmeal and steak and eggs, and then a quick walk down to the stadium for the nine o'clock call. For the noon kick-off, the Boxers gave us the early practice time on the field. We run through basic drills—nothing fancy; the media and some of the Boliat team staff are hanging about watching. At ten, the Boxers players come out. We say some quick hellos, but we're all tightly focused and talk is minimal.

In the locker room, Coach spends fifteen minutes with us and then turns us over to Steez. I work with Gerrard and Carson, and then a little bit with Zillo. We stretch and dress and sit around trying to stay loose, trying not to think about the fact that this is the biggest game of our lives.

Gerrard helps. We all know that he's been with the Firebirds for years without making the playoffs, and so this should be more important to him than to any of us. And yet he's half-smiling, calmly wrapping his own ankles in tape, and stretching. His ears are up and his tail swings freely behind him, relaxed and confident, and the rest of the linebackers take our cues from him. The minutes and hours tick by.

And then we're walking out into the domed stadium, and as I come out of the tunnel, I pause to take it all in. It's nearly deafening, full of people, and the dome overhead is a confusing background of greyish-white with steel-grey girders stretched across it. Signs dot the crowd, but all of them are pro-Boxers. I don't see any homophobic ones. I feel comforted there; it feels like they've forgotten that I'm gay, which is perfect. I'm just a football player, now.

Zillo, beside me, folds his ears down. "Always forget how loud this place is," he says, loudly enough that I can hear him.

"It's indoors. Just amplifies all the sound," Vonni says behind us.

"That's not how that works," Pace says. "It doesn't amplify it, it just reflects it back."

"Right. Amplifying it."

"No. Amplification is a completely different process…"

Zillo and I look at each other and grin. "It's fucking loud is what it is," I say.

We trot out as we're introduced, looking across the field at the big blue-and-white arch and the empty Boxers' sideline. The stadium fills with boos for us, and then gets eerily quiet as the lights dim.

The Boxers come in, anonymous in their uniforms and helmets. I know their names, but there's only one person on the team I actually know, a cornerback who was with the Dragons last year and joined the Boxers as a backup this year because he wanted to win a ring. I see antlers over the helmets and claws at the end of paws, hands on the horses and deer. They're just another team of football players like us, who won one more game during the regular season, just one.

The lights come up during the national anthem. We stand there, paws over our hearts, and then it seems to take forever for the game to get under way. There are opening ceremonial things and people coming out to speak, a children's charity, and interminable announcements about the history of the Boliat franchise in recent years. I remember what Gerrard said

about the Knights' stadium intimidating visitors, and so I tune out all the announcements.

Next to me, though, Zillo's looking tense, his tail tightly down and his weight shifting from one side to the other. I cast around the stadium and then nudge him. "Hey. You see that funny sign there at the end zone?"

He startles out of listening to the announcements and looks down at the ad (something for Chicken Fingers; it's not really all that funny). For a moment, he just stares at it, and then he breaks into a laugh. "Yeah," he says. "Reminds me of that stupid Chick'n'Biscuits ad back home."

"I hate that fucking chicken mascot," I say.

Zillo's tail uncurls and swings more freely. His posture shifts and he grins. "Everyone does."

Charm leans over from behind us and says, "You think that's bad, you should see the mascot over at Sweet Peppers."

"Yeah?" Zillo half-turns.

"With or without the costume on?" I say.

"She's better without." Charm grins.

We joke back and forth until it's time for the team's captains to go out for the coin toss, and then we cheer on Gerrard and Aston. "Come on, call it right," I mutter.

"Don't fuck up!" Charm yells as they walk out to the center of the field. Aston ignores him, but Gerrard waves a paw back at us.

The guys coming out for Boliat are a whole squad of captains: their running back, a cornerback, a safety, and their quarterback. Everyone shakes and then the referee asks Gerrard to call the toss, as the visiting team's representative. He calls heads, and the coin lands heads. "We want the ball," he tells the ref.

We cheer from the sidelines, not because it's better to get the ball first, but because we feel good about winning the coin toss. Zillo and Charm and I relax with Pace and Vonni and Carson as much as we're able to, watching all the action as the game gets under way.

I look up toward Lee's section at the breaks. He's sitting with the wives, next to Gena and Angela and their cubs. Vonni's wife is sitting with another vixen on the other side from Lee, and Aston's is there, and about a half-dozen others. It's not hard to pick out the fox in the section, as they're right behind our sideline and not too far up, and I can even see that he's looking at me at one point in the first series, because he gestures to me to pay attention to the field.

We're a little tentative on offense. Aston tries one long pass to Strike, but they're ready for it, and after that we just go short. "Taking what they give us," the coaches say, and it gets us close enough for a kick, which Charm nails as confidently and easily as if he were still out in practice.

And then it's our turn to take the field. Boliat has a powerful running game, and they go to it early on, pounding away up the field. They don't really make much effort to hide what they're doing; their running back is just really good. Our line is, too, but we can't stop him from getting two yards here, five yards around the end, another three inside. And their veteran quarterback knows exactly when he can dump off the ball for a short gain. They get another advantage by holding our guys, grabbing them a little more than is legal, but never enough for the refs to call it.

Fisher screams at one of the offensive linemen to play legal, and the bear replies that he don't see no flags on the ground. Gerrard has to calm Fisher down to get him back to the line. Our coaches take up the pleas, to no avail on this drive. The Boxers make it down to the seven-yard line and then their running back plows through us to score.

We trudge back to the sidelines. Already I'm remembering getting to the playoffs my senior year in college, only to fall short in the quarterfinals. But the coaches are upbeat. "It's a long game," they tell us.

And indeed, our offense goes on a nice long drive that ends in another field goal, so we're only down 7-6, which is where it sits at the end of the first quarter after a couple non-scoring series.

The big problem for our offense seems to be false starts; with all the noise in the stadium, it's hard for the guys on the line to hear Aston's snap count. They make some adjustments in between series, and in the second quarter they get a lot better about their starts. Meanwhile, Boliat is hit with a sudden rash of holding calls on their offensive drives—sudden, that is, if you didn't hear Coach screaming about the holding all through the first quarter. The refs just start listening, and that stalls a few Boliat drives and negates at least one big gain. "There's your flag!" Fisher screams at the bear after one penalty, and looks like he's ready to go after the guy until we pull him back.

After another field goal from Charm, he comes back to the sidelines with one fist raised. It isn't until I'm running out to defend again that it sinks in that I'm protecting a lead now. We're actually winning the game.

It doesn't last; just before the half, Boliat mounts a great two-minute drive—I mean, great in that 'when you're watching it on TV and rooting for the Boxers' way. From our side, it's frustrating as hell. We'll get them to second and long, third and long, and then their quarterback rifles one just past Gerrard's paws, or just over my head, to complete the first down. We manage to stop them from scoring a touchdown, but they get a field goal to go back on top, 10-9, as we run into the locker rooms at halftime.

Defending the run takes a lot out of you. Running around covering receivers and short passes just tires me out; when I've been plowing into their line and tackling people over and over, I feel beaten down. It's like when we played Gateway, though thank God they don't have anyone like Gateway's wolverine running at us. Everyone looks like I feel, but the coaches are encouraging. "You are doing good," Steez tells us, standing over the linebacking corps as we catch our breath. Gerrard and Carson sit beside me, Zillo and Marais behind me. "Now you need to be great."

That's the worst part of it, that we're doing everything right. They're half a step faster, reacting half a second quicker. "Need to anticipate better," Gerrard says. "We know what they're going to do."

"Line needs to stop the run," Carson says. "Their O-line is creating holes."

Our defensive line is getting its own talk a little ways away. Fisher's voice is the loudest, even over the coaches, while the rest of the line is mostly silent. "If they could slow the other guys down even just a step," I say, "we could get in there. By the time I get to the guy, he's already past the line and got momentum."

"Yes," Steez says. "Second half, you play up a little closer, charge line on running plays more aggressively. Corners and safeties will watch the receivers. Once or twice we will blitz to shake up number 12."

That's the quarterback. Gerrard shakes his head. "Not going to shake him up," he says. "But might get a turnover that way." His ears flick and he looks up at the cougar. "You think we're going to need a turnover to win."

Steez remains impassive. "Turnovers always help. Worth taking small chance for. Their offense is conservative, more conservative than on film. We think we can make something happen."

"All right." Gerrard looks around at the rest of us. "We good with that?"

"Take chances," I say. "I'm good."

Coach gathers us all for a speech to send us back out there with. "This is an important game," he says, "and it's probably the best team we've faced all year. They don't make a lot of mistakes. So we're going to need to be more aggressive and make something happen. I know we can do it. This team has the talent to beat any other team in the league. But they're not going to deliver us a victory. We're going to have to take it from them."

We head out inspired and full of energy. On the sideline, we stretch to stay loose, keeping the sore spots and abused muscles from the first half from getting too stiff. And because we got the ball to start the game, they get the ball to start the second half, so we buckle on our helmets and go out to defend.

Being aggressive is easier said than done. My instincts are to find the play, sometimes to anticipate where the play is going, not so much to charge ahead with less regard to what's happening. But that's what we're doing; we can tell in a split-second whether the play is a run or not, and then we're just driving forward into the line. When they try to run around us, we sniff that out and stop it. They break through once or twice more, but we hold them on that first series.

They figure out what we're doing, of course, and then start throwing. They've got that great tight end who helps them move the chains again and again; Carson always seems to be a half-step away from tackling him. The Boxers get two long gains, get to right around midfield, and then the game changes.

It starts out as a standard running play. Fisher's coming off the end right into the heart of the play, but their running back jukes and Fisher spins around off-balance right as one of their offensive linemen slams into him, knocking him to the ground.

I see it peripherally, but don't think much of it. I mean, most of us get tackled hard every game. It knocks the wind out of you, then you get up. Only Fisher doesn't get up.

Gerrard's the first one to notice, and then I see Fisher sprawled on his stomach, the big number 75 not moving, his orange-and-black striped tail limp across his thighs. Two Boxers are already crouched over him as Gerrard and I hurry over. *Not again, not again*, I'm thinking as I get close. "Hey, Fish," Gerrard says. "Come on, get up. We got a game to play." But the coyote's helmet is off and the cant of his ears shows the worry he's not letting into his words. Fisher's up on the Jumbotron now and the crowd has fallen silent, so we can hear all the things going on around us with eerie clarity.

"I just tackled him," the huge bear from Boliat says. He sounds defensive, gesturing to the ground, which is clear of penalty flags. "It was all clean and legal."

We ignore him, mostly; Gerrard nods quickly at him to show we've heard, and Carson stands next to him and tells him it's cool. Already our team physician is hurrying over from the sidelines with three trainers, and Strike, of all people, is leading the way.

Just as they get there, Fisher's tail twitches. He groans and gets his arms under him, trying to push himself up.

"Easy there," the doc says. "We got a stretcher coming."

"Don't need a stretcher," Fisher mutters.

Strike says, "Okay, just take it easy, bud. Think you can roll over onto your back?"

"Don't move him yet," the doctor snaps. "I need to check—"

Fisher growls and rolls over onto his back. He pushes himself to a sitting position before the doctor can do anything. "I'm fine," he says, more clearly.

"Let me just take a look at your eyes." The doc gets his helmet off and shines a light into each of Fisher's pupils. "Are you dizzy at all?"

"I'm *fine*," Fisher snaps again. He looks up at me and Gerrard. "Tell him I'm fine," he growls at us.

"What year is it?" Strike asks, crouched over with his paws on his knees.

"Do you know where you are?" the doc asks.

"I'm in…" Fisher looks around, up at the roof and the steel girders in front of it. "This is Boliat, right?"

"All right," the doctor says, and gets to his feet. "Come on, you're coming out of the game."

"I have to stay in!" With the help of the trainers, Fisher struggles to his feet. The crowd cheers, so much that it's hard to hear the next words he says. "This is an important game. I can still play!"

Strike says something, but I can't catch his words. I hear the doctor, though, still talking as the trainers, an otter and a slender ringtail, try to walk Fisher to the sidelines. "Why is it important?" the doctor says.

The trainers are having trouble managing Fisher, so I step in to help, blocking Strike, who's still trying to talk through the doctor's words. "Because…because it's the playoffs," Fisher says. "We have to win this game."

"You've got a concussion," the doctor says gently. "The best thing you can do for your team is step over to the sidelines and let the healthy players finish the game."

"We can do it!" Strike says, with a big smile and a fist pump.

Fisher looks at me and then at Gerrard. The coyote lifts a paw to Fisher's shoulder. "You've given us all you can," he says.

I nod. "Go get better. We'll finish this."

The big tiger slumps. He lets the trainers support him back to the sideline.

Gerrard turns to me. Pike is already walking out to take Fisher's place on the field. "You ready?" Gerrard says. I nod. He puts his helmet back on, and says, "Then let's finish this."

Chapter 7 – Aggression (Lee)

I feel worse than I can ever remember feeling at a football game, not only at the moment Fisher went down and didn't get up, but at Gena's cold stillness beside me. I can't even think of what to say to her as those agonizing moments stretch out into minutes. Next to her, her sons—Fisher's sons—are just as still, although I see them look at Gena while she doesn't take her eyes from the field.

Finally, when he rolls over and sits up, Junior says, "Dad's okay," and that seems to snap Gena out of her daze.

"Of course he's going to be okay," she says, and forces a smile as she turns to them. "He's going to be fine."

"I'll stay with the boys if you want to go down there," I say gently, though Bradley's probably only about seven years younger than I am.

She turns to me. "During a game?"

"Well…" I just want to make sure she won't spend the rest of the game worrying about him. "Let's see if he goes back to the locker room. If he does…"

Even then, she might not go down there. Right now they're talking to him and I don't know what's going on. Then he stands up and we all cheer, our section loudest of all. Nice crowd in Boliat. There are some things that transcend team allegiance.

"Look, he's walking off. He's okay," I say.

"They're supporting him," Gena says.

The boys lean forward to look, passing a small pair of binoculars between them. Bradley offers them to Gena, but she waves him away. Junior says, "There was a guy in one of my games who got the wind knocked out of him so bad he couldn't come back in the rest of the game. But it was just a rib contusion, he was okay in like two days."

"At least it's not his leg again," Bradley says, watching Fisher. "He's walking fine. He's talking with the trainers." He pauses. "He's angry."

Gena takes her phone out to text. When she puts it away, she says, "Hopefully he'll write back and let me know…"

They're taking Fisher back to the locker room. So he's probably not coming back to the game. It's a good game, but my thoughts keep going to Fisher and what happened to him, and how close Dev might be to something similar, some game-ending or, God forbid, career-ending injury. I try to focus on the football game to chase away those thoughts, with moderate success.

Pike's out there now, slower but more powerful. I wait for Boliat to run more quick patterns to his side, see if their runner can get around him before he can bring his weight to bear. That's Dev's side, and with some help from Pace, they seal the edge until it's clear Boliat's not going to be able to exploit Pike that way. Chevali has a bit of an advantage here; they played without Fisher for half the season, but Boliat probably only prepared for Fisher, not Pike. Plus Chevali's now playing for Fisher as well as themselves, I'm sure. The whole defense is fired up: Dev pumps his fist more than once, and his and Carson's tails lash constantly. When Dev does look my way between plays, I can see the white gleam of his fierce, proud smile.

But Chevali's offense can't muster more than a field goal after a long pass to Strike gets them down close to the end zone. And in the fourth quarter, down 12-10, Boliat starts passing the ball more, when it becomes clear that the Firebirds aren't going to give them any running room. Dev covers the short receiver, but when they split out three wide plus the tight end, they can get some passes off quickly enough to keep marching down the field. They're at the seven-yard line when the quarterback lobs a pass to the corner of the end zone.

Dev is covering the short receiver and Vonni the deep one, but of course at this distance, there's not much distinction. As it happens, the pass was to the short receiver, with the deep one running a curl in front of him as a decoy. Vonni nearly smacks into Dev, but adjusts in time to see the pass going behind him. He stops, leaps, and twists brilliantly in the air to get a paw on it. That sends the football to the left, where Dev shoots a paw up and snatches it cold. He brings it to his chest and drops to the ground clutching it as he disappears into a sea of ecstatic red and gold. I'm standing in my seat and jumping up and down and Gena stands too, her worries about Fisher momentarily erased.

Of course, there's six minutes left in the game. The Firebirds offense takes the field and does exactly the right thing, handing the ball to Jaws over and over to chew up clock; the Boxers know what they're going to do and stack the line, holding the big wolverine to two yards on first down, one on second. And then Aston does something wonderful and unexpected.

The Boxers haven't forgotten about Strike; they're too good a team for that. Aston drops back to pass on third down and fakes the long throw as Strike races down the field. There's already a corner on him, another cheetah who can barely keep up, but the fake sends the safety shooting across the field to help cover.

And there's Ty, red tail streaming out behind him, lifting a black paw over the middle, and Aston throws so smoothly that it's clear that's where he meant to go all along. It's a brilliant fake that makes me jump up again with all the wives as Ty dodges one defender, and then Strike throws a terrific block on the safety who's now trying to reverse field to catch the fox, and there's nothing between Ty and the end zone and he strolls in, tail high, and slams the ball to the ground.

Our little section is screaming and hugging while the rest of the stadium is silent. The people near us give us half-hearted boos and jeers, but they know who we are, pretty much. Before the game, in one of the rare periods when I could keep my ears up without getting deafened, I heard speculation from the next section over about which of the females over here was whose wife on the Firebirds. I didn't hear them speculate about me, but now that we're cheering and the rest of the crowd is quiet, I can hear little bits of conversation, and I focus in on the ones that say, "fox."

Like: "...that fox with the tiger—that's DiCarlo's brother."

"DiCarlo's got a brother?"

DiCarlo is Vonni. I don't think he has a brother.

"...the fox is with the wives..."

"...it's families too—he's gotta be a younger brother or something..."

After that, the Boxers receive the kickoff and the crowd gets loud again. But during the ensuing drive I sneak a look over to see if I can pick out the guys who were talking. I narrow it down to either a pair of cougars in Boxers t-shirts, both with 32-ounce beers, or a dark grey wolf chatting with a muscular brown rabbit in a wife-beater. But I can't match the voices up exactly to either pair, and so as I watch Boliat stall at midfield, I focus back on the game. They punt with three minutes left, and the Firebirds' punt returner, a quick-cutting otter, calls for a fair catch on the five. Great punt—the Firebirds are backed up against their end zone and they have to be really careful here.

Run, run, run. Jaws takes the ball and runs into the line, and the Boxers call time. It's a tedious part of the game and yet I'm still wringing my paws. Up by nine, this should be the part where we're just counting down to the end of the game. Unless they don't get a first down. If they have to punt the ball, then the Boxers get another chance, and a quick touchdown and an onside kick and a field goal...

Those kinds of endings happen just often enough to keep us nervous, as the Firebirds get to third down and take their time getting back to the line. They come up in a passing formation, which makes me curse softly, "Just run the ball again, chew up more clock." But Aston drops back and passes, and Ty reaches for the ball—

—the crowd holds its breath—

—as the ball glances off his fingertips—

—and a Boxers' linebacker, a tall fisher marten, makes an incredible diving catch, rolling over and over with the ball on the ground—

—and the crowd erupts, screams and cheers all around us, as Gena and I look at each other, as Bradley says "Shit," and Gena doesn't even scold him for his language.

"They still have to score," I say. "Twice." But the energy of the crowd is deflating for us. All down our row, ears are flat and tails are limp.

It doesn't seem to be doing our defense much good, either. Though Dev and his teammates play pretty well, the Boxers are fired up and determined. They march down the short field with screen passes to their tight end, who gets out of bounds at the sidelines after gains of four, three, five—at which point Gena cries, "Can't they stop him?"

I know she's thinking that she doesn't want this to be Fisher's last game. I don't want Dev's season to end here, either. I squeeze my paws together and don't say anything, just watch the action on the field.

They line up on the three-yard line and I feel the creeping sense of inevitability. They're going to score here, I know, whether on this play or the next. It's just one of those things you get a sense for. Sure enough, they give the ball to their running back and he drives up the middle—risky, because they'll lose precious seconds if he doesn't get in—but their offensive line creates a nice gap for him, and when Dev tackles him to the ground, he's already a foot inside the end zone. The ref raises both arms into the air, and if I thought the crowd was loud before, that was nothing. I actually put my paws over my ears for a moment.

Beside me, Gena's shoulders slump. Her boys do too, although Junior straightens up and says, "We're still winning."

Just don't give up the onside kick, I mutter. That's all you need to do. Hold on to the ball. They're out of timeouts. If the Firebirds can just recover the kick, they can run out the clock and win, 19-17.

The Jumbotron screams, "MAKE NOISE," and a piece of a popular song plays, about a boxer who knows when to fight. The crowd is on their feet, and we stand with them. "Come on, Firebirds!" Bradley hollers, and I echo him.

Our cheers might be lost in the noise from the crowd, but they make us feel better. Ears perk up (some; it's still too loud to have them all the way up, at least for me) and our tails and body language show more energy.

Uncovered

The teams line up for the onside kick. The receivers and cornerbacks are out there—the "hands" team—for both sides. The noise from the crowd escalates to a roar as the Boxers' kicker kicks the ball into the ground, sending it up through the air in a short arc as the Boxers charge madly down to get in position before the ball comes down. Ty and Vonni are waiting for it, but it's Strike—the superstar wideout, in the game on a special teams play—who leaps and swipes the ball out of the air with a paw, tumbling to the ground with it.

Players from both teams leap on him. The ball and cheetah vanish from view as the crowd around us gasps and holds their breath. The referees run to the pile and start peeling away players. All around, Firebirds are hopping and gesturing that it's their ball, and as the referees get to the final layer of the pile, one of them stretches out his arm and points toward the Firebirds' side of the field.

Chevali ball. All we have to do is run out the clock.

The crowd deflates, sagging back into their seats for the most part. A few die-hard fans stay on their feet. Bradley and Junior slap paws in a high-five and then Bradley turns and hugs his mother. In the relative quiet, as my ears come up, I catch scattered words nearby, the same voices, one telling the other to be quiet.

I turn and catch the rabbit looking at me, though he turns away the moment my eyes meet his. Next to him, the wolf is staring down at the field. Well, when your team is about to lose in an upset at a playoff home game, it's a tough thing. Still, I wonder why they're staring at me. I'm trying not to be gay-paranoid, because I've never had a problem in a football stadium, but it's hard not to read the attention in that way. That mutes a little of my excitement at the Firebirds going to their first championship in a generation or so.

Aston takes the snap and kneels immediately. The clock ticks down to 40, 30, 20...Aston gets behind center again and takes another snap and a knee, and that's the game.

The wives cheer and hug each other while the fans around us go dead quiet. I hear the wife of one of the offensive linemen say, as she hugs Angela, "Another fifty grand!" I'm just bouncing on my paws until Gena gathers me in a big hug.

"This must be exciting for you," she says.

"Incredible." I'm grinning like a maniac and feeling that burst of pride for my tiger in my chest. "The interception, just—he played so well the whole game."

Her ears flick, and I see Fisher in her eyes again. "They played great," she says, and we turn back to the field. The players in their road whites with the red-trimmed gold numbers are still jumping up and down as the two coaches shake paws in the middle of the field. Dev is out with the rest of the team exchanging pleasantries with the Boxers, but he doesn't stay more than a minute before sprinting to the locker room. I'm sure it's to check on Fisher.

"Going to go down there?" I ask Gena.

She holds up her phone. "I just got a text that he's fine, but I need to come pick him up. You can get back to the hotel okay, right?"

I nod, heading toward the aisle and out. "Sure." The other wives are dispersing. Angela waves at me; some of the others smile as well. Penny, the vixen Gena was worried about, actually comes over with Daria as we're all filing out of the row of seats and says she's sorry I couldn't make it to drinks the night before. I guess she met Dev earlier in the year at a dinner and thought he was very nice. Then we get to the aisle and are separated by the crowd; she waves and I wave back, slightly puzzled.

Bradley and Junior follow their mother out behind me. But they turn and walk down to the field as I walk up to the concourse, figuring I'll let Dev enjoy the moment with his teammates. *So proud of you*, I text. *Going to the championship!*

I get up to the concourse wedged into the crowd, the miasma of scents and greasy food and beer all around me. People spot my Firebirds shirt and some boo, others say "Good game" or "Congrats." I raise my paw as best I can, shuffling toward the exits with everyone else.

Then I feel warm liquid drench the back of my shirt, dripping over my tail, and I catch the smell of beer. I turn and the rabbit in the wife-beater, one of the ones I thought was talking about me, is there with an empty beer cup, leering at me. "Hey," I say. "Watch it."

Instead of apologizing, he says, "You like that, huh?"

Up close, I can see he's got huge shoulders. My thumb twitches. Even if I wanted to get into a fight here in the crowd, I wouldn't take this guy on. "Not really." I try to duck around some people in front of me. My heart's going faster now.

A strong paw grips my tail at the base. "Nah," a deeper, slurred voice says, and I spin in time to see his friend the wolf behind me holding a plastic bottle of beer. "He likes it under the tail." He yanks my tail up and turns the bottle over, shoving the mouth of it between my tail and my jeans.

Colder liquid gushes out over my underwear and the smell of beer rises thick and strong. I reach around to pull the bottle out, but the wolf's holding my pants with one paw and the bottle with the other. The position is awkward; I have little leverage to begin with, and it gets worse when the rabbit grabs my wrist and twists it.

Sharp pain shoots up my arm. I give up formal aikido and just swing my hips away, slapping at the bottle with my other arm, and I hit the wolf's wrist. The bottle comes out, landing on the floor with an empty clatter, and though the wolf lets go as I stagger and lose my balance, the rabbit doesn't. My underwear, my rear, the back of my legs are all soaked with beer.

People around us notice. How could they not? I'm being held half off the ground by a big rabbit, stinking of beer. The wolf backs away, stepping hard on my tail as he does. I do manage to use an aikido slip to get out of the rabbit's grip, and as I regain my balance, the wolf shoves me hard. "You fuckin' hit me," he snarls.

I slam into a jaguar, who shoves me back at the wolf. "You threw beer—you dumped a bottle of—"

"Hey," someone yells, "take it outside."

"Christ," someone else curses, looking disdainfully at the three of us.

What I'd love to do is yell for a cop, but in this crowd, the better part of valor is definitely running away. My tail hurts and my lower half is soaking, stinking wet, and I'm a little worried about what these two might do next. I'm trying to keep an eye on them as the crowd pushes us along, and so without meaning to, I stumble forward into the jaguar again.

"Watch it," he snarls, and shoves me again.

In trying to spin away from the wolf, I fall against the rabbit, and he grabs me and drives a fist into my stomach. "Faggot," he spits in his light voice.

I double over, gasping for breath. That gets a little more attention from the crowd around us, either the word or the punch or both. An armadillo yells, "Hey! Security!" and a wiry cacomistle tries to get between us.

"Calm down," he says, with broad Midwestern geniality, and then he sees my Firebirds shirt. "Come on. It's just a game. We're all fans."

"He's not just a fan." Even over the beer soaking my clothes and fur, I can smell the rabbit's boozy breath as he leans in. "He's that faggot Firebird's boyfriend."

I'm slowly recovering, still sucking down air, not really able to form words yet. The cacomistle looks at me and frowns. "Uh. Hey, you guys, just, just settle down."

I have about a half-second to think that maybe things are over before there's a hard yank on my tail, enough to pull me backwards and send a jolt

of pain up my spine, bringing tears to my eyes. I turn and see the wolf shoving his way through the crowd, running away.

The rabbit brays a laugh, and I can't help it; I run after the wolf. It's not hard to catch him, because he's making little progress through the annoyed crowd. I'm not sure what I want to do, but when I grab his shirt, he turns and throws a punch. I duck in time, and he hits a doe beside me. She stumbles against her boyfriend or husband or whatever, a big stag, and when he grumbles, she says, "He *punched* me!"

The stag sizes up the wolf for just a moment and then leaps at him, and I take advantage of the distraction to land a punch on the wolf's stomach. It's not as hard as the rabbit's was on me, but then again, it's not a sucker punch. It's enough to slow the wolf just as the stag gets to him, and maybe, maybe, the wolf thinks that the stag is the one who punched him, because he flails at the stag's muzzle with both fists. The stag lowers his head and smacks the wolf hard with his antlers, sending him to his knees with a yelp.

I'm keeping my tail curled between my legs for safety, backing away. As much as I'd enjoy watching the wolf get the shit beat out of him, I'd rather make myself scarce. The exits are about ten yards in front of us, but there's little chance I'm going to get there anytime soon, as the whole crowd has stopped to either watch, participate in, or try to stop the growing fight.

"Fuckin' Firebirds," someone near me says, and shoves me.

"Whoa," someone else says, "cut it out." Me, I just try to stay quiet and watch the wolf and deer, who are now grappling on the floor. The deer lands a couple good punches; the wolf has his mouth open, snarling, showing off his teeth, and his claws have already torn the deer's shirt in several places.

"Break it up!" someone yells, and a uniformed wolverine drops to his knees by the wolf and stag and reaches out to separate them. Another security guard, a badger, starts directing the crowd to move on, away from the fight. I start to go with them, and then my sense of morality kicks in. I tell myself that the security guys will need a complete account of the fight, so the wolf and rabbit can have charges pressed against them.

When I walk up to the badger, he says, "Just keep moving, sir."

"I was involved," I say.

He waves some other people around me. "It's all right. We're just breaking this up." The wolverine's got the wolf and deer on their feet and is talking to them. The badger looks their way and then back at me. "You can just go on."

"I want to file assault charges," I say, and point at the wolf.

The badger looks at me steadily. His eyes drop to my beer-soaked pants. "He did this?"

"Partly. His buddy helped—big rabbit, sleeveless shirt. I don't know where he went. But him, he grabbed my tail and poured beer down my pants. And then yanked on my tail after. Also he tried to punch me." The wolf and stag are still shouting at each other. "That's when he hit that guy's girlfriend."

"All right. Stay here, sir. Don't go anywhere."

The badger goes and talks to the wolverine. He keeps his voice low, but I hear him say "assault" and at that, the wolf yelps and points at me, yelling, "He started it! He fucking started it!"

I keep quiet. The crowd's thinning out, so I have room to pull out my phone and check it—keeping one eye on the wolf—without worrying I'm going to jostle someone or drop it. I have a message from Dev that's just, *YES!!!*, and one from my father that says, *Can't wait for the championship!*

And there's a voicemail from Brian. The corridor is still very loud, too loud for me to hear anything, and of all the people I don't need to hear from right now, he's at the top of the list. I put the phone away and wait.

They have a holding area where they bring me, the wolf, and the stag. It's lit with harshly white fluorescents and it smells like a stale locker room. There's all kinds of fur clumped in the corners; I guess the janitors skip this room on their rounds.

After some discussion, security lets the stag go; he doesn't want to press charges, and the wolf pretty much admits he hit the guy's wife (it turns out), if only by accident. I describe the rabbit for the security chief, an imposing bear, even though I'm sure the guy is long gone. The wolf doesn't volunteer the name even when they semi-threaten him. "You won't be coming to games for a long time, so you might as well tell us your buddy's name," the security chief says, and the wolf just shrugs and doesn't say anything.

He's pretty beat up. The stag landed a good punch in his face, or else it was the antlers that got his eye all swollen up. He has blood on his muzzle which I hope is his; the security chief photographs it before handing him a towel to wipe it with. One of his ears is nicked, but I can't tell whether that happened during the fight or if it's an old injury.

I text Dev: *Held up. Will let you know when I get back to the hotel.* Then I just sit there in the slowly-drying beer and relax. My stomach and tail feel sore but improving. Hopefully the only lasting injury was to my pride. To assuage that, I recall the punch I landed on the wolf, and make it better in my head than it probably was.

The police, a male otter with a shoulder bag and a female red fox with a sour expression, arrive half an hour later and get right down to work. The shoulder bag holds a scent-swab kit and a camera, which the otter starts using while the vixen records the statements of the security chief, the badger, and the wolverine. The wolf, who's sobered up some, tries to interrupt, but she turns with an ice-cold stare and says, "I'll get to you, sir."

The otter, to distract the wolf, hands him a scent-swab and says, "I need you to run this under the base of your tail, sir. If you need privacy to do it, you can use the restroom."

"I didn't do anything wrong!" The wolf shifts his pleading to the otter. "This fag—this guy picked a fight with me and then I hit that fuckin' deer by accident and her boyfriend started whalin' on me."

"She'll take your statement in a moment, sir." The otter's getting the camera ready. "I just need you to do that for me."

The wolf scowls and reaches behind himself with the swab. The otter turns to me with the camera. I hold out my arms for him to photograph the brown/red demarcation of the fur, and his eyebrows rise. "Someone knows the drill."

"It's not my first fight," I say. "But I don't start them. I guess I just have one of those faces."

The otter grins as he takes some pictures. "You wear that shirt down in Hellentown, too?"

"Yeah, but they didn't pour beer down my pants."

The wolf says loudly, "He spilled beer on himself! I saw him!"

"That'd be a neat trick," I say, "getting it all down the *back* of my pants."

"Hey," he shrugs, "I hear that's how you people like it."

The otter looks up at that, and the vixen turns around. "'You people'?" she says, her voice low and dangerous.

The wolf's ears go back. "Firebirds fans," he mutters.

"I was sitting with the players' wives," I say. "He recognized me."

The security guys get it then, but the two cops don't. So I say, "I'm Dev Miski's boyfriend."

It's harder to say than I would've thought. I would've said I was used to coming out to people, and the guy most likely to react badly to it already knew. But I'm still sort of steamed about the wolf and I'm in the mood to force people to deal with me.

The otter just goes back to photographing my arms, and then the whisker pattern on my muzzle. The vixen narrows her eyes and looks between the two of us, then turns back to the security chief. "What happened to the stag?"

"He didn't want to press charges. We got his name and all that."

"Good." She shakes her head and turns to the two of us. "Now, you two, tell me your story. You first." She points at the wolf.

He spins some crazy story about how I was waving beer all over and bragging about the Firebirds win and then started chasing him through the crowd until he had to throw a punch at me in self-defense and hit the doe by accident. The otter shakes his head and finishes with my photos, then gives me a scent-swab.

"I don't know how good it's going to come out," I say. "Since that's right where he poured the beer."

I time it so that it falls in a break in the wolf's story, and everyone looks at me. It has the desired effect; he falters and the vixen folds her arms, glancing at me more often as the wolf stumbles through the rest of his lie. When it's my turn, they want to see the evidence, so I have to kneel on the floor, leaning forward with my arms on the chair, while the otter takes photos of my beer-soaked rear and tail. I think about telling Dev that I was late getting back because some cops wanted to take pictures of my butt, and that brings me the first real smile I've had in a while.

"Use the swabs anyway," the otter says when they're done, and hands me two. "We'll be able to get your scent off them, and it'll help as evidence of the beer being there."

So I rub the swabs around the base of my tail and hand them back, sitting back in the chair. "Now," the vixen says, "what's your version?"

I tell my version of what happened—the real version, not leaving out my chasing the wolf after he yanked my tail. "I know I should've just let it go," I say, "but I felt like—like really? He pulled my *tail*? That hasn't happened since sixth grade."

The vixen's tail curls, I hope in sympathy. We long-tailed species come in for more abuse as cubs in school, and girls have it worse than boys. I tell the rest of the story and she takes down notes in addition to the digital mini-recorder she's using to capture it. "All right," she sighs, when she turns it off. "Shore, process the wolf. I'll get the fox's info and we can get out of here."

"Process?" The wolf's ears come up. "What's that mean?"

"We're releasing you on your own recognizance, but we need to write you a citation for fighting, and we need your address and phone so we can contact you for your court date."

"Court date?" he yelps. "No no. I'm not—What about that fag—that guy? Does he get a court date?"

"Sir," the otter says, pulling out a citation book, "you're not under arrest, but I strongly suggest you remain silent."

The vixen pulls out a similar book and starts filling out a ticket. "I have to write you up as well," she says, "because I'm sure if you press charges, he's going to. But I have your statements and I don't think you need to worry much. So where are you staying, and for how long?"

"The Intercontinental," I say, and give her my drivers license, pointing to the Hilltown address. "This isn't current, though. I moved to Chevali a month…month and a half ago. I don't drive much there, so I haven't gotten it changed."

"Huh. Okay, give me your current address, and get that updated as soon as you get back."

"Yes, sir. Ma'am."

She raises an eyebrow. "'Ma'am' is fine."

I grin. "Okay, ma'am." She writes down the info as I give it to her.

"This is bullshit!" the wolf yells.

"And on behalf of the city of Boliat," the vixen says, "allow me to apologize for our citizenry. We're not all violent bigots."

She shoots a look at the wolf that would shut me up even in one of my activist rants. But the wolf doesn't get the hint. "Violent? Me? No, I'm not like that, it was just that he grabbed me—"

"I'm sure we'll sort all that out," the vixen says. "In the meantime, you're going to come down to the station, and Mister Farrel, once you get home and cleaned up, we'd appreciate it if you could come down and give a formal statement as well."

"Of course."

I get directions to the police station (which is in walking distance of the stadium and the hotel) and go back to my room to clean up. I text Dev when I get back to my room, but he doesn't answer immediately, so I call the hotel's laundry service to clean my jeans and briefs and then hop in the shower. When I get out, he's texted that the team is still celebrating. There's also a text from Gena asking if I'm free.

Shit. I completely forgot about Fisher, what with being attacked by drunken homophobes. I call her, and the first thing she tells me is, "Fisher's fine."

"Good. What happened?"

"Concussion. So I guess he's not 'fine,' but…" She laughs, shakily.

"Could have been a lot worse." The fact that he walked off the field meant it probably wasn't a spinal injury. But there are all kinds of head trauma he could've gotten.

"God, yes."

"Is he going to be able to play in the championship game?"

She makes a noise, kind of a catch in her throat. "That's what I want to talk to you about. They say he's day to day, but…I don't want him to play."

"Is he still taking the, uh…"

"I don't know. I didn't find any in our luggage, but I can't search his locker. Did you look it up?"

"I sent a couple e-mails out to friends of mine on the Dragons, but… honestly, I don't know if they'll know anything. Or if they do, I don't know that they'll tell me. I have one other source I can try, but this stuff—it all happens behind doors, in closed rooms, you know?"

"I know." Her voice is small. "I don't know what else to do."

"I'll help," I say. "I'll do what I can. Where are you guys now?"

"He's still in the locker room. I'm in a restaurant next to the stadium."

"Do you want company?"

"If you have time."

"Sure." I grab some clothes out of my bag. "I just have to go do this thing at the police station."

"All right," Gena says, and then, "Wait. Police station?"

"I'll tell you about it later. Give me an hour? Text me if you leave."

So I go down to the police station and I file an official complaint. I give them contact information again for the court date. "Probably in a month," the otter tells me, the same one who photographed me. He holds up the signed statement. "And again, sorry for your experience here. I'd wish your team luck in the championship, but…" He gestures around at the Boxers pennants, pictures, and framed newspaper with the headline screaming "KO'D" from the Boxers' championship in '06.

"It's okay," I say. "I hope I have reason to come back to your town soon."

"But good luck to you," he says. "And Miski."

I thank him and leave with a little more wag in my still-damp tail. If I don't think too much about being assaulted for being gay, if I focus on the fact that everyone was sympathetic and the asshole is being punished, then I feel a lot better about things. I remember Dev's interception and Strike grabbing the ball on the onside kick, and that lifts my spirits still more. The day has been really up and down, and it's barely late afternoon. In fact, by the time I spot Gena in the restaurant and sit down across from her, the second half of the other playoff game has already started.

Gena follows my gaze to the TV. "I guess we'll be going to Crystal City," she says.

The score's Crystal City 14, Peco 0. "It's a long game," I say, "but yeah. Sabretooths don't give up second-half leads. Pity."

"Would we have had a home championship game if Peco won? We finished with a better record."

I shake my head. "I think as a division champ they get home-field over a wild-card team. That last Hellentown game…if we'd won that. But it's a moot point anyway, unless a miracle happens in the second half."

"Two scores down isn't really 'miracle' territory."

"Against the Sabretooths, I think it might be." I order a Diet Coke from the waiter when he comes by, and then ask about Fisher.

"I only talked to him for about ten minutes," Gena tells me. "He was in the training room and they wanted to run a few more tests on him. I guess he was dizzy…having trouble remembering things…" She stops talking and swallows, staring past my muzzle. She's larger than I am, but her frame seems unsteady, about to collapse in on itself. Her small black ears flatten, her large paws turn her gleaming silver fork over and over without looking at it, and the shoulders of her white jacket—nicer than the Firebirds warmup she was wearing at the game—bow inward.

We both know what the end of this road looks like. I've never had to deal with this kind of personal tragedy, when you might partly lose someone. Like Fisher is becoming a different person, one who still loves his wife and kids, but might forget things about them. Things they've done together, things about their lives. Their names.

"I'm sure he'll be fine," I say.

I don't think it was particularly helpful, nor insightful, but Gena draws a breath and her shoulders straighten, her ears come up a little, and she braces herself as she reaches for the glass in front of her. It smells of fruit and tequila. "Are your grandparents living?"

"Only my mother's mother, but she…doesn't stay in touch."

"Fisher's father had Alzheimer's. It was…hard."

I bite my lip. "My father's grandfather did too. I don't know much about it."

The waiter brings a plate of stuffed mushrooms just then, and Gena smiles. "I'm not hungry, but I thought you might be. And I think I should eat something."

The mushrooms smell of mushroom, strongly, and then cheese and a faint whiff of crab. I usually don't like mushrooms all that much on their own, but I take one so as not to be rude. It's greasy and cheesy, but, I realize, I haven't eaten at all since the greasy, cheesy sausage sandwich I had just after halftime of the game, and I am hungry.

"How long ago was that?" I ask. "Fisher's father, I mean."

"Oh. Three years ago, he passed." Gena picks up one of the mushrooms on her fork and holds it in front of her muzzle, looking at it. Cheese oozes down the side. "The boys didn't quite get what was going on, until it was very close to the end and he couldn't really talk anymore."

Again I feel a tightness in my chest, a sympathetic grief that I'm not quite sure how to handle. It's not mine to dismiss or confront, and I don't know how to offer comfort any more than I already have. "Where are the boys?"

"At the stadium. They wanted to wait for their father and maybe see some of the other players." She smiles. "I'm sorry to be dumping all of this on you. But I don't really know the other wives that well."

I don't either, of course, except maybe Angela. "I'm already looking into the drugs," I say. "I'm sorry I can't be of more help."

"Dev's close to Fisher, though. If Fisher would listen to anyone…"

That seems like a pretty big "if," from what I know of Fisher, but I don't comment on it. "I'll talk to Dev about it, yeah."

"About Fisher playing in the championship?"

"I meant about the drugs." I rub the side of my muzzle. "You don't want him to play in the championship."

"Well…" She sets down the mushroom without eating it. "Would you? If it were Dev?"

I think about that and I get a chill which raises my hackles. "No. But if he thought he could still play…I don't know how I could stop him."

"I don't know what to do about Fisher, either. Maybe together we can figure out something."

"I'll enlist Dev, for sure. Once he sobers up."

She smiles faintly. "At least Fisher's not out drinking tonight."

"Has that gotten worse, too?" I eat another mushroom, since she's not going to.

"Not worse, but…I think in combination with the drugs, maybe. It just seems like the alcohol affects him differently now. He gets sleepy right away, or he gets maudlin."

"At least it doesn't make him even angrier."

"No. Not usually." She takes another sip of her drink and sighs. One paw covers her phone, sitting on the table. "I wish he'd call."

The TV distracts me; Peco scores a touchdown, and then Crystal City blocks the extra point. It's 14-6. I get that little football-related spark in my chest when something exciting might be about to happen, and that makes my tail wag, but I suppress it because of what we're talking about.

Gena fills the silence. "So what was this 'police station thing'?"

"Oh…" I wave a paw. "I was around when this guy got arrested. They just wanted me to come down for some routine paperwork."

It's all true, just not the whole truth, and Gena's eyes narrow. "I've got two high-schoolers who bullshit me on a daily basis," she says.

"I'm not one of your cubs." She raises an eyebrow. "Really," I say. "It was nothing."

"So it happened right after we left you? What did he get arrested for?"

"Fighting. That's all."

I eat the last mushroom, but that doesn't stop her from shaking her head. "All right, well. If I don't read about it in the papers, then I guess it really is—"

Her phone rings, beneath her paw. She jumps and then picks it up. "Hi, honey."

Fisher's voice comes faintly through the speaker. I can hear it, but not what he's saying. Whatever it is, it melts the tension from Gena's face. Her whiskers and ears come up, and she smiles. "That's great," she says. "I'll be right over and we can meet the boys—" He talks again, and she listens, the smile fading. "Well, I know, but…yes, okay. I guess I'll see you tonight, then."

She sets the phone down and stares at it while the waiter clears the empty mushroom plate and asks if we'd like anything else. "No," she says. "Wait. Another one of these." She taps her half-consumed margarita.

"Another plate of the mushrooms," I say, "and some house bread." When he leaves, I glare at Gena. "You're going to eat the mushrooms this time."

"I'm fine," she says.

"Hey," I say. "I take care of a tiger who doesn't always eat right, too."

She glares back and then laughs. "All right. You got me."

"So Fisher didn't want to come back to the hotel right away?"

"He said it was important to go celebrate with the team. He promised he wouldn't drink anything. They told him it was dangerous with the concussion."

"I'm surprised they released him."

"Someone's walking over to the bar with him, and then I'll pick him up when the party winds down."

"If it winds down," I say. "Might go pretty late."

She drains a quarter of her drink. "Then I'll go get him. Anyway." She forces a bright smile. "Other than that, how are things with you?"

I catch her up on my life while we watch the end of the playoff game. It's nice to be able to say frankly that I'm worried about the phone interview with the guy from Yerba who might or might not be homophobic, and Gena transfers a lot of her anxiety to me. "They can't not hire you for that, right?" she asks, and I have to explain about people finding other reasons to hide the real one. I don't tell her about the Vince King lawsuit because I feel lost there and I don't know what I can say, but we do talk about Mother for a little. She has a good perspective on it, being a mother herself, and she agrees with Father that I should apologize and take the first step. Mother, she thinks, probably feels just as bad as I do, if not worse. I still have trouble buying that, but hearing it from yet another source helps.

The conversation sounds dull, but it's more exciting than the game turns out to be. After the brief spurt of life, Peco can't make anything happen. Crystal City smothers them for the rest of the game, their two coyote line-backers seemingly everywhere at once, their defensive line stopping Peco's offensive line cold when it doesn't crush them outright. I get absorbed in watching some of their plays on offense, because this is what Dev's going to be facing next week.

They don't have the fireworks on offense that they do on defense, but they're plenty good. They put another touchdown on the board after an interception leaves them at the Fraters' five-yard line, and then add on a field goal.

Gena eats almost all of the plate of mushrooms, and we split the bread. When the game ends with the Sabretooths celebrating on the field, we signal for our bill. I look at the delirious locker room, the guys patting each other on the back, and I wonder if that's how it was in the Chevali locker room this afternoon. They're still out at the bar, probably getting trashed, and I'd be the last to say they don't deserve it. I just kind of wish I'd been able to be part of it. Still, it's nice to see that celebration. Gives me a warm, waggy feeling when I think about Dev and his teammates celebrating, and I get even more of a wag to my (now dry) tail when they post up the graphic for the championship and there's the Firebirds logo, right there beside the Sabretooths. It's almost a surreal moment, like I'm going to pinch myself and find out that I've been dreaming. Even Gena gets a big smile, and we talk for a bit about what those two championships Fisher won with the Rocs were like.

When Gena goes off to find her boys, I wish her well with a promise I will look further into the drug she found in Fisher's things last week. All she knows about it is what was on the label: the name Somatotropin. That's growth hormone, a banned substance for sure, so I have to be careful how I research it; she's just worried about the side effects it might have, but my preliminary research indicated that it's probably not the only thing Fisher's taking. I didn't want to go to Hal, because once I open that can of worms with the media, who knows what'll happen next. But it's sure looking like he might be my best shot.

I go back to my hotel to do a little more research online. Dev texts me on the way back with a drunken "Limos don here." It takes me a minute to translate "limos" into "Almost." I smile and sit back in the hotel chair, debating whether to strip down for his arrival or not. At least he's sure to be happier than the last time he came to my hotel room drunk.

I settle on t-shirt and boxer briefs—sadly, my briefs from yesterday are dirty and the ones from today in the laundry—giving me a nice saucy feeling as I lean back in the office chair with my laptop on my lap and my feet up on the desk. Outside, the city is pretty quiet, though occasionally I'll hear whoops and hollers, with screams of "Yeah Firebirds!" sprinkled through the incoherent noises. I hope none of them get into fights.

There's not a lot online about somatotropin other than ads disguised as fact guides ("Did you know that somatotropin has been called the 'miracle drug' for its users' quick recovery from injuries?"). There are species-specific brands and somatotropin mixed with other things and warnings that you need a physician's guidance to take appropriate dosages. It's legal, you see, just not if you're a professional athlete.

It doesn't have any emotional side effects on its own. But it also doesn't really help maintain muscle mass after an injury. For that, you need to take it in conjunction with anabolic steroids. And those, yeah. Those have an emotional effect. Quick temper, anger…the kinds of things we and Gena have been seeing.

I put the laptop back up on the desk and set my elbow beside it, resting my cheek against my paw. Hopefully they keep Fisher out of the championship game, he won't be tempted to keep taking the drugs, and this whole thing will be over. It'd be nice if he retired after this year and settled back into a normal life.

Normal life. I trace a claw up and down my legs. A normal life like I have now, only without the prospect of a job in the spring? A normal life with nobody but Gena to be around, no game to prepare for every week, his cubs off to college? Maybe Fisher and I can hang out until I get the job in Yerba.

Or maybe once the cubs are gone, Gena will divorce him. Maybe she'll be tired of taking care of cubs and won't have the strength to take care of a husband losing his mind, prone to bouts of rage. I might just be projecting because of what's happened with my parents, but I feel like I'm picking up on faint traces of that possibility.

To clear that out of my head, I start writing up the brief I want to file with the court. Hal told me that I need to write it up as clearly as possible, and plainly state the relevance to the current case. He was working on finding me a lawyer who could submit it, although he said most of the lawyers he knows specialize in sports and wouldn't touch a civil suit like this. But getting it written is the important thing.

I funnel my anger at the stadium fight into my description of Mrs. Hedley's callous writing-off of her children and my mother's burning of my things. But I only get through a few paragraphs before the weight of bearing witness to the dissolution of three families—mine, the Hedleys, and the Kingstons, maybe—takes its toll, and I have to stop.

Even Dev's family isn't perfect, although his parents are coming around. But his brother won't accept me, whether it's a religious issue or jealousy over Dev's success. Maybe there's no such thing as a solid family these days. Maybe there's a time limit on every relationship, and Families United is just an agent of inevitable fate.

I wish Dev would come back.

PART II

CHAPTER 8 – CRACKS (DEV)

We decide to leave the celebration, Fisher, Vonni, and I, because I want to see Lee, like, really badly now, and Fisher is tired of being the only sober guy in the more and more raucous bar, and Vonni—well, we pretty much decide it's time for the fox to go. He's been trying to drink with the tigers and bears, but he just doesn't have the body mass for it.

On our way out of the bar, the fox slides as though the pavement is ice and falls against the outside wall, all puffed-out orange tail and flailing black paws, big ears askew, laughing. I reach down to help him up and stagger a little, so Fisher pushes me out of the way. "Let me get it. You guys are too wasted to walk straight. Good thing I'm here."

"We're goin' to the championship!" I yell.

"Yeah. You are." He growls, and I remember vaguely that something happened to him, but I'm not quite sure what.

So I put an arm around him and say, "Aw, Fisher. You can come. I'm gonna talk to Coach. I'll tell him you have to come with us."

"I'm going with you." Fisher gets an arm under Vonni's arm and growls. "I just don't know if I'm going to play."

He looks fine, no bandages or anything. I stare down at his leg. Then I remember. "Hey. You hit your head."

"That's why I'm not drinking. Lion Christ, fox, at least make an effort to walk."

"She's got an effor' ta walk!" Vonni sings. "An' she don' care!"

"I've got my own cubs to raise," Fisher says to me. "At least you're able to walk. Mostly."

The ground is behaving itself, though every now and then it rises up or drops down an inch. I stumble, and Fisher glares at me. "I can't hold you both."

"I am fine," I say, putting a paw to my chest.

Fine is an understatement. I can't remember when I've felt better. We didn't do everything right, but we did a hell of a lot right, and it felt like we were in control of the game the whole time. Falling to the ground in the end zone with the ball clutched to my chest was one of the best things that ever happened to me. Watching the clock tick down to zero was another. Everyone was jumping up and down, slapping each other on the back, hugging. I looked up at the stands and wished Lee could be celebrating with us, but that was the only slight stain on the moment. And after all, Vonni wasn't longing for Daria, and Gerrard wasn't saying anything about Angela. So I settled for a look his way and then enjoyed the celebration with my teammates.

And later, even though Coach took the time to appreciate our achievement in getting to the championship, he stressed that we were going to have two more weeks of hard work ahead of us. "And then," he said, "you'll get to celebrate being World Champions!"

I can't even imagine. Fisher told us on the way to the bar that the first time he won, it took a week for it to sink in, and that the second championship was even better. "Great," I said at the time, "another year to wait, huh?"

Then Strike told us not to get cocky because he'd been to the championship game, and losing was the worst feeling, and he assumed he'd be going back but then it didn't happen for three years. He said that we were a great team, although to be honest, he didn't think we were quite as good as the Hellentown team he'd been to the championship game with, but that was okay because Crystal City wasn't as good as the Port City team that had beaten them, and anyway it only took a few lucky breaks. We tuned him out after a while.

But all that's in the background now, in the happy haze of beer and camaraderie that I left behind to walk home—no, to the hotel—in the cold air. I take in a deep breath and it chills my lungs, making me cough, but over that I get the smell of the city: beer and trees, exhaust and people in a unique mix that I will always associate with this feeling. Plus, I keep thinking of getting back to Lee's room and wrapping him in a hug and then getting his clothes off, and I have a rock-hard erection from that. "I love Boliat," I announce, bracing myself against a building's wall.

"Yeah, yeah." Fisher hefts the still-singing Vonni around a corner. "You know if his wife is here or not?"

"Vonni's? I think her name is Dairy—Dairy-ah?"

"I know her name. Did she come up here or is he staying with Pace?"

I frown. "Pace is back at the bar."

"Lion Christ. Here, hold onto him for a second." He shoves Vonni at me, and it seems like he shoves him pretty hard. It's enough to stagger me backwards, and Vonni almost slides off my arm and back to the ground, but I catch him.

The fox is still singing, but now it's, "Oh, I like the party life, break out the red lights!" I hold him up as best I can, breathing in the cold air again. I'm starting to get a bit more clarity.

"Hi, honey." Fisher talks into his iPhone. "Listen, Vonni's pretty wasted. Did Daria come up? Uh-huh. Okay. Yeah, Dev's going there, too. We'll bring him up."

He brings the phone down and pokes at it with his thumb until the screen goes dark. "Damn things," he says. "What was wrong with the flip phone, the thing you just talk into and then you close it and you're done?"

"Strike gave you that. I have one too." I pat my pocket. "They take pictures."

"Yeah, and if you can find me some fucking West Coast computer nerd, I'll show you how."

"No, look, it's easy." I fumble for the phone in my pocket and pull it out, turning it on with one paw while I hold up Vonni. The phone slips out of my paw, but I catch it just before it drops. "Dammit."

Fisher steps around to the other side of Vonni and supports him. "Let's get back to the hotel."

"No matter how you slice it I'm your muthafuckin' guy," Vonni sings, and then, changing rhythms, "I ball 'til I fall!"

At which point he almost does, lurching around Fisher. Only Fisher's grip on the fox's arm saves him from face-planting. Which is the perfect time for me to lift the phone and snap a picture of them.

"God dammit, help me!" Fisher yells.

I hit the button to clear the camera function and promptly drop the phone. It lands on the pavement with a crack and lies there. "Aw, shit," I say.

Fisher pushes Vonni back up to his feet. "Get his other side," he snaps.

I pick up the phone. It's got a small white fan of cracks radiating out from the corner where it fell. "Shit," I say again.

"Dev, put the damn phone away."

"All right, all right." I slide the phone into my pocket and get back under Vonni's shoulder, helping Fisher, and like that, we walk him back to the hotel.

I'm not even sure where we're going. I just let Fisher pick the floor. When we get to the room, Gena's there and Daria, and I give them big smiles. "Hi there," I say.

Daria rushes to get Vonni in her arms, and Fisher practically shoves him at her. "Oh, boy," she says as her husband nearly topples her over.

"Hi, baby! I love you." Vonni tries to kiss her and then tries to get his paws up her shirt.

"I love you too." She wrinkles her nose and coughs, then gives Fisher a smile. "Thanks for bringing him back."

"Well, he would've ended up on the bar floor. Damn kids." Fisher sounds a lot more angry than I think he should be.

"Come on," I say. "We just won a playoff game."

"Yeah!" Vonni yells, right near his wife's ear, so she winces and flattens it. "Firebirds!"

"You need help getting him back?" Fisher asks Daria.

"It's right down the hall," she says.

I step up. "I'm going right down the hall," I tell her. "I carried him part of the way."

"Oh, well, thank you." She lets me get in on his other side.

We bid the tigers good night. Gena says, "Make sure he drinks water," and then closes the door. I help Daria get Vonni, now singing the Firebirds fight song, about five doors down the long hallway. I hold him while she opens the door.

"I think I can get it from here," she says, and Vonni actually walks into the room, though he immediately slumps against the wall, stops singing, and just exhales.

"Good night," I say, and Vonni turns to grin at me as Daria closes the door.

"What a fuckin' game," he says, and raises a paw to me.

"What a game," I echo, and turn away from the closing door.

The number beside the door is 330. I stare at it for a moment, as if I can by sheer force of will make it into Lee's room, so I can just walk in and find him. But even though it smells of fox, it doesn't smell of my fox, so I walk back toward the elevator. I'm pretty sure Lee isn't on this floor. But I stand by the elevator for about ten minutes, rubbing myself through my pocket, before I think to pull out my phone and look up his text message from Friday, where he sent me his room number. Then I get to his floor and down to his room. I know he gave me a key, but I just knock on the door to let him know I'm there. Also I'm not sure where the key is in my wallet.

He opens the door in a t-shirt and tight boxers, and I charge forward and hug him as tightly as I can. I'm a little too aggressive, I guess, because he staggers backwards and loses his balance. I hold on, managing somehow to get one foot out and stop our fall. I'm laughing, and he laughs a little with me. "Just a bit of celebrating, huh?"

In catching him, I got a paw under his tail and now squeeze his rear. "Celebration isn't over yet."

"I see." He kisses my nose and I turn it into a full-muzzle kiss, pushing my tongue in against his and pulling him tight against me. His paws rest on my hips and then tighten around my waist too. Still kissing him, I march him backwards to the bed.

"Mmmf." He pulls back and presses fingers up along my spine. "You're not sore?"

"Little bit." That doesn't matter much to me right now. My hardness presses into his stomach and all I can think about is getting it out into the air.

"You played a terrific game." He kisses me again. "I'm so proud of you."

That just sends me over the top, past even the sexual need, and I grab him and squeeze him as tightly as I can, spinning to fall on my back on the bed with him on top of me. "Oh, God," I say, "I can't believe this. It's like some kind of crazy dream. Winning the playoff game, and you're here with me, and we're together and people know it and it's okay, and did you see that interception? I saw it come off Vonni's paw and it was right there, it was huge as a beach ball and I grabbed it and nobody was gonna take that away from me. Did you see the press conference after? Nobody even asked about me being gay, they just wanted to know about the interception. It was amazing. It's the best day of my life."

He lies atop me and grins a big wide fox grin. "It's a pretty awesome day, all right."

I stroke my paw down his tail and I tell him about Vonni being drunk and about Strike drinking ginger ale all through the celebration and about Fisher showing up. "He's going to be fine, it's just a concussion so he can't drink, but he wants to play in the championship game and did you see, we're going to Crystal City? They were playing awesome against Peco, but Coach says we can take 'em, and oh man, Coach was there at the bar for a bit and he had a couple drinks." I stroke my paws down his sides and can't seem to stop talking. "And Pace and Norton made a bar bet about arm wrestling and Pace won and Ty was so fuckin' happy it was great."

"Wish I coulda been there," Lee says.

"Ah, none of the wives were there. It was just so cool. No, better than cool. It was amazing, incredible. I still can't believe it. It's like that college game, the one where we lost on a field goal, you know? Only we won."

My paws are rubbing down his back and rear, and when they get to the base of his tail, he gives a funny kind of jolt and moves my paw to his boxers. I'm glad he's that into it, and I'm happy to oblige, pushing his boxers down fast. He wriggles to get them over his sheath, and then lies down again on top of me, kicking the boxers free, naked but for his shirt. "You deserve it," he says. "And I know you guys are gonna win in two weeks. You just have to."

I kiss him hard on the muzzle, and then, because he doesn't seem too anxious to do anything about it, I unfasten my own pants and shove them down my legs, boxers and all. His shaft slides against mine through our fur as I rub my hips up and down, and he laughs into my kiss. "All right, stud, I get it."

A moment and a quick reach to the bedside table later and we've got ourselves all slickened up, and I'm inside him thrusting away while he sits on top of me. He bends down so I can fit one arm across his back while the other works at his shaft, and maybe it's not quite as good as the feel of winning a playoff game, but having that on top of this—or this on top of that—is pretty fucking incredible.

I'm so worked up that despite being halfway to smashed, I come in about two minutes of frantic, hot thrusts. His tightness around me is just too much to bear; I moan into his shoulder and squeeze him against me, bucking up into him and panting harshly as the climax surges through me and up, up, and out.

It takes me a few more minutes of stroking before he joins me, squirming and arching and then spurting into my stomach fur and over my paw, a quick convulsive orgasm followed by a slow relaxation and a kiss on my nose, a broad smile looking down at me. I slide my paw out from between us and wrap both arms around him.

"You wanna shower?" he murmurs, but I'm exhausted by the day and the words hang there in the air. Responding to them seems like it would be a lot of work. I'd rather just enjoy his warmth on top of me, rub my paws down his back, feel the soft fur just above his tail and along it, inhale the scent of our lovemaking, close my eyes...

Distantly, I hear him say, "I guess that's a no," and he chuckles.

I'm woken in the morning by my phone ringing. It sounds muffled, and at first, I don't get what the sound is: I'd been dreaming that I was playing in the playoff game, and we were winning as the time ticked down to zero, and then with a minute left, the score suddenly changed so that we were losing. I was wondering what happened, but the rest of the guys on the team all seemed to know. "We just weren't paying attention," they told me. "Turns out they were scoring all along and we just never noticed." I tell them we need to get out there and score again and they just shake their heads. "Too late now," they say. "Too late now." And the clock hits zero, and the bell rings with a weird electronic chime.

I struggle awake and listen to the chime, letting the chill of the dream fade away. It takes three rings for me to convince myself that we did actually win the game, another two for me to realize that it's my phone ringing.

Lee nudges me. "That's yours," he mumbles. "Mine's over here."

"Mm-hmm." I roll over, listening for the ring, and locate it in my pants on the floor. Of course. It's still ringing when I pick it up, telling me that Charm is calling.

When I pick up, he's singing, "I own this city, the city's mine…hey, Gramps!"

"How are you up this early?" I grumble. I'm just assuming it's early because I'm still tired and stiff, and my ribs and foot and one knee are sore, and I'm not starving for breakfast yet.

He laughs. "It's nine-thirty," he says. "Figured you were spendin' the night with Mrs. G and I should let you know you got half an hour to get your stripey tail to our hotel unless you wanna book your own flight back home."

For a moment, it's tempting. I just wanna lie in bed for most of the day, and plus I could go back with Lee. Heck, I earned another fifty grand or so just for winning the game yesterday. But I need to be with the team, and I want to be part of that flight home. "I'll be there," I growl. "Can you toss my stuff into my bag so I don't have to come back to the room?"

"Can you carry my bags to the airport?"

I snort. "Sure. Yeah."

"Deal."

I drop the phone and roll back over. Lee's bright blue eyes are staring at me. "I gotta go. Flight's at ten. I mean, we're meeting at ten for the flight, and I have to shower and everything."

He nods and leans forward to kiss my nose. "Go."

I wrap him in a hug. "I'd ask you to come shower but then…"

"You'd never get out in time." He pushes me. "Go, go! Don't miss the flight. I'll see you at home."

"All right." I kiss him and run to the shower.

I get to the team hotel at 10:02, by my cracked phone, and the team bus is already out front. Charm, lounging by the entrance to the hotel, waves me over. "I won't tell Coach you're late," he says, and indicates his suitcase and mine.

I go to pick them up, and his weighs about as much as he does. "Jesus, what did you pack in here?" I ask.

Charm turns and grins over his shoulder. "I picked up a few souvenirs while I was waitin' for you."

"Bricks from the stadium?" I mutter.

"I asked 'em for the heaviest things they had. So there's about two dozen of those lead figurines of that deer in the square."

"Fuck me," I say, tossing the suitcases at the luggage compartment.

"Hey," Charm says, getting on the bus, "Careful with those."

The bus is raucous, guys laughing and yelling and lots of "remember that play" stories going around. Some guys chirp about their own plays, but most of us on the defense talk about each other's—that time Gerrard dove into the gap, that time Carson got the brilliant sack. Vonni and I, sitting near each other, deflect praise for my interception—"Dev's got the paws with the claws," Vonni says, suffering apparently no ill effects from his drinking, and I shoot back, "Trust a fox to have a great tip," which makes Vonni wag his white-tipped tail and grin.

The plane is even worse than the bus, because they serve drinks. We're celebrating all the way through takeoff and as we get into the air. About an hour into the flight, Charm's gone to hang out with the special teams guys and the seat next to me is empty. Fisher slides into it, rubbing his forehead.

"Headache?" I say. "You didn't even drink."

"I know. Head still hurts from yesterday. Hey, is Lee okay?"

"Uh…" I frown. "I think so. Why?"

"The thing with the police?"

I stare at Fisher. "What thing?"

"He didn't tell you? Whoo. Um, Gena said he had to go be a witness or something. He saw a fight at the stadium and a guy got arrested?"

I shake my head slowly. "He didn't tell me anything about it. I mean, we didn't really have a lot of time to talk. I was kinda drunk."

"I remember." He scowls. "Can't wait 'til I can celebrate properly again."

"Two weeks." I grin. "So what happened with Lee?"

Fisher shakes his head and then winces, rubbing it again. "No idea. Other than what I told you."

So I change the subject to whether Gena and the boys enjoyed their time in Boliat, and all the while in the back of my mind I'm wondering about my fox. But I guess it wasn't a big deal, and we really didn't have a lot of time to talk. I guess that's what he meant when he said he was held up at the stadium. I'd forgotten about that message in the rush of celebration. It's probably nothing.

I call him when I land, but his phone is off—must be in the air. And I have a new rush of voicemails from Ogleby telling me about this group and that group that want to do interviews now that we're going to the championship game. I call him back from the airport and say, "Set things up for today and tomorrow, but only sports outlets. None of these lifestyle magazines."

"Sure thing!" he squeaks. "Hey, Ultimate Fit wants to come shoot another commercial this week."

"Jesus, Ogleby, I need a week off."

"Thing is, we kinda have to let them because of the contract..." His voice trails off.

I clench a fist, then relax my paw. "Right. Okay, fine. Wednesday or Thursday, just tell me when and where to be."

Some of the guys are talking about going out again and I say maybe I'll join them. I don't tell them I have interviews to give because most of them don't, and I don't want to come off as a star or anything. So I just go home and spend a few hours on the phone talking to various sports reporters about my development over the season, about how great it feels to go from the Dragons to the Firebirds, from last place to the championship game, about how I feel about our matchup with Crystal City, about making the transition from cornerback to linebacker (I give Gerrard and Steez most of the credit for my success), and, of course, a little about being gay.

"Nobody really comments on it now," I say. "It's become a non-factor. I don't think about it and I hope nobody else does. I'm just a football player."

They ask how my boyfriend is doing and I say he's fine, he's cheering me on, he's supportive. In one interview I let slip that he's active in gay rights and then I have to go on and say I support that, so I do. The reporter asks if I want to be active in gay rights.

"Maybe one day," I say. "But right now my mind is completely focused on football."

Lee calls in the middle of the interviews, and I put the reporter on hold with an apology. "Just landed," he says. "Be home soon."

"Okay. Hey, what happened with the police? Fisher said Gena told him something."

"Uh...I'll tell you when I get home. It's no big deal."

I don't quite believe him, but I get back to the interview and try not to think about it.

I'm still on the phone when he gets home half an hour later. He smiles, tail wagging, and kisses me on the other ear on his way to the bedroom. I finish up the interview while he's unpacking, and then go into the bedroom to give him a proper hug.

"Hey there, tiger." He turns and hugs me. "Championship game-bound tiger."

"Yeah." I nuzzle him fiercely and grin. "So what was this with the police?"

He goes still. "It's nothing, really," he says. "Couple drunk yahoos took exception to my Firebirds shirt."

"So you were *in* the fight?"

"It wasn't really a fight. I got beer poured on me."

I make him tell me the whole thing then, and when he's done, I sit down on the bed. "Lion Christ, Lee, why didn't you tell me?"

"Ah, it was over. I didn't want to ruin your day." He sits beside me, tail curled around my hips.

"That fucking sucks. I thought we were done with this. How did they know you were my boyfriend?"

"I was sitting with the wives. I guess they read the Internet."

"I'll get you tickets somewhere else, then. Then you can just be a fan."

"Whoa, hold on," he says. "I liked sitting with Gena. Well, except for when Fisher got hurt. How's he doing?"

"Don't change the subject. If you're going to get attacked—"

"This was one incident." He stresses the words. "It feels like you're ashamed of me again."

That stings, a hot flush under my collarbone. "I'm just trying to protect you."

"I can take care of myself," he says, and I roll my eyes.

"I thought we were past that. How's your thumb feeling?"

"How's your dad's head?" he counters.

The conversation is simmering into an argument, which is strange to me because I don't really know what we're arguing about. "I'd rather you not get into fights because of me."

"They're not because of you. This one wasn't, anyway. It was because of the fucked-up worldview of this wolf and his asshole rabbit friend." His ears are still up, but his eyes are narrowed.

"Because of us, then, because of this relationship."

"Right, this relationship." He clasps his paws together and takes a breath. "You know, I—"

I cut him off. He's on the verge of some big speech, it sounds like, and I just can't—I don't want to deal with it right now. "I know. I know, I'm sorry, I just mean…I want to win this championship, fox. I want it more than I've wanted anything in my life except for one thing." I take his paws. "And I need to be able to be a football player for the next two weeks."

He bites his lip. His eyes lose their narrowed intensity and he sighs. "Two weeks. It's…yeah. Okay. I'll…I want you to win that game too."

I don't like the reluctance in his voice. "You knew what you were getting with me. Hell, you put me on the path to be here."

"I know." Now his ears droop, just a bit. It sort of pisses me off. I should be deliriously happy today, and instead he's trying to make me feel bad about not being more proud of being gay. And the really annoying part is that it's working. No; the *really* annoying part is that he's *not* trying, he's just doing it.

"Two weeks?" I say. "Can I have two weeks? Then we can have this fight or whatever it's going to be."

"Yeah." He sighs and leans against me. "You want to get lunch with Hal, or just us?"

"Oh, does he want to have lunch?"

"He wants to say congratulations."

"How about tomorrow? Let's do today with just us."

He nods. "Okay, I'll tell him."

The morning slides into afternoon. We get a quick lunch, and going out into Chevali in the daylight is really a wonderful experience. Everyone in my neighborhood who knows me is wearing perked ears and a huge smile. I get slaps on the back, hands and paws offered for shaking, and the lunch Lee and I order at the small sandwich shop is brought to our table by the owner himself, a skinny white-tailed deer, who slaps the plates down with a clatter. "On the house," he says, beaming. "Extra meat, too. I haven't been this excited about football in years."

He points to a Firebirds pennant, and a space below it on the wall. "Gonna frame today's paper," he says. "And the one two weeks from today, if, y'know…"

He stands there grinning at us. "Here's hoping," I say. "Thanks a lot. I really appreciate it."

"Oh, it's the least I can do. You guys are bringing hope to the town. And it's so great that you come eat in my little sandwich shop. I hear Aston and those big stars all go to the fancy joints."

"Well," I say, trying not to be offended that I'm not a "big" star, "I like the food here. You have a great dressing on the sandwich."

"And good bread," Lee offers.

The deer doesn't pay much attention to Lee, but claps his hands together at my compliment. "Thank you so much!"

Lee says, "Would you like him to sign your pennant? Or something else?"

Now the owner pays attention. "Oh, that would be too much to ask. I couldn't."

I raise my eyebrows at Lee and stand up. "If you have a pen, I'll be happy to."

"What did I tell you about carrying a Sharpie?" Lee asks.

"I got a pen!" The deer pulls one out of his apron and holds it out. So I take it and walk over to the wall where the pennant is. I don't even have to reach up much, just scrawl my name under the Firebirds logo and then add the number after it.

"Thank you so much." The deer takes his pen back, and if he was beaming before, he's positively glowing now. "And if any of your teammates would like to try our sandwiches, I will be happy to make one for them for free as well."

There aren't that many other people in the shop, but the ones who are there are all staring at us now. "Sure," I say, and sit back down. "I'll let them know."

"Wonderful! Again, thank you so much." He hurries back behind the counter.

We dig into the sandwiches—they really are pretty good—and two people come over shyly to ask me for autographs while we're eating. I sign them and say thanks, and while I can see Lee bristle at the rudeness, he also smiles as we chat. And then he gets a phone call while I'm signing the second person's Firebirds shirt anyway, so he doesn't have room to talk about being rude. I catch only a little of the conversation before he walks outside with the phone: he says, "Hi, thanks for calling me."

I've finished my sandwich before he comes back and sits down. "Was that Rodriguez?"

"No," he says. "I told you, I don't think that's going to work. It was Peter, from the Whalers. He wants me to get on a call with this guy Jocko later today or tomorrow."

"That's good, right?"

"Well, it depends." He picks up his sandwich and takes another bite, chews, and swallows.

I wait for him to go on, and instead he takes another bite. "Depends on what?" I say, finally.

He shrugs, his ears down, looking at the sandwich he's holding in his paws. "The thing he says I need to convince Jocko of is that there won't be any conflict of interest. Basically that I won't talk to you about any of the work I'm doing."

I take a moment to think about that as he continues to eat. "But you won't. I mean, you never did."

His ears come up a little, and below the table, his tail swishes. "Not intentionally, but you could say something to a teammate like, 'Lee's off at Cobblestone College this weekend,' and a coach could overhear it and bring it to the front office and they could say, 'I wonder who the Whalers are scouting at Cobblestone,' and then maybe it comes to draft day and there's a kid from Cobblestone on the board and the Firebirds know they have leverage." After that speech, he takes a drink.

"That's a little far-fetched."

"Scouts can be fired for messing up one pick. That's what they say, anyway. I never knew anyone it happened to." He finishes off his sandwich.

We get up and walk out onto the street, waving good-bye to the owner. The conversation is getting close to talking about our relationship again, which I don't want to do and I'm sure he doesn't either, so there's silence while I search for football-related things to talk about. "Oh, I'm going to be filming another commercial Wednesday for Ultimate Fit." I shake my head. "It's in the contract we signed."

"You signed it," he points out. "Ogleby just negotiated it."

"Yeah." I sigh. "He really isn't that great of an agent, is he?"

"Fisher's agent sounded pretty good."

"After the season," I say. "I will look at other agents, I promise."

He half-turns toward me as we cross the street. "I'm not angling for the job."

"I know." I grin down at him. "You want that job in Yerba."

His ears flick again, and he doesn't return my grin. "Would you be okay with that? I mean, if you stay here, and I go there? We'd be apart again, for most of the year."

"Sure." I realize I may have said that a little hastily. "I mean, I like living with you. And I hope maybe you'd keep some of your stuff here. I mean, you could still consider this your 'home' and you'd just have a place in Yerba, too. But I'm not seeing you all that much during the season, and in the off-season I could come stay with you maybe."

"I'd be traveling a lot."

"Yeah, I know."

He looks down at the ground, paws still stuffed in his pockets, thinking. "I guess maybe living together is something for the future."

"And the occasional now." I wrap an arm over his shoulder, a comradely hug.

He leans into it. His tail brushes the back of my legs. "And the occasional now," he repeats.

It feels nice. The sun comes out and the breeze is cool, I have my arm around my fox, and all around me there are Firebirds flags flapping from car windows and hanging in storefronts, Firebirds shirts on people and Firebirds logos hanging in office windows. The city is really coming alive and I am part of that, I helped make it happen. It's not that I feel like the celebration is all for me; it's more like I feel that it's my family throwing a big party. It brings a big smile to my muzzle and an extra spring to my step.

CHAPTER 9 – SLIPPING (LEE)

This might be the longest two weeks of my life. I really want Dev to be able to concentrate on football, so I'm trying to avoid talking about anything that might be distracting, like about gay rights. The problem is that everything I have to talk about is distracting—well, no. The real problem is me, that this tangle of shit I'm working my way through makes me edgy, makes every little conversation we have a threat to erupt into an argument. I can see Dev's puzzlement at it, because he's not doing anything wrong, and I want him to understand all the things that are going on with me, and at the same time I can't lay all of that on him because it's the last thing he needs.

There's the interview with Jocko. And I can't tell Dev that I'm worried this guy might be biased because I'm gay, for fear of starting another argument (see above)—especially since it might be nothing. I could just be on a hair trigger because of the fight in Boliat, seeing homophobia in every hesitation when there might be a hundred other explanations. So I kind of half made up the thing about the NDA, because it's about our relationship but not the gayness part of it, and I managed to avoid an argument. And it was a half-truth, not an outright lie.

That doesn't mean I feel any better about it. I'd like to be able to say, "I'm worried that this one guy will blackball me just because I'm gay," without worrying that he'll immediately ask whether I think he should be more open, or think I'm judging him for not doing more activist work. But I really think that in this case, it won't matter that much; it avoids an argument without really misinforming him.

Anyway, Peter wouldn't send me into this interview if he didn't think I have a chance to ace it. So I'm just going to have to do the best I can.

And the NDA wasn't an outright lie; Peter and I talked about Dev signing an agreement like that, and he said he wasn't sure how that would play with the Firebirds—or whatever Dev's team ends up being next year. He hinted again that things would be a lot simpler if Dev came to play for Yerba, but didn't give me any clue whether that's something that's actually being discussed or if it's just his ideal scenario.

If you look at the sports websites, Dev's name comes up less often in connection with being gay, and more often as someone the Firebirds should try to sign in the offseason before the last year of his rookie contract. Promising young linebacker, good skills, good team presence. The gay thing is only mentioned to make the case for Dev to stay rather than hold out and test the market elsewhere: this team knows him and has accepted him, so why would he go to another team and have to start over, risk maybe some yahoo on the defense making trouble for him?

No, the best situation for him is to stay in Chevali, and if they win the championship, it's pretty much assured that they will try to lock him up for a long time. This is the year to do it, because he's only played three-quarters of a season, so the team can lower the total amount they pay him. A savvy agent could get around that, test the market and see what the going rate is for a good young linebacker. I don't think that's in Ogleby's skill set.

So I'm thinking about all that and then I had to bite back my initial reaction when he said he's filming a commercial, because I know he's been declining interviews from gay rights groups and he won't film a PSA until after the season—and I'm starting to get creeping little doubts wondering whether he'll even do it then. It wasn't even a new reaction. It's the same reaction I had to the Strongwell commercial, to him doing all these other interviews, and every time it feels like I'm struggling against a load of bricks that Dev—that life keeps heaping onto me.

The part about the phone call at the sandwich shop that *was* an outright lie is that it wasn't from Peter at all. I talked to him on Monday after Dev had left for home. The call at the sandwich shop was from a lawyer in Crystal City who works with the group Fair and Legal, responding to an e-mail about my *amicus curiae* to the Vince King case. I'd inquired on Sunday after Hal told me his lawyer friends recommended I find someone passionate about "cases like that." This lawyer, an ermine, asked me about my statement in quick, sharp questions, then gave me some general advice for making it more to the point and told me to send it to her while she looked up the case details.

Her brisk, efficient manner ended up making me feel more distanced from it. She did say she was sorry I'd had to go through that with my family, but beyond that it was all very clinical and detached, except at the end where she gave me some little mini-pep talk about standing up to bullies. It sparked a little of the fire I had when I first heard about King, but I couldn't stop thinking about how much of this still happens all over. I had an urge to call Brian, because he was so passionate about the case too; not to prove to him that I'm really doing something, but just to have someone else to say "Good job" to me. But of course, I can't call Brian anymore.

It would be really nice to have some reassurance or encouragement from Dev, but I promised not to say anything, and I already had to tell him about the fight in Boliat. So I keep quiet when we go out that day, walking beside him through the glare of the sun and the crowds, and I remind myself that I'm doing something, I'm staying active, and I'm keeping him out of it. This is our bargain, and I should be happy that it's working out.

The other thing I can't tell him is that every time a biggish guy lets his eyes linger on us for more than a second, I get tense. I see the rabbit in the wife-beater, the smirking wolf with the beer bottle, and I feel the paw on my tail again. I'm with Dev, I tell myself. I'm out in public. Nobody's going to start anything. But the words only penetrate so deep.

"Can you imagine what this place will be like if we win the championship?" Dev asks as we pass a storefront thick with Firebirds banners.

"When," I say absently.

"Crystal City's good. McCrae's only been sacked what, five times this year?" His paws gesture and then hang in the air as though waiting for a phantom quarterback in front of him to make a move.

"I haven't been keeping track."

He goes quiet and I feel bad right away. We're passing a theater, so I say on impulse, "Want to catch a movie?" It'll let me lose myself in someone else's story and not risk depressing Dev because I'm being quiet.

"Sure. What do you want to see?"

"Oh, any of those," I say without looking at the marquee, and I don't listen to the name he says when he buys our tickets.

The movie is a cacophony of explosions and blaring horns starring a leopard who won't take no for an answer and a leopardess who plays by her own rules. Or something. I'm just happy to be able to turn my mind off and sit next to my tiger for a couple hours. We walk around a little more after the movie, because Dev wants to enjoy the feel of the town with all the Firebirds gear, and I'm able to enjoy it a little more with my mind cleared by the movie.

We end up hungry and near an Italian place for dinner, and again Dev is recognized. This time he refuses to let the owner pay for the meal (on my urging), but he does allow the owner to give us a bottle of wine. The people in the restaurant are more restrained when it comes to bothering Dev for autographs, but once we're outside, he spends a good fifteen minutes signing shirts, napkins, and old ticket stubs for people.

I like watching him do that and it gets my head back into a good mindset. I can write up my statement tomorrow, I figure—Dev's going to have to work sometime during the day. We go home, beat up on each other in football video games, and crawl into bed together enthusiastically enough to get ourselves all hot, bothered, and sticky before falling asleep.

And when Hal calls the next morning about lunch, we're still in bed, and Dev is a little frisky, teasing me as I try to talk on the phone. "Where are we—ah!—going?" I try to push Dev's paw away from my sheath, but that's a fight I'm never going to win.

"I was gonna say, we don't have to do lunch today. I'm sure you guys are busy with stuff."

"No, we-ee! We want to." Dev has moved his paw down my leg, holding me still while he brushes his muzzle over my stomach. "How about Between the Sheets?"

"Sounds delicious," Dev purrs, licking his lips and then the tip of my shaft.

I squirm, as Hal says, "Thing is, I'm not sure I'm in the mood."

"How about if we play some soft music and bring wine?" I squirm more as Dev takes me between his lips.

"Nah, I mean…" He sighs. "Pol and I broke up. Last night."

"Oh, jeez." I try to push Dev off me, but my squirming just takes me deeper into his muzzle. I lie back and try not to pant into the phone. "Sorry," I say, as Dev licks along my shaft. "What happened?"

"The usual. Not going the same places, not quite right, the matchup just wasn't there. Look, you don't want to hear about this right now."

He's right, but not for the reason he thinks. Dev's got a paw under my balls now and is rubbing as he sucks, which he's really getting into. His ears are aimed back and I know he's listening and wants to know what I'll do if he can make me come while I'm on the phone. And I don't know how to mute this new phone easily.

"So te-ell me over lunch." I grit my teeth as my body shivers and tries to force out more pleasure-induced sounds from my throat. "Dev really wants to see you."

That makes Dev stop. He makes a questioning, "Mrrr?" noise which vibrates all along my shaft and makes my leg kick—the one he's not putting his weight on holding down.

"Maybe tomorrow?"

"He can't do tomorrow," I say, and then Dev goes back to sucking me off, sliding his muzzle up and down, and I have to clamp my mouth shut, exhaling hard through my nose. I think Hal's waiting for me to go on, so I try to get the words out evenly. It's like balancing on a narrow beam. "He has. To shoot. A commercial."

"Are you okay?"

"Fine," I snap out, and just then Dev catches my tip and a little whine escapes me.

There's a pause. "You're in bed, aint'cha?"

"Maybe-ee." I'm having a lot more difficulty controlling my panting.

"Oo-kay. All right, Between the Sheets at noon. Now get off the phone before I have to listen to something I ain't exactly in the mood to listen to right now."

"Sorry!" I yell at the phone. "Thanks!" and I stab at the end button and drop the phone over the side of the bed, finally able to arch my back and let the tension out of my throat in a long moan.

Of course, Dev takes his mouth off me then.

"Wh-what..." I stare down at him, dazed.

He grins with a disingenuous smile. "You're not on the phone anymore. Not as much fun."

"Oh God. Do you want me to call your Dad, then? So I can come in his ear?"

He twists up his muzzle. "Oh, ew."

The sensations are starting to subside, the urgency with them. I'm still panting, though. "Well, if you don't want to finish..."

"I guess I can." He traces a finger up my shaft. "You were a pretty good fox."

I give him a smile and big hopeful eyes, and he laughs. "Okay, okay." He bends back down and his warmth surrounds my shaft. I close my eyes.

After I come, of course I have to suck him off too, though I insist on doing it in the shower because, well, we haven't showered since last night. It's kinda fun kneeling on the tile floor with him driving into my muzzle, when I can reach up and feel the cords of muscles in the backs of his legs and his rear, when he can curl his tail around my wrist, when the warmth of the water and steam surrounds and relaxes us, when he can let out a long, loud groan as he spurts warm onto my tongue.

I swallow and wash his length and my muzzle, and then stand and put my arms around him, and he squeezes me. "You're the best fox," he murmurs.

It's a nice thought. I hope I'm worthy of it.

•

When we get to Between the Sheets, Hal is leaning on a table in a booth staring off into space. It takes Dev's bulk to get his attention. "Hi," the swift fox says, and scrambles to his feet, extending a dusky brown paw. "Good to see you again."

Dev shakes, and Hal turns to me. I take his paw and reach around to give him a hug. "Sorry," I say. "There'll be someone else."

Half of his muzzle smiles, a quirky yeah-right expression. "I know that up here," he says, tapping his ears. "Still hurts everywhere else."

"Yeah, sorry to hear it," Dev says. He starts to sit down, and I tug on his shirt.

"We order up there." I point. "Then bring it back."

So we get our sandwiches, and Dev laughs at some of the silly names. Here, amusingly, he's not recognized, and nobody offers to pay for his food, which makes him a little bit sulky, but he gets over that quickly when I elbow him in the side and say, "What's the matter, famous football player not getting every meal paid for?"

"I'm not that kind of player," he says, and leaves them a twenty-dollar tip. The sheep behind the counter doesn't even notice.

"So what happened with Pol?" I ask as we sit down, Dev beside me, Hal across from us.

Hal's ears go down and he shrugs quickly. "Not every relationship works out, right?"

I glance at Dev, whose bulk overwhelms us two foxes. He looks back at me and puts a paw down to brush my tail on the plastic bench. "Seems like you thought it might and she didn't."

"I'd rather talk about the championship," he says, and forces his ears and smile up. "You guys kicked some ass in Boliat. Great interception there."

Dev beams, and I sit back. After Hal promises that he won't write any of this up without Dev's permission, Dev talks about the team through the delivery and eating of our sandwiches, while I chime in every now and then with how things looked from the stands. Hal asks about Fisher, and Dev says Fisher sounded and felt fine after his injury and is hoping to play in the championship.

We both notice Hal's reaction to that. "Hal's writing," I start to say, and the swift fox cuts me off.

"I'm just thinkin' about writing a profile on the Firebirds," he says.

"Come on," I say. "I'm not going to *not* tell Dev what you're working on."

He glares at me, scowling. "Fine. But you can't spread it around too much. I can't afford to scare people off."

"Scare people off? Of what?" Dev looks from him to me.

"Hal's writing a story on football injuries," I say. "That's why he's interested in Fisher."

"Head injuries in particular," Hal says, "but all kinds of things. Basically the long-term effects."

"I know there's some players who can't really walk," Dev says slowly. "But we have better pads now. I mean, they played back in the seventies when you just had a sheet of plastic between your joints and the uniform. And they played with 'em cracked all the time, too. I've seen some of that old equipment, it's beat all to hell."

"That's part of it," Hal says.

"You're writing this by yourself?"

"Actually workin' with a couple other guys."

I sit up, ears perked. "You didn't tell me that."

He grins at me. "I don't tell you everything, sweetheart."

Dev turns to me with one eyebrow raised. I pat his thigh. "Remember, I was a lady for the first few weeks I knew Hal."

"Anyway, Fisher just got his bell rung," Dev says, turning back to Hal. "Wasn't that serious."

I lean in. "You haven't noticed any changes in him since he was injured?"

"He's been fine," Dev says.

"He was fine during the bye week," I say. "Well…" I hesitate, because Gena didn't want me to talk to Dev about this at all, and because this is only tangentially related to the injury. "No, I mean, that was fine. He was fine. It's just that he's seemed more irritable lately."

"Of course." Dev looks at me like I'm crazy. "He wants to be playing. Of course he's irritable."

Hal's looking at me and I feel cornered. I lay my ears back and in that second, I have to decide whether to back down and leave it unresolved, or press forward with it. If it were just Hal, I might go ahead. "Okay," I say. "It's just something I thought I noticed. But you know him better."

Dev relaxes, but Hal's eyes narrow. I look away from the swift fox, and after a moment, he goes back to asking Dev about the game. After a few minutes, I'm able to let myself relax and appreciate reliving the memory of what was really a pretty special game. I chip in some comments and get a little emotional, and long after our sandwich papers have been collected by the sheep, we're still talking about it.

And then Hal says, "So did they taunt you at all about being gay?"

Dev exhales and shakes his head. "No."

"Hellentown did," I put in.

Hal looks my way and Dev slumps back against the booth seat. "They were just trying to get in my head," he says. "They didn't mean it."

"That's not what you told me after the last regular season game."

He turns and meets my eyes. "They talked to me after."

"Okay, okay." I subside into the corner of the booth.

"So it's not an issue any more," Hal says.

"No." Dev delivers that one word like a fist to the table. "And that's the way I want it. I want to be judged on my performance on the field, not on what I do off it."

"That's what every athlete wants," Hal says, but from his look I know he can see what I'm thinking. I feel like he's trying to tell me something, but I don't know what it would be. I don't say anything, and we move on to other matters and eventually wrap up the conversation.

"He's nice," Dev says after we've said good-bye to Hal and are in the truck heading back home. "He really cares about the game."

"Yeah." I lean against the window and wonder how many things I can hold back for two weeks. The stuff about the Whalers guy, some of the things about my mother, and now the stuff about Fisher. I already didn't want to talk to him about the fight, and that kind of hangs awkwardly around us, with both of us ignoring that it happened. Do I think that if he were more vocal about being gay, that would stop a couple drunken pissed-off fans from picking on the faggot fox? No. But it's impossible to tease that thread out from the rest of the conversation.

Dev, with that kind of instinct that we've developed over the last couple years, reads my thoughts, and despite the awkwardness, forges ahead. "You were gonna say something about Fisher."

"No," I say, and then, "it can wait two weeks."

He pauses. "If you say so." There's steel and edge in his voice.

I squirm, but even if I wanted to give him something to worry about, it's not my secret. "We're going to have a lot to talk about on that plane to Disneyworld," I say, and his steel dissolves into a laugh. I relax back into the truck seat, feeling like I just cut the right wire on a ticking bomb. Today.

We both have calls to make, so we separate when we get home: he sits on the couch while I sit on the bed, the bedroom door closed. Peter gave me Jocko's number and said it would be okay to call him if I didn't hear by three today. It's two-fifty-five, so I download a game for my phone and play it, and about ten minutes later, I call the number.

"Jack Brucker." He's got a voice deep as a truck engine and about as loud. I know he's a bear, but the image of the wolf from Boliat swims into my head.

I identify myself. He pauses for a minute, then says, "Oh yeah, the scouting guy. Sorry, time got away from me."

"You on vacation?"

"Golfing," he said.

"I can wait 'til you're done."

"Nah, I finished a while ago. Get in first thing, you still got the rest of the day." He talks short and punchy, every sentence almost a challenge. "Just catchin' up with some old friends, but work comes first."

Then he pauses, and even though I'm interviewing with him, I decide to jump in and get things started. "You want to hear a little about my history?"

"Sure."

So I tell him how I got my start, watching college games. He breaks in. "So you watched 'em for the plays, right? Or the players?"

I bite my tongue—he's not supposed to ask me shit like that—and swallow the first two answers. "I watched how the players executed the plays."

He grunts, and I go on. I talk about the Dragons, some of our few successes and our many busts, and why I thought they were busts. "So," he interrupts again, "y'ever bump someone up the board 'cause you thought he was hot?"

"Um." I stare around the bedroom. The naked picture of me on the bureau doesn't help. "No. Never. I mean, I was dating Dev by then, and—"

"Sure, yeah, I'm married. Don't mean I don't tip a waitress a little more if she's smokin'."

"Of course. No, strictly business," I say. "The guys don't get paid for being good-looking."

He laughs. "They do, but not by us."

"Right." I pause, but he doesn't go on, so I tell him more about the Dragons, and eventually we come to the sticky question.

"So why'd they let you go?"

I take a breath. "Because I didn't disclose my relationship with a player."

"Miski."

In the silence, I hear the murmur of Dev's voice in the other room. "Right."

"You got any relationships with any other players we don't know about?"

"What? No."

"That's the only reason you were fired?"

"As far as I know. That's what they told me." I pause. "You hear different?"

He whuffs a short laugh. "Heh. No. Seems kinda unfair. You lose your job, he gets a big spotlight." He considers. "Do we gotta worry about you tellin' Miski what we're doin' here?"

"No. I asked him and he's willing to sign a non-disclosure agreement if required."

"Huh." He grunts again. "So whatcha been doin' since they let you go?"

"I moved to Chevali, and—"

He cuts me off. "You'd move up here if you get the job."

"Yes."

"Good."

I tell him about how I've been watching college games. He grills me on some players, then asks me about the Whalers and the game they played against the Firebirds. I think I acquit myself pretty well, but every moment, I'm aware of my heartbeat, like I'm walking a tightrope.

Finally he says, "Okay, look, the guys are heading out to dinner. I think I got what I need."

"Thanks for taking the time out of your day," I say.

"No sweat," he says. "Tell Miski good luck and we hope they knock the fuck outta C.C."

"I'll tell him." I hang up and exhale, and even grin a little. I think it went okay. I hope. His comment about me picking players based on their appearance was a little worrying, especially for someone who might be my boss. Maybe he was just making a joke, though. I can't tell and I shouldn't be paranoid. Not everyone who doesn't understand gay people is a homophobe.

Dev's still on the phone when I peek out, so I call Hal. The swift fox picks up with a chuckle. "Figured I'd be hearing from you."

"Yeah," I say. "So I'll talk to you about Fisher if you talk to me about Pol."

"Wow." He laughs again. "I dunno, can I think about it?"

"Dev's in the other room. Felt like you didn't want to talk about it with him around."

"About right." He takes a breath. "Okay. You first."

"Oh, no," I say. "You'll make some excuse to put off the conversation."

"But," he points out, "I've already told you a little bit. And this isn't something that's gonna go away."

I sigh. "Well, the thing with Fisher isn't anything you couldn't guess."

"Getting more irritable while recuperating from an injury. Sounds like anabolic steroids. Muscle growth?"

"Not sure. And there's...there's no hard evidence." Only the growth hormone, and that just indicates probable steroid use, not definite.

"But if it smells like a muscular duck and quacks like a muscular duck..."

"It's probably a duck on..." I lower my voice and turn up the music on the iPod. The bedroom door's closed and I can hear Dev talking. I know his ears aren't quite as sharp as mine, but you can never be too sure. "On steroids, yeah."

"You think there's any way he'd talk to me?"

"After the championship, maybe." Gena would talk to Hal, I'm almost sure, once the game is over, and definitely once Fisher's career is over. But I can't volunteer her.

"Well, this is taking a while to write, so I think that's okay. We want to put it out in the off-season anyway so it doesn't get eclipsed by other big football news." He pauses. "Like your boyfriend's announcement."

"Right." I sit on the edge of the bed and curl my tail over my lap, flicking the white tip up and down.

"Didn't seem to sit too well with you, him just putting it on the back burner."

"It's best for him. If he can just play the game and win the championship, it'll be a lot easier to be a spokesperson for advocacy groups."

"Unless he falls into the habit of not being a spokesperson."

"You know, that thought had not occurred to me at all."

Hal laughs shortly. "Okay, okay. You got your fox ears on it."

"Yeah. So tell me, what happened with Pol?"

He's quiet for a moment, then he says, "Oh, dang, I got a call coming in on the other line. You know, I really oughta take this."

"Hal."

"Seriously."

"You know I can hear when your line clicks with another call, right? And when it doesn't?"

"Ah, crap. What good is technology if it can't get you out of uncomfortable conversations?" He makes kind of a stretching noise. "Pol's a sweet girl and she liked the idea of being with a reporter."

"Better than the reality?"

"Ayup."

"What did she expect?"

He exhales across the phone, a slow hiss of escaping air. "Damned if I know. I think she thought we'd be working on stuff together. But when I'm on a story, you know, I got to keep things confidential and I can't really talk about it. And when a guy calls me with the information I was looking for, I have to take the call, even if I'm out at a nice dinner."

"That's all? She broke up with you because you ditched her for ten minutes at dinner to take a call?"

"We-ell." A long pause. "It was more like fifty-five minutes. And it was a double date with one of her work friends."

"That is kinda rude."

"It was an important call."

"And it couldn't have waited? Not like you have a deadline on this story."

He snorts. "I'd been trying to reach this doctor for four days and I was pretty sure he didn't want to talk to me, so when he called, I had to get in all the questions I wanted to ask him."

"While Pol and her two friends waited and waited."

"Heh. Well, they didn't exactly wait. They sat there for about twenty minutes and then they ordered. And got their food. And finished it. She broke up with me on the way out of the restaurant."

"Oh, come on," I say. "That's not a breakup. It won't stick. She was mad. You just have to let her cool off and call her back in a day or two, tell her you're sorry. Send her flowers—isn't that what you straight guys do? Chocolates maybe?"

"Maybe," he says. "I dunno."

"She's a coyote," I remind him. "It's probably just a scheme to make you want her more. She wants you to call her."

He's silent for a good long while, enough that I start to compose a sentence about how she's not just a coyote, she's also a lady whose feelings were probably hurt, but before I can get it out, he says, "Anyway, speaking of reporting, did you find a lawyer for your thing?"

I let the change in subject go. "Yeah. She's cool. I have to send over my writeup today, but she's already notified the court that I want to file something."

"You can tell them you're going to file before you do?"

"She says I have ten days now to get it in. It's pretty much all written up; I just need to work on it with some of her thoughts. She was going to look at the details of the case and get back to me with specific phrases I can use to make the court see it as more relevant."

I catch Dev's voice from the other side of the door saying something in a very "good-bye" kind of tone. Hal's saying something about how to talk to lawyers and I cut him off.

"I think my time's up," I say. "Look, really, just send Pol flowers, like, Thursday. That gives her a few days to cool off and think about what she's missing, and lets you follow up Friday for a date on the weekend."

"Really?"

"Well, that's what happens in all the sitcoms," I say. "If she were a guy, I'd say just show up at her place with a bottle of wine and an apology and you'd be good."

"You can quit with the conversion campaign," Hal says. "It's not that I ain't buyin'. It's that I don't think I even got any of the right credit cards to hand the cashier."

"To each his own," I say. "Take care and call me tomorrow if you want. Dev's out filming that commercial and I'm gonna need something to take my mind off shit."

•

"You sure you don't want to come see the commercial being filmed?" Dev's getting dressed up in a collared shirt.

I wouldn't mind it, to be honest, but I'm kind of afraid I would just start thinking about how he could be filming so many other more useful things, or about how crappy an agent Ogelby is, because I'm already thinking those things, so it's probably better I just stay home and nurture the feeling that things are going to be okay. After talking to Jocko and Hal, I feel better, and when I'm not out having flashbacks to the Boliat fight or ignoring calls from Brian, I can focus on loving Dev and spending time with him. Also, I could work on that writeup while he's gone, but I haven't heard from the lawyer yet, so I can't pretend there's a rush. "Why are you dressing up when they're going to want to film you in athletic gear?"

"I like to make a good impression," he says. "They did a seminar on that. Always dress up for media appearances."

"I guess that's not a bad philosophy," I say. "I'd come, but it'll be really boring."

"It'll be boring for me too," he says. "Come on, then I'll have someone to talk to while they're setting up lights or whatever it is they spend forever doing. I waited for hours for the Strongwell thing."

"I don't know that these guys are going to be as professional as the ones in Crystal City," I say. "They're shooting their footage in a parking lot."

"Parking garage," he corrects me. "On the roof."

"You don't have to jump off, do you?" I curl my tail, not honestly worried about this, but after I've said it, I wonder. I mean, this company had him working out on asphalt in the middle of the season.

"They haven't told me." He grins and walks over to kiss me on my nose. "Come on, fox. It'll be fun. You can talk to the director and stuff."

"I have other things I can do," I say.

"Like what?"

Finish up my statement, but I can't do that 'til the lawyer calls back, and if she calls while I'm at the commercial I'll have to explain it and…That's the problem with someone who knows you well enough to call you on your bullshit. I sigh and give in. I'm going to have to keep this stuff bottled up for another week and a half anyway. At least after today, Dev'll be out in Crystal

City practicing, and even if I go out there a couple days later, he'll be busy all day and I can occupy the evenings with dinner and sex and avoid any heavy conversations. So as long as I can make it through today, I'll be fine.

We drive up to the parking garage, which is the one adjacent to the Firebirds' stadium, and I have to admit that it's got a nice view of the circular stadium and its distinctive red and gold colors. They lucked out; it's a cloudy day, so there won't be any harsh shadows.

You would think that would make it easier for them to set up, but no. "The home-movie look worked for the last one," the director, a pronghorn wearing oversized sunglasses, explains to Dev, "but since we have more time today, we want something more polished. So it'll take a while to set up."

I'm not sure how it takes them so long, because they only have a crew of six people plus the director. I think they probably all came in the same van. Dev and I lean against the edge of the roof to one side, watching, until the director comes over and starts telling Dev what they're going to want him to do.

They've brought footballs and a generic uniform helmet, and of course a bunch of Ultimate Fit stuff in some searingly bad colors: carmine red and electric green and bright yellow-orange. They're going to show him doing more "football moves," as the director puts it. They've got footage of a football machine on another roof and the idea is it launches these footballs onto the roof of this parking garage, and there's a cheetah trying to catch them and Dev keeps leaping in front of him. Then at the end of the commercial the cheetah finds an Ultimate Fit shirt and says "Let's go again."

Honestly, the Strongwell spot sounds a million times better, and I haven't even seen it yet. But Dev's already contractually obligated, so I curl my tail around my legs and watch all the scurrying preparations and try not to make any editorial commentary on the commercial. I do make sure that they're laying down pads for the guys to run on, so Dev isn't going to do any injury to his feet. Fortunately, someone must have yelled at them about the last time, because they've got enough pads to blanket a big section of the garage concrete.

It is interesting watching the setup go on, for a few minutes, but you can only watch someone test lighting for so long. I look over the edge of the parking garage at the empty streets below. With no games scheduled and no reason to go to the box office—the championship tickets are only being sold online—nobody is hanging around the stadium and the streets are deserted. There's a brew pub a couple blocks away just opening up for lunch: a panther is shaking out floor mats, and a moment later the neon sign comes on. But nobody's beating down the door to get in.

When they start making more urgent noises, I turn to see if the cheetah actor has shown up. No; it turns out the cheetah they're using is the tall guy who was setting up the reflective light shades. He strips off his jacket and puts on a generic t-shirt, then takes off his sweatpants to reveal athletic shorts. He doesn't have a bad body, but compared to Dev he's definitely no athlete. I kind of smirk inside at how bad this commercial is going to look.

The cheetah does some jogging and stretching warmups, and then the director runs them through their paces. The boar he has throwing the footballs is pretty terrible at it, to the point that I do actually speak up once the director's done with the blocking. "Can I have a shot at throwing the football?" I ask.

Dev looks at me in surprise. The football-throwing boar looks offended, but the pronghorn says, "Len, let him have a throw."

The boar flips me the football as if he doesn't really care. As I lunge to one side to catch his terrible throw, he stalks away to inspect some little gadget or another over by the cameras. I squeeze the football, take some practice swings with my arm, then throw it to the back of the roof-slash-set.

The first throw isn't that great. The cheetah runs it down and lofts it back to me, and he throws a pretty nice spiral, actually. But then I get into a rhythm and some of my younger days tossing it with my father come back, and I get some good movement on the ball.

"Looks great," the pronghorn says. "I've got an agreement here for you to sign if you don't mind throwing footballs for the ad."

I haven't actually ever thrown footballs to Dev before. It sounds a little crazy, but when I know he can practice with Gerrard Marvell or someone who, you know, actually plays football for a living, I never thought he would want to catch my weak-armed throws. For the commercial, though, I guess it'll work okay, and anyway, it's fun.

We get set up finally and they're ready for Dev, so I start tossing balls to the cheetah for Dev to leap in front of. You can see how professional Dev is: he looks at the ground as though he's running a designed play and I swear his feet hit the exact same spots on the pads every single time he goes through the rehearsal. The cheetah just kind of runs vaguely toward the spot where the ball's going to be and makes adjustments at the last minute, which he can do because I'm throwing softly and trying to get it to him. To be honest, I'm not that great at getting the football to the right spot either, but it doesn't matter to Dev; when he gets to his spot, he leaps and grabs the ball from wherever it is in the air. It's impressive.

The director says he wants about thirty repetitions so he has a lot to choose from. Well, I can throw the ball thirty times, I guess. "This time is for real, everyone!" the pronghorn calls. I squeeze the ball again as the cameras roll for the first take, and let it go.

The two big cats run into position, and Dev leaps in from the side to snatch the ball away. As the cheetah lands, one foot plants awkwardly on the edge of the pads and he falls heavily to the ground. At first, I think I'm the only one who notices, because all the cameras and attention are focused on Dev. But when the cheetah struggles to his feet and nearly collapses again, I drop the football and run over as soon as the director yells "Cut!" and then everyone sees.

"It's my ankle," the cheetah says. "Caught my foot on the thing there." He gestures.

"Can you put weight on it?" I ask. He's about a foot taller than I am, but he can still lean on my shoulder, and he does.

"Ye—no." He tries, wavers unsteadily for a moment, and then the leg buckles again.

"Fan-fucking-tastic," the pronghorn says, throwing his arms up in the air. "There goes the day. Don't suppose you can rearrange Mr. Miski's schedule to be available when we can find a replacement, can you?"

For some reason, he's yelling at the cheetah, as though it's his fault. I try to undercut that with rationality, like, "Let's get some ice on it. Do you want me to call an ambulance?" He passes on the ambulance but does tell me there's ice in the cooler, so while the director is yelling at the boar about wasted time, I'm improvising an ice pack by wrapping a towel around a bunch of ice cubes. I get the ankle wrapped in it and kneel by it to make sure it's comfortable.

When the director comes closer and looks like he's going to yell at the cheetah again, I say, "Hey. Aren't you supposed to have medical personnel here? What would you do if Dev got injured, just start yelling at him, too?"

"What?" He looks startled. Perhaps nobody interrupts him in mid-rant, usually.

"An injury to him could be worth millions of dollars. You have insurance, right? Doesn't his contract mandate that medical personnel be in attendance at any event in which he undertakes any physical activity?"

I have no fucking idea. I know the Strongwell contract we looked at had a medical clause, but I don't know if these guys did. But I'm guessing that the director doesn't really know the contract that well either. And it turns out I'm right. His eyes kind of bug out over his sunglasses, and he blusters, "Well, look, that's not my problem. The management tells me what to bring to these things and I assume that's all in accord with the contract, so if there's no medical person here then we don't need one. Maybe he's supposed to bring his own. How about that, huh? Maybe he brought you and that means we don't need to have one."

"Okay." I stand up and shake my head. "So are we done here?"

"I don't know. Is he going to be able to run in the next hour?"

"No. Probably not in the next week."

"Fuck me."

And then Dev steps up. "Lee's in pretty good shape," he says.

I stare at him, and then hold up my paws. "Oh, no. No, no."

"He isn't tall enough to catch balls," the cheetah says.

I bite back a retort, because I was the one who just helped him get his ankle wrapped, but then it occurs to me that he's an actor and probably is worried about his paycheck. It doesn't matter; the director waves the protest aside. "Fuck that. He doesn't have to. Can he act?"

"Better than I can," Dev says. "He was in plays in college."

"That's totally different," I say.

But the director's already looking at me. "Not bad," he says. He gestures. "Take off your shirt."

"Normally," I say, "I'd be flattered. But—"

"Come on, Lee," Dev says. "If you can play the cheetah's part, we can finish this up today and it'll be over with."

I waver, while the cheetah sulks and the director says, "And he's already signed an agreement to be in the commercial."

That gets me. "That agreement said nothing about appearing on camera. Don't you have a different one for on-camera talent?"

"No," the director says.

"That's bullshit." The boar goes back behind the lights and rummages in a bag. "Jack, you can't put him on camera without this." He comes out holding a wrinkled, poorly photocopied page, and pushes it toward me while the pronghorn glowers.

"Fine," the director says, "just sign that and we'll get started."

I scan the document quickly. "A hundred dollars?"

He shrugs. "When you're a big football star, we'll put more zeroes on it." He holds out a pen. "Going to get this thing done?"

Dev mouths, "Please," at me. I snatch the pen and read the paper more closely while everyone waits. It looks like boilerplate, though I have no idea what a contract like this is supposed to look like. So I fill in my name, scan the clauses about the company owning all the video footage and me getting compensated for it. For the heck of it, I scribble an extra zero next to the number, cross out the written "hundred" and write in "thousand," and then I sign it and hand it back to the director.

"I'll do it for a thousand," I say.

Dev's eyes go wide. The director barely looks at the paper as he takes it. "Forget it," he says automatically.

I stand my ground, challenging him. I can be a dick, too. "How much is it going to cost you to bring all these people back another day? You're lucky I'm not asking for ten thousand."

Everyone stares at the pronghorn. He stares at me, and then looks down at the paper. "Fuck me," he says again, and initials next to my changes and then signs it. "All right," he says. "You're hired. Now get into costume. Sorry we don't have a wardrobe trailer."

He has kind of a malicious smirk on, as though making me take my clothes off in public is his punishment for the uppity fox who's shaken him down for what I'm sure is a minute fraction of what he's making for this shoot. How little he knows. I slide my pants down without really caring that I'm standing in my boxers, even the tight ones I bought for Dev. The pine marten behind the camera stares, and maybe the director does too, but I pretend not to notice.

They have a lot of shorts and t-shirts, but the director likes the red shorts the cheetah's wearing and insists I try them on. The cheetah looks a little uncomfortable at having to undress, so the boar finds a towel to drape over him while he does it. Maybe he's wearing rocket-ship underwear, or nothing at all. I'm starting to think this director has a voyeur thing going, which fits, given his profession.

I pull the shorts on and take off my shirt. The director eyes my bare chest and I guess his shrug passes for approval. Fortunately, the cheetah is slender and around the same build I am, so the shorts and t-shirt fit, if a little long. "Doesn't matter," the director says, smoothing down my fur around the sleeves of the peach-colored t-shirt the cheetah was wearing. "It's not supposed to look like you have muscles. No, no, this doesn't work. Your black paws just do not go with it."

"They're brown." I take the yellow shirt off and try on a black one, which just highlights that my paws and lower arms are not, in fact, black.

"No, no, no. Nothing is going to work with that brown fur coming up the forearm." The director pivots dramatically. "Why can't you just be a uniform color?"

"Your mom's a uniform color," I mutter under my breath, reaching for the electric green shirt.

"What if he rolls up the sleeves?" the cheetah says. He's in a better mood since the director told him he'll still get paid.

The pronghorn whirls and snaps his fingers. "Yes! Roll up the sleeves! No, not with the green one, that's hideous. Put the black one on again."

Finally, we settle on the black shirt with rolled-up sleeves. It looks "passable," the director assures me. "Now go, get in position."

"He's too short," the camera operator, a pine marten, says.

"So we film from the waist up, we only use shots of Miski leaping for the ball. Looks more impressive."

"Yeah, we can do that." The marten gets back behind the camera.

And just like that, I'm acting in my first paid commercial. Mindful of the cheetah's misstep, I try to run my routes as precisely as Dev does and find how hard it is. I mark spots on the pads, but I can't watch my feet landing there because I have to look at where the ball is coming, and I manage to get in position to catch the ball, but when I stop and look at where I am, it's a foot or two off from where I'd intended to be. Part of that is because the ball is going to slightly different spots every time. The boar started out throwing again, but then the cheetah said he could throw from a seated position, and his throws were much crisper, so they're letting him do it.

"This is hard," I say to Dev as we reach the side of the pads for the fourth time. He's not leaping to get the ball, just practicing being in the right spot. I'm panting already and he's just smiling, barely winded even though he's run twice as much as I have.

"Maybe you should spend some of your days working out," he says, and elbows me in the stomach.

"Oof. Yeah." I grin and go back to it, and after a few more runs, we start shooting.

We do thirty-five takes in all. Every time, I run the route, I reach up for the ball, and Dev leaps in front of me to take it away. At first, I'm just happy to be acting with him, but as the takes go on, I find myself wishing I could catch the ball, just once.

CHAPTER 10 – BROKEN COVERAGE (DEV)

I have a blast acting in the commercial with Lee. I show off a bit, twisting in the air in front of him, coming down on one foot, one-handing the ball. He grins, appreciating the show, I'm sure. I like how he looks in his shirt with the rolled-up sleeves and the athletic shorts. "You should wear that more often," I tell him, low, between takes.

The director calls for us to get back in position before he has a chance to respond. The cheetah tosses the ball in our direction, Lee jumps for it, and I jump in front of him, grabbing it and pulling it down. Then they do about five takes of Lee picking up the Ultimate Fit shirt and grinning at the camera. He says, "Let's go again," and then asks if they need him to say it again.

"No," the director says. "We're going to loop Jorgy's voice over it anyway, because he signed the contract to speak on camera and I can't afford another thousand to use your *voice*." He turns away from Lee, back to me, and gets courteous again. "I think we got enough. You guys mind sticking around while I look through the takes real quick?"

"Sure," I say. It's a nice enough day out, and I like being up here.

"Hey," Lee says to the cheetah. "Throw me one."

The cheetah grabs a football and tosses it. I grin, stalk behind Lee, and then leap in front of him to grab the pass at the last minute. When I turn, flaunting the ball, he's standing with his ears flat and paws on his hips, staring at me. "Nice catch, stud," he says, and walks over to where he left his pants.

I drop the football and walk over, but he's already shoved down his shorts. He steps out of them and picks up his pants. "Hey, you okay?" I put a paw on his bare shoulder, just below the rolled-up shirt.

"Yeah, I'm fine," he says. "This was fun."

He smiles, but I don't know whether to take it seriously. "I was just kidding around."

"I know," he says. "It's not a big deal."

"I'll throw you a football if you want."

"Maybe some other time."

The boar's already picked up all the footballs and one of the other assistants is cleaning up the pads, and yeah, maybe we shouldn't do this on the roof of a parking garage in front of a whole camera crew. "Tell you what,"

I say, "I've got some footballs at the apartment. We can head down to the park."

"Sure," he says again.

The director tells us he's got everything he needs. We shake paws and head on down to the truck, where I grab an energy bar and devour it as I turn on my phone to check it. Ogleby's left me voicemails with the times of the interviews I'm supposed to be doing, and it turns out one of them was ten minutes ago. The last voicemail is from that reporter.

"Fuck." I hit the steering wheel. "Can you drive home? I need to get on this interview."

He nods. "Sure." We switch places and I call the reporter back.

The questions are all pretty standard football questions. He asks about stepping in for Corey, about keeping the spot when Corey came back, and what it's like working with Gerrard. I talk about football, the extra practices and the schemes, and how Gerrard keeps us really focused on the game and helps us make in-game adjustments. And then he asks, "Do any of them care that you're gay?"

"No," I say.

"Really? Was there any behind-the-scenes trouble when you came out?"

"You know," I say, "this was all reported pretty thoroughly back then. I don't really want to talk about it any more."

Lee glances at me, navigating the streets. "Sorry," the reporter says into my ear. "Didn't realize it was still a sore subject."

"It's not a sore subject." I try to keep my voice calm. "It just doesn't have anything to do with the championship game, and that's what I'd prefer to talk about."

"You're going to be the first openly gay player to play for a championship," the reporter says. "That doesn't mean anything to you?"

"Well." I reach over and put a paw on Lee's thigh. "Sure it does. But what would really mean something to me would be if a few other players would come out. Then you guys could go bother them for a while and then it would all die down and people wouldn't care whether the guys suiting up were straight or gay or bi or whatever."

"Why do you think nobody else has come out?"

"Maybe because they don't think it's important. Maybe because they just want to play football. I don't know. I'm not them."

"Well, why did you come out?"

Christ. I bite my lip to stop myself from saying, *this has all been talked about already!* "My circumstances were pretty unusual. I have a partner and there had been a lot of rumors. I don't know any rumors about any other players in the league."

"What about your quarterback?"

I laugh. "Aston? Those aren't real rumors. Those are people who hate him because he's clean-cut and he said one time that he liked that one country singer, so he gets photoshopped in with him a lot."

"So you're saying he's not gay."

"I'm saying I don't know. He never talked to me about it. It's his business if he is, but I can't tell you one way or the other, and I wouldn't tell you if I knew. Which I don't."

"All right."

"Now," I say, before he can go off again, "do you have any more questions about the game?"

The interview ends a couple blocks before our apartment. I close the phone and my eyes and press my fingers to the bridge of my muzzle. "Tough," Lee says. "All those questions about being gay."

He's a little snappy, and I snap back, "You said you weren't going to do this until after the championship game."

"I didn't know I'd have to ride in a car with you while you told a reporter you didn't care about being gay."

"That's not what I said."

He pulls into the garage. "You couldn't have just said, 'I'm proud to be the first gay player,' and left it at that?"

"He wouldn't have left it at that."

"You could have talked about your influence on other players."

I look at him. "Like what other players? Who else has come out?"

He pulls into the parking spot and shuts off the car. "It'd have to be a star."

"I wasn't a star."

His ears flick as he turns to me, one eyebrow raised. "'Wasn't'?"

"Well, not that I'm that big a star now. But people know who I am." My tail flicks self-consciously.

"Yeah, they do. A lot of that—not all—is because you came out. That's why you had this commercial today."

I get out of the truck and close the door as Lee gets out the other side. "I'm a pretty good football player, you know."

He stands with the door open for a moment and then closes it softly. "You're right. And I said I wouldn't do this for two weeks, so I won't."

We ride up the elevator, and I can't help but wonder what's going to happen when those two weeks are over. If we win the game, am I going to be barraged with requests to do these interviews with gay rights papers? If we lose, am I going to be in any mood to listen to Lee's badgering? It wouldn't be so bad if we had time to spend apart. But we're going to the same apartment for the rest of the day, and I have two more interviews to do this afternoon and I don't know where I'm going to do them unless I lock myself in the bedroom.

And then we get out of the elevator and he unlocks the door, and I can't believe I was just thinking that. Because I love him, and living together is still as wonderful in a lot of ways as it was when he first moved in. Maybe when he has his own job, things will be going better. But even that thought makes me feel guilty. I want to help him. I want him to think he can rely on me. I just can't distract myself from football right now.

"I need to do some more interviews," I say when we close the door. "Should I just go into the bedroom?"

"Yeah." He pauses, looking at his laptop, then disappears into the kitchen for a moment. "Maybe I'll look at making something for dinner. Want to eat in? We only have one more day before you leave."

"Sure," I say. "Whatever is fine."

"All right." His tail swishes, and I go into the bedroom.

The other interviews follow similar lines as the first. They talk about football for a while and then ask me how it feels to be the first openly gay player to be playing for a championship. Mindful of Lee in the next room, who would probably have to be trying hard not to hear me even with the door closed, I use his lines about how proud I am to be there, how I hope to be an inspiration to other gay players, and how I hope to see more out players in the UFL soon.

They poke with some follow-up questions, but after the first interview, I'm better at deflecting them blandly, and they go back to football when they get better answers from me on those questions. I'm happy to talk about our preparations in a very general way, to talk about how great the Firebirds are and how much potential they have, and how I'm looking forward to winning multiple championships with them, no matter what happens in two weeks. Or, now, a week and a half.

And when I'm done with the interviews, I feel unaccountably nervous about the championship game. The attention focused on it from the reporters, which usually I don't care about because I avoid papers and websites, is as impossible to ignore as the sun.

The smell of roast chicken filters through the bedroom. My stomach growls; that energy bar I had after the commercial shoot is long gone. I open the door and look through to the kitchen, but Lee's not there. I sniff, then turn to the living room. He's curled in the sofa, typing on his laptop.

"I'm all done," I say.

He nods, staring down at his screen, his ears flat against his head. I lean over the back of the couch. "Everything okay?"

"Fine," he says. He flips the window he's working on to the background, but not before I catch a glimpse of the document and the name "Vince King" jumps out at me. He's writing an article or something about it.

"You don't look fine." I reach over to his shoulder.

He flinches away from me, and his ears go even flatter. "I'll tell you in two weeks."

I pull my arm back and stand up. "You know, not talking about stuff for two weeks includes not talking about how you're not talking about stuff."

He looks up. "Sorry, stud. I tried to put all the non-football parts of my life on hold for two weeks, but…" He stares at the laptop and then shuts it with a click. "Some things just wouldn't wait."

My tail lashes. I scowl and stalk across to the window. "Fine. Should I just go out until you're done taking care of your other things? Or should I go back in the bedroom?"

"You don't have to go back in the bedroom," he says softly. "I'm done." He puts the laptop on the floor, but he doesn't get up, just sits there and pulls his tail into his lap.

"You know," I say, "I'm under enough pressure this week. Having you moping around isn't going to help at all."

"I know you're under pressure," he says, an edge creeping into his voice. "I'm trying not to make it worse."

"You're not doing that great at it."

"I'm doing the best I can."

"Well, do better! Lion Christ!" My claws snag the back of the couch.

He doesn't respond, and the silence grows. I retract my claws and say, "Sorry. I'm hungry, I guess, and those interviews…everyone's talking about how important this game is."

"It is," he says quietly, and gets up to walk to the kitchen. "I'll get dinner."

"Lee…" I start, but he's vanished, down-curled tail and all, and I want to kick something, but the only thing nearby is the couch, and his laptop is there on the floor in front of it…

I stare down at the closed computer for a second, then pad around the couch and pick it up. I'm sure I can take whatever it is, and if I get it out in the open, maybe he'll perk up and be the fox I want him to be.

So I open the laptop, and it comes up with a web browser. Behind the browser, though, is a document, and that's what mentioned Vince King. I just skim what he wrote—it looks like he's talking about his mom, and how what she did reflects on the King kid. Then I see the word "court," and realize why the language is all stiff and formal. There's a court case, and he's writing something for the court, helping maybe try to sue Families United for driving the kid to suicide.

I close the laptop and put it back on the floor. I get that he thinks I don't want to hear about Vince King anymore—and I don't—but he's not asking me to do anything for it. I feel shitty then, that I made him so goddamn paranoid about talking activism around me that he doesn't even feel like he can tell me about the shit he's doing on his own that doesn't involve me.

And it's not like I just want to forget about that kid anyway. Just yesterday when I was talking to Mom, she asked what Lee was doing and I told her he was really upset by the suicide, but there wasn't a lot we could do about it. She thought it was terrible, but she agreed with me.

The other thing that makes me feel shitty is that I only talked with him the one time about *his* mom, and we didn't even get into it that much. He's so bent on this whole "I can take care of myself" thing that I sometimes forget what a whole pile of terrible things he's gone through lately—losing his job, his parents divorcing, the fight with my dad, and I guess you could toss Vince King in there too, 'cause it hit him pretty hard.

Lee brings out chicken (half a chicken for me, a thigh and drumstick for him) with mashed potatoes, peas, and carrots on two plates. I go into the kitchen and get a beer. "Want one?" I call.

"No," he says.

We sit at the table and eat. I feel like I should say something, but I don't know what. He's just staring at his plate. So I pick up my fork and knife, and eat.

"This is pretty good," I say.

"Store-bought," he says flatly, and then, with more warmth, "thanks."

I would think I'd know, after two and a half years, what to say or do. And if it were just him, then I would. I'd lean over and I'd smile and tell him I know a way to make him feel better. But I chew bite after bite of chicken, worrying that if I say anything, it'll open a floodgate or just make him feel worse. Finally, scraping the last few peas around my plate, I say without looking at him, "I know about the court case."

He doesn't answer. I look up and he's staring at me, ears flat, fork frozen in his paw. His eyes are bright and wide and—and scared? "The Vince King case," I say, and try to control my tail's lashing. "Look, it's okay. I appreciate you not talking to me about it."

His eyes don't shift. I squirm in my seat as he lowers his fork and whispers, "You know?"

"Yeah." I lick my lips, regretting having said anything. I determinedly do not look at his laptop. I can only imagine what he'd say if he figured out I was spying on him. Is that what he's so upset about? "Look, it's cool. I was talking to my family yesterday and they agreed, it's a shame."

"A shame," he echoes, and then makes a weird sound, kind of a hiccup, maybe. "They think it's a shame. Well, yeah, so do I. So I guess you didn't talk to Gregory."

"What? No." I frown. "He wasn't home. I wouldn't talk to him about it, anyway. I just...Mom was asking what you were up to, and..."

I trail off, because he's looking at me weird. "Oh," he says. "That's nice of her. I should give her a call." And he stands up, real fast, and grabs his plate and mine.

"I can do that," I say.

"I know." He hurries to the kitchen, where I hear the clatter of the dishwasher.

I follow him. His tail's bristled somewhat, and curled tightly down around his legs. "Look," I say as he finishes the last one. "I was just trying to ease the pressure on you."

"Yeah," he says. "That makes sense." He shuts the dishwasher and walks out of the kitchen without saying another word.

"Lion Christ," I mutter under my breath. I straighten up a little in the kitchen and then go back out to the living room, where Lee's starting up UFL '09.

We play in an uncomfortable silence, which isn't broken except for minor exclamations of disgust whenever one of our plays doesn't work, or one of our players underperforms. "I know that guy," I say. "He makes that play ninety-nine times out of a hundred." Or, "That guy's a stiff, and he's a jerk."

Lee just grunts curses under his breath, and he doesn't celebrate when something goes right. I thought that the game might help ease tensions, but it doesn't seem to. We didn't pick Crystal City as one of the teams, but still I keep looking at the plays and thinking about what I would do, how the Sabretooths would play it differently, and I'm not focusing on the game as a result.

Maybe for that reason, Lee wins the first game, and the last two, three out of four total. And I'm already kind of on edge about the whole argument, so I just toss the controller on the floor and get up. "I should get to bed," I say. "Maybe I'll call Gerrard tomorrow and see if he's up for some extra practice." He doesn't respond. "Unless we have something else to do."

I wait and watch him. He shakes his head, staring straight ahead at the TV. "I didn't have anything planned."

"So," I say finally, "are you coming to bed?"

He reaches down for his laptop. "In a bit."

"Lion Christ," I explode, "if you want to work on whatever the hell you're doing for the Vince King case, you can tell me. I'm not going to get pissed off because you're doing it."

"I thought you didn't want to hear that name anymore," he says. He brings the computer up and sets it on his lap, but doesn't open it.

"I didn't want to hear it as a reason for me to waste my time yelling at people about how they shouldn't hurt their gay kids! I don't care if it's something you want to do. Hell, doc, I'm glad you feel that way about it. I mean, someone has to."

"Well, if you don't, at least someone in your family does."

What the hell does that mean? Is it a shot at me? I shouldn't have told him I talked to Mom. Somehow he managed to turn that against me, and all I was trying to do was help, be understanding and sympathetic to what he's going through. "Fuck," I say. I go into the bedroom and I take my shirt off and sit down on the bed. Fuck Families United, and Lee's mom, and fuck Lee, too. He's supposed to be helping me deal with my life, not sulking so I feel awkward bringing it up and have to keep going around and around in my head about it.

I stalk back out to the living room, where he still hasn't opened the laptop. "You're supposed to be helping me," I say, standing over him. "You keep going on and on about that Vince King, well, what about us? We're still alive, we're here, right? What about our life?" He's very still. "Don't we have a life to work on?" I press.

When he talks, it's slow and deliberate. "I know you're tired of hearing about Vince King," he says. "Believe me, I wish it hadn't happened. I'm tired of bringing it up over and over. But you never asked what it meant to me. Never asked why it was so important."

I stare at him. "I know why it was important. Because you miss being an activist and this was a cause. Because you saw the kid play once and so you feel invested in his tragedy. I get all that."

"No." He shakes his head. "It's partly that, yeah. But it's more...it's more that these people destroyed his family. The parents should have been there for Vince, yeah. They should have supported him. But they didn't know how to handle it, because it's hard to find positive messaging."

"Messaging. Yeah, if only I'd done that PSA—"

"Let me finish, stud." He challenges me, blue eyes bright, but they're not hard, and the nickname lacks bite. He struggles as if the words are sticking in his throat. "His parents called these people to help, to save their family. And they destroyed it. They preach love, but when it comes down to it they're about conformity and division, about throwing away people who don't meet their stupid fucking outdated standard of living. And Vince—he was alone. He was a confused kid who might have been able to love someone the way you love me and I love you, and now he'll never get that chance because of a bunch of religious bigots. And it—it could've been—it could've been different."

There's nothing I can say to that. I mean, I can't tell him he's wrong. What I really want to say is, can we have this conversation in two weeks? But I'm the one who brought this up, so all I can really do is just nod and tell him he's right and then go to bed and forget about it. That's what I should do.

"I'm sorry about what happened with your mom," I say. "It sucks. I want to help, I want to tell you that you've got a family in me, and with mine."

For some reason, that makes his ears go flat again. "Yeah," he says. "Thanks."

"Well, god dammit, doc, what the fuck else can I do?" I'm yelling now. "Not every problem can be solved by going on TV and telling the world about it even if I had the time to do that."

He glares at me. "Some things need light shined on them. These people are bullies, plain and simple. Maybe you never got beaten up in school, but I did." He waves a paw. "Even that isn't the point."

"Two weeks." I hold up two fingers. "In fact, you know what? Forget that. Can we just get through tomorrow? After that I'll be in Crystal City and we'll be practicing every day."

"You think I shouldn't come with you to Crystal City?"

God damn him. "I didn't say that."

He watches me carefully. "You didn't say 'no.'"

"I don't think you should come tomorrow, but yeah, I mean, I want you there…" I imagine getting into a fight on the night before the championship. Lee wouldn't do that to me. Would he?

"I'm sorry," he says, curling his tail around himself. "I promised myself I wouldn't talk about this, and I guess I'm not as good at keeping it hidden as I thought I could be. This lawsuit is going on right now, and the Equality meeting was last week. I know how special a playoff run is and how hard it is to get back. I'm trying hard not to fuck that up. But I can't stop thinking about…about those kids, about their lives, all those families falling apart right now."

"That's not my problem!" The words spill out. "My problem is how to stop the Sabretooths fucking passing attack in a week and a half, how to keep that slot receiver from getting five yards on the short curl patterns, how to catch the running back when he hits the edge and stop him from turning the corner."

Lee doesn't look at me. He turns off the video game console and sits on the couch, tail curled around his legs, ears flat back. "Those are pretty big problems," he says. "You oughta get your rest."

"Look." I come back to the couch. My tail's lashing and I try to stop it, then give up. "What you're doing is important. I get that."

"To me."

"Fuck, it's important to me, too, fox. It's just—not right *now*. I mean, it's important now, it's just not the *most* important thing…" I hate not being as good with words as he is. He doesn't answer. I wait and then stalk to the bedroom. At the doorway, I turn around. "Well?"

His head comes up slowly. His eyes meet mine. "You go to bed," he says.

"What are you going to do?"

"I guess I'm going to sit here and figure things out."

"Don't sleep there," I say. "It's bad for your back." It takes me an effort to add, "And my front."

He doesn't smile or make any other acknowledgment. So I go into the bedroom, but I leave the door open.

I take my pants off, crawl into bed, and lie there, but I don't get to sleep. I wonder what Lee's thinking, out there in the living room. Probably about the court case, or his mom. Or me, and football, and the championship. Or his father, or Vince King…I don't know how that fox keeps so much going on in his head at once. Sometimes it feels like it takes all my brain just to do my job. Until I'm on the field. Then it's easy. Then it's just me and my team, and them and theirs, and the rules are bound in a big book and there are striped shirts to enforce them.

The clock shows it's been half an hour since I came in to lie down. I guess I dozed off a bit. I left the light on, but Lee still hasn't come in. So I go to the bathroom and glance through the open doorway on my way back. He's still sitting cross-legged on the couch, head down. I can't tell whether his eyes are closed or not.

I should really go out there and just bring him back to bed. But then I think, he's trying to act the martyr, and I should just let him. I'll go practice tomorrow, we'll have dinner and a nice, cuddly night tomorrow night, and then I'll be off to Crystal City and all of this will be behind us. I turn the light off and get back into bed.

Still, sleep doesn't come. I close my eyes, but I can't stop seeing Lee's expression, sad and a little scared. He's gotta do what he does, and I do what I do, right? Is it really my responsibility to be the best linebacker I can be and also single-handedly save the gay youth of the world from the forces oppressing them? Even Lee said he didn't think that. He always told me: football comes first. I mean, if we win this championship game, I can pretty much write my own ticket when my contract is up next year. I could even negotiate for an extension this year. And if we don't, I still have a year to play well and prove myself. Once I get that big payday, then I can start funding charities and doing PSAs and speaking out. In the offseason, of course.

I turn over and look at the clock: it's almost one in the morning. Lee's probably sleeping on the couch. Fine. Maybe in the morning he'll have worked something out before I go off to practice. Or maybe it'll be once we come back. I feel pretty sure he's going to apologize, and whatever he thinks of to do will be the right choice to let me play football and let him worry about his social responsibilities.

·

In the morning, my head is full of football, thankfully. I don't know what I was dreaming, but it's left me worrying about curl patterns and flare routes. And then I flop an arm beside me, onto the empty bed, and I remember.

God damn martyr fox. He slept on the couch all night. I yawn, lie in the bed thinking about how comfortable it is, and how silly Lee is for not coming back to it. He's probably going to be all kinked up.

I think pleasantly about getting some of the kinks out of his back, and other parts, and rest a paw on my sheath. The apartment is very quiet, even the usual traffic noises from outside fainter than usual, and after I notice that, the silence starts feeling wrong and oppressive somehow, like I'm afraid to make a noise in case I miss something else going on.

Stupid. I give myself a quick brush of the paw through the boxers—I'm pretty hard by this point—and swing my legs off the bed. The morning sun doesn't come through the bedroom window, but the soft light of morning (late morning; it's after nine) suffuses the room, making the whole place dreamlike.

And still the apartment is silent. Lee is a quiet sleeper, but I feel like I should be able to hear his breathing. I pad toward the doorway, my tail curling behind me as shivers spread out from my stomach. Silly paranoia, I think, but my whiskers twitch and my hackles rise. I'm convinced that when I step into the living room, I'm going to see an empty couch, that Lee will be gone.

I'm so convinced that I don't want to take that final step through the doorway, so convinced that I hang back with my head behind the door jamb so the couch remains out of sight. I can see the front door, and it looks completely normal. The half of the kitchen I can see looks completely normal. I take a deep breath and go out to wake up Lee.

And the couch is empty.

I stare at it. Car engines approach and recede outside, louder in the living room but still distant. Where the hell did he go?

The kitchen is empty too, no sound nor smell of coffee. Of course—Lee went out to get coffee. But normally, if he did that, he would leave me a note or something.

I turn around and there it is, on the refrigerator, a folded piece of paper held there by a magnet with my name on it in big letters. I take it down.

I hold it in my paws for a long time after reading it. Then I go get my phone and I text him three words. I call Gerrard and tell him I'm going to the field to practice, and he says he'll meet me there. I get dressed and I don't think of anything but football.

Chapter 11 – Shattered (Lee)

I really thought two weeks would be easy. I underestimated the capacity of the universe to lob shit at me.

When Dev goes to bed, I stare at my e-mail program, the highlighted message with the name of the lawyer in the "From" column. I can't stop myself from clicking on it, looking at it again just to make sure I read it correctly. Then I close the program and close the laptop.

If I'd only left well enough alone, I wouldn't have to keep seeing that name over and over again, even though the laptop sits cooling in my lap, powered down. If only I'd really ended things the way I did with Brian, if only I hadn't pressed. If only I hadn't been so fucking fired up to shove my muzzle into the case, to push myself at it so that I could show it off to Mother. All I wanted was to use poor Vince's suicide to make my case, to compare myself to him somehow even though I'm living with my boyfriend and he's dead. My life isn't that bad, and if I'd just realized that, I'd be lying in bed next to my boyfriend now, not sitting out here with a secret caught in my throat.

I thought I was going to die when he mentioned his family. For a half-second, I thought that his parents knew and were okay with it, and then I realized that he might have found out about the case somehow, but he didn't find out the way I thought he did at first, the most blindingly obvious way. He didn't find out from his brother, who is one of the attorneys defending Families United.

"I received a message from the court today advising that your relationship to one of the defense attorneys, Gregory Miski, will be taken into account when reading your *amicus curiae*."

That's what the lawyer's e-mail said. So short, so simple, and I can't stop thinking about it. I can't tell Dev. In fact, I have to call his parents first thing in the morning to make sure that they don't say anything about it if they find out. Because talk about your huge distractions…we're already fighting about the case, and I have gotten to know myself better over the last two weeks. I don't think I would say anything about his brother, not specifically, but I won't be able to stop thinking about it for the next day at least, and he'll notice, and he won't understand how important it is for me not to tell him. Hell, I almost told him tonight.

And then he'll call Gregory and he'll yell at him. He'll talk to his parents, he'll get involved in a family drama, and he'll blame me—eventually. Or I won't tell him, and he'll be mad at me and wonder what I'm hiding.

I wish I were as good at pretending with him as I am with the rest of the world. But Dev has always had a way of getting into my heart, getting past all the trickery and lies. Even just lying about the phone call earlier today was difficult.

He has the same problem with me. He can put everything aside and focus on football—except where I'm concerned.

In this case, it's not about the distraction of his brother, though that would be the final straw. The problem is that the things I'm doing just aren't as real to him as they are to me. He has a great life, and his team has made him welcome. The one guy who keeps giving him shit for being gay got slapped down by the coach. While he can understand that there are problems outside the team—he's not an idiot—he doesn't feel them the way I do. He didn't sit in the hospital with a best friend who was beaten up for being gay. He didn't get fired for being gay (well, sort of).

I remember sitting in a restaurant in Hilltown thinking that Dev had it right, that all we had to do was be happy with who we were, and that was enough to advance the cause, that being a positive example worked as well as being an angry thorn in the side of the status quo. But I'm not so sure about that now. Dev has football, and yes, being an ordinary football player regardless of whom you go home and fuck at the end of the day helps, it does.

I'm just not sure anymore that it helps enough. I wish I could get that image out of my head, of Vince King slumped on his bench. I wish I didn't think his thoughts every time I see it, didn't realize now what I should have seen then, that he was alone with nowhere to turn. I wish I'd talked to him, if only to say: No matter what your family says, you are a person who deserves to live a full and happy life. I wish I'd said more to Kodi when I had the chance, but I can't talk to him either, not in the middle of their playoff run.

I know I can't go talk to every gay college student. But Dev could. He could reach out and save lives, and I can't stop thinking about that.

At the same time, I know I need to. It's our life together, yes, but it's also his football career. I can stand here and say that the greater moral obligation is to the kids whose lives are in danger, but I can't tell him, at the end of the day, how to live his life. I know he's not blind to the problems kids are facing, and I know he thinks that he'll get his big football-star payday and then he'll have a lot more freedom to help. I admire that, I do. I even think he's right.

So I sit here and I feel like a complete jackass because I'm supposed to love and support him, and instead I'm just picking at everything that's wrong. I should be telling him how proud I am that he's helped his team get to the championship game—the Firebirds, who finished 4-12 last year. That's an amazing accomplishment. That he came out, the first active football player, or basketball or baseball or hockey or soccer or anything in this country to do so, is incredible. He's already done so much and here I am, mad because he's not doing a little bit more.

I could walk into the bedroom. I could walk in there and take my clothes off and lie beside him, and go to sleep. And in the morning, I could let him fuck me again, before he goes off to practice. I could tell him how proud I am, and that he's done all I could expect of him. I could tell him I'm sorry and that I'll shut up and be a good boyfriend.

I could, except I promised not to lie to him again.

And what's more, I am terrified of what will happen if he finds out about his brother. I've been on this crusade to get some concrete fact to make Mother see what she's doing; will he become similarly obsessed? Will he get into a fight with his parents? Shit, I'm going to have to call them, and what am I going to say?

I drop my muzzle to my paws and close my eyes, letting comforting darkness enfold me. Right now, I can't see myself being anything but a distraction to him in the two weeks, week and a half, whatever, leading up to the game. Even if I apologize in the morning, he'll know it's just another argument waiting to happen, and he'll be waiting for it to come up again, walking on eggshells around me every moment.

My shoulders slump as I squeeze my arms together. The room feels cold even through my fur. My brain, ever helpful, recites the litany of my crimes against Dev: the arguments, the story about him in the paper, the lying about Brian. How can he still want to be with me?

He gets up to use the bathroom. I don't look up. When he lies down again, I check the time on my phone. One in the morning.

My thoughts are leading me down a path, and I don't see much alternative to it. Outside, the city seems to be as asleep as Dev is. There's nobody I can call, nobody I can talk to. That's okay, though. This is my decision to make.

One forty-five. I unfold my legs from the couch and stand up, shaking pins and needles from my right foot. There's a pad of paper near the refrigerator; I bought it so Dev and I could leave notes about what we need to buy at the supermarket. For about five minutes, probably, I stand holding it and thinking about that, while my eyes blur. I have to put the pad down to wipe my eyes, and then they get blurry again as I think about what to write. It takes a long time.

> Dev,
>
> *I'm sorry about last night. I think it's one of those things I just can't let go of and can't stop thinking about. I can't see any way I'm not going to be a distraction for you in the next two weeks, so I'm just going to go to a motel until you leave for Crystal City. Maybe I'll see if I can stay at Hal's tomorrow night.*

I'm doing the right thing. Of course I am. It's just late at night and I never thought I would be walking out on my tiger for any reason. That's why I'm finding it hard to breathe, why my breaths sound like sobs, why the fur around my eyes is still damp even though I just wiped it.

> *I'm so proud of you, now and always.*
> *Love,*
> *Lee*

It doesn't look any better the second time I read it over, but I can't think of anything to add. I could fill all the pages of the pad with the things I want to say, but most of that wouldn't be helpful. We'll have plenty of time to talk after the championship game.

He'd go off to be by himself if he could figure out how to do it. I see him pacing around the apartment, desperate for his own space. Maybe next year, if I don't wind up in Yerba, we should get a two bedroom apartment, or if he signs a deal with Chevali, he could buy a house.

I fold up the note and slip it under one of the magnets on the fridge. Whether or not he's in the habit of looking for notes from me on the fridge, he'll have to go in there to get his protein breakfast drink. I write his name on it in big letters, so he can't miss it.

My overnight bag is in the closet in the bedroom; taking that and some clothes would be risky, because Dev might wake up and then he'd want to know what I was doing, and I don't think I could tell him to his face.

Maybe I want him to talk me out of it. Maybe I want him to wake up and say, *Don't go, fox. You can be as much of an activist as you want, I'll understand.* But I know enough to know that that voice in my head isn't the real Dev. The real Dev is prickly and complicated, and right now what he needs is peace and quiet to be the best football player he can, without distractions from his family or his fox.

Besides, I can always come back to get my clothes tomorrow when he's at practice if I need to stay out one more night. If he doesn't end up calling me and we don't end up talking out our fight and calling some sort of truce.

So I just take my laptop and computer bag, hefting it over my shoulder as I walk to the door. I lift my fingers to the bolt on the apartment door and turn it softly, then ease the door open. I slip through quiet as thought, and pull the door closed. I even lock it, though I'm worried that the bolt will wake Dev.

If that didn't, the rattle of the elevator surely would. So I take the stairs, hurrying down and trying not to think about what I'm doing. Like, if I'm so sure I'm doing the right thing, then why am I so afraid of Dev waking up to talk me out of it?

Because he wouldn't understand what I'm doing, that it's best for both of us. This way, I can't screw up his shot at a championship and he can just be a linebacker. I get to the bottom of the stairs and have to wipe my eyes again, because I come out into the elevator lobby and it looks just like it did the last time I walked out on him, after our big fight.

The elevator rattles, moves up.

I hold my breath. Did Dev wake up? Is he coming down to get me? I should leave, but I can't force myself to move. The elevator stops, waits forever. I'm just about to go on out the door when it starts to rattle its way back down.

Last time I walked out, I was sure we were going to break up, but that was mostly because I kept doing stupid things. This time, I don't think we're going to break up, but I'm scared we will because we have different priorities. Like Hal with Polly, like Mother and Father.

The elevator grinds to a halt in the lobby. The doors slide open. Out comes an old caribou. She takes two steps out onto the tiled floor and then looks at me, her eyes widening. "Couldn't sleep either?" I shake my head. "Nice walk," she says. "That always does it for me. You're too young for arthritis, though. What's keeping you up?"

My throat is dry. "Boyfriend trouble," I say.

Maybe I want her to turn away in disgust. Maybe I want her to ignore me. But she just nods and says, "Happens to the best of us." And then she goes on out the front door.

After a moment, I follow.

•

The motel is pretty much the same as I remember it. They don't give me the same room I had last time, thankfully. It would probably still smell of sex, if not for real, then at least in my memory. I take the key and stumble into it. The door swings shut behind me, its slam still echoing in my ears as I fall to the bed.

Still, I find sleep impossible to catch. The bed is alien, the smells sterile and wrong. Why am I here in this bed and not next to Dev? I have to keep reminding myself, like a child, why it has to be this way, and every time I go through it, it's only a few minutes before I reach my arm out, or rub my nose into the pillow, and I miss Dev, and the whole thing starts over again.

Somehow, I lift my head from the pillow and see the sun shining bright through the window; I forgot to draw the curtains. I'm unsure whether I slept at all. My eyes feel sore and gummy, but that could just be from the half-crying I was doing all night. I still feel frustrated at myself for my inability to not be an annoying prick.

But I'm also feeling a little more hope. I might have over-reacted a little—well, I certainly over-reacted; let's not qualify it. Problems always seem worse late at night, don't they? Dev will understand. He'll be angry, and maybe I won't see him again until Crystal City, but at least this is all out in the open and we'll be able to talk about it.

My shoulder has a kink in it from sleeping funny, or just lying on it funny and not sleeping, whatever it was I actually did. And my fur is all matted and feels gross. Well, I paid for the room, might as well take a shower.

I breathe in the steamy air and soak myself through, dousing my fur in shampoo and scrubbing myself thoroughly, taking care to soap my tail and run claws through the fur. For a good long time, I stand under the water, until I'm so soaked that the water running into my fur just pushes out more water. It's so relaxing that I close my eyes and doze off briefly before waking up with water in one ear from having tilted my head the wrong way under the shower.

That's about enough for me. I get out and dry myself with the towel, and since this motel doesn't have a fur dryer, I sprawl on the bed on my stomach, naked, letting my fur air dry. Showers really do revive one; after the soak and the sunshine, I feel a lot better.

I take out my phone to text Dev something like, *I shouldn't make decisions in the middle of the night. I'm sorry.* But the phone beeps as soon as I pick it up with a text message from him.

Fine. Stay there.

I stare at the words. It's not the middle of the night for him, it's clear morning and he's read my note, and he agrees.

I don't feel clean anymore, just damp. The sunshine is harsh and glaring now. I'm lying naked on a bed in a motel room, and there's just me, all alone.

•

"Hi," I say to Hal, an hour or so later, and my voice cracks a bit. Only because it's been so long since I talked to someone, and I didn't sleep very much.

"Hey, Miss Farrel," he says. "To what do I owe the pleasure?"

"I was wondering." I take a breath. "I was wondering if I could stay on your couch for a few days."

There's a long silence. "I gotta say, that's about number two on the list of things I never thought you'd ask me."

"Yeah, well. Me neither." I swallow a sob that threatens to come out as an embarrassing squeak, and exhale instead.

"Just a fight, I hope?"

"Me too. I don't know. I just…he needs time alone to get ready for the game."

"That's probably it." He fidgets on the other end of the line. "You know, lots of guys going to their first championship…that's a lot of stress, a lot of pressure. Guys deal with it in different ways. He'll probably call and apologize in a couple days."

"Yeah," I say. "Maybe. So how about it? I can stay here in the hotel if I have to, but…"

"Oh, hell, Lee," he says. "I just been dumped too. I mean—I sure as hell would appreciate the company. And the couch folds out into a bed, or you can have my room and I can sleep in the office."

"No, I don't want to put you out…" I press my fingers to my eyes again, and rub the dampness into the fur on the bridge of my nose. "We can work that out when I get there."

"You need a ride?"

I sit and think about it. I need to walk back to our—to Dev's place and get my stuff first. I could just drive over to Hal's, but I'd have to get directions and my mind doesn't want to deal with that.

"You need a ride," he says. "Let me get cleaned up and I can be wherever you are in an hour or so."

"Thanks," I say, and give him the name of the motel. And then I sit down and just hold the phone in my paws.

I keep turning it over and over again, wanting to call up Dev's message and read it over, to examine it for hidden meanings and somehow read into it that he doesn't really not want to see me again. But the words are burned into my mind, and the only reason for me to look is out of some hope that reality has warped and the words have changed, or that my mind doesn't remember them clearly, that the cute blue designer bubble of the new phone's message program might have changed what was really said. And I know better.

Maybe he'd meant it in a light-hearted way. But then he would have followed it up because he'd be afraid I'd misunderstood. He was angry enough last night that I don't think I'm wrong, when I think about it with my head.

We will talk again. We will have to. My imagination plays that scenario out in excruciating detail, a stage play in one act. Tearful, regretful Dev versus haughty, angry Lee. Tearful, regretful Lee versus proud but regretful Dev. Angry, shouting Lee versus angry, shouting Dev. The variations cycle around and around, none of them making me feel any better, none of them giving me a constructive way to move forward. Melodramatic Lee, that's me.

That sounds like Brian talking, which twitches a long-dead reflex to talk to him…but no, I've left Brian with the equivalent of *Fine. Stay there.* Twice now, in fact. That was different, though; even the first time, our lives were already apart, and there was nothing further for me to do but not talk to him. Otherwise I would be calling him right now, waiting for him to tell me that there are more boy fish out there in the big gay sea, that I'll have that big hole in my heart and under my tail filled in no time, that I'm better off without Dev.

I know that's what he'd say, because he's said it before about my other boyfriends and he's as much as said it already about Dev. He'd only be disappointed that Dev didn't punch me in the jaw on my way out; that would complete his self-righteous Cassandra complex.

Getting angry at Brian helps a bit. I stop leaking tears, at least, and stand up and walk around the room, still holding my phone. There's a little bit of time before I want to walk over to the apartment, so I try turning on the TV. It comes up with a news story on the championship game, and I turn it off again. Lying back on the bed and staring at the ceiling seems like a good option.

All that occupies my mind for the next ten minutes is thoughts of Dev, orange with black stripes, smiling, putting his arms around me, yelling, stalking into his bedroom, saying, "I love you" on the phone, in person, with his eyes, with a touch. My throat tightens and I have to squeeze my eyes shut again. Like thunderclouds massing above, I know that there's a big cry coming. Do I want to subject Hal to that? I may not have a choice.

I brought little to the room; I leave nothing behind save for a bit of shed fur. It would be nice to leave my sorrow and regret like a stain on the bed, a dirty towel on the floor. But all I leave behind is a little of my scent. I wonder whether the maids will be able to tell my mood from it, and I wonder whether more people leave behind stains of tears, or stains of sex. I would like to hope it's sex, but I believe it's probably tears.

Outside, the air has remained cool even though the sun is up. I flip my tail back and forth as I walk, because it forces me to sway my hips and I had always thought nobody could be really sad if he were sashaying down the street. But here I am proven wrong. I only get a few steps before the swing goes out of my hips and my tail, because I approach the corner of the apartment building and am struck with the vision of all my stuff piled in boxes on the sidewalk.

My steps slow, my tail droops. I don't want to see the pile if it's there.

But of course it won't be there. Dev doesn't have time to throw out all my stuff. Not unless he really wants me gone, can't stand to have me around any more. Things aren't that bad yet. I tell Melodramatic Lee to shut up.

Still, I avoid looking at the sidewalk more than half a block ahead of me, watching anything else: the other pedestrians coming and going, the pattern of bricks in the sidewalk (they all seem to have cracks), the stores just opening their iron folding gates. Jewelry, coffee, sneakers. Across the street, past the slow crawl of cars, there is another coffee shop and a takeout spaghetti place Dev likes. It's all such a normal morning that it makes me feel even more alienated. None of these people had their boyfriends basically kick them out of the apartment, even if only temporarily. None of them would understand why my throat tightened again, why I had to look away from the spaghetti place.

When I cross the last street, I have to look up. The sidewalk in front of Dev's apartment building holds people, parking meters, garbage cans. No box full of Forester memorabilia, no wall paintings or plants or stylish collared shirts sitting alone and abandoned on the curb. I exhale, and walk a little more quickly toward the parking garage.

Dev's truck is still there. I lean against one of the bare concrete pillars and try to plan a next move. My two options are: wait here until he leaves, or wait somewhere else and come back later, whether that's around here or at Hal's place. I don't like the idea of waiting here stalkerishly, and who knows how long it'll be before he leaves, but also I don't want to leave and have to come back.

The door to the upstairs opens with a bang, swinging free and slamming against the far wall. I shrink back behind the pillar as Dev stalks out, duffel bag over his shoulder, and makes a direct line to his truck, away from me.

His tail lashes. He's clearly upset. My first thought is, *I hope he's okay to practice.* My second is, *He still loves me.*

He throws his duffel bag in the passenger side of the truck and then stops, lifts his head. He sniffs the air.

My scent feels as thick as fog to me. I pull back and lean against the pillar, tail tight around my legs. When I glance down, I see loose shed fur floating in the air beside the pillar. Will he see it? My heart thumps. I want him to see it. I want more than anything for him to come over right now, find me here, grab me and shake me and tell me I am a stupid fox and take me upstairs to hold me and never let go.

Another car pulls into the garage, but even its rumbling can't drown out my heartbeat. I keep my ears perked straight up as it passes.

The fur drifts to the ground and lies there, still.

A door slams. Did Dev get in, or—

An engine starts. I think it's his.

And then whichever car it is pulls out, drives away, and the garage goes silent. I edge my head around the pillar so I can see the empty space where Dev's truck was parked.

Strangely, having seen him calms me a little. He's upset too, going off to blow off steam at football practice. If he were happier, more carefree, then I'd be more worried. And of course he was mad when he found my note this morning. He expected me to come to bed, to make up this fight like all the others, and instead I walked out on him. His anger, like my melodrama, will ease in time.

This peace of mind lasts all the way up the elevator ride to the sixth floor. The locks haven't been changed (of course they haven't), but the apartment when I step into it is. Nothing is out of place, but the smells that hit me all at once are angry, resentful, and sad. Unable to stop myself, I go into the bedroom and sniff around.

Dev's whole night is there on the sheets for me to smell. There's no smell of come, so he didn't paw himself off in the night. That makes me feel better, but only a little, because what I can smell is sadness and some anger. My own scent is still on the bed too, but fainter, and it is very neutral, and Dev's emotions overwhelm it.

I sit on the edge of the bed. I put him through all this. I put myself through all this. Does it reveal cracks in our relationship that we can patch, or fundamental differences we can't overcome? After two years, I would have thought we knew each other well enough to know the answers, but what about me and Brian, ending the closest friendship I'd ever known after three years? What about Father and Mother, ending a marriage after twenty-five years? Is it so odd to think that we might be fine long-distance, but when we merge our lives, we find hidden edges and jagged breaks that pierce each other in tender places?

If it were just me, I would sit here on this bed all day and I would cross my legs and fold my paws in my lap and I would get up when he came back and tell him I don't want to leave him. If it were only me, if Dev were a bewildered and unaffected construct of my imagination who simply did everything I wished, then—well, then I wouldn't be sitting here having these thoughts now.

I'm not even angry with him for the direction he's chosen to take. It would be nice if he pursued the gay rights causes with me, sure. It would be nice if I didn't feel so restless and useless, or, rather, if I didn't mind feeling so useless. But that's not the case for either of us. Dev has football, and I want him to find out how good he can be. I want him to make millions over a career and win championships, and if I had to choose between him having success without me and being an unknown mediocre player with me, I would have to choose his success over my happiness. I've never wanted to be an albatross around his neck (one of the more disturbing literary images), which is what I've become.

So, thinking of him, I pack a bag for about two weeks. At the end of that, we'll either be living here again, or I'll be figuring out a place to move all my stuff.

Hal calls while I'm finishing up the packing. "At the motel," he says.

"I'll be back there in about fifteen minutes. Just getting some things." I hang up and finish my packing. For a good two minutes, I hesitate over the picture of me naked on the bureau. I could hide it from Hal, but that's not the real issue. The real issue is whether I want to leave it as a reminder of me. But if I take it, then that's a signal to Dev that things are over, and that's a message I definitely don't want to send.

In the end, the only thing I take apart from clothes is my little plush fox in his leather jacket. I go into the kitchen to leave him another message, but when I see my original message crumpled tightly on top of the trash, I reconsider. What would I say to him? He already knows I'm going to Hal's. He will know I'm taking my stuff when he sees the clothes gone from the dresser, the shampoo and toothbrush and ear swabs gone from the bathroom. I feel an intruder in the apartment, as though it's Dev's place again, and even though the bag and the clothes in it are mine, taking them feels wrong.

Come to think of that, should I leave the key? I ponder for a moment and then decide to keep it, mostly because I still own some things in the apartment and I'll need to get at them. So I close the door behind me and I lock it, and I don't slide the key back under it.

The first thing Hal says to me when we get into his car is, "We don't have to talk about it if you don't want."

"We can talk a little," I say. "I can't not think about being an activist for a cause, and Dev needs someone who can think about nothing but football for at least the latter half of the season."

"Ah. Career. Kind of like what I went through."

"Is it?"

He pulls away. "Yeah. Pol said she'd always be second place to the journalism, and she didn't like that. Not for her so much, but if we got cubs, would they be second place too?"

"Wait, you talked to her again already?"

"I, uh, called her last night."

"Sober?"

He taps his fingers on the steering wheel. "Mostly."

"Terrific." I shake my head. "You know, if you're going to have a gay BFF giving you relationship advice, you ought to take it."

"Hey, it went okay. She said I could call her again. Sometime."

"I guess it was okay if she was already thinking about cubs."

He snorts. "We didn't talk about cubs. She'd mentioned them on our second date, but I thought...you know, that kind of thing is way down the line and maybe I'll be tired of journalism by then."

"I hear you." I stretch out my legs and sigh. "It sucks. It just sucks. If I could turn that part of me off..."

"Then you wouldn't be you. Listen, Lee, you can work through this kinda thing."

"Really?"

"I dunno. That's what people tell me." He swings a hard turn and heads for the freeway. "I guess there's some people want to be in a relationship more than they want to be themselves. But you never struck me as that kind of guy."

"No," I say. "I guess I'm not."

"Me neither." We merge onto the freeway. "Doesn't mean I don't miss her. Not as much as Cim, but it's more recent."

"You only had, what, three dates with her?"

"Yeah, but they were comfortable dates. She talked about her work and I talked about mine and I felt like I could really talk to her. It wasn't just that she was a good lay." He turns to look me in the eye. "But she was a good lay."

"Watch the road," I snap.

He snorts. "I got it, I got it."

"I don't care how she was in bed," I say. "Dev was good, too. Better than good."

"Okay, stop the reminiscing right there," he says. "You can stay on my couch, but yeah, I don't need details about the sex life."

"You started it," I say.

"You told me you wanted details," he shoots back.

"That was…last week," I say.

He drives along in silence, and I keep my muzzle shut and try to think about anything other than Dev. It's hard when every other building we pass has Firebirds flags or pennants, when the office building skyscraper you can see for blocks away has "GO FIREBIRDS" with one letter in each window, a giant message meant to scream across the city and inspire thousands. It's not their fault that the message has a different meaning for me, but I still wish I could erase it.

It also doesn't help that I don't have much else going on in my life. I could talk to Father, but that would remind him—and me—about his recent divorce. I could talk to Mother and get frustrated about the Families United thing again. I could talk to Hal about that case, but as much as I want to vent to him about it, I don't want to risk him writing up a story that exposes Dev's brother as the lawyer. That'd be all Dev needs, for that story to hit the press. He'd hate me so much after that…

It hits me without warning. I double over in the seat, pressing my paws to my face, and the sobs shake my body. "Whoa, hey," Hal says. "We're almost there."

I try to get out the word, "Sorry," but it isn't understandable through the choked breaths and high keening moans my body is making. I fight hard to get control of myself, but that thought, that Dev would hate me, that hits me worse than anything else. I can't stand the possibility of that.

The tears subside, but I'm only holding back a future flood, and I'm not sure for how long. "I'm okay," I gulp. "For the moment."

"Hey, y'know," Hal says, "when Cim left, I…" He shifts in the driver's seat and stares fixedly at the road. "I did that more'n once."

"I'll try to keep it private," I say.

"I got scotch back at the apartment." His ears swivel toward me. "But I dunno, do gay guys get drunk when they get dumped? I don't have any ice cream."

I half-laugh, but it comes out as half a sob, too. "I don't want ice cream. I don't know what I want."

That's a lie. I know exactly what I want. I also know I'm not going to get it, not today, and probably not for at least one week and—Thursday, Friday, Saturday, Sunday—four days, counting today.

Of course it's not over. But the last few months have been pretty rocky. We've affirmed our commitment to each other and both done stupid things—me more than him, yes. So maybe a week prepping for the championship will convince Dev that it's not worth the trouble to have a too-clever idiot fox for a boyfriend. Or maybe he'll realize how much he misses me. I sure hope to God it's as much as I miss him.

Wait, maybe I don't. I don't want him to screw up his mindset for the championship. No, if I know Dev, he'll just focus on practice and let everything else go by the wayside until the game is over. At least, that's what I'd tell him to do.

Not that he's made a practice of listening to me. Not lately.

"We're here," Hal says. "Think you can make it inside?"

I hadn't registered that the car stopped. "I'm fine." I get out and retrieve my bag from the back of the car, and then look around Hal's neighborhood.

It's low and sandy-colored; the tallest building is three stories, and that's the one we're stopped in front of. All up and down the street are sandy stucco walls and iron-railed balconies, some with bicycles leaning against them, others with pots of cactus and climbing vines whose waxy leaves shimmer even though the sun's behind a bank of clouds. At the corner is a 7-11, beside it a liquor store. Down the street at the other corner is a taco grill, and across that intersection is a small shopping plaza with Starbucks and other small businesses.

The building we've parked in front of us feels a little more alive than its neighbors. Bright flowers dot the cacti, and hanging decorations from the windows and balconies add more color to the desert-toned street.

Like the Firebirds pennants on the third floor balconies to the left and the ground floor patio toward which Hal is leading me. He shoots me an apologetic look, lowering his ears. "I can take that down if you want," he says. "I kind of passed them around the building after the Boxers game."

I shake my head. "No, leave it up."

We walk around the patio, down a small passage into shade and chill that smells of earth and mildew, and Hal takes out a key to open door number 13. "Lucky," I say.

"Always been." He grins and pushes the door open.

Whenever you visit someone's place for the first time, the smell hits you first. It's Hal, and it's many layers of him. I know his scent pretty well now, but it's different when he's relaxing, when he's stressed, when he's sad, and all those little subtle things hit me all at once.

I stop, step to the side to let him push the door closed, and set my bag on the floor. He sees my nose twitch and we have that slightly awkward moment of intimacy where I'm now getting to know him better than I have before. It's not just the scent, of course; it's the long leather couch with tattered armrests; it's the movie poster on one wall and the two prairie paintings on the wall facing me. It's the olive-green carpet with the light layer of shed fur on it, soft under my paws, and the rack of movies on one wall and the big TV and the coffee table with the Stella Artois bottle on it.

"Nice," I say, because you have to, and because it is.

"That's your couch," Hal says, "unless you want to sleep on an air mattress in the office."

"Which would be less disruptive?" I follow him around the couch to a short hallway that ends in the bathroom.

He gestures into a small room, about half the size of Dev's bedroom, with window shades open to let the light in. The walls are covered with framed articles and magazine covers, the desk piled with papers that almost obscure the large monitor on it. "I can move the laptop out of there," Hal says, "and that'd give you more privacy. Been writing a lot of stuff in the bedroom or living room anyway."

"You know you can get flat-screen monitors now that take up like a third of the space?" I crane my neck to look inside. The floor is clear in a large circle around the chair, though the wall just to the right of the door is covered by a huge bookshelf and books are stacked in front of it. There's a smell of salsa and cheese that comes from a wastebasket full of food wrappers. "I think this'll be fine, if you don't mind. I really appreciate it."

"Sure. I'll set up the air mattress. Just toss your bag in there."

I drop my bag on the floor, where it lands awkwardly and looks out of place. I stare at it and lean against the doorjamb. This all feels like a bad dream, except that it's not dreamlike at all. The filtered light through the open window, the smell of books, the taupe-colored walls, the crack in the paint right at my eye level in the door, and the touch of air on my tail, all of these are too insignificant to be unreal.

This is just a waystation, I tell myself, just a temporary stop. I shut out the rest of my thoughts while I help Hal set up the air mattress. He takes the laptop and some notes out of the office and dumps sheets on the bed with a towel. "I don't keep a set schedule," he says. "So shower whenever you want."

"When you're not in there."

"Heh. Yeah."

"Thanks. I'll make up the bed. Later." There is still in the back of my mind a nagging thought that Dev will call and tell me to come home before the end of the day. I have to shove those thoughts aside, because otherwise I won't be useful at all today.

He keeps watching me. "Okay. I have a couple calls to make, and then I was just going to go down to the taco stand for lunch."

"You don't have to change plans or include me in them. I can walk around on my own."

"Well," Hal scratches behind one ear. "Truthfully, it'd be nice to have some company around. And if you don't mind, I could bounce some of these story thoughts off you."

I nod. "I'd like that." It occurs to me that I have a phone call or two that I could make now, too.

So when Hal goes into his room with his laptop and I hear his muffled voice through the walls, I shut the door to his office and sit on my air mattress.

I take out the phone, where Dev's message is still up. I clear it so I won't have to think about it, and then I take a breath. I should call his family. I curl my tail around my hips and take another breath, and another, and I make sure there's no moisture around my eyes. I can get through this. I don't even have to tell them about me leaving.

Duscha picks up after three rings. "Hello?" She sounds a little out of breath.

"Hi. It's Lee." She doesn't say anything, and I say, "Dev's—"

"Yes," she says brightly. "Hello, Lee. I am sorry, I did not think you would be calling. Did you want to speak to me, or…"

"Yes." I inhale, steady myself. "I need to ask you a favor."

I tell her briefly about the Vince King case, which she says she remembers discussing with Dev, though they didn't know it had gone to court, and she clucks about why people need to sue about everything in this country. But she agrees that it's tragic, and that's when I have to tell her that I want to make sure Dev is free to concentrate on winning his football game, I don't want him to be distracted.

"Of course not." She sounds puzzled.

"I found out that Gregory is one of the people defending Families United in the King case."

The phone line is as quiet as Chevali at two in the morning. "Our Gregory?" Duscha says faintly.

"Unless there are two Gregory Miskis practicing law." Shut up, fox, don't be snappy with her. "I mean, I didn't call to find out if that's a common name, but…" Shit, just get to the fucking point. "I tried to file a brief with the court and they said I have a relationship with him, and Dev's brother is the only one I, so, um, yes. I think it has to be."

"This is…" She trails off. "Well, perhaps his company ordered him to do it."

"Maybe." I don't know Gregory a hundredth as well as she does, but she doesn't sound much more convinced that it's a mistake than I am. "He mentioned doing pro bono work for his company."

Back at Thanksgiving, that was. When I mentioned Families United to him.

"I will call him, I will find out…"

"You know him best," I say, "though I wouldn't call him, if I were you. But please, please, don't mention it to Dev. And make sure Gregory doesn't either. It'd…it'd just distract him, and the championship is so important."

"Yes." She sighs. "Sometimes your children go off in directions that you could not anticipate. They are grown up now, and they have to make their own life."

"That doesn't mean you have to stop talking to them." I say it before I realize that I don't know which of her sons she's talking about.

"No, of course not." She gets what I mean, because she says, "Lee, will we see you at the game? Misha is buying our airplane tickets today."

My throat closes up. "I hope so," I choke out in what could maybe pass for a normal voice twisted by unreliable phone signals.

I'm being ridiculous, I think after we've said good-bye. Dev's not going to just throw all this away. Once he's won the championship game, he'll talk to me and we'll work things out. We'll figure out how to make this work with me doing what I need to and him doing what he needs to, and I'll be seeing Duscha again.

That's the hope, anyway, hoping that Dev and his family don't go the way of just about everyone else in my life except for the swift fox in the next room, who is probably only letting me crash here out of kindness and because I don't have another place to go. I mean, we don't know each other that well…not really. Inevitably, I'll do something to piss him off and then we'll drift apart.

I dial another number when I've calmed Melodramatic Lee down a little. Father answers almost immediately. "Let me guess," I say. "You're about to go into a meeting."

"My Thursday morning meeting doesn't start for forty-five minutes. What's going on?"

"Well." I take a breath and then tell him. I spill everything except, oddly, the crucial bit about Gregory, for no other reason than that I don't want to tell too many people. I just say that I can't keep the activism out of my life and his, and it was starting to get destructive because we were both edgy about it all the time, and finally I just left to give him peace and he was mad about me leaving.

"Don't you two have fights all the time?" he says.

"Yeah, but. This is different. It's not just…I mean, I feel like it's something different about the way we…about our philosophies."

He laughs and then catches himself. "I'm sorry, I don't mean to make light. But you're so young. This all happened last night, and it's your first big difference. You'll talk it out."

"You and Mother didn't."

"We talked a lot."

"Really?" The word slips out before I can stop it. Of course they've talked about things. Just because I've never seen it doesn't mean it didn't happen.

Father goes on. "We had fights, we had conversations. Honestly, when you went to college, it made things a lot easier. We weren't staying together for you anymore."

"Wait, it started before I graduated?"

"Wiley. I told you that this wasn't all about you. Your mother was bored, looking for something to do with her life as you were growing up and needed her less. She turned to places that I wouldn't necessarily have thought were appropriate. We had a lot of talks. She said those groups gave her something that she wasn't getting elsewhere. Our common ground shrank year after year."

"I thought she liked to write articles for magazines."

"Yes, but…" He sighs. "There's only so much you can write about when you're not leaving the house. So she felt she had to go investigate places to write about them. She visited a lot of community organizations. Her family was always very involved with charities. When you…invited us to that dinner…" The one where I told them I wasn't going to graduate, where Dev showed up to support me and possibly, in retrospect, intimidated Mother and confirmed that I really was gay. "She reached out to people in the community who had dealt with similar issues. I thought at the time it would help her deal with it. But it went in another direction."

"A crazy direction."

"At the very least, it was less expected. Knowing her family, though, it wasn't a huge surprise."

I lean back against the wall and close my eyes. "I thought she was so proud of not being like the rest of her family."

"Age does funny things. You start missing the things you were comfortable with growing up and then rebelled against later. When cracks appear in your life, you start wondering if rebelling was the right decision. Sometimes you just don't have the energy to keep rebelling. In your mother's case, well." I hear him tapping his claws on his desk. "I think when her father died, it hit her hard. They'd never had a chance to make up."

"But they fought. They hadn't talked in years."

"Imagine if your mother died tomorrow, with your anger and hers still between you. You'd feel pretty lousy."

"Well, yeah," I say. "My mother would've just died. But I wouldn't go straight and find Jesus and…and deny who I am."

He exhales. "I don't think you would. But I also don't think that this is denying who she is. I think it's just a part of her that she kept repressed for a while. You can't do that forever."

"I can't do it for two weeks, apparently," I say, and that brings back thoughts that I would rather not be exploring on the phone with my father. "Oh, by the way, you don't need to talk to her about the court case. I got what I need another way."

"Okay. Useful info?"

"Um. Not really." Talk about cracks appearing. I squeeze my eyes shut and try not to feel the spiderweb of cracks all around me, in every aspect of my life.

He's quiet, mulling over whether he wants to ask me more about it. I forestall the question. "It's complicated. I'd rather tell you about it in person."

The thought of seeing my father in person is surprisingly reassuring, an island of stability I cling to. He says, "Okay," and then goes on. "You and Dev—Wiley, you'll talk it out. You're a passionate fox and he's got to know that. Passionate people hit highs and lows and have fights and work it out. Your mother and I kept things a little more quiet, which is great for a stable home in which to raise a cub. Maybe not so great for working out relationship issues."

I shake my head. "I don't know. We yell a lot and he seems to take it pretty hard when we do."

"You've had these kind of fights before."

"Yeah, but..." How do I explain this? "The stakes...it's the championship for him, and for me it's...it's this whole mess of stuff. I had a chance to do some real good and I keep getting it cut off at every turn."

Father chuckles again, then catches himself. "May I remind you again that you are young? You'll have more chances and they will come around again and again."

"Not chances like this one."

"Yes. Not this exact one, but others like it."

"But this..." My voice catches. "This is the one I wanted."

"Okay," Father says. "Do you have anyone there you can talk to?"

"Yeah. I'm staying at Hal's." I rub my eyes. "He's a good guy. We've been hanging out."

"All right. Look..." His voice softens. "If you need to talk, call me at home this evening. I don't know what I can offer, but if I can help at all, or if you just need to talk to someone..."

"Thanks," I say.

Hal's on his phone in the other room, his voice a low murmur through the wall. I close my eyes and lean my head back. It's not a tiger's voice, and my nose isn't filled with a tiger's smell, but it's another island, a part of my life that, at least for the moment, is solid.

Chapter 12 – Moving On (Dev)

Thursday is cloudy and cool and perfect weather for stomping around a football field and slamming into tackling dummies. "Easy," Gerrard says after I bounce off of one dummy and stand there panting. "Save something for the game."

"I've got plenty for the game," I growl, then stand up and go at the dummy again.

Gerrard and Carson do sprints and footwork drills, which to be honest are probably more useful than tackling drills at this point, but I feel like tackling things. Not that I'm imagining that the dummies are Lee. I push any thought of him out of my mind as soon as it comes in. I'm focused on football, perfecting my technique and being the best I can be.

In the afternoon, the backup linebackers come around and we go over film and formations. There's little deception involved in Crystal City's offense. They run a lot of standard formations and they run them very well. They have a quarterback who can thread the ball through a tight seam, an elk at running back who just doesn't quit, and a rabbit and fox at wide receiver who make coverages difficult. We review film of our game against them, and even though I didn't play a lot in it, Gerrard points out Korey's mistakes as though they were mine. "He's cheating here, and the quarterback sees that," he says. Or, "Here he's watching the quarterback instead of his assignment, and the wolf just looks him off so he isn't in position when the throw comes."

"I know my assignments," I say. "I know what I'm supposed to be focusing on."

Gerrard looks around the room, past me to Zillo and Marais and the couple others sitting there. "Don't put too much pressure on yourselves," he says. "Yeah, it's the championship game. But in the end, it's just another football game. The lights are brighter, the crowd louder, but the other team is the same as they were at the beginning of the year, and the football is the same, and the ground feels just as hard when you hit it." He stretches the corners of his mouth back in a narrow-eyed smile. "So make the other guys hit it."

The backups murmur behind me, but I stare ahead at the screen. "Keep going," I say.

Gerrard and Carson have to drag me out to dinner. Even then, I stay at the steakhouse until everyone else has left for one last night with their families. Zillo and I sit there nursing our fourth beers of the night, with our bills sitting on the table in their faux-leather folios, our plates long since cleared away, only crumbs and meat juice stains left on the tablecloth.

"You don't have to hang out with me," he says. "I know you've got your fox to go home to."

"Yeah." I let the beer wash over my tongue, barely tasting it. "I don't mind."

He flicks his ears back, then cups them toward me. "Everything okay?"

"It's fine," I say. "I'm just antsy to get on the road and get to Crystal City to practice."

"All right." He pulls down another drink of beer. "I don't know how I'm going to get to sleep."

That question's been on my mind, too. "Can't you just hook up for the night?"

Zillo laughs. "Probably. But sometimes I just wanna be by myself, you know how it is?"

"Sure," I lie.

He squints at me again. "You sure you're okay?"

"I'm fine," I snap. "Fine. I'm going to be great once we get to C.C. and I can settle into the hotel."

"Is your fox coming later?"

"Probably, yeah."

"He must be pretty excited for you."

I drain the rest of my beer. "You know, I think I will get on home," I say. I toss a hundred on the table and stand up. "I'll see you at the plane tomorrow."

He blinks up at me. "Sorry," he says, and his ears are back. "Look, if I said something wrong…"

"Nah." I hold up a paw. "It's not you. It's just some shit I gotta deal with, that's all."

"Okay." He digs into his wallet and covers his check, then stands up. "Lemme know if I can help. I mean, I dunno what kind of things you guys have to deal with in relationships or if that's even what's going on…"

"It's fine," I say, and we're quiet, walking out of the restaurant.

Near the cars, Zillo speaks up again. "You know how I get ready for games?" I shake my head. "I listen to Cold-T's 'Stone Cold' album like twice in a row all the way through before bed. Then I've got it in my head the next morning and like all day. It gets me pumped up for special teams and shit, it's great. You wanna try that?"

"Nah, thanks," I say. "Not really my thing."

"I didn't think so." He grins. "There's this one song, though, 'Knock 'em Down,' which just goes like, nnf!" He punches the air and raps a couple lines. When I don't respond, his grin falters. "Anyway, it's pretty awesome."

I feel bad because I know he's trying to help, but all I can do is wish him good night and drive on home. The sun's set already and the air is cool. I roll the window down and lean my elbow out, and I feel sort of like I did on the Forester campus back in the day, when the team was doing well and everyone was excited to be seen with us. There aren't many stars visible with the city lights on, but I drive past Firebirds pennants and a big "GO FIREBIRDS" in the windows of an office building downtown, and that cheers me up, lifts my spirits. The whole town's pulling for me, for us.

As I get closer to the apartment, I slow down. I stop at red lights and stop signs and observe the speed limit. I don't know what to expect. Maybe Lee will be waiting there with an apology and a bottle of wine, or maybe he'll be at the door naked and we'll just have the best make-up sex ever. He didn't text me at all today, but he's prone to surprises like that, so I wouldn't put it past him.

But then I wonder what tomorrow would be like. I mean, sure, I want to make up and fuck him and hold him and wrap my tail around his leg, so bad it almost hurts. But how long before the tension creeps back again, even if I try to do everything right? He said himself that he was having trouble keeping it in, and that was when I was trying to be helpful and understanding.

Maybe he'll get a job. Then he'd be distracted. Again, though, that just papers over the problem.

But shit, haven't we been papering over the problem for years? I mean, my parents don't have a perfect marriage, but they stay together, they tolerate each other. They don't have big screaming fights, as far as I know, but I know Mom has her local friends and Dad has his work friends and they don't overlap a whole lot.

That line of thought makes me think of Lee and his father and mother, and then I squelch that because I don't really know all that much, just that they split up. But it darkens my mood. Maybe Lee won't be there in the apartment after all. Maybe he's serious about leaving, about us spending time apart. After all, I guess we got along really well when we were living at the top and bottom of the country. So maybe he's just figuring he'll go back to that.

Still, I avoid the spot where his car is (was?) parked, so I don't have to see whether it's gone, because I kind of feel like it is. Then I pull into the parking garage and just sit in my truck. I don't know what I want, if I want him to be there so he can apologize, or if I should apologize (because I feel sort of like I should, though I'm not quite sure why), or if I want him to not be there because that would make things easier leading up to the game, or if it would make things easier or just harder.

If today's any indication, I can stop thinking about him long enough to play. If I can keep that up for a few more days, then I'll feel better about going into the championship game.

Funny. I never thought I would be better at football if I stopped thinking about him.

That thought doesn't sit well with the confused mess of anger and loss in my chest. Fuck, I am not going to cry. I'm not. I'm just going to sit here and squeeze the steering wheel.

Finally, the need to use the bathroom drives me upstairs. Four beers inside me doesn't leave a lot of room for anything else. So I slam the car door and slam the elevator door and squeeze my legs together the whole torturous slow ride up until the door clatters open and I can get my key in the lock.

Once I've finished in the bathroom, I step back outside. I already noticed that Lee isn't in the apartment anywhere. Standing in the bedroom, I lift my nose, but his scent is suffused through everything, like the fine layer of his fur all over the apartment, and I can't tell when he was last here. I think it was more recent than last night, but I can't be sure.

Then I notice the bottom of the closet, where his overnight bag is gone. And when I check the dressers, there's one shirt of his that I notice missing, which means there's probably more missing, too.

I kick the closet door shut and go into the kitchen, but there's no note on the fridge. He didn't even have the courtesy to say good-bye or anything, not by text, not by phone, not by calling me. Even after our fights, he was always the one who made sure to talk to me, to tell me what he was doing. And now…nothing.

There's still beer in the fridge, so I take one out and sit on the couch. The UFL '09 disc is still in the game console, but when I turn it on, I just sit and stare at the startup screen and I can't make myself start a game. I down the first beer and then go and get another, and still the players on the startup screen run through the same motions, over and over again, never changing.

Drinking brings back the anger and the loss. He's only been living in the apartment for a few months, but already it feels wrong without him.

My tail slaps the couch restlessly, so I get up with the beer and walk into the bedroom. The bed's sheets are still mussed from when I got up in the morning; he didn't make the bed because he wasn't here. And he didn't sleep with me that night.

God dammit, why is he so obsessed with his gay rights crusade? Why can't he just be a supportive boyfriend for two fucking weeks? And why can't I let it go, why can't I be more like he wants me to be? I do care about gay rights, if it's not already fucking obvious to the world by this point. But it can't rule my life. I have a job to do, and if I cost myself a million or ten million dollars because I've had a meeting with some senators that ultimately doesn't matter anyway, how does that benefit gay people? Once I get a big payday, I can donate to charities and causes. And the money isn't even the issue. I think about Fisher, how passionate he is about playing, how one injury cost him half the season and another might cost him a chance to play in the championship. I don't even have the history he does. An injury could leave me with nothing.

And nothing is what I feel like I have right now. When I sit down on the bed, I notice the naked picture of him, smiling at me. I remember him saying *I promise I'll never go anywhere*. Well, fuck. I lash out and smack the picture off the dresser; it smashes against the wall with a tinkle of shattered glass and falls to the floor.

Immediately I feel shitty, and the disappearance of his picture makes the real Lee's absence that much more painful. I press my nose to the bed, inhaling his scent. Before I know it, I'm crying into the sheets. There's a moment where I try to stop, and then I think, fuck it, better get it out now. So I let myself cry, while at the same time I shred parts of the blanket with my claws and then the beer falls to the floor with a clatter and I'm pulling the sheets off the bed to throw them aside. I kick them all into a pile, wiping my eyes, and drop to the bare mattress. The pillows smell like him, so I sweep them aside as well, keeping only one, the one that smells like me, and I press my face to it and shudder on the bed, gasping into the cloth.

Moments, hours, hundreds of tears later, I prop myself up on my elbows. So I'm alone, I guess, just like that. My phone lies still in my pocket, so I fish it out. No calls from Lee, no texts. Nothing. Well, fine. If he's not thinking of me, then I will show him I'm not thinking of him. I text him, though it's hard to see the letters as my thumb slides over them.

Fine them. Maybe dee you Shen I've get back. Marble.

The phone's changing my words as I type them? Is it supposed to do that? I hit Send anyway and then drop the phone to the floor and press my face to the pillow once again. I inhale my scent, only mine.

In the morning, I have a mild headache from drinking too much beer and not enough water, made worse by the chirping of my phone. "Sorry," I mumble as I answer it, vaguely remembering something I said last night.

"You'll be sorrier if you're not here in like twenty minutes," Fisher says sharply. "You know it's Friday, right? Even that damn cheetah is here."

"Wha?"

"Trying to make me take one of his fucking shakes. Listen, just get your tail down here. They're not going to hold the plane for you."

Plane? Oh shit. "Dammit. I didn't set an alarm." I scramble out of bed, still holding the phone to my ear. "And I didn't pack. Stall them, Fish."

"Fucking rookie move, Dev!" He's yelling. "Why didn't Lee make sure you were up?"

"Don't yell at me!"

"Then don't fuck up like this! Asshole. Fuck, I'll do what I can. You're on your way, right?"

"Yes, yes, fuck yes." I stand paralyzed in the middle of the room for a second and then grab my bag out of the closet, which reminds me of Lee's bag—no time for that. I throw clothes into it and then grab my toothbrush and toothpaste. I cram everything into the bag and force the zipper shut and tear out the door, locking it quickly and then giving only one glance to the elevator before taking the stairs, three at a time.

It occurs to me halfway down that if I land wrong and hurt myself, it'll be the biggest jackass move of all time—talk about a pointless career-ending injury. But all that tells me to do is stop thinking about it. I trust my body to do the things it needs to, and what it needs to do right now is get me down the stairs and into my truck.

The clock in the truck blinks at me: 9:53, 9:54. I'm not going to make it to the airfield by ten, no way. I run a red light at an empty intersection and speed down the two freeway exits.

It's 10:06 when I park in the airfield lot, grab my bag, and run to the charter building. Thank God: the plane is still sitting there on the tarmac, the stairs are still down. And Fisher's standing at the base of them.

"Thanks," I pant as I get close.

He reaches out and smacks my cheek ruff. "God damned rookie mistake," he snarls. "That's the sort of thing that'll get you fined, that screws with team chemistry. We need everyone on the same program. Get on the damn plane."

For a moment, I want to slug him back. But I lay my ears flat and run up the stairs. My seat next to Charm is open. I head for it amid catcalls from the team: "Glad you could make it," and, "Hey, your dick made us all late," and shit like that.

Charm elbows me as I sit down and says, "Long good-bye to Mrs. Gramps?"

"No." I reach for my phone to turn it off and see that there's a message there from Lee. My thumb hesitates over the button. The doors are closing now for takeoff, but we can use our phones for a while still. And hell, it'll be murder on me if I spend the whole flight wondering what the message was. So I call it up.

Did you just break up with me over text message?

Fuck.

Did I? I look at the message I sent him last night, drunk and angry. I don't think that's a breakup message. Did he want it to be? I stare at the words and feel my anger rise up again, but here I can't throw the damn phone.

Why would he go right to breaking up? Sure, I was angry, but I assumed he would be the one coming back to talk things out because he always talks. Now he's talking about breaking up and I guess I can see where it comes from, but I don't know how to react. I don't want to break up, I don't want to lose him, but I don't know what to say to him that he won't twist around and throw back in my face. So I type, *Let me just get through this game.*

Then I turn off the phone, because I don't really want to see his response. We're going to have to have a conversation, and maybe that conversation will end well and maybe it won't, but it's got to wait until I get this other thing off my plate.

Charm's being really quiet, so I look at him and he's got a big melodramatic face on, staring down at my phone. "You're breaking up?"

"Shut up!" I look in front of us, but it's just a couple O-line players and they've got headphones in. "I don't want to talk about this."

"Okay, well." His expression changes. "I know some good clubs in C.C. if you want a distraction."

The plane turns and then goes into its takeoff run. I lean back and close my eyes, pressing a paw to my head. "Right now I just want to listen to music and have a big glass of water. Or a Bloody Mary."

"Can do!" He raises his voice over the rumble of the engine and the shaking of the plane as we climb in the air. "Hey, Gramps here is hung over! Can we get a glass of water?"

Of course we can't, because we're taking off, but the whole plane breaks into laughter. Zillo says from two rows behind me, "I'd have stopped you drinking if I'd known!"

"I'd have stopped drinking if I'd known," I call back.

"I tried to tell you about that," Strike says, but I ignore him. Of all the people, I don't want to deal with him right now.

At least now they all think I was just drunk. "Thanks," I mutter to Charm.

He shrugs and grins. "For what?"

We escape the ground and soar skyward, and the comments die down. I put headphones in and turn on my music and close my eyes. When the flight attendant brings my water, I drain it in one gulp and ask for more.

An hour later, there's bright sun and hazy air that welcomes us to Crystal City before the pilot does. The plane hits the ground with a series of jolts, and Coach stands up before we're finished taxiing.

"Welcome to Championship Week," he says, ears up and a smile on his long muzzle. "For the next week and a half you're going to be eating, sleeping, and breathing football. We have a chance to do what no Firebirds team has ever done, and we will need your full concentration and participation to do it. Practice starts today with a light workout, then we'll scrimmage on the weekend. Next week, light practices and film study, and full-contact practice Thursday. Friday and Saturday, conditioning and more film study. Sunday, we're going to go out and win a championship."

We all cheer, raising fists in the air. Even I feel better. He turns to sit down, and one of the coaches says something to him. He turns back to us. "Oh, right. Tuesday is Media Day. You're all going to have time on the podiums with the reporters and you're going to get asked maybe two good questions and a whole lot of stupid ones. I only have one order for you: don't say anything about the Sabretooths unless it's about how good they are and what a challenge this is. I don't want anything pinned up on their locker room board Sunday morning to get them fired up. Got it?"

"Yeah, Coach," we chorus.

"Bunch of fucking children," he says, but his tail wags as he sits down.

I reach for the phone automatically and then shove it back in my pocket. I don't want to see what he responded. I don't want to see that he didn't respond. So I can wait. There's nobody I need to call here in C.C. unless I want to call Keith up again and see if he can recommend a good gay bar.

No. Football, just football. That's what my life is going to be for the next week. I follow the guys off the plane and onto the bus, inhaling the curious mix of millions of scents and ocean and chemical haze that I've come to know. I look outside at the dusty pastel buildings of Crystal City and squint into the sun. I walk into the Ambassador Hotel without looking to either side, and Charm and I get our room assignment and go unpack.

"So what's happening?" he asks.

I stare at the clothes I've unpacked. I have enough pants and shirts, but I completely forgot to pack underwear. I've got some Ultimate Fit gear left in my bag from the last road trip, but that's it. "I need to go shopping."

"I mean with you and Mrs. Gramps."

"What the hell do you care? You never had a relationship that lasted longer than a raunchy teen comedy movie."

"Not true." He points a finger at me. "Once I took a girl to see 'Yearbook 2' and *then* I fucked her. But that's me. You were all into the relationship thing."

"Relationships end," I grumble.

"Sure, sometimes." He grins. "I dunno, you guys seemed to have it figured out. You fight, you don't fight. Opposites attract, right? Ain't that what that song says?"

"Songs don't know shit." I play with the phone.

"Well, what'd you fight about?"

"Oh, come on," I say. "You're giving me relationship advice?"

He lounges back on his bed, hands behind his long head, muscular legs extended across the sheets. "I got lots of experience keeping relationships short," he says. "So I figure I'll just tell you to do the opposite of what I normally do. Right?"

I turn the phone on. It takes a moment to connect and get a signal. "Can't be worse than the advice I'm giving myself, I guess."

"Okay. What you gotta do is tell the truth. When he asks if you're going to call him, say yes, and actually do it. Oh—and always give him the right phone number. Definitely don't give him one for a fur-dye salon in Dry Gulch. That'd send the wrong message."

"Thanks." I watch the message indicator pop up, and the voicemails. Maybe one of the voicemails is from him. I open the text message first and read it.

"So what are you going to do?" Charm asks from across the room.

I turn the phone off and drop it on my bed. "I'm going to play football," I say.

"I mean about Mrs. Gramps."

I don't feel like listening to any of the voicemails now. I drop to the bed and close my eyes. "I'm not doing anything about him. He can do whatever he wants."

Charm doesn't say anything for a few minutes. I think he's dropped the subject, and then he says, "Well, if you don't care what he does, then you should…definitely call him up and see what he's doing. Maybe invite him over."

"Shut up, kicker," I say.

"You know, maybe you should just play football," he says.

"Thanks." I lie on the bed with my eyes closed.

There's another pause. "You know it's eleven-thirty in the morning, right?"

"Shut up."

Chapter 13 – Temporary Housing (Lee)

Wednesday night when I get Dev's garbled probably-drunk text, it takes me a minute to decipher it. "Marble"? Wait, "maybe"? *Maybe* he'll see me when he gets back? It makes me furious and desperate all at once, and I lash out back at him because I can't believe he would say something like that. And because I go all quiet staring at my phone after it beeps, Hal watches me with his ears perked and finally says, "It's from him?"

The night outside is dark and quieter than Dev's downtown place, suburban streets where the cubs are in bed by nine and last call is at midnight. Hal's curtains, plain olive-green, are drawn across the window, giving his living room a cozy close feel. We're both sitting on his couch watching some dumb action movie, which he paused to let me deal with the text message. My tail curls around my hips and my ears are down, so it's probably easy for him to figure out something's wrong. I'd guess my scent might have changed, except I've probably had that blue depressed tinge to it ever since I showed up.

I look up at him and nod, shortly. "Did you ever do something you regretted when you were drunk?"

He laughs. "Hell yes." Then he looks at the bottle in my paw. "That's only your second. You a lightweight?"

"No. I mean, did you ever do something you didn't mean? Or did you just regret it because you didn't want to say it out loud even though you meant it?" The phone is warm and heavy in my paw. I don't want to hold it any longer, so I put it down.

"Hell, mostly I regretted it 'cause I woke up the next morning with God's own headache and a screeching in my ears." He pauses. "Sometimes the screeching was the girl I'd picked up when I was drunk."

I stare down at the phone. "Ever say anything to Cim you regret?"

"More often than I care to admit. Not when drunk, though. That whole *in vino veritas* thing is a load of shit. Being drunk drops your inhibitions, sure, but it also confuses you. Well…" He leans back in the couch corner. "We had a big screaming fight once when we'd polished off a bottle of wine. It was good, though. We got it all out of our systems and then we were too tired to do anything about it 'cept crawl into bed together. And in the morning I said, 'I'll get the aspirin,' and she said, 'I love you,' and…" He spreads his paws. "These things get worked out."

"You think this'll get worked out?"

He meets my eyes, still with a slight smile. "Well, let me say this. I never saw a couple did so much to drive each other away and still stay together as I did with you two. It's a pain in the ass for anyone to be married to an athlete. It's not just that they live in a different world where they're gods, and it's hard to be in a relationship with a god. It's the travel, it's the obsession that they have to be the best there is and they can't let up even for a minute." His voice softens. "Doesn't leave a lot of room for thinking about anything else in their lives."

"Dev's different. I thought." I stare at the phone and then turn to Hal's sympathetic muzzle.

"When he wasn't starting, maybe. The reserve guys can be pretty laidback. Collect a few hundred grand for a decade, don't play that much. It's a good life. It's what I'd want to be if I were an athlete. But then you've got the starters, the top-tier guys, and well, you know how Ryan Marcher's on his third wife now."

"He's got two championships."

"Uh-huh. And he didn't get 'em by being a good husband."

I pull my knees up to my chest and feel the pressure of tears there again. My throat feels scratchy and the whole length of my muzzle feels too warm. "So there's no hope, in the long run."

"Hell, I ain't saying that. Just saying it's hard. Dev's starting, but he's got this pressure behind him because he thinks if he slips, the team'll cut him, what with the whole gay thing and all."

"You think they wouldn't?"

"I don't think they'd cut him just for that." He takes a drink of his own beer.

I don't know what to say to that. In the silence left by the absence of our conversation and the movie, I hear the low purr of a car outside, and then it's gone. There's an insect drone in the background and the smell of cactus flowers. "I hope we'll talk it out. But he's not answering."

"If he was drunk, maybe he passed out."

"Maybe." I turn the phone over and over and then set it aside. The bottle of beer isn't cold any more, but it fills the space left by the phone. I take a drink. "Let's finish the movie."

There's still no text from Dev by the time the movie's over. I sit on the couch with my tail wrapped around my legs while Hal takes the bottles to the recycling. He comes back and sits on the far side of the couch. "You want to talk about this?"

"What, more? What's to talk about?"

"I dunno." He waves a paw. "Thought I'd offer. I mean, if you were a guy whose girl'd just walked out on him, I'd just bring out more beers 'til you passed out."

I weigh the thought of that. "Doesn't sound like the worst idea in the world."

"Yeah, if you weren't staying in my office maybe."

"What, you'd rather I drive home?"

He laughs. "I'd call you a cab. You could throw up there and I wouldn't have to deal with you in the morning."

"I don't throw up from drinking," I say. "Promise."

He eyes me, rubs a paw along the back of the couch. "You want another beer?"

I reach up to rub my throat. "Not particularly. Tea maybe?"

"Right. I'm not sure what you're expecting, but I got Lipton and that's it."

"Just something hot with a flavor," I say. "Do you have honey?"

He gets up, tail swishing. "I have a jar full of some honey crystals and maybe some liquid."

"Oh, that's easy," I say. "Just boil a pot of water and hold the jar in it for a few minutes. It'll all liquidize again."

He's at the kitchen door; he turns and eyes me. "It's goin' in the microwave," he says. "Don't get all 'Queer Eye' just because I'm letting you crash."

"Why are you letting me crash?" I ask as he disappears into the kitchen.

"Where else do you have to go?" He makes some clatter, getting a pot out.

"Hotel."

"You're unemployed and I don't really think you wanna be living off his salary while you're working out relationship issues."

I lean my head on the back of the couch and close my eyes. "I have some money saved up. I just made a thousand dollars for not catching a football in a commercial."

The microwave starts. Hal comes back to lean against the kitchen door. "You're a friend," he says. "How about that?"

"Works for me." I sigh and play with the tip of my tail. Loose fur drifts away from my fingers, down to the floor. "Thanks. I'm glad to have a friend here."

"Talked to your dad at all?"

"Yeah. He says it'll work out, that we're passionate people."

"Isn't that what I said?" The microwave stops and there's more clattering.

I perk an ear, but the sounds aren't resolving well. I swallow, and my ears pop. "Fuck, I think I'm getting sick," I say.

"You better not bring anything from that skanky motel back here. Shoulda called me first thing." He's just thrown a bunch of pots on the floor, it sounds like.

"If I'd known it was such a production to make tea, I'd have taken another beer," I say.

"It's not a production. I just had to wash this one out, and it unbalanced all the others."

"I don't want to come in there, do I?"

"Probably best you didn't, nah. Give me a minute here."

So I just lean my head back and wonder if I'm going to be starring in this 'Odd Couple' drama for long. I wonder how long it'll take Dev to get back to me, or if he'll just ignore the message and call me stupid. I'd like that, for him to tell me I'm being stupid, for him to come get me to take me back. It's not going to happen; he's going to be on his way to Crystal City in the morning. But it would be nice.

In my hazy half-sleep state, I imagine Dev's scent, mixed with the sharp tang of black tea, and when the tea smell gets stronger, I open my eyes and expect to see his smile, his black-and-orange striped muzzle, one immense velvety paw holding out one of the white teacups we bought. Instead, it's a mug that says "Hang In There" and has a picture of a monkey hanging by one arm from a tree branch, there are coffee stains all around the edge of it, and the paw holding it is a dusky tan color with worn, blunt claws. Hal's got a nice smile, but he's not Dev, and for a moment I just stare at him.

"What?" he says. "I told you I had Lipton and that's all. Don't tell me you couldn't smell it."

"No, I…" I reach out and take the mug. "Just half-dozed off." I turn the mug to see the "Hang In There" picture. "Thanks for the encouragement here."

"Well, you know. Whatever I can do." He has a glass of water for himself, which he sets on the coffee table—an old piece of furniture with a fair number of what Hal calls "war wounds" around the edges. I keep the mug of tea in my paws and inhale. The steam feels good.

And I can't stop looking at the stupid monkey hanging off the branch and thinking, that's me. That's me trying to hang on, and there's no point really. I'll never pull myself back up onto the branch. The weight of my situation flattens my ears, crushes my chest. It wasn't Dev bringing me tea, and

Dev isn't coming through the door to bring me back to the apartment, and sometime in the next couple weeks I am going to have to figure out whether I'm staying here or going to live with Father or maybe waiting until I hear back from Peter Emmanuel to get a place in Yerba, which would be the best option, really, because then I'd at least have something to do.

"You okay?" Hal says.

I start to say I'm fine, and my throat closes and I can't get the words out, so I just shake my head, knowing it's stupid of me, knowing I shouldn't start crying again, knowing that there's nothing I can do about it.

"Aw, geez," he says. "Sorry about the mug. Look, if there's…" he pauses.

I wave him away. "Not your fault," I choke out. "Just…just everything."

"Look. You wanna get some sleep?"

I don't know if I'll sleep, but at least I'll be alone in the room. So I nod, and he stands up and comes over to me. He rests a paw on my shoulder and helps me up, and the touch is comforting, reassuring. I let him walk me to the spare room, keeping both paws wrapped around the mug as we go.

"Now, look," he says. "I got a meeting in the morning, but I'll take it from the bedroom. You need anything, you can pretty much help yourself."

"Thanks." I stand in the room and turn to face him. I feel drawn in on myself, my tail tight against my leg, arms close against my sides, ears flat. "G'night."

He raises a paw and closes the door, leaving me alone with my thoughts and the smell of tea, overwhelming everything in the room. I sit on the mattress and hold the cup, which is finally cool enough to sip. But after one sip, the bitterness of the cheap grocery store tea lingers on my tongue and I set the cup down.

I cross my legs and lean back against the wall. My eyes can't stay open, but my mind can't stop whirling. It's the same old images of me and Dev, of the text messages, of all the events of the last few months going around and around, his resistance to doing any of the Equality Now spots, my inability to stop thinking about it. How could I imagine that any of it would get any better? The end of football season will only be a reprieve. Maybe we can date from February to July and otherwise we're on our own, until his career is over.

If the world will let us. The news about Gregory wasn't just an unlucky chance; it is an end result, and that it circled around to crash back in on us is only poetic justice. Just as Dev's well-meaning walk to my side in that restaurant may have driven my mother to Families United, my own well-meaning standing at his side at Thanksgiving may have driven his brother to them. Even when we try to do the right thing, our actions cause twisted ripples that come back to us black and weighted with the prejudices we're fighting against. And if I hadn't gotten involved with the court case, if I'd just let it go, I never would have found out about Gregory. I'd be sleeping next to my tiger right now, he'd have his arms around me, and tomorrow morning after he left I'd be in our apartment—*our* apartment—playing UFL '09 or prepping for my trip to Yerba.

Hal moves around, getting ready for bed. My ears are stuffed again; the noises are distant and irrelevant to me. I lie down to try to force myself to sleep, through the bathroom noises, the getting-into-bed noises through the wall. Brief fantasies of going in and curling up with him, just for comfort (because sex is about the farthest thing from my mind right now), remain nothing more than brief thoughts; Hal would not be into that, I'm not in any shape to do it, and besides, I don't want to be the kind of guy who'd crawl into bed with someone else the day I maybe got dumped.

I didn't get dumped. That's ridiculous. Dev loves me too much for that. We'll talk tomorrow, or later in the week, or at least after the game.

The rational part of my mind isn't the one I feel inclined to listen to, not at two in the morning when Hal's been asleep for an hour and a half and I'm still lying half under the blanket, tossing and turning as if there's a magical position that will bring sleep to me, as though it's not the lack of a tiger in the bed with me that is keeping me awake. My throat is so dry and scratchy that I drink the cold, bitter tea, and then I lie there and wait for the taste to fade.

It takes a long time.

•

I must have slept, but I don't remember it. I remember turning over and seeing only streetlights shining through the window. Then the room was brighter, light grey. Then it was brighter still, and the next time I looked up, it was morning. Now Hal's voice comes through the wall in a reassuring murmur, and I lie and listen to the pleasant rhythms, wordless baritone thrumming life into the apartment.

It reminds me of sleeping in on Sunday mornings at home, when I could hear my parents talking downstairs and I knew I'd be called for church in fifteen minutes, ten, five. Until that happens, though, I'm in my own world, curled up here, safe from everything outside. My throat hurts more, and my head feels warm, but maybe that's just because the rest of my body feels cold. I curl my tail over my stomach and hug it to me like I did when I was a cub, sick in bed. Beside me, my plush fox watches me, and looking back at his glass eyes relaxes me a little.

My phone beeps. I crane my neck to stare over at it. The screen brightens with a message, but I can't read it from this angle. Slowly, I reach out to take it in my paw, but by the time I get it near my eyes, the screen's gone off again. I bring the phone up and read Dev's note: *Just let me get through this game.*

Get through this game. He's still thinking about football. He doesn't miss me at all. I'm sitting here miserable, throat killing me, without having slept in pretty much two nights, hugging my tail, and he's still worrying about his football game. That's just great. So I type back, *Fine. You want to be on your own, good luck.* And I throw the phone down.

Of course it's unfair of me, and I regret typing it as soon as the phone hits the floor. But lying there with my eyes closed, the importance of the game has receded dramatically. I want him to be distressed. I want him to be repentant. I want him to miss his flight to C.C. (the one he's probably already on) so he can come here and we can fix this. And I know as I'm thinking it that it's not reasonable. I know in the back of my head and in my heart that he still cares about me. But I can't stop arguing with myself. If he cares about me, why hasn't he said so? Why has he just left me here at Hal's without even asking how I am? (Never mind that I didn't ask how he is.)

And, worse, wondering what this means about me. I've been part of a couple for almost three years now, and I've put that ahead of almost everything else in my life. Without Dev, now, I have more freedom, but it's about the last thing I want. I wasn't ever *not* free with him; if I get the job in Yerba, he'll be supportive. If I want to do Equality Now work on my own, he'll be supportive. It's just that he has his own life, and now our lives are separate.

Well, not completely. I don't think they'll ever be separate. Look at me and Brian, for example.

Or don't. There was a time when I would've wanted to call Brian and complain to him about how I was being treated, but those days are gone. He'd be so gleeful at the prospect of our breakup, and then he'd offer me his couch to stay on, which would turn into his bed, and yeesh. As nice as it would be to sleep in a warm bed with someone, I'd rather stay on this air mattress being sick than be in Brian's apartment feeling his desperate clinging to the past.

And I don't want to cling to the past either. So I should just let go, at least until after the game. Let Dev play his best without me, because he's already made it clear he doesn't need me.

I curl up against the bed and try to breathe through my nose, because my throat is raw and the air is so dry, but my nose is half-clogged and I can't. I look around the room for tissues and only find a few Neutra-Scent wipes; I try one, but it makes me sneeze and gives me that weird feeling in my nose, like there's a scent there that I just can't detect. I throw the wipe in the trash can.

I despise fucking Neutra-Scent. It's supposed to make it easier to live with us strong-scented people, and easier for people with sensitive noses to live with everyone. You know, so our scents don't intrude on each other all the time, so we can live our separate lives blissfully ignorant of our fellows. Well, I'm both: I can sniff out a tiger at fifty feet, and he can sniff me out a day or two after I've been somewhere. And I get along okay without Neutra-Scent. We never had it in the house when I was growing up, not even for company.

When Hal knocks on the door, that's the first thing I say to him: "You don't even have proper tissues in here, just fucking Neutra-Scent."

"Well, yeah." He scratches below his ear. "In case I get some red foxes in here stinking up the place."

"I can't blow my nose in these." I sit up in bed and kick the box.

"Jesus Fox, no," Hal says. He reaches up to a bookshelf and grabs a box of tissues. "Why would you try?"

"Because I didn't want to blow my nose on your sheets. Thanks." I take the box and grab several out, pressing some to my nose and some to my eyes.

"Are you sick or just still, you know…"

"Both." I try to blow my nose, but it's not really that stuffed and it just makes my throat hurt more. I struggle to my feet. "I can make some tea myself."

"You okay with Lipton again?"

My tongue finds the places in my muzzle where the bitter taste still lingers from last night. "Is there a coffee shop in walking distance?"

"It's Starbucks."

"God dammit." I stand there with the crumpled tissue in one paw, staring at the carpet. "I guess their tea is okay."

"That's the spirit." Hal grins. "I got this thing almost wrapped up. Let me scribble a few more notes. You want to shower?"

"Sometime," I say. "I can wait 'til we get back."

The sun is out, bright and piercing, which seems vastly unfair to me. I have to squint at everything because I left my sunglasses at Dev's, and my eyes water from the reflections off the sidewalk, the ochre sand in the front yards, the tan stucco walls of every building. "Why can't they build dark buildings here like they do in Hilltown?" I grumble. "Everything's so damn bright."

"Any word from your tiger?" Hal judiciously ignores my whining.

I show him the phone and the last exchange, because I don't really feel like saying the words. He reads and then gives me the phone back in silence. We walk to the corner of the street and wait for the light.

"It sounds like maybe you broke up with him," Hal says carefully.

"He's the one who told me to leave him alone."

"Until after the game."

I don't feel like going into all my reasoning with him. "He didn't even ask about me. He doesn't care."

The light changes, and we cross. Hal's tail swishes, the shadow distracting me as we walk because my tail doesn't have any life in it at all. "He's playing in the championship," Hal says finally. "He's doin' what he needs to do. You oughta do the same. Then after the game, you guys can talk."

"Sure. We can." I see the green sign of Starbucks up ahead. Instinctively I look around for an alternative, but of course there's very little else around, and zero in the way of coffee shops.

We cross the parking lot and go in to the air-conditioned sameness, the bland coffee-friendly smell that permeates every one of these stores I've ever been in. I stand behind Hal as he orders and then asks me what kind of tea I want. "Don't care," I say. "Something for a sore throat."

The perky desert rat behind the counter has a smile I have to squint at. "I'll get you a chamomile. That always helps me when I'm sick. And we've got some honey packets you can put in it."

"Thanks," I mumble.

"Aw." She smiles. "I hate when I get sick, too. Don't worry, it's just a cold. It'll be over soon."

"Thanks," I say again, and then wander away because I don't want to talk to her smile any more. Maybe she's hitting on me.

I stand and stare down at the newspapers, and of course in the local Chevali Herald there is a big story on the Firebirds, and there's Dev's face staring out at me. I can't quite look away. I just stare, and then Hal is grabbing my arm and I'm letting go of the paper. "Hey," he says. "I'll buy you a tea, but you gotta get your own paper."

"Oh, shit," I say. "I'm sorry." I fish in my pocket and come out with my wallet.

He holds out a cup, condensation showing through the plastic top. The floral scent of the tea breaks through my nose as I take it. The steam feels good on and in my muzzle. "And here," Hal says.

Three honey packets lie in the paw not holding his coffee. "She said to put one in the tea and take the others with lemon juice when you get home. I said I didn't know if we had lemon juice and she said that orange juice would be okay."

"Thanks." I take them and shove them in my pocket without even checking to see if they're sticky.

"Then she told me to take care of you because you seemed really cute and we made a nice couple."

It takes me a second to parse this, and then I take a quick step toward the register, where the rat's already talking to someone else. Hal grabs my arm, but I shake him off. "I'm okay," I say.

"I thought you'd think that was funny." He shakes his head. "Didn't think you dumped your sense of humor."

"Great. Thanks." I stalk to the exit.

He hurries after me with his coffee and calls a quick "thanks" to the baristas. Outside, he catches up to me and says, "Hey, listen. If you're gonna get through this, you're gonna need to get through it quick. You can't go back to him all whiny and needy with your nose running, because that's just a turn-off."

"And you know him so well."

"No." We stop at the corner again, waiting for the light. "I know how I went back to Cim."

I swallow against the raw skin of my throat and look at him, bringing the tea to my muzzle. "I wouldn't," he says. "Still too hot."

The steam is in fact still as powerful as it was in the store. I lower the cup. "How'd you go back to Cim?"

"Well, my nose wasn't running."

"Mine isn't running." I swallow. "Will be in a day or two if this is a typical cold, though."

"Great," he says. "I'll lay in some orange juice."

We cross, the asphalt warmer than pavement under our paws. I still get moments when I look around and think, wait, it's January? The sun, the fifty-degree weather, it's all wrong for the season, and it adds up to everything else that's wrong about my life. I squint ahead and flick my ears toward Hal. "So?"

"Ah," he waves the paw that isn't holding coffee. "We had a conversation and I said some things I don't wanna repeat. I don't think she'd have taken me back even if I were all strong and independent. But I'd feel better about myself."

"So, what? I should be strong and independent?"

"Sure. That so hard?"

We amble slowly down the street. I can't see his tail's shadow now, but I can still feel its motion against my fur. "Am I not being independent?"

"Okay, well, I grant you, you've always seemed pretty strong. Maybe that's why this is kind of unsettling. Didn't think you'd be the one going to pieces over losing him. Kinda thought he'd be the one."

"Maybe he is." I think about Dev losing it during practice, or crying in his bed in some hotel. "I hope not."

Those words come out without me thinking about them, and they feel true and honest. That calms me a little bit. "Well," Hal says, "I'm just trying to get you past this initial shock so you can be more...more *you* when you face him."

"I'll be fine." I inhale more steam from my cup. "I'll be me. I'm just sick and running on like five hours sleep the last two nights."

His ears perk. "Air mattress not comfortable?"

"No, it's fine. I just..." I rub my throat. "Combination of the sore throat and thinking about stuff. I'll probably nap today and I'm sure I'll sleep well tonight. And you know what, I should call Peter. Emmanuel."

"The fox from Yerba?"

"Yeah. He was worried about conflict of interest. I guess I should tell him he doesn't have to now."

"Oh, I wouldn't do that. I'd just say that you've worked things out and that if necessary, Miski'll sign an agreement saying he won't disclose anything you tell him. Paperwork, that's what they want. Cover their tails."

"Yeah." That actually sounds reasonable and makes me feel better. I had been looking forward to the cathartically bitter statement that Dev wasn't part of my life any more, but after two days that seems extreme, and it would open up the conversation to a lot of questions I don't necessarily want to deal with in a business call.

So when we get back to Hal's, I shut myself in the office/guest room, sit cross-legged on the air mattress, and call up the Whalers. It's past eleven here, so after ten in Yerba, and Emmanuel should be in his office. In fact, he answers the phone himself.

"Secretary out of town?" I ask.

He laughs. "Whole office is taking a holiday. Can't do a whole lot until the championship anyway. That's the official position. I'm in here all the damn time. What can I do for you?"

"Well, uh. I wanted to call and talk to you about the conflict of interest thing." It's a plausible place to start, an easy way to give him new information without just calling to ask what the status is.

"Oh, yeah. You told Jocko that Miski would sign an NDA, right?"

"Right." I'd forgotten about that. "He said we never talked about prospects when I worked for the Dragons, but he understands the need for you to have something more concrete."

"I think that'd be great. Not that we expect you to be giving away secrets, but…"

"No, when two people share a life, you know, I know how things just kind of…" I trace a claw along the side of my phone. "Come out. Sometimes you don't know what things you need to keep secret."

He laughs. "I guess so. Yes, if you can get Miski to sign some paperwork, that would help. I mean, if we end up offering you the job, which we're not going to do anything about until the season's over. Not that we can't, just that DeJordy always leaves his changes 'til then. Old school. Otherwise he thinks it shows up like he's trying to take attention from the championship. Sour grapes kind of shit. So anyway. Let's straighten out this paperwork, then see where we are. Your references came back pretty glowing, to be honest."

I assume that includes Jocko, because honestly, if the interview'd gone badly, Peter would be making excuses about why they couldn't bring me on. So I guess I did okay. "You talked to Morty?"

"Flew him out here for a day. Between you and me, we might be picking him up too. But that's strictly confidential."

"That'd be terrific." My tail twitches, like it wants to wag but has forgotten how. "I'd love to work with him again. Is he definitely leaving the Dragons?"

Peter clears his throat. "Anyway, all that aside, I wanted to ask if there's a good time for you to come out here and meet the rest of the office in person. I'm guessing you're going to the game?"

I take a sip of the tea, which is now cool. It tastes pretty good. Damn. "Actually," I say, "I don't think I am."

"Oh." He pauses. "Do you want to? We might be able to swing some tickets…"

It's tempting. "No," I say. "It's okay. I'm sure I'll have other chances. I mean, Yerba's going to go to some in the next few years, right?"

He laughs. "Yeah, we sure hope so. Well, if you'd like to come up here and watch the game, I invited Morty too."

216   *Uncovered*

I swallow. My throat feels a little better. "Could I bring a guest? There's a local reporter—freelance journalist, sorry—who's a good friend of mine—really, the only friend I have down here…"

"A journalist?" His distaste shows as clearly as if I could see his ears flatten, his muzzle wrinkle.

"He's a good guy. He knows sports, but he won't publish anything he sees. Promise."

"Sports journalist, huh? He know people up here?"

"Um. I'm not sure. Maybe?"

"Has he pissed off anyone up here, is what I'm asking." He sounds amused.

"He's been out of work for a couple years, but I don't think so."

"Well…"

"It's okay," I say. "I can just come alone." I figure I have to be willing to give in, to show I can be a good employee. I'll let Peter be the benevolent future boss.

He doesn't disappoint. "What's his name?"

"Kinnel. Hal Kinnel."

Peter clicks his tongue. "He did the piece on you and Miski, didn't he?"

"Yeah."

"Look, go ahead and bring him if he wants to come. I'll straighten it out here. Just tell him he's not a journalist while he's here, he's a guest."

"Okay. Thanks."

And when I hang up, I take one of the honey packets straight up, let it coat my throat, and wash it down with tea. My throat feels better for a few minutes, and the tea still tastes good. Dammit, I don't want to start liking Starbucks.

I hold the tea and lean back against the wall, closing my eyes. I've been not letting myself believe in the job, but Peter keeps sounding more and more confident, and if they're flying me up to watch the game, maybe they do really want me. If only everyone did. The idea of watching the game with them is interesting, and with Hal along I'll at least have someone I know if I start getting emotional about the game. Maybe…maybe…

I blink. The sun is less bright, and there's a blanket over my lap. I'm no longer holding the tea, and my neck is a little sore. I straighten, rubbing it, and check the time on my phone: 3:14 pm.

So I did nap for a bit. I get up and walk out into the living room, where Hal's on the couch with his laptop and a basketball game on TV. He grins as I walk in. "Feel any better?" he says.

I press fingers to my throat, which is still raw and dry. "Not really," I say. "Not about anything. But the tea was okay."

"We'll get you a Starbucks card," he says.

"Fucking hell." I cross to the couch and sit on the far side, drawing my legs up and my tail around my ankles. I fold my arms, keeping as close in on myself as I can. "Thanks for the blanket."

"Don't mean we're engaged," he says. "Just, you looked a little twitchy and I always like having a blanket when I'm getting sick."

"I hope it's just a scratchy throat," I say, though my head feels thick and warm. My memory is thick and sludgy, too, and it takes me a moment to bring back the conversation with Peter. "I might've gotten you an invitation to come watch the championship. With the Yerba guys. They asked me up and said I could bring you."

"Well, that's right nice." He looks up from the laptop, smiling, and flicks his tail. "Lessee…" He rattles off a couple names and asks if they still work there.

I shake my head. "No idea. So you want to come?"

"Yeah, sure. Thanks."

He goes back to his writing. I watch the mesmerizing back and forth of the basketball game, all different species working together, passing and shooting the ball, until a commercial comes on for a truck that isn't Dev's model or color but still reminds me of him, of standing in that parking garage and listening to the engine rev up. I turn away and look at the swift fox, tapping away at his keys.

"Okay, so what do I do now?"

He doesn't look up from his typing. "Want to get your car?"

I think wearily about driving all the way back, seeing Dev's apartment building again, driving back here alone following Hal's car. "Not really."

"Okay then. What do you usually do?"

"Wait for Dev to get home. Go shopping. Watch college games, or movies. Play video games." Call Brian. Write up documents to a court case that has nothing to do with me. Jerk off to porn or memories of my tiger or both.

He pauses his typing for a moment, but still doesn't look up. "Wouldn't recommend the first, and if you're getting sick, you shouldn't go out, and there's no college games on and I don't have a game console." He nods toward the shelf of DVDs. "I'm not really into the game. You can throw something in if you want."

I peer at it and force myself up out of the couch to stumble over to the shelf. "You have a lot of sports movies."

"Uh-huh." He's typing again.

"And a little chick flick section. That's so cute." He doesn't respond. "Is that just for you to impress the ladies, or is it your secret shame?"

"It's out on the shelf, ain't it?"

I chuckle and then cough, and then curse myself because it hurts. I don't want a chick flick anyway, so I grab a basketball movie I haven't seen and kneel in front of his entertainment unit. I figure out the DVD player okay, but I can't figure out anything else about it. It seems like everything's in the wrong place and I miss our system at home.

"I'll get it from here," Hal says, tapping a remote next to him.

The basketball game's back on. "You can wait 'til the game's over if you want," I say, and close my eyes.

PART III

CHAPTER 14 – FOCUS (DEV)

Hoffridge University, an hour south of C.C., loans us their field and equipment for practices. There's students and media buzzing around every time we take the field, so Coach and Steez keep some plays back, out of the spotlight. The defense as a whole takes extra unofficial practice on alternate evenings from the offense. Gerrard's extra practice philosophy is catching on with the whole team, and though we're exhausted after three full days of this, everyone feels pumped up.

I'm doing a pretty good job of keeping my focus. It sucks that I'd just gotten used to living with Lee, but for the first three months of the season and the two months of pre-season and practice before that, he'd been living in Hilltown, so it's not like it's a big deal that he's not around. Going home to a hotel and not to the apartment makes it easy to keep that out of my mind. Charm helps, in his own way, but it's still hardest at night, when I pick up my phone to call him, hold it for a moment, then put it down again. He doesn't text for the rest of the week, and though I think about texting him every night, I'm worried about what it might start if I do, if I might be scratching at scabs and pulling out fur. The searing anger and hurt from the flight out to C.C. lingers in my memory, dulled now by time and distance and football. If I reach out, I might end up frustrated and angry again, and I can't blow off steam by taking him to the bedroom afterwards. So I have to let it go for another week.

Steez is happy with us when we break practice Sunday. We can tell because he only grumbles a little bit about the things we've been doing wrong, and our list of plays he wants us to focus on is down to about five. So we head to a bar to hang out, because it's the offense's night to practice, and we're all exhausted anyway. All except Fisher, who hasn't been allowed to work out, and is still on edge about whether he'll be able to play or not.

They closed the bar for us to hang out in—it's a popular college bar, and there are muzzles pressed against the window, cameras going off, sometimes with flashes. We ignore it; our media guy Vince will let us know if there are any real media around to talk to, and we're just supposed to be relaxing tonight. I chat with Zillo and Gerrard for a bit, and when Gerrard gets up to go home early and Zillo gets drawn into a conversation with Marais, Gerrard's backup, I go sit with Fisher.

He seems mellow, talking to one of the defensive linemen who's been here three years—came over from Pelagia like Fisher did—about how the league's changed. When I sit down, he laughs and says, "But Dev here don't remember those days."

"I saw 'em on TV," I say.

"Yeah, wasn't the same. Eh, Wook?"

Wook, a shaggy brown bear, downs half a pint of beer in one swallow and then belches. "Sure wasn't," he says. He sets down the empty and gets up. One paw goes briefly to the gold cross hanging around his neck. "Hey, I'm gonna go see what Brick's doin'."

"Okay. Catch you later." Fisher raises a paw as the bear ambles off. "He's a good guy," he tells me.

"I know he's great on the line," I say, trying not to think about why he chose to walk away right when I walked up. I know there are at least a few other people on the team who have a problem with me, but at least they don't make waves over it. And he's not talking to Colin, so I'm not that upset about it.

"He played against…" Fisher goes off into a football story, which normally I'd be all over. I listen patiently until he lifts his beer, when I break in.

"Hey, you've been through—wait, should you be drinking beer?"

He sets the glass down hard and licks his lips free of foam. "What? Because of the concussion?"

"Well, uh…"

"I don't have a concussion," he says, a little loudly. "In fact, they might clear me to play in a day or two."

"If they haven't cleared you to play…"

"Are you my doctor?" I just stare at him. "Well? Are you?"

"Fish—"

"Because if you're not my doctor, then keep your fucking medical advice to yourself."

I'd really like to just walk away at this point. I mean, really. My claws are extended and I have to force myself to pull them back in. "I wanted to ask you about Media Day."

"Can I drink my fucking beer while you ask me?"

"Yes. Fine. Whatever."

I wait while he orders another one, and then he turns toward me, a smile lifting his whiskers. "What do you want to know?"

"Well…do you have to answer all the questions? I mean, I've seen your Media Days on TV, and it looks like you answer all the questions, but they're always cutting in and out. Can you ignore the ones you don't feel like dealing with?"

Fisher shrugs. "It's just a press conference, really. You call on the people you know, and you call on some of the weird ones to see what they're going to say. Give 'em the same bland answers and you'll be fine."

"Yeah, I guess." I rub my paws together.

"You've already dealt with all the gay stuff," he says. "What do you think they're going to ask you?"

I shake my head. "I don't know. I don't want to be 'the gay football player.' I just want to be a football player."

He snorts. "Good luck with that." The bartender brings him a beer and he drinks right away, not even looking at me. "They will sniff out any angle they can use to ask you the most inane questions, and when you just hand 'em an angle on a platter like that…well…"

"I know." I sigh. "So just be bland?"

"Like you always do. Unless…" he grins, "unless you wanna put on a show."

I snort. "Thanks, Fish. Enjoy the beer."

I walk away wondering whether I should call Gena and tell her he's drinking. I'm sure he's only having the beer now because she's not around to smell it on his breath when he gets home. But fuck it, it's not my problem, and his snide little comment about putting on a show makes me even less inclined to worry. Let Gena talk to Lee about it. Seems she'd rather talk to him than me or Fisher anyway.

Out of perversity, I go sit near Strike, who is by himself. I know that he tends to drive people away with his attitude, and I'm one of the few people on the team who can stand to be with him for long periods of time. Not that he looks unhappy, sitting at a high table against a window, leaning back into the curtains. He looks like a monarch surveying his people, pausing every now and then to look down and play with his iPhone.

He greets me with a smile as I come up. "Anyone sitting here?" I ask of the obviously empty seat next to him.

"Help yourself." He taps his iPhone. "How are you liking the phone?"

"Oh, it's great." I don't want to show him the cracks in mine. Less than a month and I've already broken it.

"Check it out, I got this game for it. It builds mental fitness and reaction time." He shows me some game with interlocking pieces that you have to identify quickly before they explode.

"Cool," I say.

"You can get it on yours, too," he says helpfully.

"I'm okay for now. Let me know when you can get UFL '09 on them."

"Ha." He grins. "You joke, but it's probably not too far out. Not drinking?"

I shake my head. "Not really in the mood right now. Trying to keep loose." Also I don't want to get over-emotional in front of the whole team, and it's hard enough to keep a rein on my emotions when I'm sober. I point to his glass. "You are, though."

"It's just a gin and tonic." He brushes his fingers along the glass. "Game's far enough away that I can have a drink. It'll be purged by Sunday."

"Okay." I sit quietly, resting one arm on the table, looking out at the team. Every so often I'll catch a smile from someone, or a wave, or just a look. But nobody wants to come over here and talk, not with Strike next to me, and that suits me fine.

"What's on your mind?" the cheetah says.

I drum fingers on the table. "I'm not sure. I'd like to be able to get through the rest of the week just playing football, not talking to anyone about my life or any shit like that."

"Really?" He turns to face me, grinning. "You know, if you want to build up your image, you need to talk to people."

"I guess," I say. "But I don't particularly want to do that."

"Oh." He turns his whole body now, leaning across the table. "I thought that's what you were doing with the commercial. Oh, tiger, listen, you have to work on your image. That's a five million dollar difference right there."

"Between what and what?"

"Between the contract you'll get as a good football player and the contract you'll get as a good football player with a good image. Like with all the fur dye and everything I do, you know? Only don't you start dyeing your fur." He laughs. "It's expensive if you want to use organic chemicals that won't wear out your fur."

"The dyeing thing is not me," I say, with maybe a little more snap than is necessary. "I know I'm gay and all, but—"

"Whoa." He leans in a little closer. "You know what the dyeing is about, right?"

I frown. "I know it's not about being gay."

He laughs again, but differently this time. Maybe I'm just imagining it, but the laugh sounds a little nervous and condescending all at once, kind of like he's wondering, *Wait, do they really not know?* Or maybe, *Wait, do they think I'm gay?* "Look, I like you, so I'm telling you this, but don't spread it around. It's not about me. It's just keeping my name in the news."

I stare at the red and gold designs drawn around his eyes, down the bridge of his nose. "There's not a better way to do that?"

"There's a lot of ways to do it," he says. "I got this idea from that warthog in the basketball league. But he just changed the top of his head." He rubs between his ears. "I thought, why not change all of it? And now, before every game, people want to know how I'm colored, what it looks like. I've done modeling shots for GQ, too. Me!"

"You've got a good body." I regret saying that right away, but he doesn't take it as a come-on.

"So do you. So does everyone in this room. But they picked me. And so lots more people saw me and know my name."

"But they just think of you as that weird cheetah who colors his fur."

He taps the table. "But they think of me. Sure, you gotta back it up on the field, but how many of my Firebirds jerseys you think they've sold?"

"Uh…" I shake my head. "I don't know. Where would I even find that out?"

He grins. "You'd get your agent to ask the front office. Number one Firebirds jersey the first half of the season was Aston's. Number two was Jaws. Number three was Marvell."

"Makes sense."

He holds up three fingers. "In three weeks with the team, they sold more jerseys with my name than they sold of Aston's all season."

"New player," I say. "Lots of fans already have their number 12."

"You're not doing too bad with sales yourself," he says. "Though not as well as I would have thought. Talked to your agent about that?"

"Not really." I haven't talked to Ogleby at all in the past week other than to tell him that I'm not doing any non-sports-media interviews. He's certainly never mentioned jersey sales to me.

"Might be the gay thing," Strike says. "You were in the top fifteen of players on the Firebirds when I checked. Might have gone up. It usually spikes after you make a really good play in a win."

"Sure. I'll look into it." I scratch the table with one claw. "But the jerseys don't actually make you any money, do they?"

"A little," he says. "The point is, they make money for the club. You know the owners aren't just trying to put a winning team on the field, right? They want to make money. That's why I wouldn't be surprised if Yerba goes after you in the off-season."

"They need a linebacker, I guess."

"They need someone who can attract the gay community. You know how many jerseys you'd sell? How many people would come to games or come out to Whalers events? It'd be epic. If I were gay, I'd be signing with Yerba or I would've stayed in Port City."

My claw scratches deeper into the table. I picture a frenzy over the beginning of each game, not because they think I give them a better chance of winning, but because I'm gay. Lee would be so proud. My chest tightens. "I like it here."

"Oh, sure. This club is tremendous. Coach has a great rapport, the front office doesn't fuck with you every week, locker room is super mellow, and we're winning games. Best trade I ever asked for. And they have really loose curfews. It's great. Hey, are you going to look up Keith? Or is Lee coming out?"

"Lee's not coming out." I retract my claw and look at him. "Hey, you said something about tantric meditation…"

His expression becomes serious. "You can't just start meditating because you miss your boyfriend."

"No, I—" I back off instinctively and then say, "Wait, why not?"

"Well, it's a discipline. I mean, would you shoot baskets in your back yard and then go try out for an FBA team?"

I frown. "Are you competing against anyone with this meditation?"

"I'm just trying to say, it takes a long time to get good at it. You're not going to properly sublimate your frustrated energy if you're just starting it this week. You're much better off looking up Keith, or heading over to the West End and going to one of the clubs there."

"Oh," I say, "is that where they are?"

He shrugs. "I have some gay friends. There are terrific restaurants there. I don't care if the waiters think I'm cute, and they know not to hit on me."

"Makes sense." I slump back in my chair. I guess I'll just jerk off a lot this week, then.

"Hey, you know what else would help?"

I perk up my ears. "What?"

"There's a restaurant around the corner. Totally organic vegan. They make the best tofu burgers."

I slide off the chair. "You know, I think I do want that drink after all."

Chapter 15 – Sick and Tired (Lee)

It's probably crazy to think that my relationship with Dev was keeping my immune system up. After all, I had colds while we were together. I just can't remember one this bad, and I say so, often. Frankly, the last three days have been so bad that to call them "crappy" would be putting too positive a spin on them. My throat got progressively worse on Friday, to the point that Hal got me a small bottle of Southern Comfort to help me sleep. I drank half of it and started crying about Dev and locked myself in his office out of embarrassment. But I did sleep, albeit kind of passed out half-on, half-off the air mattress, and woke up with my muzzle open and my tongue lying across his carpet, which was damp and smelled pretty gross. As a reward for one good night of sleep, my throat improved slightly, while my nose, the whole length of my muzzle, started getting warm and congested.

Saturday, I stayed in Hal's office most of the day blowing my nose and playing a solitaire game on my iPhone and trying hard not to think about football at all. I caught stories about Dev here and there, unavoidable in Chevali, but not in the newspaper when Hal dragged me to Starbucks (God help me, I like their tea), and not on TV, which was generally set to non-football sports or movies.

Sunday I feel more miserable, but well enough to drag my laptop out to the living room and listen to music while Hal goes out for groceries. I leave some money on his counter but he doesn't take it; he's as stubbornly fox-proud as I am. It took me two days just to give in to the cold and admit I should be resting and not doing anything. I did send my legal brief to the lawyer, mostly so I wouldn't have to think about the court case. She e-mailed back Friday night to say it was fine, and that's the last time I checked my e-mail.

"Doing any better?" Hal asks when he comes back and sees me nestled in a corner of the sofa, tail wrapped around me.

"No," I say dully.

"Not sleeping for three nights in a row will do that," Hal reaches into his grocery bag and tosses a canid-strength decongestant onto the couch next to me. I fumble with the box, tearing it across the silhouette of the fox with the glowing red masses in his nose and muzzle, and then scratch with my claws at the foil seal around the pills while he goes to the kitchen and gets me a glass of water.

"I've got orange juice," I say, huddled in my blanket. I reach for a tissue and blow some of the endless supply of crud out of my nose. "How many of these do I take?"

"What's the box say, genius?" Hal brings the water out into the living room and sets it down next to me. "You should take the pills with water. Gulp orange juice the wrong way and it burns. That's what my mother told me."

I peer at the box and rub my watering eyes. "Says two pills every four hours."

"Then I reckon that's what you ought to take."

"If your ass was any smarter, your tail would be a mortarboard tassel," I grumble, popping two pills into my paw.

"Is that some kinda college wisecrack? They didn't have them at Whitford where I did my journalism Masters," he says, with an exaggerated aw-shucks accent.

I toss the pills onto my tongue. They catch in my rough throat, and I gulp water, working at swallowing until they go down. "God, I hope these work," I say.

"Gal at the pharmacy said they're the best," Hal says. He swishes his tail and sits on the other side of the sofa.

I turn away from coverage of some Kanatian arctic fox preparing to compete in the Winter X Games and hold a tissue to my nose again. "Hope you don't get sick."

"Oh, I don't plan on it." He grins and lifts a paw to scratch his whiskers. "Say, um. You gonna be okay if I head out for dinner tonight?"

"Sure." I wipe my nose. "I can, uh, walk down to the taco place. Where you going?"

"Just out, you know. With a friend."

"Okay. You don't have to tell me who it is." But from the way he's acting, I think I know. My ears flick; I make an effort to keep them forward. "You know, just because my relationship is in the toilet doesn't mean I won't be happy for you. So what happened?"

"Well, Pol called back." He flicks his ears back and loses the grin. "Um, she liked the flowers. Said we could go on a date again. Talk about shit."

"That's great." But instead of being happy for him and leaving it at that, I imagine Dev calling me, maybe agreeing to talk about things for a bit. With a small flare of pain, I shake those thoughts free. After all, he's been in Crystal City for—what, it's Sunday, so, three days? If he were going to call, he would have. Anyway, if he called right now I would be blowing my nose every five minutes, coughing and miserable, and either I'd be snappish because I'm sick, or he'd feel sorry for me, or something. It's not the ideal frame of mind to have.

"Thanks for taking care of me," I tell the swift fox, and he snorts. "I mean it. You can have an evening off. I won't die or anything. I hope you guys work things out."

"Yeah, me too. I mean, it's nice having you around to produce snotty tissues, but I kinda miss someone I can kiss."

I make kissy-lips at him and try for my husky female voice, but I only get as far as "You can kiss me—" before the rasp in my throat makes me cough, and snot explodes into my paw. I fumble for a tissue as Hal laughs.

"Sexy as that is…I'll hold out for Pol."

"Straight guys," I mumble through the tissue. "No sense of adventure."

"I got plenty sense of adventure," Hal says. "If I wanted snot blown on me, I woulda had cubs."

"Cubs." I remember Gerrard's cubs and Fisher and Gena's older cubs. "Glad I haven't had to deal with all that."

"No younger brothers or sisters?"

I shake my head. "You?"

"Older sister. She's married and lives in Pelagia working for a game company. We talk on holidays. I'll get you another box of tissues."

I've just pulled the last one out of the box and emptied my nose into it. "The trash is full, too," I say, dropping the used tissue onto the pile. At his baleful look, I flatten my ears. "I'll empty it," I say.

"Nah." He shakes his head, picking it up.

"When do I need to be out of here by?" I call after him as he takes the can out to the back patio where the big garbage bin is.

He comes back in and drops the emptied can by the couch. "You can stay here. We're going out to dinner and if we go back somewhere, it'll be her place. I'll tell her I have a sick friend staying with me."

"Should win you sympathy points," I say.

He winks. "You'll be useful one way or another."

"So…" I pause, not sure how to bring this up. "I mean, you still have those differences, right? She still doesn't want to be second-fiddle to your work?"

"Yeah." He says it slowly.

"Are you going to be able to talk through that, you think? It's not going to be too big a thing?"

"Not if we don't let it."

I think about that. Is it possible that Dev and I are just letting a little thing spiral out of control? But then again, I mean…what do we really mean to each other? Are we just together because he can't find anyone else and I've lost touch with everyone else? I don't think so, but it's really hard to think clearly when you have to blow your nose every two seconds and breathe with your mouth open. Reminds me of a story about a society where everyone has to be the same intellect, so the smart people are handicapped with distractions.

Good lord, us English majors are pretentious when we're sick. Even non-graduated ones. Apparently a cold is enough to burrow down through two layers of working in the sports world to remind me of esoteric things I read five years ago.

"Hey," Hal says, "mind if I change the channel? This is only slightly less boring than the actual Winter X Games."

"Sure." I sniff, and rub my watering eyes.

He finds an action movie and we watch for a while, because I can't muster up the energy to do anything else. My nose clears up as the decongestants start to work, and I get a floaty light-headed feeling that makes me a little dizzy and uncomfortable.

Eventually he goes to get ready for his date, and when he comes out in his blazer, shirt, and tie, I look up from my third mindless action movie of the day. The color combination is enough to stir me from the lethargy of the cold and its medication.

"Really?" I say. "That's what you're wearing?"

He stops in the middle of adjusting his collar and looks at me. "What?"

"What?" I cough, trying not to laugh. "Um, okay. Let's start with the blazer. Are you going on a date in 1990?"

He frowns down at the blazer. "What's wrong with it?"

"Oh, the cut, the stain on the inside of the left sleeve…"

His ears flatten. "You can see that?"

"Oh my god, Hal, please don't wear that thing. Did you wear it on a date with her before?"

"Once," he mumbles, starting to slide the blazer off.

"Then you should thank your lucky stars she's agreeing to see you again." I blow my nose. "Maybe she thinks she can help make you over or something."

"Maybe she thinks it's cute," he snaps, but he tosses the blazer onto the couch. "Better?"

"Do you have a tie that doesn't fight with that shirt so much?"

"I have that gator-skin one you got me." He folds his arms and looks down at his tie.

I shake my head. "You were married, for Fox's sake. What about that thing you wore the first time you came and met me at the sandwich place?"

He frowns. "I wasn't wearing a tie then."

"No, I know. I mean, that shirt. That would go with that tie."

"I have to go in two minutes."

I stare at the shirt with what I hope is heavy meaning, but is probably ruined because I have to wipe my nose in the middle of it. "Better to be late and look good than on time looking like that."

He glares at me, grumbles, and then goes back into his bedroom. Five minutes later he comes out in the other shirt, adjusting the tie. "Now? Can I go?"

It's kind of cute. The shirt is rumpled, so ideally I'd tell him to press it. I have the feeling he probably fished it out of the dirty clothes pile. And he should have a nice tie pin for his tie, and his fur is a little mussed still. But overall, he'll do. "Brush your headfur down," I instruct him. "Then you can go."

He stomps out the door a moment later, but his tail is wagging, so I feel better about things overall. And his blazer on the couch suggests something I could do to repay his kindness.

I haul my laptop out of the office and look around at some online stores. I check the blazer size and find him a couple nice jackets that will go well with his shirt, but hopefully won't look too fancy to him.

When I complete the order, I notice that it's using Dev's credit card, the one he just pays every month without really looking at the bill. I hesitate. I really should use my own credit card, the one I haven't touched in ages. So I start to add a new credit card to the site, and then realize that I have no idea whether I changed the address for it. I sit and stare at the computer screen, trying to work it out, and after what seems like not too much time to me, I go back and decide to use Dev's card, hell with it, and the transaction's timed out because I was sitting there too long.

I feel miserable on just about every level. I force myself to scrounge for some piece of mail with Hal's address on it so I can finish the purchase. By the time I'm done, several of my laptop keys have snot on them and I'm not even sure I've managed to buy the things right.

Someone is blowing something up on the TV, and it's about time for me to take another two pills, but I feel so incapable and helpless and like I've ruined everything in my life that I don't want any more medication that makes me feel stupid. The only thing to do is to grab the remainder of the Southern Comfort bottle and retreat into the office with my laptop. I drink the bottle and pull up some of my favorite porn, but I really only enjoy the aesthetic value of the pictures. I don't get turned on at all.

So I start crying again because I'm sick and I'm never going to feel healthy again, and I haven't had any sort of sex drive since leaving Dev and I'm starting to worry that maybe I'm completely broken now. And Dev is going to go on to be famous and he'll find some gay version of Angela or Gena who will just subordinate himself to the football life and the worst part of all of that is that I want desperately to be able to do that, to just close my eyes and hold my breath and sink into domesticity. And I can't, I can't. I always end up thrashing for air, fighting, clawing back to the surface and breathing, and it's not that I don't want to be in that life at all. It's just that I need to have my head clear and out of it, and right now my head is just a giant mucus factory and my ears haven't heard properly in two days and I can't smell anything and I feel useless.

Of course, drinking half a bottle of Southern Comfort doesn't do much to make me feel better. In fact, I'm pretty sure that a lot of that stuff I'm thinking is amplified by the alcohol into unreasonable self-pity. So it's kind of a miserable hour or two, drinking booze that tastes like cough syrup and watching porn I'm not enjoying in the right way and unpicking all the stupidest, worst aspects of my life.

I come close, then, to writing a maudlin e-mail to Dev telling him that I'm leaving him for his own good and he's better off without me. And by "come close" I mean that I actually open up the e-mail program and start typing it, with some difficulty as my laptop still has snot on the keys and my claws keep skittering across to the wrong letters, and even when I hit the right letters, my brain is sending the wrong words to my fingers. I feel all desperate and noble and self-sacrificing and tragic.

The last thing I remember writing is "your life trajectory is a shining comet and I am Marley's chains on your tail." Even drunk, I can work in pretentious literary allusions, although every third word is misspelled and the metaphor is so strained as to be nonexistent. It makes perfect sense to me at the time.

Not so much when I wake up with a familiar tightness in my skull. Not a full-on hangover, but certainly the reminder that they exist. The sun streams through the windows of my temporary bedroom, and Hal is snoring in the room next door. I'm not even disoriented, waking up on the floor of this room full of someone else's life, not on the fourth day.

I sit up and blow my nose, and for a few seconds it is actually clear. Scents come flooding back to me, my ears pop, and I remember what it is to feel normal. As the mucus collects back in the cavities I've just cleared, I reflect back on the previous night and rub my head. The shadows have retreated from the room in the harsh sunlight, and the illuminated clutter of Hal's office, smelling of swift fox, reminds me that I do have a friend. There is another morning, and another. Life is not that bad. Life always gives you another chance.

Unless you leave a voicemail or send an e-mail, I remember. No second chances there. Fur prickling, I reach for the laptop and wake it up.

Well, at least I didn't send the damn message. But there's two more full paragraphs after the "shining comet" line, and I mean "full" as in "verbose mode on." I stare at the text, which I have absolutely no recollection of, while shame builds up at my self-pitying rambling. Jesus Fox, I'm glad I didn't send it. Dev would definitely dump me if he read something like that. Not only is it full of things like "all that you've done was in you all the time and I just latched on to your success," but that "shining comet-Marley's chains" thing is the least of my literary transgressions. I even wrote at one point in what I think is supposed to be French.

I erase the text and cancel the message, because I never want to remember that I did something like that. "Thank God for Mondays," I mutter, shutting the laptop, and set about distracting myself with trying to clean up Hal's place. He's out of coffee, so I take a trip to Starbucks, where to my dismay I actually feel excited at the green sign and awnings, and then come back, sweep up stray fur in the living room, and tackle the kitchen. The work makes me feel good, or at least useful.

He comes out sort of bemused an hour later, after I was making noise putting away dishes in the kitchen. "What're you doing?" he yawns.

"Cleaning. And not blowing my nose every five minutes. Sorry about the noise." I put away a saucepan.

"So all my dishes have germs on them." He scans the kitchen back and forth. "Where are my coffee mugs?"

"Up here," I say, "and I washed my paws with hot water and soap."

He reaches into the cabinet and retrieves a mug. "I'm not going to tell you to stop," he says, holding the mug and looking lost, as though it's my kitchen. "But, um."

"Want me to make coffee?" I give him a bright smile.

"Do I have coffee?" He blinks at me.

I show him the bag of Starbucks. His eyes widen. "You went to Starbucks? Voluntarily?"

"Their tea is okay," I say, measuring out the coffee. "And you like their coffee. Also, I got you some blazers."

He sniffs the air. "At Starbucks? That smells pretty good, by the way."

"It's their strongest blend. I thought maybe it wouldn't taste like piss."

He makes a face at me. "You going to have some?"

"I'm still on tea." I point to the Starbucks cup on the counter.

"Oh, that's what I smell. I thought you'd left the garbage out."

"No," I say, "but I can put some in your coffee if you want."

He leans against the kitchen door frame, swishing his tail back and forth. A smile creeps along his muzzle. "Sounds like you're feeling better."

"A little," and of course, I barely get the coffee started before I have to run past him out into the living room to blow my nose.

But yes, Monday is better. I get Hal to open up about his date, which he's reluctant to talk about, I think partly because he doesn't want to rub it in my nose as well as because he just doesn't want to talk to me about his private life. Eventually he says they had a nice dinner, they went back to her place and had a serious talk about their priorities.

"How serious?" I say. "I can't smell anything and I was asleep so I don't know when you came home."

He makes a face at me. "We decided we like each other's company and maybe that'll be enough."

"Uh-huh," I say. "So. How serious?"

"I don't know that I want to talk about that."

"Oh, come on. I don't have a love life of my own. Shirts-off serious? Naked serious?"

He flicks his ears. "We just held each other on the couch."

"Uh-huh. And?"

His tail flicks. "And a little bit of petting."

"There you go." I leave the coffee to percolate and go sit on the couch. The TV comes on to a sports channel and I think it'll be okay, because I can always flip away when they start talking about football. The national ones aren't as relentlessly Firebirds-heavy as the local stations are, although the Firebirds are a great underdog story and Dev is a great story and they're not shying away from it by any means.

I'm in a better mood to deal with it than I have been in days, and when they flip to talking about Dev, I stay on to test myself. They rehash all the same old things, play a clip from his coming-out press conference and footage of him getting flattened by Bixon, followed by some of his interceptions, ending with the one in Boliat, to create this illusory arc that coming out made him seem weak until he got his head on straight. At least they don't pull out footage of the Millenport fight where he tackled the boar that gored Fisher, which is kind of funny because that was one of the turning points of the season. It let his teammates know he was backing them up, and it let the rest of the league know he wasn't going to let them fuck with him.

The piece makes me feel moody, but more nostalgic-moody than depressed. I only feel the pressure of tears at one point. Hal goes into his room to write, and I pull up the laptop and open Dev's e-mail account, which I'd been avoiding doing. I was pretty sure nobody'd been looking at it since I left, but on the off chance that someone had, I would've been crushed and I didn't want to deal with that. I'm not sure I'm still allowed to read his e-mail, but as long as nobody else is doing it, it needs to be answered, and he's not going to do it.

Nobody has been accessing his e-mail; a small relief. I read through the letters to him with as much detachment as I can muster and respond to the ones that need responses. The volume's gone up steadily throughout the playoffs, with lots of e-mails from local Chevali cubs saying how awesome they think he is, and three requests for interviews that I route to Ogleby. There's some abuse and some praise and guys wanting to hook up with him, which makes me pause. Should I pass those on now? Will he want to try out someone besides me? One of the guys is a fox, too, or at least the picture he sent is of a fox, a red fox, in tight white underwear.

The thought of him with someone else makes me sad, not angry, so I pull up my solitaire game and play it until my mind is more or less clear. I'm still congested, but better than yesterday, so I don't take any more of the pills, which Hal notices when he comes out. "Did you only take two of those?" he says, pointing at the packet on the side of the couch.

"Yeah. They make my head feel stupid."

He puts his paws on his hips. "You could've told me that before I spent thirteen bucks on them."

My ears go back. "I left you grocery money," I say. "Anyway, you can get the generic store brand for like six."

"You telling me how to shop?"

"Oh, come on. What are we, married?"

His jaw hangs open and then snaps shut. "Yeah, well," he says gruffly. "Glad you're feeling better."

I mimic his voice. "Sure am, bro." Then I cough and have to blow my nose again.

"Jesus Fox, seriously, take the pills." He comes over to stand by the couch and picks up the box.

"I'm getting better."

"Not fast enough." He pops two pills out of the foil (easily, the bastard) and holds them out.

"I finished off the Southern Comfort last night," I say. "I feel better." My nose tickles, but I resist the urge to blow it yet again. Timing is everything.

"Trust ten years more experience," he says. "Take the pills."

I sigh, but I'm staying on his floor, so what else am I supposed to do? I take the pills and wash them down, and wait for my head to get warm and muzzy again. In the meantime, I think seriously for the first time about what my long-term plans are going to be. I want to move back in with Dev when he comes back from the game, and I'm gonna try like hell for that, but I have to face the fact that realistically it may not happen.

So what are my options? I can't impose on Hal for too long. After the championship, I can hopefully get a better sense of the situation in Yerba. I mean, they wouldn't invite me up for the game if they weren't serious about hiring me. Or I could go back to Hilltown and sleep on Father's couch. If he has one. Does he? I can't remember whether he told me that.

After about ten minutes of trying to figure out if my father owns a couch, I remember that I slept on it when I went up to get my stuff from Mother's. The pills are working again, I guess, so I shelve the thinking process for another day. "Make things go boom," I instruct Hal, and he throws on a DVD of a terrible movie with good explosions.

The urge to blow my nose decreases as the day goes on, and though I hate the hollow, dry feeling and the crazy, skittering paths my thoughts take, I do appreciate not having to live with a tissue box grafted to my side. I take more pills at the appointed time, and when my head throbs with a headache, I go and lie down, and Monday slides away from me easily.

Tuesday I get up, throw a t-shirt on, and march out to the living room to announce to Hal, "I think I'm over the worst of it."

"Good," he says from the kitchen, and sips his coffee, reading something on his laptop, already accustomed to my presence.

I pull out my iPhone. I would've heard if there were a message from Dev, but I still check—there isn't. I decide I may as well figure out how to get my e-mail on the phone, so I pull out the laptop and do that.

"Want to turn on the TV?" Hal asks, coming in with his computer.

I don't look up. "It's Media Day."

"Yeah?"

I sigh and pick up the computer and phone. "I should just go in the office. You might want to watch this."

"I'd like to."

Dev would've said he didn't have to, maybe. Or I would've realized it was important to him and not been waiting for him to say he didn't want to. At any rate, it's fine. I tune out the muffled TV noise with the door closed, and work on my e-mail, which is more complicated than I thought it would be and involves looking at a bunch of different web pages and typing server names into programs.

"Going to grab lunch," Hal says in a little bit. "Want to come?"

"Sure," I say, bringing the phone with me. "I think I have this set up right."

He snorts. "Fancy things."

"You'll have one before long," I say, showing off the mail. "It gets e-mail and plays games, and has a camera, too."

"If I want to read e-mail, I'll sit down at the computer. I just want my phone to take phone calls." He pauses. "And send text messages."

"Really? You never text me." I shrug on a jacket.

"It's warm out."

"I'm sick," I point out. "Who do you text?"

We walk out into the sun. "Pol," he says. "She likes to text."

I grin and elbow him. "So you're adopting new technology for her."

"I didn't say I liked it," he says.

"Your tail says otherwise." I grin, and he stops wagging it, but by then it's too late.

He takes me a little farther than the taco stand, to a burger place—not the fast food one that I growl at as we approach, but a little mom-and-pop place that he swears is run by an actual mom and pop, a pair of raccoons. And it smells really good, all grease and beef and cheese, and the female raccoon behind the counter is pretty friendly. We sit in the window with the sun on the table and enjoy the sandwiches, the crispy fries, and the onion rings. It's horrible and unhealthy and I don't care. I only have to blow my nose twice, and my throat is all better.

I'm starting to think that it might be a pretty nice day when my phone rings, and I see Brian's number on it. "So much for that," I say aloud.

Hal glances at the phone in my paw. "You don't have to take the call, you know."

"I can handle him." But still I hesitate a second, because it's Brian, and I don't want to talk to him until I get my situation resolved with Dev. I wouldn't say anything to him about it, but I wouldn't put it past him to know, somehow, or to figure it out from talking to me.

Then the phone stops ringing. "Problem solved," Hal says.

I feel the weight of the phone in my pocket the whole way back to the apartment. It beeps to let me know Brian left a message, but I wait until we get back to listen to it, because somehow I don't want to hear his voice or his words under the bright sun.

Back in the apartment, Hal turns on the TV and I retreat into the office. I sit on the air mattress and curl my tail around my legs and pull up the voicemail on the phone.

"Well, I'm not surprised you're not talking to me, Tip," Brian says. "I mean, I'm sure you've heard what he said by now. I was just calling to see if you had any comment on it before I write it up for our newsletter. Let me know if you'd like to give the boyfriend's perspective." He pauses. "If you still want to, that is."

I'm not sure what he means, but my fur prickles with foreboding. And then Hal calls from the other room, "Lee? I think you might wanna see this."

CHAPTER 16 – IN MEDIA (DEV)

Monday goes by in a blur of film study and light practice. Monday night, Charm goes out and I stay in the room and jerk off and then study the playbook and get restless and think about Lee and jerk off again—it's mechanical and unfulfilling and halfway through I almost stop, but I don't want to go to bed hard. So I finish, with little more thought than "finally," and still don't sleep all that well.

Tuesday is my first Media Day. All the members of the team have to give some time to the media, and someone like me, who's been in interviews all year, gets a more prime spot (though still not as prime as Strike, or Aston, the actual stars, the ones who move jerseys, as Strike would put it). Because there are fifty-three of us, they have ten at a time, podiums lined up along the field with canvas backdrops, separated just enough that one crowd of reporters doesn't run into the other. When I walk up to my podium for the allotted half hour at 11:30, I'm still a little bleary. I sit down in front of the Firebirds backdrop and look up and down the length of the field. It's a sunny day, and I'm second from the end; to my right, our special teams otter is fielding a crowd of ten or so reporters. To my left stretch eight more interviews, the most crowded being Jaws all the way at the far end. I can't tell how many he has, but my crowd looks at least as big, with probably some fifty muzzles all pointed my way.

It's okay, I tell myself. Bland answers, that's all I need to give.

They don't make it easy. The first question is, "What kind of pressure do you feel, being the first openly gay player to play in a championship game?"

"The same pressure my teammates are feeling," I say. "We're all excited to bring a championship home to Chevali." That's pretty good and bland. Go me.

I try to pick the reporters, but they all blurt out their questions, and the next one is, "But doesn't being gay mean anything special to you?"

"That's part of my private life," I growl out into the sea of muzzles. "It has nothing to do with what I do on the field."

"What does your boyfriend think about that?" The high, sneering voice is familiar. I look through the brown and gold and tan and red and there, at the back, I spot a black-and-white muzzle.

"I thought this was only for reporters," I say.

"I think you know my media credentials," Brian says.

A hundred gleaming eyes turn on me. I can feel the energy in the crowd pick up. *They know each other! What will Miski do here? This could be a story!* Already some of them are jotting notes or muttering into their phones.

So I take a breath and relax. I picture Lee in the stands at a game, not huddled on the couch as I last saw him. He's standing and smiling, and his tail wags in the sun. "My boyfriend is proud of me. He believes I'm a pretty good football player, and that's what I intend to be on Sunday."

Someone else asks a question about the Crystal City offense, thank God, and I take my time addressing that. Then there are more football questions, and someone asks if I had any pets growing up, and someone else asks what other tigers I've modeled myself after (Fisher is the obvious answer, but I'm also careful to say that I admire a lot of players, not just those of my species). And then Brian again, asking, "Why do you think no other gay players have come out?"

"I don't know," I say. "You'd have to ask them."

"Do you think it could be because you haven't embraced your sexuality?"

"I don't know," I repeat. I turn to someone else, but it's become a theme now and they're all asking about it.

"Do you think there aren't any other gay football players?"

"I'm sure there are," I say. "Now…"

"Why do you think no other players have come out?"

I fidget. "I've answered that question already."

"Sorry," Brian says, "but you really haven't. You just said you didn't know. But you must have a thought."

"I can't tell what other gay players might be thinking," I say.

"Well, then," a sheep near the front says, "why did you come out?"

"I've talked about that a hundred times," I say, and glare at Brian. "There was a threat—there were allegations, and I wanted to address them."

"But you could have just denied them."

I rub my eyes. "I could have, sure, but…" But that would've been lying. But I would've disappointed Lee. But I would've disappointed myself. But none of that seems as important right now as the overwhelming desire to get the fuck out of this Media Day and stop talking about why there aren't more gay players or why more gay players haven't come out or any number of other things I have no control over. How much time is left out of my half hour? Eighteen minutes? That can't be right.

They don't wait for me to finish my answer. "Is your boyfriend going to be at the game?"

"I don't know," I say without thinking, and then regret that. Lying would have been the better option there.

"You don't know?" "Hasn't he told you?" "Are you fighting?" "Did you break up?"

The questions come scattershot and I can't focus on any of them. "No," I say, and lift a paw, trying to get a moment of peace. I'm feeling stretched thin and I don't like it. "Can we talk about the game?"

But they keep at it. A few gamely put some football questions up, which I pounce on, but I only get to talk about the Sabretooths' running game for a few minutes—and believe me, I drag those out—before someone's asking me about my boyfriend, or what brand of lube we use (really?), other things like that.

The sports reporters drift away about twenty minutes in, even though I was trying to give them good lines about our planning. Left behind are the supermarket rags and Brian, for ten more minutes, and then there's nothing but questions about my lifestyle. I resort to bland "No comment" and "I don't know" answers, hoping they'll get bored, but Brian is always ready with another question, and my nerves are frayed.

And when he says, "How does it feel being the only player to have come out? Do you feel pressured?" for the hundredth time in half an hour, that is just about all I can fucking take.

"I wish I hadn't," I snap. "Then I could just talk about football."

In the silent seconds after that, I'm aware that I've done something pretty wrong. But I can't call attention to it or backtrack; that'd look worse. So I just go on, saying that we've got a great team, that they're all being overshadowed by this lifestyle question, that all I want to do is play football.

Brian calls, "Do you really want to go back into the closet?" I ignore him, and the second my thirty minutes is up, I stand, thank everyone, and walk quickly off the little stage, behind the screen with the Firebirds logos printed on it.

To my surprise, Zillo is standing back there. I'm out of sight of the cameras, so I take a deep breath and close my eyes. "You next?" I ask.

"Nah." He doesn't move. "Just want to see how the starters handle it. I'm going in another half hour."

"So how did the starters handle it?"

I open my eyes and he's shaking his head, with that kind of wide-eyed look, like he had when I came off the field after getting steamrolled by the wolverine in the Gateway game. "They really push on the gay thing. I mean, why hasn't someone else come out—well, maybe nobody wants to sit through hours of inane questions about who they fuck in a football press conference, huh?"

"Yeah. Sort of my thinking." I sigh. "I let them get to me."

"Hey." He gives a little smile—as little as a long coyote muzzle can manage. "If I had people badgering me for half an hour about the girls I fucked, or if Gerrard—well, you know—I mean, I bet we'd let loose with a good, hearty 'Fuck you' too."

"It's not that." I start to walk back, and Zillo walks alongside, somewhat to my surprise.

"So what is it? I thought you did pretty well."

"Saying I wish I hadn't come out. I mean, you get that coming out is a big deal, right?"

His ears twitch. "Sort of?"

I sigh. "Being gay, it's like—like being a Unicorns fan in Chevali. You know everyone would hate you if you told them who you root for. But it's not something you can put aside, you can't just say, 'well, we're all fans of the game,' because people get fanatical about it. And it's…it's about living your life, not just who you root for on Sundays. Right?" He nods. "So lots of people just hide those relationships. And that's like saying that all those other guys are right, that we deserve to be marginalized," there's a word I definitely picked up from Lee, "and hidden in shadows and 'straightened out' and shit like that. And beaten up, sometimes."

His ears go flat at that, and the smile disappears. "And have people call you shitty names."

"Yeah. But coming out, it's a big deal, it's standing up and saying 'Fuck you, bigots, I am not ashamed.' So you know, me saying I wish I hadn't…"

"But you didn't mean it." I give him a weary look, and he laughs. "Right, right, it's the fucking media. Can't you just go out and apologize for it?"

"I'll call my agent and have him send out a statement, yeah." I cringe at the thought of Ogleby handling the press, and I wish I could just call Lee and have him issue a statement. He'd write it so much more elegantly. Also he would give me a whole pile of shit for saying something like that in the first place. And I'd feel better about it, afterwards, because I'd know that he still loved me in spite of all of that. Now I don't have that to fall back on, and it's bugging the hell out of me that I lost control like I did. What if Lee sees it? Is he going to think it's his fault, that I wish I hadn't come out because of our fight?

Well, maybe it'd serve him right, walking the fuck out on me like he did. I take out my phone to text him and then I think, I'd better handle this first. So I call Ogleby and tell him I'm handling the situation ("What situation, Dev?" he says, and I hang up). I call two sports reporters I trust, who aren't answering their phones because they're probably outside listening to Aston or whoever's out there now. So I leave messages telling them to call me back, saying I want to apologize for my remarks, that I just got frustrated because football is so heavily on my mind and that one so-called "reporter" wouldn't leave me alone.

One of them calls back right away and we have a pretty good conversation about football and about the idiots they'll let into Media Day nowadays. I don't mention that I know Brian from way back.

The other reporter calls me back when the day is over, and though he's brisk, he sympathizes with my situation as well. Both these guys are veterans of the reporting business and have talked to me in the past about being "the gay guy." So I feel comfortable sitting down in the locker room talking to him about how the press conference went. He has a column that's updating all week, and he promises to give me some space in it on Wednesday, or Thursday at the latest.

Nobody else in the locker room really gets how important this was. Everyone talks about the stupid questions they got asked, and I don't want to talk about any of it, so I go off and sit in the film room and stare at the same loop of the Sabretooths' running offense for hours, at the running backs hitting the gaps and the slot receivers running formations. I try to impress the patterns on my mind.

When I come out and go back to the locker room, Fisher comes up and tells me I'm an idiot, and I say, "Tell me something I don't know."

We're standing eye to eye near my locker. Charm and Zillo are talking next to us, but stop at my remark. "Did you even listen to me? Don't ever try to control a press conference," Fisher says. "Just makes 'em madder."

"Right," I say. "Next time I'm losing my temper, I'll remember that."

"You can't lose your temper with the press, *rook*." He tries to poke my shoulder, and I dodge it.

"Obviously, I can. And keep your paws off me."

I remember the fight we had a few months ago, but that was when we were alone in the weight room and it was about me bringing Lee to an event. If I hadn't wanted to do that…if I had just kept myself in the closet… but I didn't, I fought for him, and for me. But Fisher won't do anything like that here in the locker room, I think.

Wrong, it turns out. He shoves me harder in the chest, knocking me back into the massive bulk of Charm, who acts quickly, pulling me to the side. "Hey, hey," he says. "We're all on the same team. Come on, Gramps, Fish, let's not play like that 'til we're out with the Sabretooths."

"We?" Fisher snorts up at him. "We? Only opponent you ever faced was a leather ball." He puts a paw to his forehead and closes his eyes for a moment.

Strike hurries over, too, just as Charm is saying, "Yeah, but some of those balls are tough customers." The cheetah assesses the situation and puts his paws up between me and Fisher, even though we're already clearly settled down.

"You boys need to take some rest," he says. "Worst thing can happen in a championship game is the stress gets to you. It's just another football game and we're all on the same side, remember."

"I'm fine," I snap.

"Listen, maybe what you need is—"

"So help me God," I say, "if you tell me a vegetable smoothie I will personally force a cheeseburger down your throat."

Strike looks as offended as someone can be with bright gold fur and red firebird markings on his muzzle. He looks like a fucking clown. "I was going to say, you need to get away from this for a bit. Listen, I'm going out with Iva tonight. You want me to get hold of Keith? I'm sure I can track him down. You guys can come along."

"Wait," I say. "Wait a fucking minute. You're going out with Iva?"

Charm nudges me. "Might do you good to get out," he says, which I think is as close as he's going to come to telling me to cheat on Lee even though maybe we're already broken up. He's got to have seen that interview and quote by now—Lee, I mean, not Charm. He didn't text me to give me shit for it, which was the right thing to do but I'm mad at him for it, because I'm turning it into thinking he's given up on me. If he'd texted me to tell me I'm an asshole, at least I'd know he still cared. Shit, now I'm hearing his lectures in my head, and that is not what I need, not this week. I'm glad he didn't text me. But why didn't he? Fuck. Fuck fuck fuck.

I shove those thoughts aside to deal with the cheetah clown. "What about your tantric meditation and all that bullshit?"

"Oh, that's fine for the regular season," Strike says. "But we have two weeks off, and it's the championship. Lot of stress can build up here. Anyway, I didn't say I was going to sleep with Iva. Just going to dinner, getting away from the football crowd."

"And you," I say to Charm. "I don't know if I want to 'get out.'"

He shrugs like he always does and grins his horsy grin. "I just said I thought it might do ya good," he says. "I mean, you need to unwind somehow."

"I can think of a lot better ways to unwind than…" I don't want to say "going on a double date with Strike," but I can't think of another way to end that sentence.

"I can't." Charm elbows me again. "G'wan, get out of your head for a bit. This 'Keith' guy sounds pretty hot. Is he a bunny?"

"He's a wolf."

"Ah, well. Bunnies are the best for getting out of your head. Reminds me…" He takes out his phone and scrolls around. "Ah, Davinya. Thanks, guys, now I know what I'm doin' tonight."

"Don't you mean 'who'?" Zillo's wandered over from his locker. I bet he didn't say anything stupid in his interview like wishing he wasn't a coyote.

"Or 'whom'?" I say.

Charm laughs. "Who, whom—she's a Sabretooths cheerleader. You guys can argue 'bout what to call her. I'm just gonna call her." He puts the phone to his ear. "Hi, Davi? Guess who's in town?"

When he steps back, Zillo looks between me and Strike and seems to realize that he's very close to getting into a conversation with Strike. He checks the clock and says, "Ah, I gotta go too—sorry, set up a meeting with—um, I told Mace I'd play Xbox with him," and before we can say anything, he's taken off.

"I'm really glad I get so much one-on-one time with you," Strike says, getting his phone out when everyone else has cleared away from the two of us. "Hi, Iva?" he says, and starts making plans.

I could still back out. But like he said, it doesn't mean I have to sleep with the guy. It's just company, just something else to do for a night. Fuck it. I can either be miserable and entertained or miserable and alone. And I've done the miserable and alone bit.

So when Strike hangs up, I barely hear what he says about Iva not knowing Keith's number, but having another gay friend who wanted to date a football player. I just say, "Sure," and tell him we can take a taxi to wherever it is.

In the taxi, I tune out Strike and watch the apartment buildings fade into department stores and small strip malls. When I say 'strip malls,' I mean Crystal City strip malls. They're as much like the strip malls back home as the fashion-show wannabes walking around here are like the girls in my high school. The ladies walking around these malls in glittering jewelry and bewildering swaths of cloth and color look perfectly assembled, unbelievably thin at the waist and arms, coordinated from the delicate shawls around their heads and necks to the trim at the bottom of their skirts and the decorations on their anklets. Whatever the species, they are so similar that their fur colorations look like just another fashion accessory, as though this one chose red fur and a long muzzle while this other one chose a shorter muzzle and golden-brown fur. It's a little unsettling, and the guys aren't much better. They're either packed into identical business wear—charcoal or light grey suits, or shirts and brightly-colored ties—or else they're jogging shirtless in athletic shorts down the sidewalk. My eyes linger on the latter; my first thought is that Lee would say they were hot, and then I actually make the leap and think to myself that yeah, those guys are hot, and if we were alone in a room together…

I shift in the seat, surprised at the reaction in my sheath. The truth is, I've never been with any guy but Lee, and I never really wanted to be. But now, even though I'm missing him, I'm mad at him, too, so I'm taking the horniness from missing him and turning it into wanting other guys.

That's how my mind spins it, anyway. I look at this leopard guy jogging down the street, hard abs, powerful legs, and I imagine his body twisting under mine, and it's a little exciting, but not heart-thumping passion exciting. He's not a fox, but that's not what's tempering my attraction. What's tempering it is the same thing that tempers my attraction to any guy I see who's moderately attractive: I don't know him. He's not the guy I fell in love with.

The restaurant turns out to be some glitzy place, all tinted windows and silver chrome supports, called The Raven's Nest. Strike tells me as we pull up to the curb that movie stars hang out there, though usually only in the upper floors where there are more private booths. "And that's where we'll be," he says with a little smugness.

I take a moment to examine the warped reflections of the other buildings in the restaurant's windows while the taxi pulls away, and then I follow Strike inside.

My first thought is that it's kind of like what a goth cub would design given unlimited money. The whole place is draped in black curtains with brass feather ornaments around them. The staff are all black-furred, either natural or dyed, I guess—the hostess is a panther, which could be natural, but the waiter at the host stand is a weasel and I don't think they come in black—and they wear black feathery decorations on their wrists and around their collars. The carpet, though, is a wine-red plush that my feet sink into, and behind the host stand, I see white tablecloths with gold trim, black plates and glasses, and gold candlesticks. The air is thick with Neutra-Scent, but over that is a light, flowery perfume.

"Posh," I say under my breath to Strike.

He just smiles and gives his name to the pantheress. "Party of four?" she says, and taps a small device—is that an iPhone? I crane closer to look. It is.

"The other two are at the bar," Strike says, and I turn with him to look in that direction.

The bar is the dimmest part of the restaurant, which makes the smoked glass shelves and collection of bottles on them look somehow eerie. A black wolf behind the bar polishes a glass with a rag, talking to a customer in a trenchcoat with a long white-tipped red tail emerging from the lower hem. A little away from the bar, at a high table, a busty leopard swirls a straw in some pale green-colored drink. I think that's Iva, but I can't be sure in the dim light, too far to catch her scent. There's another drink across from her, but nobody's sitting there.

"I'll get your companions from the bar," the hostess says as a black rat appears. "Carmen will take you to your table."

The rat gestures with one paw so that the feathers around her wrist flap slightly. "This way," she says with a bright smile, and leads us around to the right, through a black-curtained doorway. The wine-red carpet continues up the stairs and ends at the second floor, where a glossy black tile replaces it. Apparently even a ritzy place like this doesn't want to lay out the money to clean a full building's worth of carpet every week.

The upstairs is considerably less crowded than the downstairs. Not that there are more empty tables; there are just fewer tables altogether, and they're split into several rooms. Our room has two tables in it and three booths, two of which are occupied by couples (if they're famous, I don't recognize them). The Neutra-Scent is still as thick here, so we can't smell our fellow diners, but the flowery scent is gone, replaced by the very light aroma of wine. Carmen brings us to a square table—apparently we don't rate a booth—and holds the chairs out for both of us as we sit down.

The tablecloths up here glimmer with mother-of-pearl iridescent trim, and the silver centerpiece is much more elaborate than the candlesticks downstairs: a stand that looks like a silver monument topped by three curved arms that each end in a base decorated with carved silver ribbons. Carmen lights the black candle above each base, says, "Your companions will be right up," and then leaves us.

"Don't we get a menu?" I say.

Strike grins. "They only serve four dishes a night, plus starters. The servers just recite them all. And the sommelier will be over to discuss wine with us. If there's a vintage you like, you can ask for it, otherwise he'll be happy to recommend something."

I feel lost without a menu, something to occupy my eyes and paws, so I tap fingers on the table and look around the room. The other couples are all eating already, so I give them a cursory glance—two sheep at one table, a coyote and a kangaroo at the other—and then just sit down to look around the room.

Like the rest of the restaurant, it's understated and mostly dark. The floor-to-ceiling windows are bordered with silver partitions topped with small clusters of silver feathers. Through the tinted glass, the lights in the Nordstrom's across the street glow darkly, and the people shopping inside flit like shadows. Even the people on the sidewalk look unreal, as though they're in a movie I'm watching. I guess there's a certain amount of power in being able to look down at all those people without them knowing it. If that's what you're into.

"Hi, boys!" The busty leopardess from the bar slides into the seat next to Strike, across from me. So it was Iva. And to my left, as I look up, the black pantheress from the host stand is holding out the chair for—

—a bunny.

He sits down, a slender white-furred rabbit with black-tipped ears and a bright smile. "Hi," he says. "I'm Iva's friend Machaine. Like 'machine' but with an extra 'a' in the middle."

He's wearing a blue silk shirt and some kind of chain under it. I can only see the glint of a few links that aren't completely sunk into his lush white fur. The paw he holds out to me is immaculately manicured. Usually non-retractable claws are cracked and dull, but his are polished and almost sparkle in the candlelight. I take his paw, unsure whether to shake it or kiss it. I shake, and he doesn't seem offended. "Devlin Miski," I say. "Pleasure to meet you."

"The pleasure's mine, dear," he says. "Do you know who was in the bar downstairs?"

I frown. "Besides you two?"

He giggles and gestures dramatically. "Ford Flame!"

"The fox?" I know the name from movie posters, though I'm not sure I've seen any of his movies.

"Oh God, he was in a trenchcoat, but I saw his muzzle and he is *so* much handsomer in person, I could've *died*."

Iva leans over and grins. "He's straight, dear."

"Well." Machaine—whatever kind of name that is—sits back in his chair and smirks. "Maybe he is, and maybe he isn't."

"This isn't a gay bar." They argue for a few excruciating minutes about Ford Flame's sexual preference, and then the black rat comes back to rescue us.

"Tonight," she says without preamble, "we have four delicious dishes…" She describes a mushroom-saffron risotto, a portobello mushroom roasted with red peppers, a sauteed eggplant with a balsamic vinegar reduction, and a sweet curry with tofu.

"Um," I say, cutting her off as she starts listing the salads and other appetizers, "so there's no meat entrees?"

"Oh," she says with a smile. "We're an organic vegetarian restaurant."

I glare at Strike, who says, "Didn't I tell you that?" He doesn't even put on wide-eyed innocence. Maybe he really did forget. Not everyone is plotting all the time, I remind myself.

"No." I look back up at Carmen. "Sorry, it all sounds delicious."

"I recommend the portobello," she says. "It's got the consistency of steak."

Machaine looks faintly disgusted, then loses the disgusted face and cheerfully orders the curry. Strike takes the eggplant and Iva takes the portobello as well.

"Sorry," Strike says. "I could've sworn I told you."

My reply is forestalled by the wine guy, whatever Strike called him. I leave Strike to choose the wine and take the time to talk to Machaine, who is, after all, supposed to be my date.

He's a nice enough guy. Works as a key grip in the studios but wants to act and has been an extra in three films. When he's talking just to me, he slowly loses the 'fabulous' affectations, but when Iva breaks into the conversation, they're all back again: the hand gestures, the outraaaaaageous semi-flirty comments, the head tilts.

When he asks me about my boyfriend, I hesitate. Lee and I haven't officially discussed our relationship, but he's pretty much told me to go it alone until the game. Still, I don't want to give this rabbit the wrong idea. I mean, Iva brought him to be my date, and I don't know if that means only that we talk to each other while she talks to Strike, or if I'm expected to take him home at the end of the night, or what. So I just say that Lee's staying home to not be a distraction.

"A little distraction is good every now and then," the rabbit says. "Helps you focus when you get back to what's really important."

"I guess," I say.

Strike jumps in then to echo that sentiment, and we slide into a conversation about football, which it turns out Machaine doesn't know much about. It's kind of fun trying to explain it, and that takes my mind off the social pressure I might've only been imagining. Then the salad courses come, and we pause the conversation.

I stare down at the glossy black plate that has what looks like about three lettuce leaves and a drizzle of dressing on it. "Fabulous," Iva says, eating slowly.

"I love the presentation," Machaine says.

"Is this, like, the teaser for the actual salad?" I say. I'm starting to wonder if I should've ordered two entrees.

Strike gestures with his fork. "You don't want a lot of salad to start the meal. Eat the main course and then the vegetables that come with it. This is just enough salad to start your digestion flowing."

"It's just enough to make me hungry," I say, and spear two-thirds of the salad on my fork, finishing it off in one mouthful.

This makes Machaine giggle again, only it seems more like a real giggle and less like the affected ones he was making earlier. "Slow down," he says, nibbling on one of his lettuce leaves. "It's a fifteen-dollar salad."

"That's okay," I say. "He's picking up the tab." And I gesture at Strike, whose whiskers flick for a moment, then relax into a smile.

"Sure," he says.

The mushroom I get is much more reasonably sized (and for forty bucks, it should be). It's still not enough to completely fill me up, but at least it takes me more than one bite to eat. The wine is good, too, and in fact, the first thing I think when Carmen pours the wine is that Lee would really love this place. Then I think, too bad for him, because he could have been here with me and Strike and Iva, and we'd have made fun of it afterwards, in bed.

"Devlin?" Machaine rests a paw on my arm, lightly.

I snap my head around to him. "Uh, sorry. What?"

"You looked all spacey there for a moment." His nose twitches. I wonder if he can smell me thinking about Lee. Probably not over the wine and mushroom and Neutra-Scent.

Strike and Iva get along great, and sometimes seem to be so much on the same wavelength that I wonder if he's been in touch with her on the phone since our commercial. Machaine and I do all right keeping up the conversation, though it feels to me more like we're two separate people struggling to join in. Still, once I get over thinking about Lee and remind myself that nothing needs to happen, it's okay and even a little bit fun.

At the end of the night, Strike pays the bill, and we troop downstairs, Iva gushing about how lovely the place was. Machaine is a little quieter, hanging back, and out of courtesy, I hang back with him.

"Thank you for a lovely night," he says quietly.

"Oh, uh. You're welcome, I guess."

He laughs. "You know, I kind of thought you'd be like everybody else in this town. Don't know why. I mean, you're a football player, and you're not from C.C. But it was just nice talking about real things. Even if I don't really understand football yet."

"It's not that hard," I say. "I mean, some of the guys I play with can't do basic math, and they understand it."

"I don't know." He waves a paw. "I can coordinate an outfit like whoa, but I've never been able to catch a ball, much less throw it. Never cared much."

"Not everyone can."

"See, I also thought you'd think less of me if I didn't care about football."

"You're a pretty good guy." I hold the restaurant door for him. "If the flouncy bit is just an act, why do it? Why not just be you?"

"Oh, honey," he says, and giggles—the sincere giggle. We stop just outside the restaurant, and about ten feet in front of us, Iva is draped all over Strike. He's got one red-and-gold paw on her butt. "This is C.C.," Machaine goes on. "People have expectations. If you're gay, you flounce." He follows my gaze. "If you're an actress…you put out."

"I don't expect you to put out," I say.

"I didn't offer." He winks.

I can't help smiling. "I just think you're a pretty nice guy without the, you know." I flop my paws around. "Limp-wristed bullshit."

"Well, thank you." But his smile fades a bit. "But the 'limp-wristed bullshit' is part of me, too. I like playing that role. I like saying, 'Oh, *girl!*' and 'She said *what?*' and all that. I like dressing fabulously. Maybe I don't want to do it all the time, but I like it, and it's part of me, too."

"But you said…"

"Oh, it gets tiresome when people expect it. I want to play the role on my terms, you know what I mean?"

"Do I." I think about that Media Day, and about the barrage of questions at every press conference. "I guess it's like you said. People have this framework of how they expect you to act. They want you to fit into their view of the world."

Machaine tilts his head. "I bet you get that a lot. Jocks, must be difficult."

"Kind of. I mean, my teammates are great." I sigh. "Mostly. It's the rest of the world that won't leave me alone."

"You're famous, though. You can make them accept you on your terms. Or am I buying into a 'famous athlete' stereotype?"

I chuckle. "I'm not that famous. I can still lose my job pretty easily, and football players who lose their job wind up with…" I make the "poof" motion with my paws. "Nothing."

"At least you have a boyfriend waiting at home. That's good."

"Yeah," I say, and somehow it feels easier to talk about the situation with Lee here, to this almost-stranger. "I don't know if I do."

His eyes widen a bit. "You want to talk about it?" he asks with gentle, experienced kindness.

I slump back against the wall. It doesn't look like Strike and Iva will be done anytime soon—he's got a paw pretty much right on her tit—nor are they making a move to take their groping elsewhere. We're a little away from the entrance to the restaurant, but not so far that the people walking in can't take a moment to gawk at the couple. I could just call my own cab, and I'm about five minutes from doing that, but I don't mind talking to Machaine for a bit longer. "He wants me to be more active and more out about being gay. I just want to play football."

"Sure," he says. "Buckle down and do your job."

"It's more than a job." I'm aware that I'm arguing against my own words. "It's…it's a thing only like eight hundred people in the country can do. Three hundred fifty or so if you only count starters. And I'm good enough to be one of them."

"So you have to keep proving it?"

"Well, yeah, but it's more…I'm really proud of it. I love being one of those guys, someone everyone else can count on. When we stop the other team's offense, we do it together, and it's…it's the best feeling. When I get an interception, it's great, but when one of my teammates does, it's great too."

"You're like a family," he says. "I wish acting were like that."

"Like a family…" I think about last Thanksgiving, with Uncle Roger and Gregory and Auntie Za. "With all the sniping and stuff behind the scenes. But we're doing something out on a big stage—the biggest stage, in a few days—and we all want to see how good we can be. We want to get to the top together. And who I'm sleeping with shouldn't have any bearing on that."

"It shouldn't," he agrees. "In C.C., being gay is an asset, as long as you behave the way they expect you to. And you got to do a commercial."

"That was nice," I say, "but it was also a pain, kind of a distraction."

"Wish I had more distractions." He examines his claws, and the next question comes out very casually. "What'd you get paid for it?"

I'm surprised at the blunt question. "A lot," I say.

"Iva got two thousand dollars."

"Really? That's all?" He inclines his head, long ears flicking. I scratch my muzzle, and blink as someone takes a picture of Iva and Strike. "Well, if I'd known…"

He shakes his head. "She doesn't care. I wouldn't. That's how it works here. You want to get paid, you do your time and you get famous and then you can get a million dollars for thirty seconds of commercial time." He grins as I lay my ears back. "It was close to that, wasn't it?"

"Something like."

"Good for you. Get paid, sister."

The term "sister" unsettles me enough that I don't answer right away, though my ears do come up. Right then, Strike and Iva break apart and make their way over to us.

"Hey," Strike says, "I'm gonna get my own cab back to the hotel. Looks like you guys are having a fun conversation. You going to be okay?"

He's still holding Iva by the paw. I don't have Lee's nose, but I can smell the sex between them, and Machaine's nose twitches as well, which is kind of cute on the bunny. "I'm fine," I say. "We're having a good talk."

"There's a good ice cream place near here," Machaine says. "They serve low-fat milkshakes. For real."

"Okay," Strike says. "You guys have fun. Thanks for coming along, Dev."

I raise a paw and watch the two of them wander out to the street.

"He's going to fuck her," Machaine says.

"Yeah," I say. "Hypocrite."

"What?"

"Oh." I gesture. "He's just got this whole 'tantric mantra' or meditation thing or whatever, and says he doesn't need to have sex, and he's clearly going off to get some." They get into a taxi. I think I see him pull her top up before the door's even completely closed. I remember groping breasts, back in college. I wonder if any of the ladies really enjoyed it. I try to remember if I did.

Machaine stands still. "We don't have to get ice cream," he says, and though he's still got a little swishiness to his voice, it's deeper and more sincere.

Charm's words about bunnies echo in my head. I half-turn and really look at him. He's brushing a paw down his blue shirt, and his pants are pretty tight, not leaving much to my imagination. I'm reminded of being back in a bar on the Forester campus, cruising for a girl to take home and spend the night with. It didn't mean anything then, and I'm pretty sure this wouldn't mean anything now. It'd just be a way for me to get off, to get rid of some of the tension I've got stored up, not just over football and Lee, but the natural "I haven't had sex in a week" tension that I haven't felt since—well, since early on in the season, when Lee made a bet with me that I'd be starting soon and promised not to have sex until I did. Then it was motivating. Now it's just distracting.

And he's cute, he really is. Those long ears would be fun—not quite as fun as black triangular ears, but different. His body is pretty similar to Lee's, too, though his tail is short and fluffy rather than long and bushy. Maybe that'd be nice; it wouldn't get in the way as much.

But I like the way Lee's tail gets in the way, and I like his ears, and god dammit, as much as I'm getting hard thinking about fucking Machaine, there's still a part of me that knows I wouldn't enjoy it all that much. Well, I mean, I'd *enjoy* it, sure. He's got a nice butt and seems like a fun guy. But would it really be that much better than just jerking off? Would I feel like I was betraying Lee?

He did give a hand job to Brian that one time. So maybe I could jerk off Machaine and call it even.

He's still looking at me and the smile grows. "Okay, so, just the milk-shake then."

"Sorry," I say.

"Nah." He grins. "Much as I'd like to have a football player, I know where to go if I want one. College boys are more fun anyway."

My ears perk up. "You know other gay football players? I mean, you know that there are some?"

"My heavens, no." He laughs. "But I have friends who go down to UCC campus every now and then, you know. They say it doesn't mean the guys are gay, though. They'll just take a blow job if it's offered. They're young."

"Huh." I sink back against the window of the restaurant.

"But I wouldn't do that, myself," he says.

I turn. His ears are askew—down, kind of. "I thought you said you'd like to have a football player."

He nods. "But not that kind. Not the 'any mouth in a storm' kind. They don't want me, they just want a no-strings blow job, and if they get it from a female, then they feel like it means something, because they're straight and they're supposed to have a relationship."

"I know a stallion who doesn't think that at all."

His right paw lifts, waves airily. "They're not all like that. But there's some that are, you know. They don't really like us gays, but they'll come in our mouths. Because we're happy to lick it up. Not like the girls they know, probably."

I think about that. "That's kind of sad."

"And that's why I don't go to the colleges." He smiles. His ears come up. "I may be a fag for show, but I'm a fag with pride."

"And you're cute. And that friend of mine, he'd kick me for turning down a bunny. But—what?"

He's glaring at me. "Come on," he says. "I know you're a fangy big tough tiger, but at least get the species right."

"What?"

"I'm a snowshoe hare. I guess if you grew up in the desert…"

"Um." My ears are getting warm. "I grew up around Hilltown, up north."

He swats my shoulder. "Shame on you. Didn't you have any snowshoe hares up there?"

"We called them all bunnies!" I mock-cringe, and finally he laughs.

"All right," he says, and shakes a finger at me. "But you're going to buy me a milkshake to make up for it."

"Deal," I say, and I feel a lot better as he leads me off down the street. As tempted as I was—which was not all that much, I tell myself as we get farther from the restaurant—we're just going to have dessert. And I have someone else to talk to about what a fucking pain in the ass it is to be gay in this fucking world.

CHAPTER 17 – REACTIONS (LEE)

I drag my feet out into the living room. Hal's looking at his laptop, not the TV, which is showing one of the Sportscenter anchors. On the laptop screen is a picture of Dev and the headline, "Gay Player Wishes He Hadn't Come Out."

The room drops ten degrees. My fur prickles as I hug my arms around myself and lean closer.

It's a short story, only two paragraphs. The gist of it is that after being questioned for half an hour about his sexuality, Dev said he wished he hadn't come out. That's all there is.

Hal's looking up at me with what I think is pity. I step back and find myself breathing more easily. "Is that all?" I say.

"Um." He scratches behind one of his ears. "Seems like a big deal."

Brian was there, of course, hence the smug voicemail. I want to take the photo of Dev and rotate it so I can see the crowd of reporters, but I'm as sure as if I could actually see his black and white muzzle and shiny black eyes that Brian was one of the people asking questions. Goading Dev, probably, one of the things Brian excels at. And Dev just snapped, like he does sometimes. I swish my tail, making sure I'm really as relaxed as I think I am. "He wants to focus on football and be treated as a football player, and all they were doing is asking him about being gay."

"Uh-huh." Hal looks at the article again. "Shouldn't he know how to handle the media by now?"

"He's passionate." I smile, sadly, and then I have to sit down on the sofa. I land just near Hal's tail, but he doesn't flip it away. "He's passionate and he wants so much to succeed. And I was getting in the way of that."

"Hey, uh." Hal sets the computer down. "You were helping him. Didn't you tell me you coached him?"

"Yeah." I stare down between my knees. "And he doesn't need me coaching him anymore."

"That doesn't mean he don't care about you." Now Hal does flip his tail away from me.

I exhale. "No. But I don't know if we can make it work. That's going to be all over the place now, and I don't know if he'll be able to apologize for it. I mean, of course he will, but I don't know if he'll want to. I think he does—the Dev I know does, or would, but… He's just going to want to play his game, and I can't…I can't." I swallow and stop rambling.

The whole thing overwhelms me, what's gone between me and Dev, what he wants and how he probably won't be able to achieve that with me in his life. He's passionate, sure, and in the long run this comment probably isn't a big deal in the media. He'll apologize after the fact (probably already has), he'll explain that what he meant was that he wished he could just answer questions about football at a football press conference, and talk about being gay at somewhere appropriate for that. Everyone will forget, his Strongwell beer commercial will come out, his new agent—because he'd better fire Ogleby—will advise him to do PSA spots in the off-season and he'll be fine. But I can't stop thinking that he would much rather have had me as a good friend than a lover, even if we were both pining for each other, because it would've made his life less complicated. After football, there'll be time for love and such, but I feel like he's just reached out and told me that he doesn't want me back.

And I can't articulate that. I press my fingers to my eyes and feel the tears leaking out again, and I think, how stupid of me, am I not done crying yet? But apparently the answer is no, because I'm shaking, and then Hal has an arm around my shoulder and I'm leaning into him getting his shoulder damp with silent tears. He's warm and solid and he smells good and it just feels so, so good to have someone hug me that that makes it worse. The crying seems to have a momentum all its own, so even though I want to stop, I can't.

He's a good friend. He holds me through the whole thing. I finally manage to get myself under control when I feel the warmth building in my nose and have to reach for a tissue. "Sorry," I mumble, and he lets me go as I blow my nose.

"Not a problem," he says. "Like I said, when Cim left, I was kind of a mess. Though I drank more than I cried, I think. Threw up a lot, too."

"I haven't done that yet." I laugh, shakily. "Not for lack of trying. Oh god, Dev." The picture's still on Hal's laptop screen.

He closes it quickly. "Sorry."

"No." I shake my head. "I mean, I need to get over it. I'm going to watch him play a championship game in five days, for heaven's sake. I can't start bawling in the middle of the Yerba offices."

"They'd be impressed," Hal says. "Means you're a sensitive guy."

"Oh, screw that." I blow my nose again. "No, I'll get it together. Sorry. Uh. Thanks for the shoulder."

"Didn't have a whole lot of choice." He grins at me. "All happened so fast."

I breathe in and out, grab a couple more tissues and clean up my muzzle, and sit back on the couch. "I don't know why it hit me like that. It's not about me, I know. Except…it sort of is, you know?" He just nods. "I don't know what to think. I want to believe we're still together, or can get back together, but it just seems like it'll be too hard."

"Hard don't mean it's impossible," he says. "Hard don't mean it's not worth trying."

"No, I know." I hold my tail in my paws and rub the fur. It feels good and soothing, and I'm not even shedding that much anymore. "But if he doesn't want to…"

"If he didn't want to," Hal says, "likely he woulda stopped long before now."

"Yeah. I guess…"

"I'm right," he says firmly. "Now let me get some work done, and you do somethin' other than watching a movie or reading the Internet."

I have no idea what that might be, but after half an hour, I think that maybe I could do some preliminary work for Yerba. So I spend time reading up on the bowl games from the end of the year, looking at the college athletes and the draft, and at Yerba's team by position. That's what I'm doing when the phone rings.

I haven't used the phone much in the last few days. I don't have anyone to call, and it just reminds me that it was Dev's gift to me. But when I look down and see Mother's phone number, I pick up the phone and stare at it.

Great. Just what I need. *Just* what I fucking need.

I stand up and head for the office, swiping the bar to answer the call on the way. I don't even know why I'm doing it. Brian I can ignore, but Mother—the flood of emotion chokes my throat as I slide the mic out and put the phone to my ear. "Hello," I say finally.

"Wiley?"

"Yes. Hi, Mother." If I close my eyes, I see her standing in the hallway, feel the shouts building in my chest. So I look around the office at Hal's stacks of papers and books, and try not to think about the things behind my locked door.

"How are you?" she says, and though I'm usually snappy about people who dance around with small talk when they clearly have something else to say, this is a welcome respite for me to collect myself so I don't start, I don't know, bawling or yelling.

I take a breath. "I'm fine," I say, and then I repeat it. "Fine. How are you?"

"I'm fine. It snowed here. Six inches."

"Did the plows come around?"

We talk about snow and the weather, the conversation calm like the air on a day when thunderclouds are gathering. And finally I feel emptied of emotion, strong enough to say, "Why did you call?"

She pauses. "Harold said you wanted to talk." When I don't say anything, when the silence stretches on and on and I start zoning out, she says, in a smaller voice, "Did you?"

"Yeah," I say, even though I never told Father I did. I know why he lied, though. Now I wonder if she really wanted to talk to me, if she was really crying when she called him, or if he made all that up. I give her all the time in the world to apologize for locking my room, burning my things.

Finally, she gets tired of waiting for me to talk, I guess. "He said you were upset over that boy who killed himself. I…I thought you were making it up. But there was a lawsuit."

"Yes." I sit up straighter. Keep a rein on yourself, I think. "Your friends got sued by the family."

"It's a terrible thing." It sounds like she means it. "Celia says the family is just lashing out. They're hurt and want someone to blame, and they're abusing the courts."

"I—" I swallow. "I think that's partly true. The family should have supported him. But they also expected the people they brought in to help, not to—not to drive him to such despair that he wanted to kill himself."

"We don't—" She catches herself. "They would only have offered messages of hope."

"If he changed who he was."

She exhales across the phone. "Celia said…that one of the lawyers is your football player's brother." I draw my knees up to my chest. "Wiley?" Mother says, after several seconds. "Is it true?"

"Go ahead," I say. "Tell me that even my boyfriend's family doesn't agree with his lifestyle."

"I assume you know that." Her voice is cooler. "Why would you need me to remind you?"

"To try to get me to leave him. The way you left Father." It's not fair, of course it's not. It's just way more true than I want to admit.

"I didn't *leave* your father. He's the one—"

"I've heard the story. You're the one who changed, who grew apart."

"Did you ever think," she says, even colder, "that perhaps it was the two of you who changed? That you two left me behind? Were you homosexual in grade school, Wiley? Did Father encourage you to behave unnaturally—"

"There's plenty of evidence that it's natural," I say, loudly.

"Really," she says. "Celia told me there was some news about your 'natural' friend today."

Of course. The timing of the call—this is what had to have triggered it. "He's under a lot of stress."

"Yes, and stress is where true character is revealed. What did he say, exactly? That he wished he didn't have to go through all this? That he was praying to be relieved of this affliction?"

"What? He didn't—" I lurch forward off the air mattress because I can't just sit down at that, I can't keep myself curled up tightly. Emotion overrides my speech, sending my thoughts out a half-second before I'm ready for them to go. "He didn't say anything about praying, about being relieved—about it being an 'affliction'—what the hell are you—where are you getting—"

"People change, Wiley."

"Not the way you're thinking, they don't. Was I homosexual in grade school? Yeah, I was. Absolutely. Did I know what it meant or how to express it? No. But I was. I have been ever since I was born. Or before that, or whenever it is you think life starts." I stomp up and down.

Hal appears in the doorway, ears askew. I ignore him, focused on Mother's reply. "Studies have shown that you're influenced by popular culture—"

"That *I* am?" I yell. "You have studies that show what I'm influenced by?"

"—that young men in search of an identity to rebel against their parents with," she goes on as if I hadn't spoken, "will often choose a homosexual lifestyle for its unconventional and shocking effect on the family—"

"It didn't seem to shock Father all that much."

"Your father," she says, "was as shocked by it as I was. He thought we should let you do what you wish and find your own path, and I said that our duty as parents was to show you the proper path. I take no satisfaction in being proven right—"

"You think you're right? Still?" I grab at a tissue and hold it to my nose, and then have a short coughing fit.

"I've read the studies that Families United references and they all show that my instincts were correct." She talks faster now.

"I know about those studies," I say. "The ones that are discredited by just about every serious researcher in the field."

"Discredited by the homosexu—"

"I swear to Jesus Fox if you say 'agenda' I will drive back up there right now."

Hal's eyes widen. He leans against the hallway wall, watching me like a ref at a hockey game wondering when he needs to come in and break up the fight.

Mother's quiet. I wonder if she's reliving the memory of our last confrontation now, like I am. I stop pacing and lean against the wall, eyes closed, ears down, my tail lifeless. I don't feel good about the implied threat, and finally I say, "Sorry."

"Well," she says, softly. "I guess we always knew we would never reach agreement. But I hope you know that all that I'm doing is out of love. I didn't want you to be hurt. I just wanted you to find the joy in life of meeting a vixen and starting a family."

"I can have joy without a vixen," I say.

"Not real love," she says. "I wish I could explain…"

"You want to explain?" The pressure of the day clamps around my chest and squeezes the words out, tumbling as fast as I can think them, and I keep my eyes closed, imagining her standing there listening. "No. Let *me* explain. True love, real love, is letting someone go. It's realizing that you might not be the best thing for him in his life and stepping back so he can have a better life. It's sitting at home with your heart tearing apart because you want so much to be part of that life and you think you might have already ruined not only your own chance at that, but his chance at having anything worthwhile. It's—" I wipe my eyes. "It's standing by someone no matter what your family says, no matter what your job says, because you know in your heart that that's where you want to be. And when it all falls apart, it's feeling sadness and grief without an ounce of regret."

She doesn't say anything, but she's still breathing, still listening. I collect myself, though my voice is starting to crack. "Did you feel that with Father? When you defied your family to move to the Midwest and live with him, did you feel that it was the right thing to do? And when you grew apart, did you regret it? Do you? Do you wish you'd stayed in Port City, wish you'd stayed in Grandma's society circles and grown up the proper vixen your parents wanted you to be? Or are you proud of the choice you made, not to be a different person, but to express the person you are?"

I sit down hard on my air mattress, back to the wall, and close my eyes. Seconds tick by. I can feel Hal still there, still watching, while Mother breathes on the other end of the line and I force air through my mostly-clear nose because I don't want to breathe across the mic. I'm tense, gripping the phone, ready for whatever she's going to say, and finally she answers. "It's not the same," she says, wavering, uncertain.

"It's exactly the same," I say. "It's why Vince King killed himself, because he told his parents who he was and they brought in specialists to tell him he was wrong and twisted and he never thought he would have a normal life. He didn't have the strength you and I have, he didn't have the friends and the love that has gotten us through those times, that's made up for disapproving parents and friends and whatever else."

Silence on the other end of the line. Silence in the apartment. She's breathing into the phone, and I can't breathe through my nose so I'm breathing into the mic, the hell with it. I open my eyes and meet Hal's. He's completely still, even his tail.

"Are things falling apart?" Mother says softly. "For you?"

"Maybe." I wipe my eyes again and curl my tail up against the wall. "Maybe. I hope not, but I don't know. I have to wait until after this game."

"That's the championship? On Sunday?"

"Yes."

"Well." She pauses. "Good luck."

"Thanks."

I drop the phone onto the mattress and close my eyes again. Motion stirs my whiskers, and Hal's scent comes forward. "Sorry." I reach up and press fingers to my eyes.

"Don't worry about it." He's a foot away or so. "Could hear you no matter where I went. Figured I'd remind you I was here. It was either that or just go outside, and, um." He's looking all awkward when I open my eyes, muzzle pointing away from me, down at his printer. "You, ah…need another hug?"

"No," I say, but I lean forward and I can't hold back the pressure on my chest, on my eyes. I grab a tissue and hold it to my face, and he kneels and puts an arm around my shoulders anyway.

CHAPTER 18 – SWITCHING ASSIGNMENTS (DEV)

Machaine sits and listens to my troubles with Lee, and I sit and listen to his troubles with his on-again, off-again boyfriend, a Jewish fallow deer who hates when Machaine flirts with predator species, which is partly why he agreed to go out on the date with me (partly, like Strike told me, he was just curious about football players). I don't just talk about the troubles though. I mention Lee getting into the fight in Boliat and Machaine shakes his head and says, "That's why I moved out of the Midwest. Mostly lovely people until they've been drinking a bit." And I guess I talk a little more about Lee, because when we finish the milkshakes, he squeezes my paw and says, "You know I don't really care what Geoff thinks about who I date, right?"

"Uh." I'm not sure if that's a come-on, so I don't say anything.

The hare gives me a smile. "It's just fun to tease him. But someone who gets under your skin the way that fox does…well, there's a reason for that."

I sigh. "I know. I love him, I do. I just don't know if that's enough."

"It's not." He says it plainly, quickly, and I stare at him. "You have to love yourself, too."

"I…" I pause. "I like myself."

He gives my paw another squeeze and then lets it go. "That's a start. But you have to do better. I'm surprised none of your gay friends have told you that yet." At my expression, he puts one paw on his hip. "Oh, honey. You *have* to have some gay friends."

"When would I have met them?"

"Through your fox? No? All right, then. Now you have one." He pats my shoulder.

When Charm asks me with a friendly bellow how my date went, I say truthfully that I got his number. He laughs and claps me on the back and says he knew I had it in me. As if it were just that easy to pick up and date someone else, for someone who isn't a big, confident, straight stallion.

So I let Charm think what he wants and I try to deal with the problem of being all pent up, not from wanting Machaine or any of the other athletic guys out there, but just from wanting some kind of release. It's not like I haven't jerked off enough times on this trip. It's that that isn't enough. I thought it would be, but I'm increasingly edgy in practice on Wednesday, and it's not just because of the coverage of my embarrassing comments the day before, or the half hour I spent talking to people and clarifying and apologizing and saying the right things about being gay and coming out. It is, I think, because all during that apology session, I felt Lee over my shoulder, nodding, and I wanted to take that shadow and hold him and kiss him and feel him against me, and at the same time it made me grit my teeth because I knew he would say something abrasive.

I almost call him Wednesday night after practice to tell him I was thinking about him while I jerked off in the shower. But I don't want to be the first one to call. He's the one who walked out on me; he can call me when he's good and ready. And I have no idea when that will be. He's probably still mad about the remarks Tuesday. I have no idea how much coverage my apologies got; all I did was return the calls I got from a Chevali local paper and from a gay sports website. I hope they posted the things I said, but I don't have the energy to spare to go look for them.

Coach talks to us Wednesday night to tell us again how practice is going well, how we have to be careful not to wear ourselves out, how it's just another game. Nervous laughter all around. We all try to believe it. But I see Kodi and another guy duck into the bathroom, and we all pretend not to hear the retching sounds that follow. By Saturday, from what Fisher tells me, more of us will be in that state.

I never had to throw up before a game, but I played with people who did. Not that I've been in an important game in a while, but in college, before the playoff game, well, I'll just say that the locker room bathroom smelled pretty foul. This year, during the playoffs, I guess a couple guys probably snuck into the bathroom, but by and large it all seemed so improbable that we were there at all that I don't think any of us felt pressure.

Now it's been two weeks, and the Media Day interviews really brought it home to us. We can ignore the radio and TV and print and web pretty effectively—you have to, if you want to play a full season in the UFL—but when every one of us has to be available for press conferences, it's hard to ignore those outside forces, hard not to feel the weight of millions of eyes watching your every movement. And then you start thinking ahead to the game, wondering what you're going to do, becoming hyper-aware that something as small as a foot planted wrong can snowball and cost you, and your team, the game.

Kodi throws up. Me, I fidget and I think of Lee, because he'd be the one to ground me in this case. But I can't think of Lee, because right now that's too stressful. So I have to shut out everything else and find the place inside myself that lets me focus, that lets me concentrate. The problem is, that place has always been "next to my fox." With that gone, I can only focus on where it used to be.

Wednesday night I go out with Gerrard and Carson to a burger joint Gerrard has heard recommended. It's pretty good, with thick burgers and a fixings bar three yards long. Like lots of places in Crystal City, it has a wall of photos up of famous people who've eaten there. We joke that we should have our pics up there one day.

Going back to the hotel, Gerrard stops a block away at a different hotel and says he'll see us later. I don't peer past him into the lobby, but as Carson and I walk on alone, I ask, "What's that about?"

Carson shrugs. "You know," he says.

"Maybe." I look back. "You got a girl here?"

The leopard shakes his head slowly. His tail twitches. Maybe I should let it drop. Maybe.

But hell, it's just the two of us. So I say, quietly, "Got a guy?"

He snorts, and then looks at me with a grin. "No," he says clearly.

"Would you tell me?" We stop at a corner to wait for a light. I feel conspicuous, not only because we're both six-foot-plus, but also because our t-shirts and jeans stand out beside the other pedestrians waiting: a pair of hedgehogs in business shirts tailored to accommodate their back spines. But they're both absorbed in typing out text messages on their phones and barely spare us a glance.

Carson gives me a long look, but doesn't say anything until the light changes and we're walking across the street, and then he says, "Probably. Think so."

"Lee thinks someone else on the team does. Er, is." My ears flick back to the hedgehogs, even though there's almost zero chance they're listening, even if they can hear us over the traffic.

The leopard just shrugs. "Chances are," he says, and then, as we reach the curb, he looks up again. "So what?"

"Well, I dunno," I say. "It'd be nice to not be alone."

He nods. We get to the lobby of the hotel, where he holds the door for me, and walk across the fancy lobby. Some of the groupies are there already—word leaks out on the Internet about where we're staying, I guess. I spot Argonne talking to a vixen. He's almost become a fixture of my games now; I think if I didn't spot him before one of them, I'd start to worry about him.

Carson doesn't spare them a glance, just goes straight to the elevator. We get one all to ourselves and go up to our floor, and on the way up, he says, "You're not."

I've completely lost the thread of our conversation, so I blink and say, "What?"

"Alone. You're not."

We step out onto our floor, and I'm still looking at him. "You mean, you know someone…"

He smiles, as much as I've ever seen Carson smile. "You're a Firebird," he says. "And you're a helluva linebacker. And a friend. You're not alone."

"Oh," I say. "Thanks."

"Anytime." He stops at his door. "Now shut the fuck up and let's get ready to kick some ass Sunday."

I'm still grinning as I let myself into my room. Charm is out, of course, which means I can lock myself in the bathroom and let off some tension. But it's more work than it has been the last few days to get myself off, and it's not that my cock is sore from my rough paw rubbing it (it's not, but it makes me wonder if Lee's gets that way, and then I remember that I usually have lube on my paw). It's more that it's lonely, unsatisfying. I keep wanting to smell fox, to hold him, and his absence works like reverse oysters or something. I'm stroking myself, but my mind's not in it. And, well, you know what they say about sex: when it's good, it's great, and when it's bad, it's still pretty good. Yeah. By the time I get myself off, I'm seriously wondering about that. There's a flash of pleasure, but mostly relief, and the relief doesn't last all that long. It sends me to bed, where I take out the video iPod Gerrard gave me and look at film of Crystal City next to the playbook, and when Charm comes in reeking of sex, he calls me a teacher's pet and I throw a hotel bible at him. And he gets to sleep in five minutes while I lie there in the dark staring at the ceiling.

Of course, I tell myself, it's just the sex. I just have to train my body to get used to it. Like when—like what Strike's always talking about, training himself to live on healthier proteins and whatever other shit he eats. Of course, he talked about tantric meditation too, but apparently that's no match for a good pair of tits.

Iva was pretty too. I think about her lying in bed with me, and wow, it's been years since I had a female in bed. I used to like the feel of tits, myself, and now I mostly think about how they'd get in the way. I like the lean lines of Lee, the way I can stroke down the fur and feel the warm skin and the muscle underneath. Was I always gay? Was I born like this? Or am I just training myself to love this one fox because of all the other things he does for me—did for me?

Regardless of the greater implications, I need to get some rest and some focus. And Thursday I'm still stumbling around the field. Not critically; I mean, it's only once or twice. But I notice it, and so I stay quiet all during dinner, imagining stumbling during the championship as the Sabretooths run for a touchdown.

Strike wants to go out again that night, but when he mentions Iva, I pass. Gerrard is nowhere to be found, and as encouraging as Carson was, I can't imagine trying to hold a conversation with him for an entire dinner. So I join Ty and Charm, for old times' sake, on their way to a strip club Charm's been to three times already. Zillo tags along at the last minute.

We talk about the game, and the two of them keep pointing out different dancers to me. One's a tiger, and Ty, a few drinks left of sober at this point, asks me, "You don't feel nothing?"

I tell him that if she came up and offered to suck me off, I'd probably let her, but I wouldn't take her home, and that leads to a longer conversation than I would like about the difference between guys and girls giving blow jobs. Charm insists that although he'd never try it, he thinks guys would be better at it. "Because you guys sucked your own dicks at least a few times in high school, right? I mean, I haven't done it in years—I outsource that now—but man, in ninth grade I was worried I'd end up hunchbacked."

Ty just grins and nods, while Zillo sticks his tongue out. "Gross."

"You did it too, don't try to pretend you didn't. That long muzzle and all." Charm elbows him.

"Yeah, yeah." Zillo gulps down the rest of his drink and grins, and shoves Charm back.

I clear my throat. "You have a point?"

"Yeah, just that…you know, guys know what to do. I mean, don't get me wrong, I've had some girls who had a lot of practice. A lot. But I just think a guy would have the advantage."

Ty bumps his shoulder into mine. "Dev, you had both. Whatcha think?"

I bury my nose in what is still my first beer of the night. "You know, I'm not drunk enough to talk about this."

Charm raises a hand to the waitress. "My buddy here needs another beer," he yells.

"No, I mean—that's not—"

"Shuddup and finish your beer." He glares at me.

For a horse, he's got a mean stare. I gulp down the beer and slide the empty mug across the table. "So which one of these gals do you guys like? Going to get a lap dance?"

Charm laughs. "Why pay for the merch when you can get a free sample? Nah, we'll just hang out and then see if one of the waitresses wants to party after. But don't avoid the question." The stallion grins down at me.

Zillo waves him off. "C'mon, Charm, he—he don't wanna t-talk about it."

Charm leans in. "I got blown by a guy once."

His breath stinks of beer. He's on his fourth at least. Ty puts his drink down, big ears swiveling forward, and I raise an eyebrow. "You never told me."

"Nah," he says. "Not the sort of thing to brag about, y'know. But in college. Guy comes up and says he thinks he can show me a good time, and you know, I like me a good time."

"So was it a good t-time?" Zillo leans in.

"He was damn good, tell ya that," Charm says. "Ain't sayin' I didn't have girls who were better, but maybe that's just cause of the tits and I like watchin' 'em more."

"I guess so." Zillo shrugs and rubs his muzzle. "Don' make you gay, right?"

Ty glances my way and grins. "Not that there's anything wrong with that." He might not be fully sober, but he's quite a bit less drunk than the coyote.

Charm just throws his head back and laughs. "Hey," he says, "it'd take a guy with great tits to make me gay."

"Probably not even then." I raise a glass to him.

"But hey, that's just how I am, and Dev here likes guys—at least one guy—and that's cool. Whatever."

Ty licks at his cocktail glass. "If you look at it just, like, what kind of person you wanna be with…I mean, that's not so bad at all. There's guys on the team, married guys, who sleep around, and nobody says shit about that."

"Well," I say, "I mean, that's how some people have their lives. Couple of the wives I talk to, they know it goes on."

"Don't know everything that goes on," Zillo mumbles, and then ducks his head, ears flat.

"You want a refill?" Charm asks.

I'm intensely curious to ask what Zillo means, but it's something he got in confidence, I think, so I'm not going to push him. He's drunk anyway, so it wouldn't be fair.

But I think about it again in the taxi on the way home, after I leave the three of them to hit on a pair of waitresses who are impressed with the size of their drink bill (right as I'm leaving, Charm invites them to share some of his $1,000-a-bottle champagne, and I know for a fact that he doesn't even like the stuff). Ty, the most sober, tells me with a wink and a wave that he'll get them back home. Zillo doesn't show much sign of being two days away from the biggest game of his life, and Charm, particularly, whose job is maybe the least demanding physically and most stressful mentally on the whole team, has an amazing facility for being able to relax that I envy.

Not that my job isn't stressful, but it's multiple small points of stress. One mistake can be costly, sure, but I have a whole game to make up for it. Charm comes in, often with the game on the line, and if he misses, he might not get to try again that game.

That doesn't mean I can afford to make any mistakes. I lean back against the seat and close my eyes, and I think about what I'm going to do during the game. For the first time, it really hits me that Lee isn't going to be up there in the stands watching me. I clench my paws and breathe in. He'll be watching on TV, of course he will. And I know...I think I know...that he still believes in me.

I never gave a lot of thought to love, in high school. That was something the girls wanted. I just thought someday I'd find a girl I could hang out with after sex, and we'd have a family. Treated it the same way I did football, really: just a game to learn the steps of, to go through the motions, to win or lose. But losing wasn't that big a deal, before Lee. I was still getting to play football, still getting to walk around with the team and get excused from homework and stuff. If I lost, well, the team was partly to blame for that. There wasn't much I could do, me alone, to make a bunch of other guys play better and win games. And what was the point? There was no football life after college for me anyway. I wasn't good enough.

Except he showed me that I was. I liked that feeling and I haven't stopped chasing it since.

I exhale. And then, I remind myself, he showed me that he wants to pursue his life, and I want to pursue mine, and it's fucking hard to make that work. But I can't blame him for it, because I think what he wants to feel is the same thing I want to feel: that he's important, that he matters, that he's good at something. When you uncover all the things we chase through this life, doesn't it come down to that? Don't you want people to admire you and friends to know they can rely on you, no matter what you're doing? Machaine said I have to love myself too, but I guess when Lee was around, he loved me enough that I didn't worry about that.

I miss him. I want him so badly that my teeth grind and my claws prick my paw pads and it takes a deep breath and a real effort to get myself to relax. I'm wound up and thinking about Charm and Ty fucking those waitresses, and Strike with his holier-than-thou tantric bullshit fuckwaddery still groping Iva, and Gerrard doing whatever it is Zillo doesn't wanna tell me about, but I'm sure it involves him getting laid. So I'm going to go up to the room and jerk off and it'll just make me angrier because it's not what I want; it's just the only thing I can have.

The taxi pulls up in front of the hotel. I pay the driver and stalk inside. I know I've gotta do something. I just have no idea what. My paw slides into my pocket and curls around my phone. My fingers brush the cracks in the screen. Maybe I'll call Lee, tell him I want him to fly out here.

Right, and then how would that go? "Hey, hon, can I just fuck you a couple times to keep myself loose for the game?" Oh, he'd love that. He would just fucking love that. I let go of the phone in my pocket and round the corner to the elevators.

I get there right as one dings. The doors open, and Argonne steps out.

He's wearing a white cotton short-sleeved shirt with pink trim on the collar and cuffs and sleek tan slacks, both a little rumpled. He's just lifting a paw to his muzzle, but when he sees me, he puts the paw back in his pocket. His ears flick back and he murmurs, "Going up, handsome?"

The long brush of his tail clears the elevator door. I stand there and watch it in the empty elevator lobby. For a moment, the need in me pulls me back to college. I'm a horny football player, and he's just a girl I want. And I can have any girl I want.

He's walking away. From behind, he could almost be Lee, with that little satisfied strut, that swish to his tail. What would Lee tell me to do, if I need to get laid to be effective in the football game? I come to an immediate decision. "Yeah," I say. "You coming?"

He turns. His eyebrows rise, eyes widen. But he doesn't decline or walk away, so I grab his wrist and pull him into the elevator, then stab the Door Close button and my floor.

At about the fifth floor, he regains his composure and his smirk. "Well," he says, "boyfriend away, tiger can play?"

"Something like that." I eye him. "No *ascot*?"

He pulls the filmy scarf from one pocket. "Didn't want to get anything *on* it." He winks.

I don't want to stand too near him in the elevator, don't want to think too much about what I'm heading toward doing. It's a sign that he was walking out as I was walking in, just as I was thinking about Lee.

I push thoughts of Lee aside. If he cared about me, he'd be here now and he wouldn't have pushed me to this. Anyway, it's not that big a deal. Argonne's already said he's discreet, and he has to be, if he's been seeing someone else on the team. And he's a fox, and if I were a little more drunk this would be perfect because I could tell myself he's Lee, and I might even remember it that way in the morning.

When the door opens, I push him back against the elevator wall and step out to check out the hallway. It's deserted; still too early for most guys to be coming back.

"I know the drill." He steps out behind me, quiet and graceful.

"Shut up," I say.

"I know that, too," he murmurs, just low enough that I can hear him.

I walk fast down the corridor to my room, and he hurries behind me. We get into the room without anyone seeing, and I lock the door behind me. If Charm comes home early, then he'll just have to see Argonne in the room, but at least the lock'll give me time to get decent. And Charm is maybe the one person who won't judge me.

"Well, well. So patience does pay off." Argonne puts a paw on my hip as I turn.

I growl and push him against the wall, not too roughly, but firmly. "This is how this is gonna work," I say, my nose inches from his. "You're gonna shut up. One more word and I toss you out in the hall."

He loses a little of his smirk. I can smell him strongly now, that musky fox scent, so like—so familiar and yet different. "Otherwise you can just leave right now," I say. "If you wanna stay, just nod."

Slowly, his muzzle moves up and down, his eyes never leaving mine. "Okay," I say. "Then get over there on the bed on the right."

I can't fuck him, probably. Well, he might have lube—probably does, now I think about it. But just a blow job, that'd be enough, wouldn't it? And it's not really cheating. Not really. It's not like I'm going to fuck him, no matter how tempting it is, with that bushy tail of his swinging back and forth as he gets up onto the bed, just like Lee's, that smirk on his muzzle that's so much like my fox's—

My fox? Can I still call him that? Of course I can. Maybe just not right now.

Argonne is younger, his ears a little larger. He holds them up, looking back over his shoulder at me, on paws and knees on my bed. His tail flicks back and forth slowly, and I step forward. "Not like that. Turn around."

Now that I've gotten to this point, I'm less sure. I need this, I know—or I think I know—but the fantasy in my mind that I could just close my eyes and imagine Lee, or forget who I was with, is receding. The smell is different, even to me with my short tiger nose. The lights are on in the room still, and there's just something off about the whole thing even as he turns, angling his head to look up at me and then down my body.

And then Argonne puts a paw up to my pants, without saying a word. He lets the tip of his tongue stick out of his lips, a little pink flicker whose meaning I get right away, and his fingers brush my pants next to my sheath. Not touching, but the vibration of his claws on the fabric makes its way across, and I get a little harder than I already was. I swallow. Maybe this won't be so hard to go through with after all.

When I don't stop his fingers, he reaches up and undoes the fastening at my waist. Then the zipper. The air is cool through the fabric of my underwear, but his paw is warm.

I close my eyes. Just another fox, I think. Even if he smells different, there's still an underlying familiarity to his musk. Maybe it's something all foxes have in common. Though I'm still having trouble thinking of him as Lee, even with my eyes closed.

His paw tickles my sheath through my underwear, and then he pulls down the waistband. He exhales a soft breath over my stomach fur. And then I feel his tongue wash across my tip, and his paw holds my shaft at the base.

I think about sucking off Lee when he was on the phone with Hal, about him returning the favor in the shower. "Hang on." I push Argonne off, step back from the bed. My heart's pounding, my cock is throbbing, and I don't know what the fuck to do.

I don't want to open my eyes to look at him, so I hear the bed creak as he gets off it, and then my whiskers shiver as he steps close to me, muzzle against my chest. Fingers slide up my cock and then curl around it. "You need this." His breath washes over my muzzle and whiskers, a warm, insistent message that I feel I should be listening to, only most of my attention is focused on those fingers, their soft pads and gentle claws. "And I won't tell anyone. I'm very discreet."

All my wiring is short-circuiting. Discreet, he says. Fuck, the last thing I'd need would be for it to get back to Fisher or Gerrard or their wives. But it'll be just five minutes, a quick suck and coming in his muzzle and then he'll be gone and I can relax. What if Charm walks in on us? Lion Christ, that paw is rubbing and I can't think. What if Colin finds out? He'll sure as fuck use this against me—no, I can't do this, but I can't make him stop, and if I just do nothing it'll be over soon...

The smell of Argonne's breath tickles my nose again, and this time, this time I finally understand what it's trying to tell me.

My eyes open. Argonne's smile is inches below mine, a sly fox grin in a lithe body. "Oh, shit," I say.

Chapter 19 – Final Round (Lee)

Hal and I fly to Yerba on Saturday. In comparison to Tuesday, the rest of the week actually went pretty well. I only broke down crying one more time, I didn't have any thoughts of sleeping with my gracious host (okay, I did have one kind of guilty fantasy that night, lying on the air mattress, that he would come in and lie down with me and put his arms around me, but there wasn't even any sex involved, that's how pathetic my fantasies are these days, and the only reason it was Hal was that I couldn't bring myself to wish for Dev even though I wanted to), and I didn't yell at Mother on the phone or make any more embarrassing emotional revelations.

Father called Wednesday, though, and while he didn't specifically say, "You upset your mother," he did say he'd talked to her and that they'd discussed me, so I sort of read between the lines. And I have managed to follow some of the buildup to the championship game without getting all emotional about Dev.

Partly it's because I'm forcing myself to confront it. I know I can't just hide in a corner. Either Dev and I will get back together or we won't—or, to look at it another way, either we'll formalize our breakup or we'll make up like we usually do. In either case, I'm going to be working in football and watching football and I can't just pretend like he's not a part of that world. I need to get used to watching him and not thinking, "That's my tiger."

Even though I still think that, deep in my heart. And near the surface of my heart, and also in my mind and in other places too. Speaking of which, I also confirmed that I am not completely broken: I managed to jerk off in the restroom at Starbucks. Okay, I don't recommend it to everyone, but I didn't want to jerk off at Hal's; I remember from college how I could smell every time one of my roommates did. And I didn't want to use his bathroom because it smells strongly of him and I don't want to start associating him with sex. So I sat in the bathroom, thought about some porn, and when I was done, sprayed around a lot of air freshener. Not my finest hour, but hey, it's better than not being able to jerk off at all.

By Saturday I feel like I am under control enough to watch the game with the Yerba people and not break down crying when Dev's introduced. I manage to watch his whole Media Day interview and it just makes me feel sorry for him, because clearly he's being goaded into an outburst. I recognize Brian's voice, though he doesn't show up in the video, and I go so far as to call the White Witch—er, Paula at Equality Now and try to explain that Dev didn't really mean what he said, that he was under a lot of pressure. But she never responds to my voicemail, so who knows if that did any good.

The only other hitch comes on Friday, when Hal says that Pol wanted to watch the championship game with him. He's close to the point of backing out of the trip, which would be fine, but I kind of would like the company. I don't pressure him, though, and a while later he says that making the connections in Yerba would be good for his career and so he wants to come along on the trip. I don't point out that he's choosing his career over Pol, because I can tell from the guilty flick of his ears and the flattening of his whiskers that he already knows.

So Saturday at the airport, he's on the phone with her for twenty minutes once we're through the security gate. I play with my phone, which at least I can use without thinking about how I got it. Mostly.I download two or three new games, mindless diversions I can use to distract myself from life.

And when we land and get to the hotel, Hal calls her again to let her know we arrived safely. "Jesus Fox," I say, teasing, "you're only dating, you're not married yet." I have a couple messages on my phone, too, but neither of them is from Dev. One from Gena, one from Father.

He sweeps his ears back and says, "When you—" and then stops. "Ah, shit," he says, "I just feel bad leaving her behind."

I don't ask what he was about to say. I think I can guess at least generally. "Long as she doesn't think you're desperate," I say. "That kinda scent doesn't wash off."

"Hah." He shakes his head. "Don't worry about me."

We check in. The Whalers are paying for the hotel, as this is technically an interview visit, so it doesn't cost anything. But it's a hotel chain where I have a lot of points, so the clerk is really nice to me, welcoming me back as a "special guest." On our way up to the room, I show off the "special guest" perks to Hal. "Free breakfast, free Internet…see, when you travel with a real VIP, you get treated nice."

"I see that." Hal takes the envelope and rifles through the coupons. "Free drink at happy hour. Too bad they don't do that on Saturday."

"Maybe we can talk them into it." I grin at him. "Think like a fox."

"Don't need you to tell me to think like a fox." Hal hands me back the envelope. "Damn reds, think you're the only real foxes."

I swish my tail pointedly as I step out of the elevator ahead of him. It's nice to be in a different location, in a hotel where I'm called a special guest even if it's only because I've spent a lot of money with them, even if it isn't the nicest hotel in the world. And I'm glad it's not up in the city of Yerba proper, where Dev and I made love and looked out the window and dreamed about what it would be like to live there.

The room is clean, and they don't overcharge foxes to stay there (not VIP foxes, anyway), and right now that's paradise to me. I drop my bag on one bed, Hal takes the other, and while I call Peter to get directions for the party tomorrow, Hal unpacks. I watch, amused at how familiar I am with his clothing already. When I hang up, I restrain the urge to ask him if that's what he's planning to wear for the game tomorrow.

Instead, I turn and look out the window, at the frontage road (the highway is behind us), the low flat grassy park, and the grey-blue of Yerba Bay. Only a few boats break the plane of the water, and there are no waves, but the air's hazy and I can't see the other side, so if I squint and imagine the sound of breakers, I can imagine it's the ocean as I put the phone to my ear and listen to my voicemail.

Gena asks if I'm okay; she hasn't seen me around and Fisher doesn't know or won't tell her what's going on with us. There's a note of worry in her voice about Fisher, too, which flattens my ears with a guilty flush because I've pretty much let that slide while I've been recovering from walking out on Dev. Father says he is looking forward to the game and hopes it's a good one, and offers to be by the phone if I don't have anyone to watch it with.

Father is the easy call, so while Hal is setting up his computer, I sit by the window and make that one. I tell him I'm in Yerba, meeting with the Whalers front office guys to watch the game, and he laughs.

"You don't have to impress me with your football connections anymore," he says.

"I'm just trying to tell you it looks hopeful for the job."

"I knew that. You're smart and good at what you do."

"Thanks," I say, watching the wind pick up over the bay. White-capped ripples chase silvery shorebirds around until the birds take wing in a massive, coordinated flight. "Where are you watching the game?"

"Few of the guys from work are getting together at Wild Wings." I can hear the face he's making.

"Hey, their wings aren't bad," I say. "I hear they're pretty wild."

"Ha. I'll bet you get better wings at the team-catered lunch."

"I dunno. It's the Whalers, so they don't really go in for spending for the sake of spending anymore."

"Yeah, but they treat their players well." He pauses. "Couple reporters said Dev might get traded there."

The pang is just a twinge in my chest. I don't think my voice betrays any of my emotion. "Maybe. I think he'd be better off staying in Chevali, though."

"Even if you get the job?"

I think about that. Wouldn't it be great, being able to work for the same team, live in the same area? It would, but it wouldn't be the best thing for Dev. It'd just be better for me, and I've already gone through figuring out that what's good for me might not be good for Dev. Then again, if the Firebirds lowball him and Yerba makes a good offer, maybe it would be good, financially. It's just a risk for him because he'd have to start over again with a new team. Players do that all the time, but not players with the kind of risk he has.

"Yeah," I say to my father. "It's the switching teams. He's got a lot of really good teammates, and he could easily wind up in some situation where the coach or a couple key players are hostile. I mean, if more players start coming out, in a year or two, when it's not a big deal any more, then maybe…" I trail off. "But that's not happening."

"I think it will," Father says.

"I hope so."

There's silence. Hal's listening to me as he types; I see the insides of his ears. Outside, a pair of kangaroos hops slowly along the walk down to the park, and a red wolf family—no, dholes, actually—pass in the other direction. Cars speed up and down the road. This whole area feels much more energetic than Chevali, or sleepy Hilltown. "You know," Father says, "I think you should call your mother."

"Why?" I make the question as dry and uninterested as I can.

"Because she was upset."

"Good."

"Wiley." He sighs. "She loves you."

"I know," I say. "She only hates the sin."

"Yes, actually. But that lawsuit you won't shut up about…"

I shift on the chair and rub fingers against the window pane. "Don't tell me she actually read something about it."

"We talked for an hour."

"Seriously?"

"It's a serious subject," he says. "Of course we talked seriously."

"Ha. So…I mean, how did it end up?"

He takes a breath. "I think. I think she understood that a boy doesn't just kill himself because he's weak. I think she started to understand how difficult it is for someone to be different."

"Even if she doesn't like the way in which they're different?" I curl my tail around into my lap and rest a paw on it.

"Even then."

"So does she think the way I'm different is okay, now?"

"I wouldn't say that, exactly—"

"Then I don't know what we have to talk about."

He sighs. "Dear Lord, how did the two of you not kill each other?"

"We almost did, remember?"

"I know it's difficult. I know that you and she don't see eye to eye—"

My reflection hovers in the glass, over the park and the street and the water and the haze. "We don't just not see eye to eye. We're not even on the same floor of the same building."

"—but the way to make things right is to talk about it. Or did you not learn that this past fall?"

I bite my lip. "This is different. Mikhail was just angry that Dev didn't come talk to him first."

"He wasn't thrilled with his son's lifestyle, either. The real question, Wiley, is whether you care about your family."

"It's not whether I care about my family. It's whether I care about her. And I'm finding it pretty hard to care about her when she clearly only cares about me to the extent that she can stop me being who I am."

"You know that's not true."

"No, I don't know that's not true!" In the window, I look angry, but also desperate. My paw clenches around my tail. "I haven't had a single conversation where she's been interested in me and supportive of me since—since I decided what college to go to."

"And have you supported her?"

"She's a parent. She doesn't need my support."

He laughs. "Wiley, now that you've graduated college, I can let you in on a little secret. Parents are actually just people who had cubs. We get scared, and sad, and insecure. We like it when the people we care about show that they care about us."

"How long, though? How long do I have to beat my heart against that wall?"

Hal, openly looking at me now, raises an eyebrow and nods approvingly at my metaphor. Father sighs again. "I wouldn't be telling you to call her if I thought it was going to hurt you. I would hope you would think better of me than that. I really think she is struggling right now, and talking to you would help her."

"Struggling?" I sit up straighter. "Is she leaving Families United?"

"I don't know. She just said she was struggling with a lot of things."

"I should call her—"

"Wiley, don't call and start going on at her about your cause and what's right."

I scratch claws through my tail fur. "First you tell me to call, then you tell me not to."

"I'm telling you to call with the right attitude. I know things are hard for you right now and you may be tempted to take it out on her. If you have to wait until after the game, then wait."

My tail looks ragged now; I smooth it down. "I don't know what difference the game will make."

"Maybe you'll be less tense. Maybe you and Dev will have talked." When I'm quiet, he says, "Strike that—you will have talked."

"Thanks. I hope so."

"You know, Lee, you do have some control over whether the two of you talk." He sounds vaguely amused. "Those new fancy phones make outgoing calls, I've found."

"I know. I just have to decide whether I think it's a good idea."

"Why would it not be a good idea?"

"Wouldn't it be better to end it now, rather than trying for years to make something work that's just going to fail anyway?" There's a lull in traffic outside. The dhole family is out of sight, but a small group of feline cubs plays in the fringe of the park.

"That's a point," Father says. "Of course, if your mother and I had believed that, you might not have been born."

I watch the cubs play, running after each other in some weird form of Tag. They don't seem to be playing by the rules I learned, but they're screaming and laughing all the same. "So you had misgivings from the start?"

"Every relationship has misgivings at the start."

"But I thought you said she changed over the last couple years."

He exhales. "Dammit, Wiley, I'm trying to be encouraging. You want to stop analyzing everything and just listen?"

I smile at my reflection, down at the cubs. "You think I can?"

"I don't know. But it'd be a good skill to pick up."

"I'll work on it. Promise."

"Not just with me," he says.

"I know, I know."

Hal glances over after I hang up. "Nice to have at least one supportive parent."

"He's changed a lot in the last two years. Went from not wanting to hear about my love life to encouraging me to get back together with Dev."

"Uh-huh." Hal returns his attention to the computer. "Sure he doesn't just want more free tickets and invitations to owners' boxes?"

"I'm not really sure of anything. But I have to call Gena." I call up her number. "How's that story coming? That still the injury one?"

"Part of it. There's like five cases I'm writing up and then the overall frame. This one's an old offensive line guy from the seventies."

"Who?"

He glances at me again and his ears flick. "Can't tell you. Confidential until the story goes live."

"Fine, fine." I thumb Gena's number. While the phone rings, I say, "Is it Silva?"

"No."

"Hi," I say as Gena answers. "Thanks for the call."

"Are you in Crystal City?"

"No, I'm in Yerba."

She digests that for a moment. "Did you get lost?"

"I'm up here for a job interview. Don't tell anyone."

"With the Whalers? Good for you. You're not missing much here. Well, I mean…there's a lot going on, but the boys are all kind of crazy running around and focused and we're just shopping."

"I like shopping." The traffic outside has picked up again.

"The stores here are amazing. So expensive!"

"That's C.C. How are the wives doing?"

"Angela's coming in tonight with the boys. Daria's comparing everything to Freestone, and Penny—Colin's Penny, the vixen—"

"Right." I hate the fact that Colin is a fox.

"She's been coming along with us, and I'm not sure she's ever been in a city bigger than Chevali. We went to the South Center Mall and she got lost. Didn't realize there's a whole other section of the mall on the other side of Nordstrom's."

"I haven't been to that one."

She tells me about the mall for five or ten minutes, about all the specialty stores and the three levels and the bizarre hanging art and the movie posters and the fountain, and then I get to ask the question I'm really interested in. "How's Fisher?"

"Oh, you know." Her energy drops. "He's…he's focused on the game. I haven't talked to him much."

"So he's going to play."

"The doctors cleared him."

She puts just the slightest emphasis on the word "doctors," enough to get my ears perked up. "You don't think he should play."

"I wouldn't dare try to stop him. It's the championship. And he probably gives the team a better chance to win. He says so, and Dev said the team felt more energized with him in there. So I guess. I mean…how much more could he be injured in one game? And it would mean a lot to the city."

"The needs of the many outweigh the needs of the few?"

"What?"

I shake my head. "Line from a movie."

"Do you believe that?"

I stare out the window again, past my reflection. Do I? "I don't know," I say finally. "I don't think it's always that clear-cut. But you have to decide. I mean, if I knew that the Dragons were going to win a championship but that one of the players would be crippled for life…"

Hal's typing stops. I turn, and he's looking at me down his long, sharp muzzle. "I don't know," I say. "I don't know how I'd feel about that."

"I don't know what I can do about it." She must have moved the phone mic away from her muzzle. She sounds distant, as though she's talking from the other end of a long hallway. "He's going to play. If I hound him about it, he'll just resent me."

"Yeah." I wish there were more I could say. I wish I could tell her that he'll come around, that he'll see reason. I wish I could tell her that she would feel good about her decision to do the right thing for him, that the feeling she has of being trapped with no good way out is an illusion, that there's a right answer and that she can choose it. Instead, I choose humor, or as close as I can get. "Men, right?"

The pause between trying to make a joke and the other person's laughter can be the longest, most painful silence in the world. She does laugh, shortly, and bring the mic back to her muzzle, but her voice also feels close to an edge of some sort, as though she's going to start crying or shouting pretty soon. "Every other wife is probably feeling that," she says. "But I don't feel like I can talk to them. They'll just think it's domestic violence or something. I wish you were here."

I should be there. "I'm sorry," I say.

"Oh, no, I hope you get the job. I know that's important. It'd be nice if you could work for the same team, but…well, you don't have a family to look after, so you need something to keep you busy, right?"

"I love scouting," I say. "Since I can't play."

"When do you go in for the interview?"

"We're going to watch the game tomorrow, and I think it'll just be informal conversations. Get to meet the guys, and so on. They already have my work history and everything."

"They know about Dev, I guess?"

"Yeah." I still don't know how much difference that's going to make by the time I actually start the job.

We talk a little longer about Crystal City and the atmosphere surrounding the game. She thinks it isn't fair that one team has home field advantage, and I say that's how it's always been done, that the better team during the season gets the home fans. "When we played the game in Highbourne, it was fine," she says with a laugh. "But the away game was terrible."

"You still won."

"Yes. Hopefully we win this one and…everything's fine."

I tell her I'll be wishing my best, and she wishes me luck again. When I hang up, Hal turns his chair to face me. "You know that's how those Dragons championships were won, right?"

"Some things I don't really want to know all of."

"And all the championships, really. That's what I'm writing about, the price that we pay for this entertainment."

I turn so I'm sitting cross-ways in the chair, legs draped over the arm and tail hanging off the front of the chair. "I don't know if I want to know these things. But I don't not want to know them."

"I know it ain't gonna be very popular." Hal sighs. "But I feel like I gotta write this story. This shit's been covered up, whitewashed, ignored too long."

"I think you should, too," I say. "Sometimes you have to do the right thing even if it's not the popular thing."

"Just wish it wasn't so damn hard," he grumbles. "Half these guys don't want to talk about their injuries. Don't want people thinking of them as broken-down. Their games still play on cable sometimes and they want to stick in the public image that way."

"People get stuck in time," I say. "It's hard."

"And some of the rest of them say they'd make the same choices even knowing how it would turn out. They'd trade the chance to be healthy and happy for most of their life for those few years of glory."

"You know," I say, "I kind of know how they feel."

•

I don't call Mother that night. I'm not sure what it'll accomplish to wait until after the game, but at least I don't want to add any more emotional baggage to my life the day before the interview if I can avoid it. Hal and I drive up the freeway to a place one of his friends recommended, in a small neighborhood that looks like the main street of a small town. The whole Yerba area is dotted with these small towns that have fused together into one giant suburb, but still retained their own identities. The sheer volume of people in this area is overwhelming (though not as bad as Crystal City), but I like the fact that these small towns are surviving and recognizably different, even if I can't tell one from the other.

Sunday, we drive down through a slightly chilly morning to the Whalers' offices. Peter meets us at the door of the building sporting a maroon polo with the Whalers logo in gold over the heart. He grasps my chocolate-brown paw in his with a firm, warm grip, and matches my smile. We lean in to refresh our memory of each other's scent, and then the other fox releases my paw. "Peter Emmanuel," he says, extending a paw to Hal.

"Hal Kinnel." The swift fox shakes. "We've talked once or twice."

Peter holds the door for us to enter. "You did that piece on the Firebirds a few years back. Nice job."

"Thanks." Hal takes it in stride, and I raise my eyebrows. Peter hadn't mentioned that on the phone; either he was holding back on me or he looked it up in advance of our visit.

It's warm inside and has that clean smell that all office buildings have, though here it's also tinged with a cloth-and-paper smell that I can't quite place until I walk around a corner and into a gallery of uniforms hanging on the walls, a maroon and gold tapestry of famous Whalers players.

"Wow," I murmur, going up close to the jersey of one of the quarter-backs I used to love watching when I was growing up. "He beat the Dragons in the playoffs in '97. I still couldn't hate him, he was so good and so much fun to watch."

"Take a little time if you want," Peter says, "but you can also look on the way out. I want to hurry back for some of the pre-game betting." He glances at Hal. "Friendly wagering, of course."

"Of course." Hal keeps that polite smile on.

"We can go." I step away from the jerseys. "We didn't have a gallery like this in Hilltown, that's all."

"No trophy room?" The other fox seems surprised as he leads us up a staircase on the opposite side of the room.

"Oh, we had one. It was just smaller. Had the Super Bowl trophies, some pictures, a few footballs." I think back. "We had Cunningham's 300th touchdown ball."

Peter whistles. "Nice. Come on, everyone's in here."

He doesn't need to say that, because the din of chatter is audible even before he opens the door to the second floor hallway. At the other end of the hall, past some office doors, a big double door with the Whalers logo on it stands half open, and beyond I can see a bunch of people, most dressed in maroon and gold.

"So what do you bet on, pre-game?" Hal asks as we come up to the room. "I mean, when we were down in Hellentown, I tossed a few twenties in on the Firebirds." When Peter stops, Hal gives him a cocky, foxy grin. "Y'know, when Lee here got us into the owner's box."

Peter relaxes, shoulders losing some tightness as his tail swishes. "I'll show you. You're welcome to get in on it." When Hal hesitates, Peter's grin widens. "Oh, don't worry. You're a fox. They won't take advantage of you too badly. Even if you're not a red."

Hal rolls his eyes at me as we walk into the mass of people. On one side of the large meeting room, the pre-game show is being projected onto a screen that takes up half the wall. The wall directly across from us is one huge whiteboard, where a bunch of prop bets are written for the game in blue and red and green and black: Firebirds number of interceptions over/under 1½, Sabretooths turnovers over/under 2½, Total number of plays for each team (Sabretooths over/under 62, Firebirds over/under 71), and of course there are bets on which team will have more tackles, sacks, interceptions, touchdowns, yards, first downs, and so on. There's also a section for prop bets on the pre-game show and the hosts: how many times Archie (one of the broadcasters) will say "ultimate"; how many times John will use the telestrator; how many touching personal stories they will refer to. One of the bets is "Number of times Miski called 'first openly gay player,'" and the number beside it is 12. On the far left side of the whiteboard wall, there's another door; I see someone walk into the room through it carrying a hot dog bun.

A lemur with a marker poised in one paw stands near the board, watching the TV intently. On it, Archie, a polished, smiling raccoon in a purple tie, says, "this is the ultimate crucible for the UFL's first openly gay player," and the lemur makes a quick mark beside the "ultimate" bet and the "first openly gay player" bet, making it six for the first and three for the second.

I turn away from the TV as a picture of Dev comes up on it, and look around the room. There must be about thirty people here. Peter hesitates, maybe thinking I want to watch the bit on Dev, but when I turn away he takes me by the arm and walks me around, introducing me rapid-fire: Director of Player Personnel, Director of College Scouting, Director of Pro Scouting, West Region Scout, and so on. Jocko, the Director of College Scouting who was vaguely hostile on the phone with me, is indeed a brown bear; he takes me in with a neutral look and then goes back to his conversation. The others are wolf, stallion, bear, wolf (this wolf reminds me scarily of the beer-throwing wolf, to the point that I find it uncomfortable to talk to him), an array of familiar football species, and, incongruously, a fruit bat named Jalili.

She's the assistant to the director, and we hit it off within about two sentences. "You didn't play football," she says, first thing.

"No," I say. "Did you?"

She laughs and tells Peter, "I hope he's the guy you told me about," and he tells her I am indeed that guy.

"Good." She takes a moment to glare at Jocko, but doesn't say anything, and when he sees her he gives her a shrug. They both turn away from each other, and before I can ask her about it, I've got a leathery wing draped around my shoulders.

"So," she says with a grin, "who you got in the game?"

"Oh, I, uh." I look at Peter and then up at the screen. "Well, I'm kinda rooting for the Firebirds."

She laughs, a high, sharp sound, and pats my shoulder. "'Cause of your boyfriend, yeah, I know, but who do you *think* is going to win?"

This becomes a theme as we go around meeting people. "Should we bet the over or under on INTs?" I'm asked. "Is Fisher a hundred percent?" people want to know. "Are they going to use Strike primarily as a decoy?"

"Come on," I say to that last one. "I know the Sabretooths have a good corner, but…come on."

His friends laugh at him too, and the little group disperses, Jalili with them. I look for Hal, but he's mingling very well, over in the corner talking to two people who are—I press my fingers to my head and force my memory to work—a Contract Administrator and…Senior Personnel Advisor.

Peter finds me again, holding a hot dog bun with something in it that smells better than a hot dog. "Hey, want something to eat? We've got sausages and beer in the other room, and nachos."

"In a bit." I look around. "Is there anyone in particular I should be talking to?"

He grins. "They'll find you. Don't worry about it, just relax and have a good time."

"I shouldn't worry about Jocko?"

He raises his eyebrows. "He say something to you?"

"Er. No."

"Then no." He indicates the betting area with his muzzle. "You putting down any bets?"

I look at the whiteboard. "I think I just want to enjoy the game, but thanks. This is fun."

"Not a problem. So tell me what you think of the matchups?"

The studio analysts are dissecting some of the matchups on screen, but I start with my own order in my own head. "Sabretooths' offense is better than the Firebirds', but the Firebirds' defense is a little better. The main reason the Sabretooths do well on offense is their left guard, and the Firebirds won't be able to make a lot of headway against him, but they're stronger on the weak side, where they have Fisher and Brick."

"And Miski." Peter smiles. I notice that Jocko and a wolf—shit, I can't remember his title, something to do with Player Relations, but his name is Cormier, and he's not the one who makes me uneasy—have drifted over to listen to me talk. I'd been expecting my interview to cover available college players to draft, but I do have some opinions on the game, and I hope they're good ones. I take a breath, think of Dev as a football player and not as my boyfriend, and go on.

"He's pretty good, too." I smile back. "And Gerrard and Carson will cover the strong side well. I think the real trick is going to be whether the tight end can slip their coverage on short yardage. If the safeties and linebackers can bottle him up, that really stalls the Sabretooths' offense. On the other side, well, if they get Strike the ball ten times, they have a pretty good chance of winning. Jaws can move the chains, but things will really open up for him if they establish the pass and those coyote linebackers have to back off the rush."

"Use the pass to establish the run?" The wolf half-laughs. Jocko doesn't say anything.

"I know it's usually the other way around." I try not to get nervous. Do I have to impress Jocko? Did I do something wrong on the phone? If so, what? Peter smiles encouragingly, and I go on. "But everyone knows the Firebirds can run. They don't know if Aston can get the ball to Strike regularly."

"What's the matchup to watch on the line?" Peter asks.

I talk about the offensive line and the Sabretooths' defensive line for a few minutes, and then the wolf and Jocko start arguing between themselves.

Peter claps me on the shoulder and brings his muzzle close to mine. "Good work," he says.

"Thanks." My mouth is dry. Jocko's the guy who'd be my boss, and he still hasn't talked to me.

As Peter and I turn to walk away, though, Jocko calls out, "Hey. Farrel."

We both turn, two fox muzzles looking back at him. The bear jerks his head toward the TV. "Who you like?"

The wolf digs an elbow into his ribs, and Jocko snorts. "I don't mean like that, asshole," he says, shoving the wolf back. "I mean, who's he like in the game? To win. C.C.'s favored by six. You take that?"

His tone is casual but his eyes are serious, and Peter, beside me, is still. I don't look at him or the TV, or anyone else but Jocko. "I'll take Chevali," I say, "and I'll give you three of those six back."

Jocko squints. "You makin' that call with your head or your dick?"

"All right," Peter says. "Let's cut this off before I have to call HR over here. Again." He takes my arm and heads over to the food room, but I stop him. I know I have to stand up for what I believe, and Jocko's the kind of guy who wants people to stand up to him, I think. I hope I'm right.

"You been listening to what we were just talking about?" I challenge him. "It's gonna be a close game. C.C.'s got a great D and a steady offense. The game-breaker is Strike, and if they hold him to a hundred and a score, they'll keep the game close. If he gets free, Chevali wins. These guys aren't scared to play on the road. They just won at Hellentown and Boliat. The spread is based on record and home field, and my pick," and here I tap my head, "is based on looking at the guys on the field right now."

Peter and Cormier both look at the bear, who nods. "We'll see," he says.

"I'd put down some cash—" I start to explain that I don't have all that much, and Jocko shakes his head.

"Nah, no cash. Just a friendly bet. We'll see if you're right."

Friendly. Maybe if I win. I turn to Peter. "I think I'll have that beer and sausage now."

They're chicken sausages, it turns out, and they're delicious. Hal comes into the food room as I'm heading back out. "Doing okay?" he asks.

"I think so." I look back out toward the main room while Hal picks up a sausage. "I'm already getting interviewed."

"How'd it go?"

"Well, nobody laughed at me…check that. The one guy did, but I think it was okay." I tell him briefly what I said. "And I have made a bet that might be the difference between me getting hired and not."

Uncovered

"You got a pretty good track record betting on your tiger. Anyway, I wouldn't worry about it. Don't think they'll leave it to something like that." He checks through the door, looking at the screen. "Fifteen minutes to the game. You ready?"

I picture Dev running out onto the field, the cameras on his face during the national anthem, the handsome stripes and proud muzzle. I think about what he must be going through now, the nervousness, the strain, and how I'm not there to tell him that I'm rooting for him and that I believe in him. I think about whether he'll be okay anyway, and I nod to Hal. "Think so."

"Good. Because nothing you can do now is gonna change anything." He nods toward the screen. "He'll have his phone off already."

"Guess so." I could still send him a text, a note he'd see once the game was over, so he would at least know I'd been watching him.

I take out my phone and start to compose the text, and then I worry that he hasn't turned his phone off yet. What if I send him a message and it distracts him from the game? I start to put the phone away and then I wonder, what if he's waiting for a message from me? What if...

"Go ahead and send something," Hal says.

"I'll wait 'til the game's going on," I say.

But as we step back into the main room, I wonder. Do I have the right to send Dev a message? Can I really write something like "I love you" or "I believe in you"? Wouldn't I have to start with "I'm sorry, and I want to talk to you again"? But then, if I start doing that, it becomes something I shouldn't write in a text message. Maybe if I just write, "*All the other things aside, I still believe in you and you're a great football player. Wishing you the best of luck.*"

That sounds pretty good. I type it out with my thumb, and then Peter comes up to me and asks me something about college players. "Just texting good luck to Dev," I say, and he lets me have a minute to finish the message.

I stare at it there on my phone before sending it. All the different ways he might take it run through my mind. Do I really want to send it? Is this how I want to express myself?

"Yes," I say aloud. Fuck the consequences. This is a big game and I'm not going to just sit here and not let him know I'm watching. I press Send, and the message goes off.

As if in response, the network coverage switches to Sabre Field in Crystal City. The game's about to start.

PART IV

Chapter 20 – Warning Signs (Dev)

Lion Christ, the list of things I'm trying not to think about as game day approaches is way too fucking long, starting with Lee, through my parents, who flew in this morning for the game with tickets I got them (I love my parents but I don't want to think about playing in front of them), and ending with the identity of the guy whose jizz I smelled on Argonne's breath. I feel like I'm chasing the quarterback around the field and there's all these guys coming to block me, and I have to ignore them and focus on the target. So I show up early on Sunday, and I'm not the only one. Gerrard's there, Carson too, Aston and Jaws and Strike, the whole offensive line, Ty, Rodo…it's almost shorter to list the people who aren't there, which is most of the backups, Charm and Fisher, one of the defensive line, Vonni, and a couple others.

We do some warmups until everyone else gets in, hit the training room for bandages and painkillers for those guys still in pain—Jaws is nursing a sore wrist, Pace has a sore groin muscle, and the guys who file in behind them have wrenched fingers or sore ankles. All the usual stuff. I get my ribs taped up, but I turn down the painkillers even though doc says it's good to take one for prevention in case the ribs get hit. I don't want anything fucking with my judgment.

On the way out of the training room, I pass Colin and he gives me a look and an exaggerated flinch. And I almost lose my shit right there, but I force myself to take one more step, one more, and then he's in the training room and I'm out in the locker room.

Kodi comes back in from throwing up in the bathroom and sits next to Pike. "All better?" Pike says. The brown bear nods without saying anything. I look at the two of them, sitting together, and wonder that I never wondered about them before. They could be a couple, sure enough. There could be more gay guys on the team than just the one I found out about last night.

Strike tries to hand out some new energy bar he's found, a hundred percent vegan with soy protein. I take one just to shut him up. Jaws tells him what he can do with it, and looks about ready to help him do it. The cheetah shrugs and moves on to the next person.

Aston walks around the locker room fist-bumping each of the starters, muttering, "Game time. Game time. Game time." I watch him walk by, eyes half-shut, in his own little world, and I feel good about contributing to his confidence, if only with a little fist-bump.

Vonni keeps his headphones in. He won't tell anyone what he's listening to today.

Ty sends text messages to his parents or whoever his current girlfriend is, I don't ask. Maybe one of the waitresses from that strip club.

The coaches stay in their office until about an hour before kickoff, and then they come out, remind us to shut off our phones, and talk to us. Just about general stuff, not plays. If we don't know the plays now, we're not going to.

"I know you know what to do," Steez says. "Heads all in the game. Listen to Marvell." He stabs a finger toward Gerrard. The coyote takes our looks impassively and nods. We turn back to Steez, whose ropy tail is lashing. "We take these guys. Stop the run, stop the short pass. Give our corners and safeties room. I know you can do it." He grins, points toward the coaches' office. "We watch lots of film. This is the smartest group of coaches I ever work with. These plays," he pokes a finger at the playbook, "these work. Trust the plays. Game will come to you."

We all put our paws out and he covers them with his. We expect him to give us a cheer, but he just looks around, at me, Gerrard, and Carson, at Zillo and Marais and the other backups. "I would not trade this group for any other," he says softly.

"We wouldn't take any other coach," Gerrard says. The rest of us all nod.

Steez gives us a warm smile. "Win this game," he says, and then we all chorus, "Team!" and turn our attention to Coach Samuelson.

His speech is pretty good, if not as personal as Steez's. He tells us about the history that we're going to be a part of, and tells us that when we strip all that away, when we forget the lights and the media and the crowd, that this is just another football game. "We played here five months ago," he says, "and we lost. But we're a better team now. We're healthy, we've got young guys with experience and veterans with stamina, and we've played together for a whole season. I don't care if this is their house—we're going to walk in and take what's ours. I believe in you guys. I believe we're going to win."

We all put our paws and hands out, even if we can't get into a small group like the linebackers did, and Coach says, "I have never been prouder to stand in front of a group of players. I have never been more confident in the abilities of a team. On three. One, two…"

I'm focused, I'm jazzed, hopping on my feet. The guys around me are hopping too, tails flicking, ears up, grinning. We can feel each other's tension, smell the excitement of the team, and the white jerseys and gold-edged red numbers bring us together as Coach builds the energy to a peak with his count. "FIREBIRDS!" we shout, and it's in our throats and chests and ears and the shout echoes around the locker room even as we disperse, hurrying back to get ready. Helmets come out of lockers, last-minute taping of shoes and jerseys and tails happens, and we're all standing, hopping, waiting to get out there.

My phone buzzes.

Because everyone's talking, only Gerrard and Vonni, who happens to be nearby with his fox's ears, hear it. They both turn toward me, and Gerrard says, "Thought you were supposed to turn that off."

"Damn new phone," I growl, and reach for it.

One of the championship officials comes into the locker room. "Firebirds, on the field," he says.

"Leave it." Gerrard beckons me to follow him.

"Probably just Ogleby," I say, although Ogleby doesn't text. Neither do my parents, who called me last night to let me know they'd gotten into town and to wish me luck (Gregory hasn't called me; in true tiger fashion, he's keeping to himself, and in true tiger fashion, I'm fine with that). Caroll sent me a text last night, and so did Machaine, and Mom called this morning to tell me they'd gotten their tickets and she wasn't going to bother me for the rest of the day. In fact, there is only one person who would be sending me a text message who hasn't already. I stare at the locker and then pull my arm back. I don't look back at it as I follow Gerrard out onto the field.

The roar is unlike anything I've heard. I've been in full stadiums, I've been in full indoor stadiums, but there, people get tired after a minute or five of screaming. Here it just goes on and on and on. We're introduced over the PA to mostly boos, but there is a large section of Chevali fans who've made the trip, a cluster of red in the sea of navy blue and gold, and they cheer loud enough for us to hear. Each of us turns to acknowledge them with a wave.

Neutra-Scent misters are running full blast along the sidelines, and even they can't mask the multitudes of scents from the crowd. Vonni rubs his nose, and I see him point at the misters when Pace says something to him. And overhead the sky is a pure, clear blue, the sun blazing gold, and white fluffy clouds drift just visible over the top of the stadium.

To sing the national anthem, they bring out Kika, an ermine who's the top-played artist in the dance clubs, and she does a kick-ass rendition (later I will find out it was taped and lip-synched, but we're pretty close to her and she is not just lip-synching, she's full-on belting it out even though her mike is off). A squadron of Blue Angels roars by overhead as the last notes die out, sending the crowd into another round of deafening cheers, and I wonder if I'll ever hear anything normally again.

I wonder what Lee had to say to me. I wonder if he's watching.

Is it even possible for me to remember the feeling of wanting to do well for him without having the annoyance at his nagging and the guilt over that annoyance, the admiration for all he's done and the conflicted debates with myself over what the "right thing" for me to do is, the balancing between being a good football player and a good gay person and a good person overall? Can I just go out and do my best for me, for my teammates, for the fans back in Chevali?

Sure I can. It's empty and its hollow, but that's okay. Nobody outside needs to see that hollowness. These last few games, I've done pretty well even though we were fighting. Sometimes I do better when we're fighting.

I latch onto that. If I do better when we're fighting (*I don't always*, a voice inside says, and I tell it to shut up), then as we're fighting worse than we ever have, maybe so badly that we're not even dating anymore, well then, I should be doing my best here today.

The logic is shaky, but I don't give a fuck. For the next four hours, all that matters is that I go out there and play hard, play well, and win the damn game.

And even after all those mental gymnastics, as Gerrard and Aston come trotting back to the sideline after the coin flip, I still, still, look up at the stands. I don't want to see my parents, sitting with the other players' families, so my head turns from the stands just above our sideline to the island of red and gold, as if I'll spot a red-furred head and chocolate-brown ears in the middle of all of that.

There's a fox in the stands, wearing red and gold.

I freeze for a second, just a second, because the Sabretooths won the toss and as soon as Charm kicks the ball to them, I'm going to have to run out there and play. But if that's Lee...

It couldn't be. He wouldn't come to the game, not after the fights we had. Or would he?

The Sabretooths return the kickoff to the twenty-two. I tear my eyes away from the fox, put my helmet on, and run out onto the field.

It's been forever since I've played a football game. The fight with Lee, the date with Machaine, the night with Argonne, the practices and evening run-throughs and film sessions and lectures from the coaches, all of that blurs and stretches out into what feels like a month since we celebrated on the field at Boliat.

The first play, it all comes back, and it's like I never left. They start out cautious, with a run to the strong side. I cover Carson and get blocked by one of their boar linemen—no tusks, just a clean block—but Carson wraps up the deer at a two-yard gain.

As we saw on film, the Sabretooths aren't trying to trick us. They're just really good. The left side of their offensive line is a pair of boars who are great at pulling to create running lanes for their two backs. The power running back, the white-tailed deer named Runningwater—he's Native American—switches off with the quick, darting back, an otter named Hob. It's pretty funny that the otter isn't the one called Runningwater, yeah.

At the quarterback position, it's hard to get more conventional than a wolf, but McCrae is a superstar. Great pocket awareness and he can run a little, so the last three years in the league he's been in the top three fewest sacked quarterbacks. He throws a good long bomb, but he's also got a really fast release.

That's one of those sports-announcer phrases Lee and I used to joke about, but in a football game, it's a good thing. And on second down, he shows it off, dropping back three steps and whipping the ball out to the tight end almost before we have time to react. I'm shadowing the slot receiver, a jackrabbit named Crais whose jerky stops and starts make him a difficult target to throw to and an absolute pain in the ass to cover. On film, I watched him juke three times and then catch a ball for a touchdown. In person in week one, I watched Corey try to tackle him and whiff, more than once. I'm determined not to let this guy beat me.

The Sabretooths' top two receivers are a red fox and a cheetah—again, pretty conventional. They don't have great moves, but they're both fast. Fortunately, we have a red fox and a cheetah at cornerback, and they match up with their counterparts. I don't have to worry about the speedsters, usually. Just the jackrabbit, the running backs, and that quarterback.

One of the things about jackrabbits is that they're really twitchy. It's hard to hide when they're excited. Something we noticed on film is that this guy's right foot stamps a lot of the time when he's going to be targeted on a play. Just a little bit, but it's something I keep my eye on, and on third down, Crais's right foot stamps and his nose twitches.

"Little blue," Gerrard calls, which is our new signal that the play's coming to my side; he's seen the foot too. I don't react, just set and watch for the snap. When it comes, I'm supposed to play the gap to stop the run. Instead, I leap forward at the jackrabbit.

He's not expecting that. He leaps to the side, avoiding my tackle, but that means he's out of position for the quarterback's throw. The wolf sees this and throws the ball anyway, but with more height and speed so it goes out of bounds. A moment later, Fisher's in his face and would have sacked him if he'd kept it.

As we head back to the sidelines, Fisher says cheerfully, "Got damn close that time."

"Yeah," I say, finding myself staring up at the Chevali section of the crowd. "Five years ago you'd have had him."

He shoves me in the shoulder. "Fuck you, hotshot. It's a long game. I'll get him."

"Not if I get him first."

"You're both full of shit," Pace says. "We got a couple safety blitzes in the playbook and I'm gonna get him before either of you do."

By this time, Brick's caught up with us. He only hears Pace's comment, but he knows right away what we're talking about. "McCrae, right? Yeah, none of you cats is going to get him."

"Oh, like you are."

The bear grins. "Nah. If I had money to put down, I'd bet on Gerrard."

Down the line, the coyote flicks his ears, but doesn't chime in. Fisher waves a paw. "Ah, what do you know? You wanna put money down?"

"Can't," I say before Brick can answer.

"What do you mean?" Fisher says. "We did in the playoffs."

We look at him. "No, we didn't."

"Sure we did." He turns to me and frowns. "I bet you that I'd get four tackles…wait. That wasn't you, was it?"

"The coaches talked to us before every game about betting and bounties and shit," Pace says. "Don't you remember?"

"Yeah. Yeah." Fisher shakes his head. "That was another playoff game, back in Highbourne. Goddammit."

"S'okay." Brick punches his shoulder. "Just remember what team you're out there playing today."

Fisher swats his arm away, hard. "I know who we're playing," he snaps, and walks off toward the Bolt-Ade cooler.

Brick and I look at each other. "What the fuck was that about?" he says.

I look at Fisher, at the big number 75 on his back. He doesn't come back over to talk to us. "Maybe he's not all the way back from his concussion," I say.

"Should we tell someone?" Brick hesitates. "I'm s'posed to tell the senior guy on the line, but…that's Fisher."

"What about your line coach?"

Uncovered

Brick glances over at the other bear, huddling with Steez and the defensive coordinator, and lowers his voice. "He told us all this concussion bullshit was, uh. Bullshit."

A little ways away from us, Pike and Kodi stand watching the game. Pike turns and meets my eyes as though he can hear what we're talking about. "Fuck," I say. "Let me go talk to Gerrard."

I try to make my way over to where Gerrard is, but as I'm walking, something lands behind me with a wet impact. Someone behind me curses, and up in the stands there's a yell of "Fuckin' faggot!"

My chest tightens. When I turn, there's already a blue-coated security tiger heading toward a clump of deer, big stags whose antlers just shed. Their crowns are bare and their eyes are staring daggers at me.

Zillo and Brick come to stand around me, and we just watch as the security tiger is joined by a ram, asking questions of the people around them. They pull two of the stags away, and the others yell obscenities while the rest of the crowd stays quiet.

When they're gone, there's a small smattering of applause. The remaining stags glare at me, but then Gerrard's there at my side. "Come on," he says. "We're going back out."

I know I was supposed to talk to him about something, but I forget what until we're out on the field and I see Fisher take his position on the line.

A few plays later, Brick comes back to the huddle with me. "Don't let it rattle ya," he tells me.

"I'm fine. How's he playing?" I indicate Fisher.

"Good." Brick doesn't need to turn to see who I'm pointing at. "Picking up his blocks, keeping it clean."

"What's going on?" Gerrard looks between the two of us.

"Some fuckhead threw beer at Dev," Brick says.

I cut in. "It's nothing, security took him away. Fisher's acting weird."

"He's playing okay?" Gerrard directs that to Brick, who nods. "All right. Get back up there, just play. I'll talk to someone about it."

Brick nods, and heads back to the line. Gerrard turns to me. "Stick on 85," he says. That's the jackrabbit. "Looks like a run formation but be ready if they throw."

They don't, not this time, but the jackrabbit has obviously had some time to think about the last series over on the sidelines—or else he was getting ribbed about it. As we're getting back to the line of scrimmage after a three-yard run, he calls to me, "Don't think you can catch me, faggot."

The twinge of fear of discovery, the reminder of my difference and isolation, is surprisingly faint. Maybe it's because I've put aside all the gay stuff to be just a football player, and I know I've got fifty-two teammates who'll back me up. Whatever it is, I think about what Lee told me, to give as good as I get. With a glance toward the red-shirted fans, I say, "If I catch you, I get to kiss you."

"Jesus Hare," he says. "Keep the fuck away from me."

"Like hell." I line up across from him and stare.

His foot stamps on the next down, and I prepare to cover him. But when the center snaps the ball, the wolf drops back five steps. The jackrabbit zigs and zags, and I run to keep up, but the play was never going to him. The wolf cocks his arm and heaves the ball downfield a moment before Fisher flattens him.

I turn in time to see the fox catch it, number 83, and shake Vonni off him, speeding into the end zone with little trouble.

"TOUCHDOWN SABRETOOTHS," screams the PA. "McCrae to Bridger for sixty-eight yards!"

The Jumbotron shows the ball floating down just in front of 83, the fox putting his arms out and snatching it out of the air. Vonni turns and leaps for the ball, but it's perfectly placed and there's really nothing he can do.

"That is the fiftieth touchdown between McCrae and Bridger," the PA announces, and while the crowd roars approval, we are treated to a montage of the other forty-nine touchdowns.

"What the fuck are you guys doing up there?" Vonni yells as we come back to the sideline. "Get some pressure on that wolf. You're killing us!"

We know it's just game-day frustration boiling over, and most of us snap out half-hearted "we're pushing, we're trying." Fisher, though, flares up. "I almost got to him," he snarls. "Knocked him down. Made him think about next time."

"That doesn't do me a fucking bit of good now," Vonni snaps.

It looks like Fisher might go after him, so I grab his arm and Brick puts himself between the two of them, and by that time we're at the sidelines and the defensive backs coach takes Vonni and Norton aside with the safeties.

Coach greets the rest of us with a "Good effort" and a nod, keeping his eyes on the field for the extra point. The Sabretooths have a good solid kicker, and though our guys jump bravely toward the ball, the kick goes through. Coach and the rest of us exhale, slightly disappointed, and the old wolf turns a little more attention to us. "Great work on the line. Keep it up."

It's hard to feel like we're doing good work when we've just given up what felt like an easy touchdown, but Coach's words give us a little energy.

Fisher seems okay, so I don't worry about him, though I don't see Gerrard go and talk to Coach privately at all.

This series, I make sure to stand away from where the group of stags was, and spend a little more time watching the Sabretooths' defense. The two coyotes at linebacker look as determined as we are, flying all over the field, near the action everywhere. Yates, who plays my position, is second-year like me, but was a third-round pick (not seventh) and played for a top ten Division I school (not a middling Division II school). And the middle linebacker, Polecki, has been in the league five years and played on the University of Lakewood national champions, as well as the Sabretooths last championship team, his rookie year. I don't know where the media ranks him as far as linebackers go; I think Gerrard is better, but Polecki and Yates together...they're really good. They and the cougar who plays strong side linebacker have the kind of rapport that Gerrard and Carson and I have now, and even though our offensive line is pretty good at opening holes for Jaws, the coyotes and cougar close the gaps really fast.

Jaws manages to squeeze through one for a fifteen-yard run, and then Aston finds Ty for a seven-yard gain, and we cross into Sabretooths territory. On the sidelines, we get excited, yelling encouragement at the offense and at each other. Aston tries to hit Strike in the end zone, but the Sabretooths corner, playing great coverage, knocks the ball away. There's a short pass to Ty again, and Polecki drops him after five. They expect a pass on third and five, but instead Aston gives to Jaws on a delayed draw, and the wolverine finds lots of room to run. He gets down to the twelve before Yates drags him down from behind.

From there, the drive stalls. Another shot to Strike, broken up. Another run, stuffed. A short pass, not enough for a first.

"I got this one," Charm says. He stomps out to the line and backs up his words with a straight, true kick to put us on the board.

It's 7-3 at the end of the first, but we feel good. They're not running away with it, and we're keeping it close. At the break, I take Gerrard aside and ask about Fisher.

"Let it be," he says. "If it's going well, don't mess with it."

"You sure? He doesn't seem okay."

"He's fine enough to play. I kept an eye on him. He knows his assignments."

"What if he gets hurt?"

Gerrard's ears go back. "You know him. How do you think he would feel if we made him come out of the championship game, especially when he's playing well?" He doesn't need me to reply. He already knows the answer. "Would you come out of this game, if you were in his place?"

I shake my head. "No fucking way."

"All right. Don't worry about him. Concussions go away. That ring on your finger doesn't."

"Right." Of course that makes sense. And the reason I didn't go to a coach myself is that I didn't want to be the one to yank Fisher out of the game. If I would take myself out, in his place, then I wouldn't have hesitated. But this is a championship game, maybe the last one Fisher will ever play in. It's only three more quarters. I can't ruin that for him.

The second quarter gets interesting. We've been feeling each other out, running conservative plays, and now the coaches try to take each other by surprise. I stick mostly to the jackrabbit, abandoning him to help stop the run when needed. They don't run to my side a lot, but the two times they do—once with Runningwater and once with Hob—I bring down the runner before he gets more than a few yards. They do try the long bomb again, but whatever adjustment Vonni and Norton were given works well.

Fisher, maybe still embarrassed or worried about his slip, doesn't talk to me or anyone. He listens to the coaches and otherwise stands by himself on the sideline, drinking Bolt-Ade and watching the game. I don't go up to him because I'm afraid of what he might say.

And I still find myself looking at the Chevali fans for support, at the fox in the tenth row. It's not Lee, I tell myself. Only maybe it is.

The other yahoos in the stands keep pretty quiet, even when Charm gets another field goal before the half to make it 7-6. Guess when their team is winning, they don't care so much who I fuck. On the field, the jackrabbit lobs a few more "faggot" bombs my way, but those don't bother me as much, strangely, because I know he's just trying to get into my head. When I do tackle him, he shoves me off him and stalks away.

"You owe me a kiss," I yell, loud enough for my teammates to hear.

"Fuck off!" he yells back, and our side bursts into laughter. Brick slaps me on the back and even Fisher, I think, smiles.

At halftime, Coach is all fire and brimstone, but a nice kind of fire and brimstone, if that's possible. "We're holding our own!" he shouts. "We're showing these guys how we play football in Chevali! We gotta keep doing what we do, clamp down and stay focused, and I promise you we will prove everyone who doubted us wrong!"

We cheer, and then meet with our individual coaches for our specific adjustments. Steez doesn't have much to say. "Good work on 85, Miski," he says. "Omba, good work holding the edge."

Carson nods. Steez turns to Gerrard. "They make good adjustments. Probably try to run more to weak side, delayed run to strong side. Maybe switch up matchups. You see something you don't like, call time out."

We talk a little more about strategy and plays, and then he lets us go. "Five minutes," he says. "Back on field."

I sit next to my locker and think about my phone. I could just reach in, look at the message. It would take ten seconds. We're supposed to have our phones off, but nobody would notice or care.

But I don't know that I want to do that. The fox in the Chevali section could be Lee. Probably he's not, but maybe he is. I'm playing well, and if I find out for sure it's not Lee, that might upset the game. So I won't mess with it.

Chapter 21 – Fitting In (Lee)

I'm sure nobody else sees it. But when Dev comes out onto the field and looks up into the stands, I have to look away from the TV. God dammit, I should be there, no matter what. I should be supporting him. But he knows that I do, even if I'm not there in person. He knows I'm watching.

And then, in a rush, I remember that my presence isn't necessarily supportive, that he probably now associates me with tension and Equality Now and Brian and people who make him think about being gay when all he wants to think about is football.

Not that I think it's right for him just to think about football. But I'm tired of going round and round that particular post. So I take a deep breath and a drink of beer, and continue talking to Jalili and some of the Whalers' scouts.

We've been discussing college prospects, which is kind of like playing Battleship in reverse; we all know where the ships are (the college players), but we can't tell each other what the Dragons (me) and Whalers (them) are planning to guess (target in the draft). So we have to focus on the players and their performances, and make only hazy general references to where they might fit in well.

"He's one of the better centers I've seen," I say about one prospect, just as an example. "But I'm not sure how well he'd do with a quarterback who improvises a lot. Word from the coaching staff there is that it takes him a while to learn the blocking schemes, so they have to keep it simple for him."

"We hear the same thing," one of the scouts says. "So is there a team where you think he'd be a good fit?"

I think about the teams in the league with steady QBs. "Port City's where I see him going," I say. "They need to think about a center once Shalick retires, and they run a pretty conservative offense right now."

The scout nods. "Fits with what we're thinking, too. What right guards have you been impressed by?"

And on and on. I know the east region best, so it's that scout, one of the bears, who spends the most time talking to me. We compare notes while the game is going on, and miss the occasional play because we're getting so involved in discussions. After a while, I forget that I'm interviewing.

Peter circles back to check on me every now and then, sometimes just a glance if I'm involved in a conversation, sometimes coming over to ask if I've gotten a chance to talk to some other person and taking me over to them whether I have or not.

And Jalili comes to talk to me when I'm free, so as a result I haven't gotten to check on Hal much at all by the time halftime comes around. I keep an eye out, and he's usually talking to someone in the room. Once I see him come out of the side room putting his phone away. He meets my eye and grins, so I know he was talking to Pol.

Jalili mostly is excited at the prospect of another non-football player on staff. She talks about all the things there are to do in the Yerba area and asks me about Hilltown and Chevali. It turns out we have a good deal in common: she likes the theater and goes on and on about the last show she and her husband went to. She's also active in gay rights, so I assume she has a gay brother or something, but it isn't that simple.

"I have a couple gay friends," she says, "and it's just so ridiculous that they can't get married the way I did. I mean, what's the difference?"

"Exactly," I say. "It's just so hard to argue when the logic is so…"

"Illogical." She laughs and I join in, the short kind of laugh that indicates a small joke in a larger, less funny matter. "So you're right in the middle of it." She nods at the screen. "You and that tiger. How's it been going?"

I can't help but read that question personally at first. A moment later, I place the frame of context around it. "Surprisingly pretty well. People are willing to let him play. He gets shit talked at him on the field."

"Not from our players, I hope."

"I don't think so. But you know, football players talk shit about each other all the time anyway. So it's just something else for them to latch onto."

She has a little tic of shaking her wings when thinking. They make a leathery rattling noise. "You feel like the culture's changing?"

"A little. Slowly. But that's how things change, until they change fast."

The TV shows the section of Chevali fans at Sabre Field. Jalili looks up, nods, and shakes her wings. "So tell me. Why aren't you at the game?"

"Oh, it was a big ordeal, and I had the chance to come up here. I'm just looking out for my future career, and this was a good opportunity."

She folds her arms across her chest so that her wings spread out like a black dress. "You know that anyone here would understand 'I have to go to the championship game' as a reason to postpone the interview."

"I guess so, yeah." I flick my ears.

She studies me. "Okay. Well, I won't ask any more. I just hope you're doing okay."

"I'm fine," I say. "Glad to be here."

"Hope to see you back." Jalili unfolds her arms. "Not that I have any say in it."

I grin. "I hope to be back."

That's when Jocko comes over and asks Jalili to excuse us. She mouths "Good luck" at me as she goes, and I flick my ears in reply.

"You're lookin' smart so far." The game's just gone to the half at 7-6, Sabretooths.

I glance at the halftime show, which is all fog machines and blue lights and some singer my father used to listen to. "It's a long game."

He nods. "So tell me about your work with Morty."

I talk for a while about our work on the Dragons, going back over some of the things I talked about on the phone with him. He nods, arms folded over the Whalers logo on his t-shirt, asks a few questions here and there. "What else did you do for Morty?" he asks when I'm done.

"What else? Um." I frown.

His dark eyes fix me again. "Like, after hours."

Oh, fuck. Seriously? "Morty usually just went home to his wife," I say, with stress on that last word.

"Uh-huh. They still together?"

I'm pretty sure he knows the answer before he asks. "Split up this year. I think it was because he was working too much."

If he didn't know, he doesn't react to it. "He made a big deal outta recommending you."

"Because of my football knowledge." I tap my head again. "Nothing else. Him and his wife, that was just about him working too much."

"Hey," Peter says, walking up to us. "Who's working too much?"

"Just talking about Morty," Jocko says. "I ain't heard much from him since I left the Knights."

"Wait, you worked with him?" I wonder why he didn't mention that before. Maybe he didn't want me asking Morty about him.

Jocko nods. "Scouts in Kerina. I left to come here in '02. Morty took the job at the Dragons a year later."

So I tell them about Morty and the Dragons and how I told him about Dev and he told me I could come work with him at the combine if Dev got an invitation. This is the first time I see Jocko smile, and Peter laughs out loud. "He really said that? 'If he comes, you can come too'? He pulled the 'League of Their Own' crap on you?"

Jocko shakes his head. "He loved that fuckin' movie. It came out in what, '92? He was still talkin' about it in '01 at the Knights."

"That's hysterical." Peter's ears cup forward. "I'm gonna tease him for that one."

"Wasn't he going to be here?" I'd forgotten until just now.

"Here?" Jocko's eyes widen. "Why?"

"Yeah, the Dragons haven't officially let him go, so he's watching with them. Damn loyal bastard." To Jocko, Peter says, "We're talking about bringing him over."

"No shit." Jocko scratches his muzzle. "Heard he was a director now too. What position we hiring for here? You forget to tell me something?"

"You'll find out when you try your key card tomorrow," Peter says with a bland smile on his slender muzzle.

"That's okay. I got one of yours." Jocko grins back.

"You heard about Dex, right?"

"Yeah—oh!" Jocko's eyes light up. "Oh, Morty'd be awesome for that."

"For what?" I say.

"Consultant on Player Development." Peter scratches behind one ear.

Jocko breaks in. "Dex is pretty good, but he's moving on to do some private thing."

"Private consultant to college athletes. Basically he'll go around to college programs and advise their top players on what to do to make themselves more attractive to pro teams. Between the colleges and the agents, he's going to triple his salary."

"Needs it, too. Laci picked up another charity."

I think about Morty's divorce, and maybe I'm not the only one. "Hey, how's Alexa?" Jocko asks.

"She's good. She's with her mom today. How about Kim?"

"Spa." Jocko waves a paw out at the door. If I knew the area, I could figure out whether it was toward the city or the 'burbs. "Guess today is one of the hardest days to get an appointment, but she got in with her sister and they're doin' the whole fuckin' day up there."

"Jocko married money," Peter tells me. "Kim's dad invented…well, you tell him, Jocko."

The bear coughs. "Thanks, asshole. It's just a surgical procedure, and he founded a company that makes the things."

Peter nudges me, a grin still on his long muzzle. I ask, as innocently as I can, "What things?"

He coughs and unfolds his arms, sticks his paws in his pockets. "Well, uh. Prosthetic enhanced claws."

The fox points at the TV. "You ever see any of Kika's videos from this last year?"

"Yeah. Oh, wait." I remember now the claws she had, how they lit up and blinked in patterns. "I thought those were just Press-On Claws."

"Nah, these are way beyond that. They bond with the keratin and they're durable as all shit." Jocko seems less embarrassed when he's talking about the technology. "But the cool thing is that felines can use 'em. You know, they can't use the press-on kind because they don't retract. But these things, you can bond them and shape them to the claw, and they're non-fucking-reactive so they don't irritate. They're kind of hot shit."

"Hot shit enough that he's making bank." Peter shakes his head. "Hey, game's starting up again. What do you think they're going to do different?"

We talk about the adjustments both teams should make. I think the Firebirds should open things up. They're not getting to Strike, but it looks like they're not letting that bother them. They need to keep pushing so they get that one big play, because all that frustration is worth it when you get a touchdown. Peter says he thinks they should use the tight end more, and Jocko says the Sabretooths need to just pound the running game. "Firebirds D-line is a little soft on the weak side," he says. "You got Fisher, but he's past his prime and he's just back from a concussion. Then you got Partchan, whatsisname, Brick, he's good but he's green. I think they're afraid of Fisher."

"They got Miski that side, too," Peter says.

"Yeah." Jocko looks at me. "He's playin' pretty great right now, but I'd still run at his side. I mean, Omba's kickin' ass on the other side, so it's kinda pick your poison, right?"

"Totally agree," I say. Dev's good, but Carson's more experienced. We watch as the Firebirds come out on offense. They march down the field looking pretty good, and then Aston has a ball tipped over the middle. One of Crystal City's coyote linebackers leaps and spears it with a paw, and the crowd screams. He dodges and darts past Firebirds, but Aston, of all people, dives for his legs and wraps him up, saving the touchdown.

"That is what Polecki brings to this defense," the announcers inform us. "Always in the right place at the right time."

"Bad luck," Peter says, patting me on the back. Jocko seems about to say something, but gets pulled away by a colleague.

"It's a long game," I say, to cover my worry. I'm saying that a lot, and realizing that it's getting less and less true every moment.

The Chevali defense takes over deep in their own territory, and Dev and his teammates hold the Sabretooths to three yards on the first two downs. Then Crystal City comes out with a four-wide formation, and the jackrabbit and cheetah both line up opposite Dev. Norton, the Firebirds corner, lines up next to Dev and I see them talking about the formation.

"This is new," Peter mutters as a pudgy leopard comes over to stand near us. Director of Player Personnel, I remember, and his name is, um. Shit.

"Farrel, right?" He lifts his beer and takes a sip, and I remember his name—Travis—just as he says, "Pulling out new formations, huh?"

I haven't studied a lot of film of the Sabretooths. "They don't have a four-wide?"

"They do, but…" Peter shuts up as the play starts.

I'm watching Dev, as usual, so I see him try to shadow the jackrabbit and get cut off by the cheetah. Norton races behind Dev to keep pace with the cheetah, and the jackrabbit springs into the air, catching a perfectly placed pass from McCrae. It looks like a sure touchdown, because Pace ducked down to follow the cheetah too, but Dev makes an amazing recovery, pivoting almost as fast as the jackrabbit and speeding upfield. I don't think the rabbit notices him until he's at the five, and then he dodges fast—but because he's running up the sideline, the dodge takes him out of bounds.

"Ni-ice," Travis says. "That boy can play."

"Dev or Crais?" I say, because the announcers are gushing with praise for both of them.

"Well, both. That was a great play to spring Crais on the outside, but Miski—phenomenal reaction. Just incredible. Can't teach that shit." He looks over my head at Peter.

The fox looks back. "Lee already wants to come work here," he says. "You don't have to compliment his boyfriend." They laugh, but it feels like they're covering up what they're really thinking, and that's got to be something like making Dev an offer to come here. Maybe their interest in me is just to entice Dev to come here.

If that's the case, then I really shouldn't tell them how things are between us. I laugh inwardly with a little bitterness, and then shake my head and tell myself to shut up. They're interested in me, whether or not I come with Dev. They talked to Morty. The interview's going pretty well, even with Jocko. I think.

As good as it was, Dev's great play only delays the inevitable. Hob, the sleek quicksilver otter, darts through the Firebirds line and into the end zone two plays later, and they kick the extra for a 14-6 lead.

The good thing is that Chevali doesn't let it bother them. They come back with a great offensive series that ends when Aston executes a brilliant play-fake and finds Strike uncovered at the Sabretooths' 40. The room goes quiet as the cheetah dodges a tackle at the thirty-five, another at the thirty, and then flat-out races the Sabretooths cornerback to the end zone. Well, I say "races" because they're both running in the same direction, but Strike gets to the end zone fifteen yards ahead of anyone in a blue and gold uniform.

The announcers can't stop playing the video back of the run, and the room is still silent, so we hear all of it. "Look at that! That's not bad tackling, that's just incredible running! And look at him hit fifth gear here!"

"I don't think anyone else *has* that gear, Tom."

"That is what he brings to this team, if you can stand the headaches."

"And he's been well-behaved so far for the Firebirds."

Peter shakes his head, the first one around me to talk. "Jesus Fox," he says.

"We almost got him, you know," Travis says. "Haggling over draft picks and Lion Christ I wish we'd given up the second-rounder."

"They're still behind," I point out.

"And we weren't that close to getting him," Peter chimes in. "Not everyone was on board."

"It's only a point." Travis is responding to me, I think.

I don't say anything, because as fun and relaxed as the discussion is, and as much as I feel like I'm fitting in here, I'm aware that I'm still being interviewed. But I think, *one point can make a lot of difference.*

The announcers show the Sabretooths sidelines. "Looks like they're still arguing over the coverage," one says. "But with zone coverage you have to make the tackles after the catch, and Strike is just too good."

"Sometimes you do the best you can and it doesn't make a difference."

Amen, I think, as Dev trots back out to the field. The Firebirds have some swagger on defense now, even as the Sabretooths try to match the big play. Gerrard, particularly, looks ferociously motivated, running and leaping for the ball carrier. Even if he doesn't end up getting the tackle, he affects the play. He grabs Dev and Carson between snaps, barking commands at them, and his excitement is infectious: the Sabretooths get one first down and then have to punt. The corners are sticking to the receivers, the line is getting good pressure, and the linebackers are everywhere they need to be. Even without me in the stands, without knowing I'm watching, Dev is playing great.

I wonder if this is how my father feels about me getting a job with the Dragons, and then, hopefully, the Whalers. Or if it's how he would feel if I did something he was really proud of.

The Firebirds get the ball back on their thirty, and now the conversation in the meeting room stays low, because it's a good game and because people want to see if Strike will get the ball again. He catches one pass, but doesn't break loose, and then Ty catches one to the outside and it looks like Chevali's going to score again.

But the Sabretooths are fired up on defense, too. The middle linebacker, Polecki, bursts through and sacks Aston, and that leads to a third and long, which leads to Aston heaving a pass downfield for Strike.

The Sabretooths are ready. The corner and safety both run along with the cheetah, pushing him off his route, and for a moment it looks like the corner is going to get to the ball. But Strike jumps too, and they get tangled together, and the ball drops harmlessly to the grass.

One guy yells, "Dammit, get that!" I see him looking up at the prop bet board; I guess he bet on the interceptions.

Conversation in the room picks up as the Firebirds punt. I keep an eye on the screen, and I think everyone else does too, as the Sabretooths' kick returner, a swift fox, sheds a tackle. And dodges another. The announcers get excited as the room goes quiet. "He's almost in the clear!" the announcer says. "Only the punter to beat!"

And the Firebirds' punter, an otter, isn't fast enough to tackle this fox. The Sabretooth plants, jukes, and is around him in a moment, leaving the otter spread out on the ground watching that black-tipped tail stream into the end zone.

"Amazing!" shout the announcers.

Smatterings of applause break out, which I don't join in with. A jaguar jumps up and down and points; following his finger, I see a prop bet on kickoff/punt returns for touchdowns, and the lemur reaching up to circle in red the word "Sabretooths" under it. Hal catches my eye and wags his swift fox tail. I bow in his direction, and he comes over.

"Still a long ways to go," he says. "We can do this."

Twenty-one to thirteen. Almost at the end of the third. The Firebirds get one more offensive sequence, but nothing comes of it, and they kick the ball back to the Sabretooths as the fourth quarter starts.

By this time, the room is a little louder, and there's a haze of beer breath all around. I've limited myself to one beer just to make sure I keep my composure, but it feels friendly and congenial, and I hardly even feel like an outsider, except I keep looking over at Jocko, worrying about our bet and his attitude. It was bad enough working for Paul at the Dragons, where he casually dropped "faggot" references all the time, and then after I came out, was mostly worried about harassment. If I have to work for this guy and he keeps insinuating that I find players hot, or that I'm blowing Morty or whoever just to keep my job...

Travis and Peter say they'll talk to me later and walk over to the prop bet board to talk to one of the guys there. Jalili comes back to stand next to me and Hal, and the two of them talk while I watch the Firebirds on defense. And so I'm not sure if they notice it immediately, not until the announcers mention it, but I see the play right away.

Fisher's grappling with one of the offensive linemen, a tapir, I think, and he gets thrown to the ground. It looks like he lands on his shoulder, but when he gets up, he staggers and drops to one knee again.

The play is a run for short gain, and only after it do the announcers mention Fisher. "Looks like he was shaken up on that play," one says.

"He's just back from a concussion."

"And the Firebirds are making a substitution. Number 72, the polar bear, is going to come in for Fisher Kingston, and he's getting applause from the Chevali fans."

"Great player, legendary career."

Fisher doesn't even raise a paw to the cheers. One of the trainers tries to help him off the field, but he's walking fine and he almost throws the guy off him. "And he does not look happy about being taken out of this game," the announcer says.

"Would you?" his partner says.

"Oh, you'd have to drag me out. Kicking and screaming." They both laugh.

"We'll see how this affects the Firebirds on defense..."

"Hope he's okay," Hal says.

Jalili turns to me. "You know him?"

I nod. I wonder if I should call Gena. Fisher's still standing there on the sidelines, so he's not unconscious or anything. "Yeah, I..." The game is still going on. "I'm gonna call Gena. Just real quick."

Hal nods approvingly and explains to Jalili while I step back into the food area. I try to find an angle where I can still watch the game, but there are people in the way, and I don't want to be talking too loudly.

"You should be here," is the first thing Gena says.

"I just saw Fisher," I say. "Is he okay?"

"He looks okay," she says. "But you know as much as I do, I think. Maybe more. Are the announcers saying anything?"

"No."

"He's still standing up, so I'm not going to worry. They'd call me if anything—"

The crowd around her roars; in the other room, cheers erupt. Gena's yelling, "Oh yeah!" and I hear her sons screaming beside her.

"What happened?" I scramble to look at the TV.

"Go watch the game," she says. "I'll call you after."

Chapter 22 – Fumbles (Dev)

Fucking amazing is what happened. The defensive line had the white-tailed deer stopped, but he kept fighting forward for that one more yard, and Carson just poked the ball out of his arms and grabbed it. They tackled him right away, but we're all leaping on him and jumping up and down as we race back to the sidelines.

"That's what we need!" Coach yells, and smacks Carson on the shoulder. "Let's get back in this thing!"

The offense goes out and we are just buzzing. I know it's the fourth quarter, but I am so caught up in the game that it doesn't register that it's going to be over soon. I feel like we're going to keep playing for days and days. Everyone on the sidelines is pacing, staring out at the field, yelling, "C'mon! C'mon!"

I don't see Fisher at first, and then I spot the orange and black striped tail, lashing near the end of the bench. He's sitting with his head down, not even watching the game.

I walk over to him, walking in front of where the stags are. Someone there calls half-heartedly, "Hey, faggot-ass." It's easy to pretend I don't hear him as I make my way down to sit next to Fisher.

"Hey." I nudge him.

"Leave me alone," he growls.

"Look, you did great out there. You helped us stay in this game."

"I should still be out there."

I listen to the rhythm of the crowd's cheers, the swell of the roar and the dying down that means we got some yards, moved forward. "Don't shut out the game. Didn't you tell me to enjoy it, because who knows if it'll come around again?"

"I *know* it won't come around again. Not for me." He growls and shoves me away. "So go watch the game, go play. Leave me alone."

I stand there for a moment, looking down. "Fine," I say, and walk back to Zillo and Gerrard and Carson.

Zillo is pumped. He went in for me briefly in the second quarter and he's hoping to get back in. "But this is the most amazing thing ever," he says. "This game…this feels incredible. You know?"

"Yeah. I still can't believe it."

I look at Gerrard. He's savoring this too, following every movement on the field, pumping his fist. Even Carson is animated, if less vocal. When we stall, and Charm runs out to kick a field goal to bring us within 21-16, we still yell and cheer and mob him when he comes back to the sidelines.

And I look up at the Chevali section again as I run out. If it's not Lee up there, at least I know he's watching somewhere.

(And maybe it is. Maybe it is.)

So are my parents, so is Caroll, so is Brian, so is Argonne, so is Machaine. The people I love, the people I don't love so much, and all the people in between, they're all watching me and there are eight minutes and twenty-four seconds left on the clock for us to pull out a miracle.

Most importantly, though, this is my game, my team, my moment. If I'm not doing this for anyone else, I have to have the confidence to do it for myself. I don't want to end up like Fisher, head down on a bench because I feel like I didn't give it my all (even if in Fisher's case I think he's wrong).

"We can do this," I say to Gerrard, and he flashes me a feral grin.

Of course, they run. They run and run and run, and they march down the field and one minute, two minutes, three minutes tick by. "We need more pressure!" Gerrard shouts in the defensive huddle. "This is it! There's no next week. You need to make a stand now!"

Five minutes to go. We stop them on first down at the forty. They're close enough for a long field goal, and they might try it. Second down, they run to my side and the jackrabbit tries to block me. I shoulder him out of the way and drop the otter for a loss of one. We're too focused for more than cursory congratulations, even though they're taking their time lining up. It's third and long, and Gerrard thinks they're going to pass. "Short," he says, "so you guys come in." He motions to the safeties. "Take 88 and 85 and let these guys," he motions to me and Carson, "rush the passer."

Eighty-eight is the tight end; eighty-five is the jackrabbit. "Watch him," I say to Pace, who's taking my side. "He likes to hop and change direction."

"No problem." The jaguar claps his paws together. "I'll shadow him."

"You guys stay on the wideouts," Gerrard says to Norton and Vonni as the offense comes to the line. The play clock is down to twelve.

We get into our set. Gerrard looks at the offensive set and shouts nonsense syllables that mean that he was right and we're sticking with the play. Pace and I trade places to make it look like we're adjusting to the offense. The jackrabbit looks between us. His hind foot stomps, just once, and he's trying to hide it, I think, but I still notice. I run to Pace and talk into his ear, facing away from the offense. "It's going to him! Stick with him!"

"Got it," he says as I back up, staring at the jackrabbit.

When the ball's snapped, Crais jumps away from me, which is fine, because I leap right past him. Pike's bulk as he pushes forward hides me from the quarterback until I come around him, and by then I'm a yard away. He's got his arm back to throw, but hasn't released the ball.

Later, when I look at the footage, I'll see that McCrae still has the ball because Pace is right behind the jackrabbit, ready to jump on any pass; later, I'll identify the flash of white on the other side of the wolf as Carson. But in that moment I see nothing but the navy blue uniform with the gold 10 looking big as a target.

McCrae brings the ball down and tries to dodge me. I've got a lot of momentum, but not too much. My arm flies out around his stomach, my helmet lowers when I'm sure I've got him, and we go crashing down together. I knock the wind out of him and crush him to the ground, and though my own ribs creak, I think maybe his will, too.

The crowd's silence is the first thing I notice as I start to get up, but it's not a complete silence. The little red section of Chevali fans is screaming, almost loudly enough to fill the stadium. I stand up and see a white uniform with red numbers streaking down the field, a gold and black tail flowing behind. Two blue uniforms are chasing, but they're not going to catch him. Carson runs into the end zone, spreads his paws, and lets the ball fall out of them as he does a U-turn, coming back to us with his arms out.

A moment later, he stops short and runs back to the end zone to pounce on the ball. I laugh and join the rest of our team running down the field to mob him as the P.A. says, mutedly, "Touchdown Chevali. Carson Omba, fumble recovery."

I reach Carson, or at least the pile of people he's at the bottom of, and I leap on it as he's struggling to get back to his feet. We pull him toward the sideline, and when I get close, he throws his arms around me, still holding the football. "Half of this is yours!" he yells. "I almost threw it away!"

"It's yours!" I yell back, watching the replay on the Jumbotron. The ball didn't pop up clean; it bounced, and Carson snagged it on the run and never let go. Amazing play.

Gerrard comes up and smacks me hard on the back. "You got the sack!"

That's the cue for the rest of the defense to come up and mob me, having already given Carson his due. I'm buffeted back and forth, slapped on the back and shoulder-bumped, and only as I'm laughing and looking up at the sidelines do I see the 4:14 ticking down on the clock and realize that the game's not over. Not only that, we have to go back out, because Charm just kicked off and Crystal City has it on their own twenty-four.

We're only two points up. All they need is a field goal, and they have plenty of time to get it. "Come on," Gerrard says. "Let's go out there and hold on to this victory."

CHAPTER 23 – FOUR MINUTES (LEE)

I'm jumping up and down and then pacing back and forth, tail wagging up a storm. I can't stop staring at the screen. Hal, next to me, is hardly any better, and in general the whole room is buzzing. They're Yerba fans first, of course, but they hate Crystal City, and besides, everyone loves an underdog story. So the noise level is high, and even the guy watching the prop bets has forgotten to update them in the last five minutes. Nobody's reminding him. The game just got exciting.

I know it's a team effort, I know it's a well-designed play and good coverage and pressure from the strong side and all of that, I know it the same way I know that the airline pilot isn't solely responsible for getting me home safely, but my heart is thudding against my ribs and all that keeps running through my mind is: *he* did it, he *did* it. I want them to show that sack a hundred more times. I want to videotape it and leave it running in an endless loop on our TV at home. I'm so proud of him I think I'm going to explode, or collapse, or scream.

But I keep it together, and even Hal, I think, doesn't quite get why I'm so excited. He knows that I'm proud of my boyfriend making a big play. Heck, more than one of the Whalers staff came over to pat me on the back. And I didn't even mind it, didn't feel awkward or uncomfortable. But none of them know how hard we've worked for years, how that play is something I knew he could do, and how I convinced him to believe in himself, too. The rational part of my brain kicks in with *hey, you know, he might not even be your boyfriend anymore*, and I tell it to shut the fuck up, for the next half hour he's my boyfriend, and after the game, when reality reasserts itself, then we'll see where we stand.

It doesn't even matter what our relationship is. I can still be proud of him. I can still bounce on my feet when the announcers say, "Miski made that play happen," or, "That was no easy sack—McCrae is elusive—but Miski would not be denied." And Dev would be happy: after the player introductions, they have not once mentioned that he's gay. He's right: while the game is going on, it's irrelevant.

"Three and out," I mutter. "Three and out."

"They can do it," Hal says.

Jalili comes over to stand near us. "You boys must be over the moon," she says.

"In four minutes, we will be." I point to the clock as the Firebirds line up on defense.

CHAPTER 24 – TWO MINUTES (DEV)

The scoreboard reads: Firebirds 23 – Sabretooths 21. The clock reads 4:08. The crowd is chanting, "Here we go, Sabretooths, here we go." The PA system plays some kind of stupid big cat roar, and a clip from some old movie where a pudgy sheep is yelling, "It ain't over! It ain't over!"

I hear it with my ears. Inside my head it's calm and quiet and Gerrard's instructions and Steez's coaching and Lee's words are clear as bells. *We can do this. Head in the game. I believe in you.*

My tail lashes, but the rest of me stays stock-still, alert and ready. Crystal City can't just kill the clock now. They need to gain about forty yards to have a prayer, fifty to have a real shot. And we're in a balancing act with them, because what they would like to do is get into field goal range with five seconds left. If we can force them to go out on downs, then we can try to kill the clock. If we let them get into field goal range, then we want to slow down the clock so we have time to answer if they score.

I'm not the one who has to figure out all that strategy. I'm the one who has to stop the plays.

Specifically, I have to stop the jackrabbit, who basically ignores me as we line up. "Hey," I say. "Wanna step aside and let me get to your quarterback again?"

His ears twitch, but he doesn't say anything. I hope I'm making him think. If he's good, he'll shut everything else out, but he's a rabbit. I'm hoping he's nervous.

They run it up the middle with the deer, and Pike and Gerrard help collapse the hole, limiting him to three yards. Carson and I slap paws as we go back to the line. "Watch the short pass," Gerrard says, coming up behind us. "They're not desperate for clock yet, but they will be soon."

And when I line up across from the rabbit, his back leg stamps. "This play," I say. "I'm going to get sack number two."

He doesn't react. But I watch his eyes and I see where they flick to, and when the ball's snapped, I jump in the same direction.

He and I collide. He spins away from me, but by the time he turns to look for the ball, he's well off his route and the pass sails behind me. I make a stab at it, but I'm off-balance and I miss by a foot.

Third down. Clock's stopped at 3:44. We come back to the huddle. "Short pass," Gerrard says, "but watch the draw play."

There's no draw. McCrae passes to his number one wideout, the fox, and Vonni tackles him right away. Fourth down, two to go.

Crystal City calls a timeout, as much to stop the clock as to discuss what to do. "Think they're going for it?" I ask Gerrard as we congregate on the sidelines.

He looks at the Sabretooths' sideline. "I'd be surprised. They probably think they can hold us and get the ball back. Also, they have to know they might not make it, and then we could just hold the ball and kick a field goal from here. Too risky."

They come back out with the punting team, so we stay back while our special teams go out. So many things can go wrong: we could muff the return, fumble on the runback...I guess there's really not that many things, but they all seem huge to me.

The other guys feel similarly, I think, because we're quiet until our returner has the ball safely in his arms and is down. Then we cheer, and we call after the offense as they run out: "Two first downs! Just get two first downs!"

Ty looks back and waves a paw to let us know he's heard us. His tail wags as he gets into position.

The chants of "DEE-FENSE! DEE-FENSE!" from the crowd are deafening. But our offense knows what plays to run, and they don't need to communicate much. Aston checks the defense, gets the ball from the snap, and hands it off to Jaws. The Sabretooths are expecting the run, and they collapse around the middle. Hard as Jaws works, he can't get through any gaps. Polecki and Yates back up that ferocious defensive line, and the Sabretooths call time out when the play's over, stopping the clock.

Second down, Aston floats a short pass over the middle, and Ty makes an incredible catch. But Yates grabs him around the waist and spins him back and down to the ground, two yards short of the first down. The Sabretooths take their second time out.

We hold our breath. I watch Aston talk to Strike in the huddle. "They're going to him," I say.

"Who?" Zillo asks.

I point out onto the field. "Strike."

He follows my finger. Charm, behind us, says, "Good. We could use another touchdown."

The teams come up to the line, and it doesn't quite work out that way. Strike does shed a tackler and get the first down, but the safeties are playing behind him and were alert to the short gain, so they come up and pin him in on both sides. He tries to dart between them, and almost makes it, almost. One of them grabs at his ankle and slows him just long enough for the other one to pile into his body and knock him down.

"That's one!" We jump and fist-bump and get more jittery as the referees move the chains and reset the down marker to 1. The Sabretooths take their last timeout, stopping the clock at 3:01. The play clock is 35 seconds, so we'll be able to run two plays and then the two-minute warning will stop the clock. After that, we'll need to get a first down or else they'll get the ball back.

Coming out of the time out, it's a running play again. Jaws lowers his head and charges up the middle for two as seconds tick off the clock. Second down, he delays and tries to run around the end. He gets three, four, and then is forced to the ground by one of the coyotes—it's Polecki, I see as he gets up and hurries back to the line.

Because Jaws stayed in bounds, despite Polecki's attempt to get him across the sideline, the clock ticks down from 2:20. Aston doesn't bother assembling the huddle, just walks to the sideline to talk to the coaches as the refs wait twenty seconds and then signal the two-minute warning.

It seems to take forever. I want it to be finished, I just want our guys to go out there and get four more yards and then the game will be over. Everyone's edgy, everyone feels the same way. Tails lash and curl, ears sweep forward and back, guys hop from one foot to the other and joke. A little way down from me, I hear Pike say, "What are you gonna do with your bonus?" and someone tells him to shut up so he doesn't jinx it.

The crowd noise is what I might call a "hushed roar." They can't wait for their team (mostly; the Chevali rooting section is loud as a jet engine) to get back on the field, and they're saving their energy to scream when the plays are on the field, to disrupt the offense, but they're so excited they can't help making noise. It escapes like the air from a shaken soda bottle, seeping out in cheers and calls, and the cheers are contagious: "KNOCK 'EM DOWN" starts in one section of the field and spreads all around, followed by the recurring "DEE-FENSE! DEE-FENSE!" Behind us, on the sideline, I think I hear a couple yells of "faggot" and "cocksucker," but to be honest, I might be imagining them, the voices are so insubstantial through the din.

Third down looms. Aston marshalls our offense, and we're on the sidelines full of nervous energy, wanting to be out there so badly and yet unable to do anything. Up and down the line, we point out things on the defense, or bet what play they're going to run, because really, only Aston and the offense know.

"Bootleg."

"We never bootleg."

"Exactly. They won't be expecting it."

"Gotta stick with what we know."

"Look at the way they're lined up. They're expecting short pass."

"Aston's going to keep it. He can get four yards if Jaws blocks for him."

"Hard count. Try to get an offisdes."

"Oh God, if they jump…"

"We gotta make this."

"We will."

"We gotta make this."

"We gotta."

We clench our fists and curl our tails around our legs, strain forward and stare. If sheer force of will could affect a game, we would carry Aston over the line of scrimmage to the first down. But all we can do is sit and watch as the lines set. Aston walks up under center, shouts at the linemen—I doubt anyone can hear him over the crowd noise—and then hurries back three steps to the shotgun position. He barks out the snap count, and we watch the Sabretooths' line intently now, ready to yell if any one of them flinches. Jumping offsides, as long as our guys don't flinch first, would be a five yard penalty, and from here, that would be a first down and the ballgame.

But the lines stay immobile and the play clock winds down: 4, 3, and Aston stamps his foot and the ball flies back into his paws like it has a thousand times before. He drops back and we're trying to follow the action: there's Ty across the middle, there's Strike racing down the seam, there's Rodo stopping and coming back on a curl route.

The sidelines are alive with screams. "Get rid of it! Throw it! Throw it!"

And there's Yates and Polecki staying with Ty and Rodo, the cornerback and safety blanketing Strike. Aston scrambles, avoids the first rusher, avoids the second, heaves the ball desperately toward Ty.

It's not a good throw, not even close. But Ty sees it and stretches for it, and his fingertips graze it. The ball goes wobbling backwards.

Our screams change from "Yes! Yes!" to "No! No!" Yates and Rodo see the ball at the same time and leap, and Yates bats it backwards, out of the deer's hands.

The ball seems to hang forever. Then it falls to the grass.

The crowd explodes. We deflate, but only momentarily. "Come on," Gerrard says. "We're still leading. Let's go out there."

Our Chevali cheering section screams approval, but we just seat our helmets on our heads. It occurs to me that with 1:43 left, this is probably the last time I'm going to put my helmet on for months. *Make it count*, I tell myself.

Our punter pins them back at the ten, but they aren't fazed by the long field in front of them. McCrae runs their offense without a huddle, just coming to the line and setting up. Of course they're going to pass, and of course they're aiming for the sidelines. I stick to Crais, the jackrabbit, who looks about as hyped up as I feel, but McCrae doesn't target him on the first series. He throws over the middle and completes to Bridger. The fox darts around Norton, but that slows him enough that Pace tackles him at the thirty, and the clock keeps running.

McCrae runs up and spikes the ball to stop the clock. One minute ten left to go. They come up to the line again, fast, and Gerrard makes sure we all know our assignments. As I line up across from Crais, his back foot twitches and his ears flick.

I backpedal when the ball is snapped, giving him some room and waiting for the ball, thinking I can make an interception if I time it right. He runs a short route and I shadow him, close enough that McCrae changes his target and throws to the tight end on the other side, but Carson knocks it down.

They line up again, fast, and McCrae throws to Bridger immediately. Vonni drops his fellow fox at the line of scrimmage, no gain.

Fifty seconds. "Hold them short!" Gerrard yells. "Guard the lines!"

And ten seconds later, Bridger runs down the center of the field, drawing the coverage as the tight end sneaks under it. The tiger turns, grabs the throw from McCrae. I chase him, with Gerrard, but he makes it across midfield before we tackle him.

At least we get him inbounds. The clock tick-tick-ticks as they run up to the line to spike it again. They're at our 46, a possibly makeable field goal, but we know they're going to want to get a few more yards.

On the next play, Runningwater fakes a block, turns and catches a short pass, and scrambles for seven yards, getting out of bounds to stop the clock. They are definitely in field goal range now. Long, but makeable.

The whistle blows. I look around, startled, and then hear, "Timeout, Chevali."

"Come on!" Gerrard yells.

We follow him back to the sideline, where the defensive coordinator and Coach huddle us up. "We need to knock them back," Coach yells. "We're going to send everyone. Just swarm them, try to get a sack. If you can get a fumble, great. But knock them back five yards, ten yards, and if he throws it, try to tip it and look for the interception."

"We never blitz big," Norton mutters, right behind me, but if Coach hears it, he ignores it.

"Play good defense," he says. "Go out there and make us proud."

"Coach." Gerrard speaks up. We turn to him. His ears are up, but his muzzle is creased and I think I see the reflection of Norton's comment in it. Shouldn't we stick with what got us here?

Samuelson looks across the huddle at Gerrard. "If we don't knock them back, chances are we lose the game on the next play. We need to gamble here."

Wolf and coyote stare at each other and then Gerrard says, "Then we'll knock them back."

CHAPTER 25 – TIMEOUT (LEE)

I feel like a swarm of bees is buzzing in my chest. I can't stand still. The timeout seems to go on forever. "What are they gonna do?" Hal asks.

He might as well have asked the question of the entire room, because everyone is answering it. "C.C.'s gonna go for the field goal right here," someone says.

"No, they're gonna run it for a few more."

"They can't run it, they don't have enough clock. They'll pass it."

"They can't pass it, that's too risky. They're just going to go for it."

"What's Chevali doing? What a dumb timeout, letting C.C. set up their offense."

"No, it's smart. They're setting up their defense."

I bite my lip and then chew one of my claws. If I were Crystal City, I would do a short out to the sidelines. Quick pass, low risk. That's what the announcers are saying. If it gets them a few extra yards, makes the field goal easier, great. The key thing is to throw it to the outside of the receiver so that if he doesn't catch it, the defender can't.

I hope Crystal City isn't that smart. I happen to think it's a pretty good timeout for Chevali. Gets the Sabretooths out of their rhythm, gives the defense a chance to settle down and prepare for what's coming. I want to tell Dev how much I believe in him.

Peter comes over. "Hell of a game! Think your boys gonna pull it off?"

Or maybe he says, "Think your boy's gonna pull it off?" I'm too excited to parse it correctly.

"Don't know." I stop biting my claw and squeeze my paws together. "I'm just happy they made it such a good game."

"Ha," he says. "Better if they win, though, right?"

I look at him and he just laughs. "Right," he says, and points at the screen. "I'll shut up."

CHAPTER 26 – BIG BLITZ (DEV)

We trot back out onto the field just like it's any other time in any other game. "You heard Coach," Gerrard says, watching the offense come back out. It's not the field goal unit. They're going to run one more play. "Don't jump offsides. Let's go get him."

In my head, I hear Steez, from the Boliat game: *Now you have to be great.* I think of him and then I think of Lee watching me, maybe from the stands, maybe on TV. For a moment, just a moment, I'm back before all the shit between us, and the pure feeling of wanting him to be proud of me overwhelms me. I want to communicate it to my teammates, but all I can think to do is put my paw out, pads down, and hold it there .

Gerrard recognizes the gesture immediately and puts his out as well. The rest of the defense all join in a moment later, and we look at Gerrard. "'Firebirds' on three," he says. "One, two, three."

Our paws dip and rise as one. All eleven guys, all together. This is our season, right here, and we shout together, as loud as we can in the deafening noise of the stadium, and it seems to me that our "FIREBIRDS!" takes on a life of its own, going up against the crowd and silencing it, exploding out from our huddle. I hold it in my chest and see my teammates doing the same. There are grins, ear-flicks, and one "Hah" from a lineman.

The offense is already getting set. We hurry to our spots and face our offensive counterparts. I don't have time to look at the stands. I don't need to.

Crais has both ears turned back toward their quarterback. Neither he nor I is up for any banter. I don't know how he can hear anything. The crowd's not as loud as when they were trying to disrupt our offense, but they're still loud. Maybe the big ears help. I can't hear anything except the crowd and the humming in my ears of the thrill of anticipation. So I watch the jackrabbit, and his hind foot stamps.

"Little blue!" I yell, but that's one second before the ball's snapped.

I need to make the decision. Do I bump him or just rush the quarterback? In an instant, I see the play last time, the one I disrupted, when McCrae found another target. When we're all rushing, that leaves people uncovered, and if I slow up, if I'm covering the rabbit and not bringing pressure, maybe that'll give that wolf a precious half-second to get the ball to someone else.

I don't have time to think it through. The jackrabbit starts moving, and I leap past him.

White jerseys swarm the blue. A big rack of antlers gets in my way—Runningwater—and I spin around him. I'm two steps from the wolf. He's got his arm back to throw. Behind him is another white jersey: Gerrard.

His arm comes forward. I crash into McCrae, knocking him back. A second later, Gerrard knocks us both down. The wolf grunts in pain. My ribs complain, but I barely feel it. What I feel is a sinking in my stomach as the crowd roars at jet-engine levels, screaming and cheering and hollering, and I know that we failed.

I roll off McCrae and extend a paw down to help him up. "Hell of a throw," I say, without even having seen it. "You okay?"

Gerrard helps him too, and slaps him on the back. The wolf looks from one to the other of us with a huge grin as his teammates leap toward him. In the two seconds he has, he says, "You guys played a hell of a game." He looks up, puts a paw to his ribs, and laughs. "Win or lose. I'm doing great."

It seems pretty clear which way he thinks the game is going to go. We step back and let the rest of the team mob him. Gerrard and I just stand there for a moment, and then I hear Crais behind me. "What do you think of that, faggot?!"

We're right in front of the Crystal City sideline, a sea of navy blue. Gerrard grabs my arm. "Don't," he says.

"Don't worry," I say, and I follow him across the grass to our sideline. My tail doesn't have any life in it, and the field seems to go on forever.

On the Jumbotron, I see the play: McCrae whipped the ball to the uncovered rabbit. He grabbed it over his shoulder and ran down the sideline ten yards before Vonni chased him out of bounds. They're in easily makeable field goal range now. Nothing we can do, not anymore.

They send out the kicking team with ten seconds left on the clock. That means that probably they will have to kick it off and we will have a chance at a miracle. For a fleeting moment, I think about going out on special teams again like I did back in week 7. But I was fresher then, and the kicker was shakier. Now I'm beaten up by the season; not that I couldn't jump if I needed to, but there's not much point. Their kicker is as confident as Charm.

But I don't want to leave anything untried. So as the special teams go out to try to block the kick, I run over to Coach. "You need me out there?" I say when he turns.

He shakes his head. His ears are still up, but he's lost some of the energy he had two minutes ago. "You've done all we could've asked and more.

Coach Martin has a good blocking team out there and they're doing what they can."

Zillo's out there, and so is Marais, and I see now that Marais is doing what I did in that game: he's jumping up and down, and they have the rabbits on the other side of the line. But their kicker, a small, compact burro, doesn't even take any notice. He steps back and to the right, nods, and the holder turns to the long snapper. The ball sails back and the holder takes it out of the air, sets it down, turns it quickly as the burro runs toward it.

Gerrard grabs my paw. I grab Charm's hand. We watch the kick sail up, over the outstretched paws of the rabbits, toward the goalposts—and through.

The stadium explodes. I feel the ground shake and wonder if this is what earthquakes are like. Probably. Just not as fucking depressing.

We all let go of each others' paws. Nobody says anything.

Coach runs along the sidelines. "We gotta receive a kick!" He yells to the special teams players, which includes Zillo and Marais. Strike jumps up and says, "Let me go out there, too."

They talk strategy, about whether the Sabretooths will kick it in the air or squib it along the ground. Gerrard and Carson and I, with Vonni and Pace and Norton and Pike and Brick and the rest of the defense, stand on the sidelines waiting. I toss my helmet to the bench, where it rolls to a stop before one of the equipment guys, a short weasel, grabs it and puts it away somewhere.

Fisher's still sitting on the bench, a yard from where my helmet stopped. I don't go talk to him.

If I'd just trusted my instincts, I think. If I'd just gone after the jackrabbit. I did the safe thing, I did what I was told to do, what the coaches and Gerrard all said was best. But I will always remember that I might have had a chance to change the outcome of the game. I might have been great.

CHAPTER 27 – SIX SECONDS (LEE)

"He couldn't have done anything different," Hal says, and I'm inclined to believe him.

"He shouldn't have left that jackrabbit," Peter says.

"He almost got to McCrae," I point out. "And if he'd given him one more second—"

"True," Peter says. "McCrae's a beast under pressure. He had Bridger about to shake free."

"Or he'd have just thrown it away." Hal feels like he's trying hard to put the best face on it. Clearly a struggle for him.

Peter pats my shoulder. "You can't beat yourself up," he says. "Football's like that. And hey, they still have six seconds."

"Miracles don't happen at the end of championship games." I say this so that I won't get my hopes up.

"Miracles can happen at any time," Hal says. "Just, usually, they don't."

"Look, whatever else happens…" Peter grins down at me, his tail wagging. "People aren't going to forget this game in a hurry."

"No," I say. "I don't think they will."

I know I won't. I want so badly to be able to see Dev, but I only catch him in quick shots on the sideline, when he's hard to pick out from the glum, shoulders-slumped white jerseys. The navy blue Sabretooths jump excitedly, despite their coach trying to calm them down. And the announcers are already talking like the Sabretooths have won, although every few seconds one of them reminds the rest that the Firebirds have six seconds left and remember that one playoff game where the Boxers won on a kickoff return for a touchdown as time expired?

The players take the field. I force myself to breathe.

Chapter 28 – Sitting Down (Dev)

It's hard to watch, but we can't look away. I keep envisioning Ty or Strike catching the ball, running it back through the defense. Ty did it once before. Strike—well, he hasn't returned kickoffs in years as far as I know, but if he gets into the open field, he can do anything. None of us dares talk, but I look at the pricked ears and the paws being squeezed again and I know everyone's thinking the same thing.

The burro kicks the ball along the ground. It skips and hops toward Zillo and past him, toward Ty and Strike. Ty's in better position, and he scoops it up in front of Strike, dodges one tackler and starts to get up a good run. We strain forward and start to cheer, but as soon as we do, a pair of Sabretooths converges on him. Ty stops, tries to reverse field, looks for someone to lateral to. It looks like Strike is clear behind him, but he pitches it instead to Zillo, who fumbles the pitch and drops it.

Jerseys pile on top of the ball. The whistles sound and the clock reads all zeroes and the crowd screams with one ecstatic voice that goes on and on and on. I hear the P.A. but not what it says, the words drowned out in the joy of seventy thousand people—minus one red-shirted section and fifty-three guys in white jerseys trudging dejectedly toward the locker room.

There's no post-game mingling, no mixing and back-patting. I prepare my statements, as I'm sure Gerrard and everyone else is doing, about what an honor it is just to have competed, about how great the Sabretooths played, about how disappointed we feel to have come so close. I can't think of anything else or else I might just break down completely.

I'm not the only one. Back in the locker room, nobody's crying noisily, but at least five guys have their paws over their faces, and more rub damp tracks into the fur around their eyes. A bunch just stare into space. Even when Coach gathers us all around, we shuffle like zombies.

"I'm not gonna lie," he says, and his voice has cracks in it too, which just makes it worse for the rest of us. Someone catches his breath in a definite sob. "This one hurts. I feel like I let you guys down, like there was one thing I could've done differently so we would be celebrating now instead of thinking about that other team celebrating."

We murmur, "no, no," and he holds up a paw. "I want you to leave here with this thought: we did not lose this game because you didn't play hard. We lost this game because they made some outstanding plays, because their players are talented and their coaches are smart, and because they had the ball last. You have done as much as you could, and the city of Chevali is going to remember you for a long, long time. Nobody expected us to be in this game, much less be leading with ten seconds to go. So walk out of here with your heads high and your ears up, and when the reporters talk to us, congratulate the Sabretooths on a terrific game, because they played their hearts out the same as you did. And this team has proven that it's no fluke, that it's going to be a force to be reckoned with for years to come. We're young, and next year we're just going to be better and have more experience."

Murmurs around the locker room. "One last thing," Coach says. "For some of you, this is the last time I am going to talk to you as your Coach. Some of you will move to new teams, and we'll have new faces in these uniforms. So I just want to tell each one of you here in this locker room: thank you all for the effort you've put in this season, for the blood, sweat, and tears you've shed to make this football team great. I have never been more proud of a group of football players than I am of you. I will never forget how much I have enjoyed the privilege of being your coach."

Now I feel the pricking of tears. Charm, steady-voiced and loud, calls out, "Let's hear it for Coach!"

He claps with steady, fast beats of those strong hands, and the rest of us join in with hoots and cheers, and the ones nearest Coach hug him and pound him on the back. "We love you, Coach" and "You're the best" sound through the cheers, and the old wolf presses fingers to his eyes and hugs back, his tail wagging.

When I make it through the mob to give Coach a hug, he says into my ear, "You're a remarkable guy."

"You're a great coach," I say back, and then Carson takes my place and I move on, back to my locker.

And you know, I feel a little better. I find that I also want to hear those words from another voice, a fox's voice, but that will wait for later. I sit there and wonder if I'll be a Firebird next year. But even that is a remote concern. I'm thinking about how I did everything right, I worked as hard as I could and I focused on football, and at the end of the year I'm still left feeling that there's a big hole in my life. Is it always going to be like this? I look for Fisher, because I want to ask him if winning a championship, winning two, dulls the pain of losing. But I don't see him anywhere.

"Where's Fish?" I ask Gerrard.

He shakes his head. "Trainers, probably."

I look toward the trainers' room. "I'll catch him later, I guess."

"Yeah." Gerrard is slumped against his locker, and he looks old, just staring at the floor, still in his game jersey and pads.

I feel the need to try to take his mind off things. "What are you gonna do in the offseason?"

He shrugs. "Play with the kids. Try not to remember this."

"I hear you." I look up at the video screens in the locker room, mercifully dark.

"What about you?" He looks up. "Going to work on your contract?"

"Maybe." I shrug. "Might be traded somewhere, right?"

Gerrard shakes his head. "Doubt it. Maybe if someone comes in with an offer that blows them away."

"I'd like to stay," I say. "I think we work well together."

The coyote doesn't say anything in response, but he smiles a little and nods.

My phone rings. I pick it up and look at the number. It's Dad, so I answer. "You played well," he says. In the background, I hear the noise of the crowd, and then they go silent.

"Thanks."

"Er…" He seems at a loss for words. "You are watching the field?"

"No. I'm not watching any of it." My phone beeps again. Another call coming in.

"Perhaps you should." The crowd behind him roars again, the silence broken.

My phone buzzes: a text message. "What's going on?"

PART V

CHAPTER 29 – STANDING UP (LEE)

When the ball tumbles out of Zillo's paws and the whistle sounds, I just stand there and stare, waiting to wake up. The whole room was focused, some cheering, some just watching silently; now they come back to life as though released from a spell. The lemur turns to the board to tally up the prop bets, and someone turns the sound down a little. It's still audible, just not overwhelming.

"Well," Hal says. "Least that was better than '85."

"Better?" I can't parse that. "I feel like my heart's been ripped out."

Peter nods at the screen. "You know that anyone in this room would kill to be in the championship again, right? Even if we end up losing? Just getting there is so rare."

"I would too," I say. "Rather taste it than never know what it's like, right?"

"Right. Excuse me a second, I'm going to collect on my prop bets."

The commercials end and the TV cuts back to the triumphant Sabretooths. I don't want to watch this. "Yeah, I'm going to, uh, get a beer."

Hal walks with me into the other room and cracks open a beer with me. "Hell of a game," he says.

"At least there's that," I say.

"And your boy got a highlight for sure. That was a pretty sack. People will remember that."

"They will," I say. "And they won't blame him for that last play. It was the coach's call."

"Right. And they've got a bright future. Defense is looking good, and maybe Strike will stick around another year."

"They'll be a tough out in the playoffs. If they stay healthy."

"Even if they don't make it back next year, they'll be back in two or three. They'll always be in the mix."

We say these kinds of things knowing they're supposed to make us feel better, knowing that they're not going to do much. But it's better than watching the other team celebrate, or watching the downcast Firebirds interviewed.

We've only gotten a third of the way through the beers and platitudes when a couple people in the room outside start shushing the crowd. Everyone goes silent, and Hal and I look at each other.

Peter sticks his head in the room. "There you are," he says to me. "Get out here."

I run out with Hal close behind, and stare at the TV. One of the Sabretooths is front and center, a coyote, number 55. Polecki, I remember before reading his name along the bottom of the screen.

"…had not intended to use this stage for that purpose," he's saying. "But as the game was winding down, I heard a teammate call Dev Miski a 'faggot,' and even in the middle of the greatest moment of my life, I felt like a coward. I wish I had had the courage to do this before the game, so that this would be recorded as the first game in which two openly gay players faced each other."

What the fuck? I stare at the screen and feel my jaw drop.

"But it will have to be just the game in which the first openly gay player played, and the game that gave the weaker one the courage to step up and join Devlin Miski in coming out to the world, with confidence that you will still support me," and here he has to pause, because the crowd roars, and he starts to speak again, but they're still cheering and cheering and they won't stop, and his eyes glisten with tears as he says, "Thank you. Thank you."

His voice cracks, and I feel matching tears in my eyes. His teammates stand behind him, McCrae holding the MVP trophy in one arm and draping the other across the coyote's shoulders, all the others crowding up to pat him on the back and they're all smiling and tails are wagging and it takes him a good thirty more seconds before he can keep talking.

"Thank you." He turns to his teammates. "Thank you all, and thank you most of all and most heartfelt to Devlin Miski, who I hope is watching—or maybe will see this on tape later—" His teammates laugh. "For showing me that pride is not just for parades. That it was time to make a change, and that I was the one who had to make that change for myself."

The cheers are not as loud as they were at first, but they're still there. I wipe my eyes, trying to be discreet and masculine about it and failing, I'm sure. Peter, next to me, says, "Holy shit," and other people around the room are echoing the sentiment. More than one of them are looking at me, including Jocko.

"All right," Polecki says, and wipes his eyes, looking *way* more masculine than I just did. "That's enough about me. Someone else talk."

He gives up the mike to Bridger, the fox, who looks back at him and says, "Jesus Fox, dude, how do I follow *that?*"

There's laughter, and he starts in thanking his family and the team, and I stop paying attention. Jalili and Cormier and few of the other guys I talked with come over to me, as Peter's saying, "That's amazing."

"About fucking time," I say, and they laugh. "No, I mean it. I felt like—I know Dev isn't the only gay player. I know it. But none of the rest would say anything, and I just wondered, what the hell are they waiting for?"

"To win a championship, I guess," Jocko says. "Nobody's going to fuck with Polecki, not after the game he had."

"They cheered for him, too," Jalili says.

"He just won them a championship." Peter grins. "He could've confessed to the Robbins murders and they would've cheered him."

"Thanks," I say.

He holds up his paws. "Not saying it wasn't sincere. Just that he kind of stacked the deck."

"When the other side holds all the cards," I say, "sometimes you gotta do that."

He nods, and Jalili says, "So what now?"

"Well…" I think for a half-second she means about me and Dev, then I mentally slap myself. "I dunno. Maybe more players will come out in the off-season, when there's less attention and less heartache and strife about it."

My phone rings: Father's number. I excuse myself and walk to the back wall to pick it up.

"I saw," I say.

"Pretty interesting," he says. "How does this change things for you two?"

"I don't know. I haven't talked to Dev yet."

"But you're going to?"

"Yes."

"And your mother?"

"Yes, yes."

"All right. So, what do *you* think?"

"I think it's about effing time. Everyone in the league seems to be scared of something happening, even though nothing happened to Dev, and well, who knows? I'm sure people will say it was easy to come out when you'd just won a championship, but you never know how crowds are going to react. A couple people could start booing and the whole crowd could turn."

"I don't think that would happen. Not anymore."

"Maybe not, but…" I search for words. "It's like this childhood fear that never goes away, of being the outsider, and even if you know with your mind that people aren't going to turn their back on you, it's so hard to give them the perfect opportunity to. I rag on these guys for not coming out, but I understand it."

He hmms into the phone. "I do, too. I'm surprised he chose that stage. I can see where it would be safe, like you say, but I can also see how he's going to be ripped for making the celebration all about himself."

"I think his teammates knew," I say. "At least, some of them did. They didn't look too surprised. Maybe they told him it'd be okay."

"I guess we'll find out as they all get interviewed to death. Oh look, speaking of, the reporters have found Devlin."

Dev's up on the screen. "Looks like it."

"Well, I'll talk to you later. Let's watch it."

"Thanks, Father."

I watch Dev answer questions, holding my phone. I wonder if I should call Kodi now, or wait until later. Maybe having his phone ring right away would be too suspicious. I'll wait. But as I'm thinking that, my phone lights up again: Brian's number this time. I send it to voicemail, because fuck him. I am done with him.

Jocko catches my eye as I put the phone away, and excuses himself from the people he's talking to. We meet by the wall, and he puts a paw out. "Congrats."

I shake paws, and tilt my head up at him. "On...?"

"Chevali plus three," he says. "Our bet."

"Oh. Thanks." I search his expression. "You know that even people who are really smart about football will get those bets wrong like a third of the time."

"Then I guess you're lucky, too," he rumbles, and it almost looks like he winks at me.

The wink makes me uncomfortable, though, because all his comments about college kids being hot and me and Morty "after hours" come flooding back. So as he starts to turn, I say, "Um, Jack? Jocko?"

"Jocko's fine." He looks back and then shifts his big barrel chest to face me again. "What's up?"

Faced with the moment, I quail for a split-second. I can live with a bigot, I think, I can make it work, I'll do it for the chance at this job...and then I think about Polecki up there on the screen, and Dev, and the chances they took. I breathe in. "I used to work for a guy who didn't know a lot about gay guys," I start.

He tenses up in his shoulders. I wish he had a proper tail so I could see if it was curling or relaxed. I forge on. "And he was kind of an asshole about it sometimes. But that's cool. I just want to know, if I take this job...are you going to be constantly asking if I like a guy because he's hot, or asking if I'm having sex with random guys I like to spend time with? Because if you are, you know…" His eyes widen slowly as I talk. "…then that's gonna be a problem."

"I knew a gay guy," he says, his voice low. "Usedta come to the locker room and open up his muzzle for anyone."

I'm guessing that "anyone" included him, but I am not prepared to go there. "Uh-huh," I say, and just then I catch sight of Jalili. "I know a straight guy who fucks anything on two legs. Anything female, that is. That mean I should ask you if you had sex with Jalili over there? I mean, you guys know each other, right?"

He opens his mouth, angry, and then snaps it shut. "I'm married," he says.

"Yeah, well, if it were legal, I might be, too." This is less true than it would have been at any other time in the last three years, but tossing that "might" in there makes it at least not an outright lie.

We glare at each other, and Peter and Hal come over, Peter holding a laptop. "Hey, look at this," he says.

Jocko points at me. "I think this guy just called me an asshole."

"I didn't mean—" I start.

Peter talks over me, barely reacting at all. "Told you he was a quick study. Here." He shoves the laptop at me. "Check this out. The article on Polecki is going nuts. Two hundred comments already."

Jocko looks over my shoulder as I skim the comments, which range from "way 2 go!!!!" to "fuck you faggot stealing the spotlight." But there are fewer of the latter type, and they have a lot of responses telling them to crawl back into their cave.

"I can't believe it." I shake my head and hand Peter the laptop back. "I mean, here I was all set to be depressed the whole way home."

"Huh." Jocko scratches his muzzle. "Maybe sometime you can teach this asshole about how gay guys work."

"I didn't mean—" I start again, and he waves me off.

"Just fuckin' with ya." He laughs. "I am an asshole."

"Well, I have it on good authority that I'm kind of a prick," I say. "So I think we'll get along fine."

Hal sighs and buries his muzzle in his paws, while Peter and Jocko look puzzled, and then stare at me. "Well," I say, "if you're going to hire a gay guy, you'll get some off-color jokes."

"Fine," Peter says, "but not in any official communications, okay?"

Jocko snorts. "That was an internal e-mail, it just got copied to the wrong people."

My grin widens. "I think we'll get along great."

The bear looks down, and then he extends his paw again, and when I take it, he shakes it firmly and with more energy than the first two times that day. "Looking forward to it," he says. "By the way, new guy brings bagels every Friday."

"Until when?"

"Until there's a new new guy." He grins and lifts a paw. "See ya."

So that's it. I did it. Warmth builds up in my chest, confidence and pride, as I keep my ears straight up. Hal punches me on the shoulder, and I shoot him a big smile.

Peter shifts his laptop to his other arm. "Of course," he says, "we haven't made a firm decision yet, but unofficially, if Jocko's okay with it, I don't see anything standing in the way of hiring you. This thing with Polecki... well, I think it'll help a lot to have you on board. There might be room for outreach after all—not to the community, but within the team and to college prospects."

I nod. "If there are gay college players..."

"And if they're any good, we don't want 'em going to Chevali or C.C. automatically. Got to make sure they know they're welcome here."

"They should be welcome anywhere," I say.

"Yeah." Peter grins, showing all his teeth. "But you're going to be working here." His eyes sparkle and in that moment, I want to work for him more than anything in the world—except one thing.

Hal knows what that one thing is, too. As Peter leaves, the swift fox murmurs very softly, in a fox-whisper at my cheek ruff, "You going to call him?"

I look at the TV. Dev's long gone, but the anchors are still buzzing about Polecki. I think about my tiger—*my* tiger—sitting sad in his locker room, or being besieged by phone calls from reporters. "I don't know," I say.

CHAPTER 30 – ANSWERS (DEV)

It takes me a while to figure out what's happening, because nobody wants to put on the TV, even after I say my dad told me to watch it. A couple seconds after we get it on, Vince runs into the room with a laptop in the crook of one elbow and a phone cinched against his ear with his shoulder. He's talking into the phone but stops when he spots me and yells, "Miski! Get out here!"

"I don't know what's going on!" I yell back.

"Polecki just said he's gay." The locker room goes dead silent. "In front of seventy thousand people. Get out here! They want your take on it."

The murmurs start around the room. "Polecki?"

"Fifty-five."

"The coyote? Shit."

"He's good."

"Did he feel you up when he tackled you?"

Charm elbows me. "You only did it in a room of fifty people," he says. "This guy did it in front of seventy thousand."

"Seventy million including the TV," Ty points out.

I'll say one thing, it's taking our minds off the loss. "What did he say?" I ask Vince as I pull on a shirt and follow him out.

"I'm working on it." He gestures me forward, types something on his laptop, and yells into his phone, "Send the fucking video over!"

The media room is much less formally set up. Coach is in there talking to two reporters about Aston's arm as Strike listens. "...complete confidence in him going forward..." The wolf turns his head and sees me and Vince. "Uh..." His brow furrows and then he shakes his head. Strike, beside him, flashes me a smile and a thumbs up.

"Yeah," Vince says into the phone. "I got 'im. Let them in when you're ready."

"What's happening?" one of the reporters says.

"Hang on." Vince taps some keys on his laptop. He points to the podium. "Miski, get over there. They'll be here in a minute."

"Who will?" Coach says.

"Polecki—fifty-five—just came out," I tell him as I take his place at the podium. "I guess. That's what it sounds like."

"No shit." His ears go back and then come up again as the two reporters scramble to ask me questions. "Well, if it means I don't have to sit here and talk about this game anymore, I'm all for it." He walks toward the exit, but doesn't leave; he just stands at the door and watches. Through the door, the shapes of Charm and Gerrard and Pike are visible, and others shifting behind them.

Strike, of course, stays sitting at the chair by my side. "Came out on the post-game, huh? Brilliant. The guy knows how to pick his moments."

The two reporters jostle. "What do you think about—" "Did you know about—"

I start to talk, but Vince stops me. "Fair's fair," he says. "We'll let you ask first, but let's wait 'til everyone gets here. I don't want Miski to have to repeat himself. Here, I got the video."

The sound on his laptop isn't great, so we all cluster around. It's a video of Polecki, the coyote still panting from the game, the "55" gold on his navy blue uniform, as a beaming Runningwater gives way to him.

"This should be the best moment of my life," he says, "and I have to thank all the fans here for supporting and believing in us this year. We haven't played a better game than we did right here today, and part of that is because of the level of competition we faced. The Firebirds are a great team, and you will be seeing them in championships for years to come." There's a less enthusiastic cheer, but still pretty loud. I feel a nice swelling of pride in my chest.

"And there's one Firebird in particular who has inspired me. I'm sure you all know the story of Dev Miski, who came out earlier this season and has played inspired football while dealing with all the fallout from that. I want to thank him especially for the game he played. I know how hard it must be to concentrate on football with the scrutiny of the media all over your private life." He takes a breath, and I do, too. I'm used to the attention focused on me, but it feels strange to be called out at a moment like that, when he should just be excited about his championship. And there's tension too, because I know what's coming, and he's put me in his story, made me responsible for part of it. "It's something I have run from my whole life. But my colleague on the other side of the field has made me feel ashamed of running, so I won't be doing that any longer." The crowd is silent except for scattered cheers. "I'm gay. I've known for as long as I've been playing football. I just want to say that, and I don't want to take away from this moment for my teammates, though I know there will be questions."

The guys behind him don't look surprised, except for Yates, the other coyote linebacker, whose bug-eyed "WHAAAT?" reaction is so comically over the top that it has to be fake. McCrae comes up and wraps an arm around Polecki's shoulder. "Really," the coyote says, "I hadn't intended to use this stage for that purpose…"

A crowd of people surges into the media room as we watch the rest of it. My throat gets tight at the cheers for him, how loud and enthusiastic they are. Maybe it's just sympathetic reaction to his own emotion, maybe it's the support and acceptance, colored though it is by the giddiness of a home crowd that's just seen its team win a championship. Still…it could have gone wrong. I watch his teammates laughing around him, slapping him on the back, and I don't see any with Colin's sulky expression. Are things changing? It'd be nice.

Vince closes his laptop. "There you go," he says. "Miski, I'm sure they're going to want to interview the two of you together, but I insisted you stay in our media room for now."

"Okay. Hey, can you get someone to grab my phone out of my locker?" I ask him.

"Sure." He points to the two reporters who were here first. "Answer these guys, then whatever order you want. You," he beckons to Strike, "c'mon."

"I'm Dev's friend," Strike says. "I'm staying as a show of support."

Vince looks at me, and after a moment, Strike does too. I know why Strike feels he needs to be there—to keep himself in the spotlight. But at the same time, he is supporting me, and as selfish as I know his motives are, I can't bring myself to alienate any friends right now. So I just turn to the first two reporters and say, "Go ahead."

There isn't really a lot I can say about this, so it only takes forty minutes to answer all their questions: No, I didn't know about Polecki. I am glad that I inspired him to come out. I think he was very brave. I plan on talking to him soon.

Strike actually stays pretty restrained. In fact, he only talks when one of the reporters asks him about his experience playing with a gay teammate, and that's right when Vince comes back with my phone. Strike goes on like he does, of course, but I'm grateful for the break. I don't know if Ogleby reads texts, but I can't talk to him yet and I don't want to wait. I just type, *Get me Polecki's number*, fingers tapping delicately across the cracks as fast as I can, and I send it off to him. The message indicator is lit up with text messages and voicemails, and two more texts come in just in the time it takes me to type, saying, "*Any comment…*" and "*did you know about…*"

I turn off the phone and answer more questions from the reporters in the room: I don't know how this will change. I do expect more athletes will come out. Do I still wish I hadn't come out?

Do I?

"Of course he doesn't," Strike says cheerfully when I don't answer immediately, but the reporters kind of ignore him, still staring at me.

I take a breath. "I was under a lot of stress when I said that. I've apologized since then. I am very glad I did. I've had—there have been a lot of challenges since then, but the changes I've seen have been very encouraging. My teammates have been supportive and so have most of the fans. I get e-mails—" I assume I do. Lee always looked at them. I pause, wondering if the e-mails have been piling up while we've been apart or if he's looked at them and sorted through them. "But overall it's been a great experience and I'm glad that I'm now the first gay player instead of the only."

They laugh. I relax. The questions get easier, and a few of them are about the game. Strike says we will be back in the championship game, and says that once he gets integrated into the offense better, we'll be unstoppable, something like that. While he's talking about how he had a good seam on that last return if only the ball had come to him, Coach comes up to the podium, and Gerrard and Aston and Jaws come into the room as well. Most of the subsequent questions go to them, so I step aside except for when there's a question about my sack and I get to say how great it felt to get the only sack on McCrae. I talk about how talented he is, and how I'm looking forward to seeing the film of the game so I can really see his quickness and decision-making in play.

The questions shift away from me just as my phone buzzes. I see a text message from an unfamiliar number. *Hey, it's Aran Polecki. You want to grab a drink? :)*

Holy shit. Ogleby came through. Fifteen minutes later, when they let us go back to the locker room, I text back. *Sure, just getting away from the press.*

Yeah, I'll be in the middle of it for a while yet.

I imagine.

How long are you in town for?

I pause. *Don't know. Don't really have any plans for the next three months.*

Know the feeling. :) I'll text you in a couple hours.

It's kind of weird talking to him. Football players are all part of a pretty exclusive club anyway, so we can talk to each other about things that nobody else understands, but now I'm talking to this guy just because he's gay. I wonder what we'll talk about. Techniques? How he hid his life from his team? Does he have a boyfriend, too? Or—can I say "too"? What do I say when he asks me about my life?

I think about my dinner with Machaine and how easy it was to talk about relationships and homophobia and…gay stuff. A little weird at first to have that matter-of-fact talk about dating guys and what we find attractive about them, but ultimately it was relaxing. I hope this'll be the same. Better, even, because we're both football players *and* both gay, and even if we don't have to talk about that, I'll know we can.

Checking the messages, I see one from Lee. The timestamp says it's the one from before the game. I hesitate over it, because I'm not sure I want to see what he has to say, and then I think, what the hell, I might as well. So I read the message. *All the other things aside, I still believe in you and you're a great football player. Wishing you the best of luck.*

Strangely, that depresses me. "All other things aside." That's a lot of shit to put aside. "Wishing you the best of luck." It sounds like we haven't known each other for three years, like we haven't been sleeping in the same bed for months. Will he be there when I get home? Do I want him to be? I should answer him, but I can't think of what to say. Do I just say, "Hey, how about that Polecki, huh?" Or "Thanks for the wishes?" There's so much I want to say to him, it's like trying to run plays around a giant hole on the field, only the hole doesn't stay in one place; it opens up in front of me and to the side and where I expect it and where I don't. I can't ever get a good run up to think about this problem, and eventually I put the phone down.

The locker room isn't as quiet as I'm used to it being after a loss. People are chattering, and I hear the words "gay" and "coyote" and "Polecki," and I get the feeling of a lot of eyes on me.

"Hey." I look up and see Carson beside me, in street clothes. "Circus of a game."

"Yeah." I smile at him. "You got that ball?"

He nods. "You played great. Don't forget that."

"You too." We bump fists. "What are you doing in the offseason?"

"Ah, you know. Working out. Playing video games. Golf. Maybe do some work on my grandmother's property."

I nod. He doesn't ask me what I'll be doing, just raises a paw and walks out.

The room is emptying quickly. I look for Zillo and find him in a heated, low-voiced argument with Colin on the other side of the room. The coyote has his ears up; the fox has his ears back, and when Colin pauses in his argument to glare at me, I am left with little doubt what the argument is about.

Well, that's okay. I've got something to say to him, too. I stalk over to the two of them.

Colin sees me first and steps back, holding up his paws. "You just stay out of this," he says. "Doesn't concern you."

"Really," I say. "Because you kept looking at me."

"It's not." Zillo stays beside me, facing down Colin. "It's just about... he's just...being him."

"Yeah," I say. "About that. Can I talk to you in private?"

Colin stares at me as if I'd asked him to bend over and drop his pants. All the traits that I find so attractive in Lee are like a photo-negative in him. The black ears flick with contempt, the muzzle crinkles in a snarl, and his eyes are brown, not the clear blue of Lee's. Fuck, I have to stop thinking of them together like that.

"I don't have anything to say to you," he says, and turns away.

"I just want to talk about Argonne," I say.

Zillo cups his ears toward me. Colin stops, half-turns, and shrugs. "I have no idea what you're talking about."

He's lying, I think, especially because his tail snaps curled the way Lee's has been recently—had been recently—I stop that line of thought and wonder if Colin ever stopped to ask Argonne's name. It doesn't seem like Argonne would wait to be asked. "Oh," I say, "I think you do."

"I told you, I have nothing to say to you. After tomorrow, I won't have to see you for two months. Hopefully longer."

"Yeah, well," I say, "We'll see how the offseason goes. But you and me need to get something *straight* before we take off. If you want, I can just say it out loud in front of all your friends here." I emphasize the word "straight" deliberately.

He stops and stares at me, one paw reaching up to hold his cross. The teammates nearby prick their ears curiously, but stay silent. Colin scowls, scans the crowded locker room, and points one dark brown finger into the now-empty showers. "There."

"I'll just be a minute," I tell Zillo. "Catch you after."

"Yeah, sure." He shrugs.

I follow Colin into the shower, still thick and warm with the smell of soap and disappointment, as if we'd been able to get it all off of us there. We stand away from the damp walls, near the drain in the center. The moment we're out of sight of the locker room, before I have a chance to say anything, he gets all up in my face. "Listen," he says, "I only agreed to come in here so you wouldn't start slandering me in front of the team. They don't need to hear that after this game."

I stand there and look coolly back. As coolly as I can while wanting to punch him in the throat, anyway. "You do know that his name is 'Argonne,' right? The fox who's been blowing you before road games?"

He steps back, and his tail is so tightly wound it looks like a spring. "If anyone told you that, they're lying."

"Mm. No, that'd be difficult." I don't want to lean against the wet wall, so I just fold my arms. "No, I got up close to him the other night. Smelled his breath. It smelled real familiar."

"Like you can tell from smells," he snorts derisively.

Fucking foxes. Despite his attitude, his nostrils flare and his eyes are wide. If we weren't in the shower, I bet I'd be able to smell the change in his emotion. I take a breath. "Yeah, well. When I realized who it reminded me of, I asked him about you. He's discreet, didn't want to tell me, but when I told him your name and mentioned your…jewelry," I gesture at the cross around his neck, "he told me he's been your regular, how did he put it, 'muzzle check-in' before road games. Some home games, too."

His eyes flicker, and he starts to walk past me and out. "I don't have to stay here and listen to whatever stories your little road-whores make up."

I don't chase him. "I'm guessing—just a shot in the dark—that Penny doesn't know."

That stops him. He edges to one side, out of view of the locker room again. "Are you threatening to tell my wife lies?" His voice is louder and higher, echoing off the tile.

"No. I'm not threatening to tell her anything. I'm just wondering how you justify being such a bigoted prick when you're not only letting a guy blow you, but also cheating on your wife. I never cheated on Lee."

"Sure." He sneers again, and again I'm reminded of Lee in a negative way, the twisting of words and the cleverness without the caring behind it. "What were you doing so close you could smell the breath of that little slut, if you weren't cheating?"

"Talking to him," I say. "Not leaving any of my scent on him. Or in him." It was a near thing, but Colin doesn't have to know how near.

"Right. Because he's so good at conversation."

"I guess you wouldn't know what else he can use his muzzle for. But it sounds like you do know him."

He drops his mouth open, says, "You—" and then snaps his jaw closed, giving me a momentary flush of satisfaction at having outwitted a fucking fox. His ears flatten, and his paw reaches up to grab his cross, then lets it go. "I am not cheating," he says in a low, vicious hiss. "I'm not lying with another vixen, or letting her touch me inappropriately."

"But you are letting another male touch you—"

His eyes narrow. I marvel that he and Lee are the same species. "Even if that were true, it wouldn't count. It's just a—a thing that doesn't mean anything."

"I'm not going to tell anyone." I don't like saying that because what he's saying is kind of pissing me off. "But you are cheating, you know. You are having sex."

"I am *not*. It's not real intercouse. It's not what relationships are founded on, no matter what you and that coyote have deluded yourself into thinking. And you're trying to convince cubs all over the world that you're right, that they can have families with anyone they let touch their privates. That's not God's plan for the world." His paw twitches through his chest fur just short of the cross and then drops to his side again.

"So because you really like sticking your dick in a boy's mouth—"

"Shut up!" His ears flatten. "I am not going to be talked to like this." He points a finger at me, inches from my nose. "And if you try to tell this despicable lie to anyone, I will make your life miserable."

He starts to walk away. I say, "Seems to me it'd make your life pretty miserable, too. So what say you lay off my private life? Then I won't feel any need to discuss yours."

"I don't make my private life the world's business," he hisses over his shoulder, at the exit.

"Neither do I!" I have to raise my voice. "The fucking world makes it their business!"

He's already out in the locker room. I stand there, tail lashing, and then I slam one fist into the wet tile of the shower wall and stalk out.

And almost smack right into Gerrard and Coach. Both of them say at about the same time, "What's going on? Everything okay?"

"Yeah, it's fine." I'm not sure why my paws hurt, then I realize my fists are clenched and my claws partly extended. I force them to relax. "Everything's fucking fine."

I stalk past them. Behind me, Gerrard says to Coach, "They weren't fighting."

I don't look toward Colin's locker, because if I see his smug smile or his big black ears, I'm going to want to punch him. And we'll be off soon enough, and I won't have to see him until the flight back home. By then I should have calmed down.

Gerrard comes up and puts a paw on my shoulder. "Look," I say, "I'm leaving this in the locker room. He's a good corner, I know that. The team needs us both. I was just trying to settle something before the off-season. I don't have football to take up my life now, not for three or four months. So just lay off."

He removes the paw, then settles it down on my shoulder again. "I was only going to ask if you wanted to come out for a drink. Just the linebackers. Steez wants to take us out."

I glance at my phone. I want to figure out what to text Lee, and I agreed to meet Polecki later, and probably Mom and Dad will want to get together. But Polecki won't be free for a while and I want to stay part of this team for as much longer as I can manage. "Sure," I say. "Should have time for that."

It takes two hours, and it's a really nice two hours. It feels strange to think that we're not going to be on the field again in a week or two, but we start comparing minor injuries and talking about things we want to catch up on. "I'm actually looking forward to spending time with the cubs," Gerrard says, and laughs. "In a few months I'll be ready to get back to football."

"What," I say, "no off-season workouts?"

"Oh, there's workouts, and you're coming." He grins at me. "Just not football."

Carson remains fairly quiet. Zillo is going to some tropical island with his family and a girl they want him to meet, and Marais is going to work on a charitable foundation for Vidalia youth, out where he grew up.

They ask me what I'm going to do, and I can't say, "Figure out my relationship," so I say, "Probably start working with the Equality Now people and maybe do some PSAs, appear at schools. Try to help gay kids."

I'm not worried about football anymore, and, I realize, not worried about how anyone in this group will react. They react just the same as they did to everyone else: with nods and approving noises, and moving on to Steez, who says, "Good work," to me before talking about coaching pee-wee football camps back in his hometown.

I think about Lee, and about Polecki, and how just the fact that there's another gay player now makes me feel less self-conscious. Why couldn't I get that from Lee? Maybe it's that plus the lack of pressure for an upcoming game. Or maybe it's both those things plus six months of learning to rely on each other. Whatever it is, it feels good, the linebackers all as close as any family gathering I've been to in years. As we talk, I slowly process that nobody else thinks of me as the odd guy out even when I talk about being gay. I'm just Dev, sitting between a couple cougars and across from a couple coyotes. Every one of us is different, no one more different than the others, gay or straight, monogamous or less so, from poor or middle-class families. Maybe that was always true. Maybe that's what Lee was trying to teach me, and I just couldn't see it.

By the time I have to grab a cab to meet Polecki, the rest of the guys are taking off to do their own thing, meet up with other teammates or go visit some C.C. hotspots. I know I'll see them on the plane, but I take a moment to look around the table and remember this group, these guys who were with me all season long. It's a special group, and talking about our lives outside of football, even for this brief time, has reinforced the bond we have.

It's illusory, I know. Gerrard's under contract, Carson is too. Probably none of us are going anywhere. But any of us could be traded, or someone else could be brought in. Steez could be promoted or could get a better job. Life wears down the bonds we form, sometimes almost as soon as we form them.

CHAPTER 31 — DEPARTURES (LEE)

Dev's probably busy, I keep telling myself. But at least there's one thing I can do. I track down Peter. "Hey, do you have the number of the GM in Crystal City?"

"Sure," he says. "But you might want to give him a few minutes."

I pull up Dev's number on my phone. "In case Polecki wants to get in touch with him. I'm pretty sure they don't have each others' numbers."

"Oh. Yeah, that might be handy. Thanks." He takes my phone and walks off with it, pulling up a number on his own phone. "Gil? Hey, congratulations, possum! Listen, I was looking at Polecki—yeah, hell of a thing, right? Well, guess who I got here? Miski's boyfriend. That's right. So if you want to pass along Miski's number…yeah." He reads off Dev's number, gives me back the phone, and pads out of earshot.

Hal pats me on the shoulder. "So now there's two."

"And more to come." I exhale. "It's only going to get easier from this point on."

"So I'd think." He beckons me back and leans against the wall, the two of us removing ourselves somewhat from the post-game party going on. A lot of people are on their phones; I guess everyone knows someone connected with Crystal City. The ones who aren't on the phone are half-talking, half-watching the screen, or else settling up prop bets with the lemur. Every now and then, one of the people I've met walks by, but they leave us alone when they see us in conversation. "So look. Your tiger, he's going to need some support."

I eye him. "Really? You're going to try to get us back together *now?*"

"Been trying a while." He grins. "Guess it was a little subtle. I know you reds like things direct."

I scowl, and he goes on. "So you got this job sewn up, and you'll be moving out here soon, but I want my office back."

"Yeah, sorry about that. Another week, tops." My tail brushes the wall, back and forth, a soothing rhythm. I could probably stay with Father for a while. That reminds me that I should call Mother soon and find out what's going on with her.

"Other thing." Hal points at the screen. "Less pressure on him now. Someone else is out, so he can worry about his life. Let other people be activists. Or not. But it should be more relaxed, and you can be you, and he can be him. Seems to work pretty well for you when that happens."

"Maybe." I follow his finger to the screen. They've moved from the Sabretooths' trophy presentation to the crowd, talking to people while the players move back to the locker room. Polecki is still surrounded by reporters; they cut back to show him every now and then. One of the announcers sounds a little disapproving, but the sound is down and the room is loud. I catch the phrase, "disrespecting the game, he could have waited a day," and then the response, "seemed to be from the heart, you can't fault that."

Hal nudges me. "Maybe?"

"Well, I don't know," I say. "Being me didn't work out. Not being me didn't work out. I don't know what I'm left with."

Hal sighs. "Well, being a martyr don't suit you either. So drop that."

"I'm not." I turn from the TV to glare at him. "I'm being realistic."

"You're being emotional."

"Says the guy who's been divorced."

"Not my decision." He shrugs as I just stare at him. "Little bit my decision."

"Didn't you say that I'll get over this emotional thing in time?" I fold my arms and slump against the wall.

"Mostly. But all I'm sayin' right now is that I think you should send him a message or something." He talks softly but firmly.

"I did send him a message." My phone is warm in my pocket. "He hasn't replied."

"You sent him a message before the championship game," Hal says. "Before the biggest game of his life, which ended, what, half an hour ago?"

"So why should I send him another message now? Give him a chance to reply, if he's going to." The thought that he won't gnaws at my stomach. I tell myself rather brutally that Dev not responding to me is something I'm going to have to get used to.

"You don't think he would have something to say about this?"

"I'm sure he does." Just maybe not to me. Too close to our fight, too wrapped up in gay activism, too much of the two worlds intersecting and colliding. I hope he has a good conversation with Polecki. I hope the coyote is as nice and genuine a guy as his speech indicated.

Hal shrugs. "Okay, then," he says. "I guess you know best."

•

Uncovered

When I do finally get the message from Dev, it's hours later in the hotel room. Hal's back to researching his story, and I've just been lying back on the bed playing some stupid game I downloaded for my phone, which is terrible, but I don't have anything else to do other than think about the day, the Firebirds losing, and so on. I have e-mail from Brian but I don't want to read it yet because I know pretty much what it's going to say, and I have a voicemail from Kodi, which I should answer sometime.

But the message from Dev, that one I want to see. I call it up and read it, and then I read it again.

"Huh," I say.

Hal looks up from his laptop. "Message?"

"Yeah. From Dev."

He turns his chair, faces me. "And?"

I stare down at the text again. "I don't know. I mean…we're talking. I guess."

"Are you going to message him back?"

"Yeah. Eventually." Once I think of something to say.

"Should do it sooner than later."

"And you should stop trying to make up for your failed marriage through my relationship," I snap, pulling the game back up on my phone.

I notice that Hal isn't typing much, but I don't think anything of it until he says, "Maybe that is what I'm doing. But I don't think it's such a bad thing to be doing." I don't respond to that, and he goes on. "You guys still have a chance, you know. I'm tryin' to help with the lessons I've learned because you have it about a thousand times harder than me and Cim did."

"Not a million times harder?" I don't look up from the game.

"No," he says. "No, I'd say about a thousand. We had lots of our own problems that you two don't. Thing is, you got a lot of advantages we didn't."

Now I put the game aside. "Like?"

"For one thing, your families don't expect you to have cubs anytime. That's a big one."

"Mine does."

He shakes his head. "Not the same. I mean, it is sort of because with your family, it's like an indictment of your whole life, but it's all or nothing. They can't say, 'We love your boyfriend but when are you going to get him pregnant?' Accepting you means accepting the 'no cubs' thing. And you're three for four on that."

"Cubs aren't the big issue anyway. The big issue is that we want different things. Like you and Cim."

"Or like me and Pol. And we're working on it because we both like each other a lot." He reaches up to scratch behind an ear. "Not as much as you guys like each other."

"Your differences aren't as strong either." I don't know if that's true, but it makes me feel better about where Dev and I are if it is.

"Maybe, maybe not." Hal's smart enough not to get sidetracked into that discussion. "I guess my thinking is you should at least talk it out face to face. Now that the game's over and all."

"Yeah, I kinda think we will. But…" I draw my knees up and curl my tail around them, trying to figure out how to vocalize what I've been trying not to think. "Maybe this is just rationalization, but I think it's also important for us to learn that we can live apart. I mean…I don't want to end up one of those guys who can't function without a boyfriend."

"At the risk of bein' flip," Hal says, "I've been pretty happy for thirty-some years without a boyfriend."

"Yeah, well, you just haven't had a good one." I stick my tongue out at him, not suggestively.

"Maybe." He chuckles, and nods at me. "Go ahead."

"Well, ever since I came out, in college…" I think about it. "I had Brian as a best friend, I had a series of boyfriends. I wasn't seeing anyone when I met Dev, and partly that played into what happened. Brian was gone, I'd broken up with—shit, what was his name? Some fox. Anyway. I was doing fine. I was independent and I was on my own, but I was also a little bit scared. I've always wanted to prove myself, that I could get out there and be my own person and succeed without help, and I've always been scared that I couldn't. Dev helped me get my job as much as I helped him get his, and then I lost it again. And these last few months I've been scared that I'll never be anything but his boyfriend."

"Those guys at Yerba thought you were plenty smart," Hal says.

I nod. "It helps. And I'm starting to think that maybe—maybe—I'll be okay whatever happens."

He rubs the side of his muzzle. His whiskers flatten and then spring back. "Okay, then I'm gonna say my piece. I haven't seen you two together all that much. But when I've seen it, you guys had a joy about you that I don't see much anywhere. Cim and I had it for a year or two, then it disappeared." He looks down at his paws.

"I'm sorry," I say. It's hard to meet his eyes when he lifts his muzzle, but I make myself do it. "For saying that about you reliving your marriage. It was a shitty thing to say."

He nods acknowledgment. "Apology accepted. But it wasn't wrong. I'd give just about anything to have that time back. So I don't want you to waste the chance at it."

"What if I've already had my time?" I drop a paw to the tip of my tail, where the red shades into white. I've sifted claws across that border more times than I can count, trying to see where one ends and the other begins, and I can never sort it out. The first white hair is deep in the red side, the last red hair deep in the white. From the outside, it looks stark and easy, but when you look closer, it's not that easy, not by a long shot.

"Then…" Hal pauses. "I dunno. I think you never know it's over until you look back. But don't stop fighting for it. Take it from me. You don't know when it might come around again."

I smooth the fur over slowly. Red and white, plain as day. "Thing is… every time I dated someone else, I got more of those moments, and better. I couldn't imagine them getting better, and then they did."

"That stops." Hal laughs. "It doesn't keep getting better."

"What if there's someone else? I mean, I love Dev. I do. But can he really be the only one out there who makes me feel this way?"

"What if you never find that other person? Why not stick with the one you know?"

"What if there's someone out there who's the right person without all the fights and the conflicting goals?" But even as I say that, I know it's not the fights that are the problem. Dev and I fight, but fighting is our way of pushing each other, of challenging each other. We both enjoy that. Plus, the make-up sex.

It's the goals that are the problem. None of our fights uncovered issues the way this last one, which wasn't even a fight, did: communication, goals, methods. So the question is, is that something we can work out? Can we figure out a way to live together even with these differences? Or should we just stay friends and start over?

I close my eyes and imagine his arms around me, the warm fur and tight muscle, the scent of tiger and athlete. There's no-one like him, not anywhere, that combination of tough jock and vulnerable kid, the strength and weakness, the way he approaches sex with such boundaries and then with such enthusiasm and energy inside them. The way he won't let me be less than what I am. A different guy would have told me to cut out the activism altogether, to just sit around the house and be his fuck-toy because he could afford it. Or another guy would have just told me to go do whatever I wanted and distanced himself from it. But Dev…what caused him that stress is that he wanted to be part of it, that he felt guilty not doing the things I asked him to. And I love that about him.

"You know," Hal says softly. "You can create the perfect partner in your head. Have dreams, write in your diary, whatever you do."

"I don't write in a diary," I say.

He eyes me. "Guys write in diaries."

"Guys write in journals," I say, "and I don't do that either."

"Fine." He rolls his eyes. "For someone who puts on a dress, you're pretty touchy about it. Whatever. The point is, that perfect partner doesn't exist anywhere outside your diary, or your dreams, or your head."

"I know." I squeeze my tail tip in both paws, my ears flat against my head. "But if your partner doesn't want to call you back, then what can you do?"

"What you don't do is you don't give up."

"Easy for you to say."

He shakes his head. "All right, all right. Go ahead and mope. I know that feels good, too."

"I have to make a call." I go out into the hallway, as much to avoid the conversation as to not let on to Hal whose number I'm dialing.

"Hi," Kodi says when he picks up. "Thanks for calling back."

"What are you up to?" I ask. I walk near the ice machine, but it's too loud, so I head down the other direction.

"Oh, sitting around. Not thinking about the game. Whatever losers do. Where are you?"

"Up in Yerba. Just had a job interview-slash-championship game party-slash-gay rights discussion." I find an elevator lobby with a nice view out onto the park and the bay, the same view as our room.

"Yeah." He fidgets. "That's why I called."

"I figured. So how are you feeling?"

He takes a moment. "I don't know. The coyote, he's a superstar."

"I don't know about that," I say, not meaning to interrupt, but he talks pretty slowly. "He's a starter, but he wasn't better known than Gerrard."

"But he's a starter. And guys like me…"

"You've got a whole off-season," I say. "Guys like you are going to be able to come out eventually."

"You think I should announce it?"

I rub my whiskers. "I wouldn't right now. But I do think you should tell Dev. He'd be cool with it. And I think you'd find the rest of the team will be, too."

"Pike," he says.

"Well, yeah. You're gonna have to work out that one for yourself," I say. "I don't know how he's going to feel about it, but I'd bet he'll be okay hanging out with you still. He likes you, doesn't he?"

"But what if he likes me because he doesn't know that I'm...like that?"

"Are you attracted to him?"

There's a long pause, which is an answer in and of itself. "Never mind," I say. "Not important. Just tell him you're not if that's what he needs to hear."

He gives a long, slow sigh. "Listen," I say, "you've got a long off-season. But do tell Dev, at least. The thing about Polecki is..." My call waiting goes off. I check the number: it's Gena. "Sorry, I need to take this other call. The thing is," I say quickly, "that Polecki's teammates all look like they knew about it already and were fine with it. So keep that in mind."

"Thanks," he says. "But I don't think I can do it yet. Go take your other call."

"Sorry, I'll call you later." I cut him off and pick up the call. "What's up?"

Gena sounds calm, not too stressed. I take that as a good sign. "Hi, Lee. I just wanted to let you know I'm with Fisher now. The trainers let him go, but he's got some medication and..."

"He's going to be okay, right?"

"Well, yes. I mean, they seem pretty sure he'll be okay. He sounds fine, but he's really angry."

"I saw him sitting on the bench. He didn't look happy." There's not much activity at night in the park. Streetlights cast little circles of warmth in the cold, and people hurry from one to the other. Out on the bay the water is mostly dark.

"He says it was just one point and he should've been able to do something about it." She sighs. "I don't know. It wasn't his fault."

"No. I don't know that there's much else he could've done." Though my mind is replaying that last blitz now, wondering if two tigers coming around the end instead of one would have made more room, if Pike's slowness wasn't a handicap for that play.

"So I just wanted to let you know that he's...he's okay for now."

"I'm sure he's going to be fine."

"I'm glad he's coming home." Home, where he won't be able to keep illegal steroids in a locker. Home, where he won't have the pressure of the game calling to him. But there's next season. He'll want to keep playing, won't he?

"Me too," I say. "You guys have a safe flight."

But she doesn't hang up. After a moment, she says, "What did you think about that coyote?"

"I thought it was great. About time."

"Right. I was glad to see it. I hope things get easier for you and Dev." She hesitates again. I think she must suspect that something's not right between us. "Would you like to come over this week, once things settle down?"

I don't know if she's asking for our sakes or for hers. "Sure. I'll…I'll work it out."

"Okay, good. We'll see you then."

I hang up and think, well, maybe that'll be a good excuse to have a talk with Dev. Or maybe it'll end up just being me going over to their place. I rub my whiskers and wonder whether I should tell Hal to interview Fisher.

On my way back to the room, I go back to the conversation with Kodi, and I get a chill in my chest, remembering Kodi slumped against the wall of the hotel, remembering the resignation in his voice. I go back to the elevator lobby and dial his number again.

"That was fast," he says.

"Yeah." I try to sort my thoughts into the right words. "I just wanted to say, even if you don't come out to the team or to Dev or anything, you can always call me. I promise I won't give your secret away."

"Thanks." He sounds puzzled.

"I mean…you're not alone. I know I can come off pushy, but I won't think less of you if you stay closeted. Maybe you're right and it'll be best for you. I'd hate to keep it from Dev, but it's more important that you feel you can trust someone. Me, I mean."

"Yeah. Okay. I think I want to keep it quiet for now. But I will talk to you. Thanks."

I feel better after that. I walk back to the room, where Hal is back at his research, and I sit on the bed, staring out the window at my new home town. After a few minutes, I find myself smiling.

CHAPTER 32 – LOOKING FORWARD (DEV)

Polecki is waiting for me in a quiet corner of a café across the street from a bar sporting rainbow flags all over the front of it, and a bookstore with pink neon triangles and those gay marriage bumper stickers with two male and two female symbols. The café is much more neutral on the outside, named the Portrait Coffee House, but when I get inside, I see portraits of gay writers and entertainers—at least, I recognize several from Lee's collections, and I assume the rest.

The coyote is sitting in the back, and though he's in a blue button-down shirt, he has a gold Sabretooths pin on the collar and is bigger than anyone else in the café—football-player sized. He grins when he sees me walk in and stands to shake my paw. The blue shirt fits him neatly—one of those things you notice as a rookie is how much better the veterans' shirts fit, because they get them custom tailored.

It also sets off his blue-green eyes nicely. That's something Lee taught me to look for.

Otherwise, he's a coyote through and through, with tall brown ears and tan fur and a long tail with a black tip. The resemblance to Gerrard goes beyond species and the position they play: they have a similar build, a similar energy, but where Gerrard keeps his tightly reined, Polecki is grinning fit to burst and can't stop his tail wagging. He bounces from one foot to the other in the short time it takes him to grip my paw tightly, warmly, and then let go.

"Hell of a game," I say to him before we even sit down.

His grin gets wider. "It's still like a dream."

"This is two for you, right?"

"Yeah, but the first was my rookie season. Didn't really play in the game that much." He points at me. "You, mister, got a pretty impressive sack. McCrae was *pissed*."

That makes me feel a little better. "I'm gonna watch a ton of your film."

He flicks his ears back. "Thanks, but you got a good teacher there. Marvell's the best. Wanted to be like him all through college."

I nod. "He's great. Steez is awesome too."

"Yeah."

And then we just look at each other. "So," he says.

I laugh. It's so weird sitting across from him, having a bond like I did with the guys I just left, only definitely not as deep, not as strong. But still, even though this is the first time we've talked, I know we have things in common and I want to ask him about them. "How did it feel coming out to seventy thousand people?"

"Almost didn't get it out." He grins. "I had to say it right out, because if I didn't, I wouldn't do it at all, and then once I started I had to finish. But holy shit, I have never had more difficulty saying two words. I kept thinking, what if they boo? What if the Chevy guys kick me off the stage?"

"Yeah." I remember the feeling. "Your teammates knew?"

"That I was going to come out? I told Rich—Yates," he clarifies. "I said, 'I think I gotta say it,' and he said, 'Do it,' and Bridger was right there and he said, 'Yeah.'"

"I meant that you're gay, but I guess so."

He laughs. "Yeah, some of 'em. They were mostly like, 'Don't bring it in the locker room and it ain't a problem.' Couple of 'em wouldn't shower with me for a while."

"Shit, me too." I tell him about the period when I showered alone, and how some of my friends stepped up to show the rest of the guys there was nothing wrong with it.

"That's great." He smiles. "With me, I think it just stopped being a thing."

"Good for you. Get ready for it to start up again."

"Ah." He waves a paw dismissively. "By the time the season starts, it'll be old news. Half the team'll be gone anyway. Happens whenever you win a title. Everyone thinks they deserve more money."

I nod. "You seeing someone?"

"Uh-huh." He looks down and taps the table. "He's another player. I talked to him a little. He's still not sure he wants to come out, but he said I could tell you. As long as you can keep it under wraps…"

"Of course."

"His name's Jay. Jay Cornwall. He's a running back for the Whalers. So I get to see him twice over the season." He lowers his voice. "We got a tradition of making good use of halftime."

I laugh. "Really? I never have more than ten minutes to myself." He winks, and I shake my head. "Wow, and I thought I had it bad only seeing Lee on weekends."

"Yeah, so, that fox of yours. Is he in town?"

I hesitate. "No."

He inclines his head. The barrier of trust is already lowered by his confidence in me, so I plunge on. "We fought a lot, the last couple weeks. I haven't talked to him in a while. He sent me a message before the game."

"What'd you fight about?" His ears stay low, his eyes sympathetic.

"He wanted me to be more active, to do all this gay rights shit. It was starting to distract me from football."

Polecki nods. "You got a contract year coming up. Need to stay focused. I mean, you played well in the game, but you gotta keep it up. If you backslide next year, everyone'll be like, 'Well, that season was a fluke.'"

"Right, exactly. And I told him that, but he didn't—well, I mean, he got it, but it's just the kind of guy he is, he kept pushing me, and finally we had a fight."

"You kicked him out?"

"Not really. He, uh. He left."

The coyote frowns. "He got fed up with you?"

"Maybe." I sigh. "I think…I think he felt like he was distracting me and it was better for him to be somewhere else."

"So…are you broken up?"

It's my turn to stare down at the table. "I don't…*think* so?"

We're interrupted by one of the servers, a ferret who bounces over to ask what we want and then gushes over Polecki. She keeps saying, "I'm sorry, but you were *so good!* And then after, you were *so brave!* I can't believe it! I went and ordered your jersey online and I'm going to wear it every day and if you come back will you sign it?"

He says he will, and grins at me when she's gone. "You get this in Chevali?"

"Not so much anymore." I watch her leave. I feel a little hurt that she didn't recognize me at all. Didn't even barely look at me.

"I'm sure it'll wear off." He laughs. "My agent says I've got some hate mail but a lot more supportive mail."

"That's what I'm seeing, too."

We look at each other across the table and he grins. "Maybe it really is changing, you know?"

"Lee—my boyfriend—my ex—" No, that doesn't sound right. "My fox. He'd say we're the ones changing it."

"I dunno. I was afraid for so long. My boyfriend still is. He doesn't even want to come out to his team…well, he didn't. Maybe he will now. Even though you're out and I'm out and our teammates are all cool with it." His fingers tap the table. "And places like Millenport, Kerina, the south, the middle of the country. Who knows?"

"You don't seem afraid." I curl my tail around the leg of the chair, uncurl it again.

"It's easy now it's over." He leans forward. "Did you find that? Did it get easier for you once it was over?"

"Well, um." I scratch the surface of the table. "Do your parents know?"

"Oh, yeah."

"Great. Then I think it should get a little easier, yeah."

He perks his ears up. "Wait, did you—did your family not know until you came out on TV? Oh, Jesus Dog. That can't have gone well."

I shake my head. "Worked out okay, I think, but…yeah."

He laughs and settles back. I like the light tone of his laugh, and can't help smiling along with him. "So," he says, "we're the UFL Gay Alliance or something, I guess."

"Guess so. Want to do some PSAs together?"

He nods, the laughter remaining as a sparkle in his eyes. "I'd like to do that. Talk to teens, record announcements. You know, all that stuff you're supposed to do. Grow this alliance of ours a bit."

"It'd make Lee happy." Honesty compels me to add, "And me too. I'd love to." I feel again the relief at not being the only one, the gratitude to this coyote for opening up a world where I can say, "*We're* gay," instead of, "*I'm* gay."

He starts to ask another question, but as if on cue, the ferret comes back with our drinks. "On the house," she says. "Oh God, I've always wanted to say that. Would you sign one of our napkins?"

"Sure." His Blackberry rings as he finishes and smiles up at her, a big long bright smile. "So sorry, but this is my agent. Gotta take it."

He nods apology to me as well. I sip the coffee and take out my own phone. Might as well look at the messages, if not listen to the voicemails.

The first one is still that short one from Lee. Then there are a bunch from some of the beat reporters I know, and a couple from my parents. One from Gena, and one from Ogleby. *working on it*, he wrote. *will get asap*.

Working on…I check the history. Oh, I'd asked him to get Polecki's number. If it wasn't him, then…I scroll up and look at Lee's message again. Free from the pressure of the game, I look at each word and I can see him typing them slowly, composing the message in his head carefully because he wants to say something, but he doesn't want to upset me or distract me before the game. I can see the focus in his eyes, the concentration, the importance to him of walking that line, and then I imagine him after the game calling up Corcoran or Rodriguez and saying, "Hey, give Dev's number to Polecki."

The coyote is talking about booking an appearance on some late night show, and hangs up a moment later. I put my phone away too and come back to the present. "Surprised it's not ringing more often. Mine's full of messages and I didn't win a championship *or* come out."

"Oh." He taps his phone. "I have it set up so my agent and boyfriend and family get through. Most of the other calls just go to voicemail."

"No shit. How do you do that?"

He laughs and puts the phone away. "My little sister showed me. I'll see if I can get her to give you a tutorial too. What do you have?"

I show him the iPhone and he whistles. "Those are hard to get hold of. Still, should work okay." He runs a finger over the screen. "Cracks pretty easy?"

"I'm hard on phones." I put it away. "So how did you get my number?" I say.

He frowns, and his ears flick forward. "Gil—our GM—sent it to me. Said I should talk to you."

"How does your GM have my number?"

"I dunno. He's got your GM's, I'm sure."

Corcoran probably has my number, or a way of getting it. And maybe he was watching, and figured I'd want to talk to the coyote. Or maybe a fox called to tell him. "Oh, of course. That makes sense."

He lifts his coffee and blows gently on it. The smell is rich and full. "So how did you and your boyfriend meet?"

I tell him the story—actually, I don't start out telling him the whole story. I use the version I give publicly, that this girl I picked up in a bar introduced me to her gay friend and we hit it off. But then I feel weird, so I say, "Actually, Lee was the girl. He liked to dress up and he was, uh, pretty convincing."

He leans forward again, voice low. "So that was the first time you did anything with a guy?"

I nod. "And then I…just kept going back."

"You've never been with another guy?"

I think of Argonne, half-naked in my hotel room. I shake my head. "Not like that, no."

"Ever wanted to?" He laughs again and holds up a paw. "Not offering. Just curious."

I shake my head. "Recently, I mean, since we've been fighting, I've been maybe a little curious. But I had a lot of other shit to think about." Saying the words together, linking our fighting to my curiosity, makes me wonder if there really is a link. Does our fighting get me worked up? Am I conditioned now to want sex after I fight with my fox? Not sure how I feel about that.

"I hear you." He takes another sip. "I met mine in college too—well, when he was in college. He went to Hoffridge U., a little south of here."

"That's where we practiced this week," I remember.

"They have a good football facility. And team. Anyway, I used to go to the gay clubs down there because it was far enough from here that people didn't recognize me. Not that they recognized me that much before, but you know. Less chance. Anyway, he recognized my build or something, saw that I was a football player, and he bought me a drink. We hit it off, and when he got drafted, we just kept dating, because we both live in the same world, you know?"

Briefly, I let myself imagine that. "That'd be nice."

"I dated some other guys, but they were always either starfuckers or idealists who wanted me to take them around the clubhouse or come out to clubs and didn't really get the life, you know?" I nod, and he tilts his head. "Your boyfriend worked for the Dragons, right? I read that. Well, that's cool. He knows the life, too."

I startle. "You read—?" Well, of course he did; as a closeted gay player, he would've been following me and therefore my boyfriend. "Kind of. He hasn't lived it, though." Even as I say that, I wonder if it's really that big a deal. Lee's smart. He's talked to plenty of athletes, he does know what it takes.

"Well." Polecki laughs, takes a bigger drink of coffee. "Don't know what your chances are of finding another player. I got really lucky."

"I did too. I thought." I bury my nose in my own coffee and inhale the sharp, rich scent. Lee would like this. I can detect traces of other flavors, subtle and nuanced, just at the edge of my perception, but he would be able to appreciate them fully.

"I mean, they've gotta be out there, right?"

I take a drink and snort. "So there's one guy on my team…"

In the pause where I'm trying to decide whether to tell this story, the coyote chuckles. "The leopard, right? Omba?"

I blink. "Um. No. No, there's one guy—I just found out recently he's got a steady blow job…um, guy? I don't know, is there a name for it?"

"Date?"

"Well, he's married. But he meets up with this guy a lot. And he pissed me off. He gives me shit for being gay, so I went to talk to him, like, I know this about you. And he said it wasn't serious. That it didn't mean anything."

"Probably didn't, to him." Polecki nods. "A lot of these guys have trouble seeing how you can actually make a commitment to another guy. One guy on my team asked if I wanted to blow him. Actually…" He grimaces. "He asked if I *needed* to. You know, like I was going to go crazy if I didn't have a cock in my mouth from time to time."

"Christ."

"Yeah. Welcome to the Age of Enlightenment, right?"

"Nobody asked me that." Although, as I recall, some came close. "Mostly they just left me alone until they realized I wasn't going to, y'know, jump on them and rape them in the shower."

I never said anything out loud like that before, and I get a flutter of "oh shit" in my chest as the words come out, but the coyote barks a sharp laugh. "Yeah, being a tiger, you'd probably get that more. Me, I'm a big guy, and mostly people don't assume shit, but I had one guy ask me how I could stand to have something shoved up under my tail. 'That's a one-way road,' he said."

I don't want to admit that I've never done that. Not all the way. Lee's played around a little with fingers now and again, but not—anyway, I don't want to assume that Polecki's been fucked, either. "So what'd you tell him?"

He winks. "I said, 'I guess we have different zoning laws.'"

It's so unexpected that I laugh, and my chest loosens. "That's really all it is, right?"

"Absolutely." He grins. "Most straight guys are so fucking paranoid about it, they won't even try with a finger or anything, and they can't believe it can feel good. Their loss, huh?"

The coffee is almost finished. I kill it and put the empty cup down on the table, and check the time. Polecki does, too. "I should probably get going," I say. "I have a lot of phone calls to answer, and I can't imagine you don't have a million and one things to do."

"Yeah, probably." He shrugs. "I don't mind. I've been wanting to talk to you for months, and I'm glad I got the chance to come out before we talked." He raises his cup. "I'm still kind of shaking. But you know, talking to you has me more relaxed than I've been in…God. Months."

"That's probably the championship ring," I say, with just a little jealousy. Maybe more than a little.

"You'll get one." He grins at me. "In the meantime, accept the compliment."

"For what? Being gay? I didn't choose that."

"No." He looks over the coffee cup with penetrating turquoise coyote eyes that in that moment remind me unsettlingly of Gerrard's, despite the color. "For being a stand-up guy. For coming out—you did choose that. For reminding me that this is part of who I am, not just part of me that I have to hide. And for coming to a coffee shop after a gut punch of a loss just to talk with one of the guys on the other side of the ball who has no right to ask that from you."

"Well." I shift in my seat. "I mean, I couldn't not, right? There aren't that many of us. We need to stick together and…" I grin. "Anyway, you're making me feel better too. Not about the loss, but about…lots of things."

His lips curl back into a wide smile. "Go-go Gay Alliance."

He drains his coffee while I laugh. "Anyway," I say, "let me know your plans in the off-season. We can do this again for sure. And I'll keep in touch about doing some PSA spots or visits. Maybe a commercial or something."

"Have your flea call my flea."

He waits for me to ask an explanation, but I just grin, startled at the familiar phrase. "Mine's half-useless, but yeah, I will."

"And if you work things out with your fox, bring him along." He smiles at my hesitation. "I hope you do," he says. "He sounded like a pretty good guy from that article."

I don't have any hesitation about what to say to that. "Yeah. He is."

We shake paws, walk past the cooing ferret, and out onto the street. "Hey!" someone says. "Hey, it's Polecki!"

A couple guys, a ringtail and a porcupine, run over to get a picture. This time, they recognize me, too. After a little ribbing about losing the game, they ask if both of us will be in the picture. "Fine," I say, "but you have to cheer for the Firebirds now. Unless they're playing the Sabretooths."

"Deal," the slim ringtail says, and we stand together. Polecki, a little shorter than me, puts his arm around my waist, and after a moment, I drape mine over his shoulder. It's easy and feels good. Reminds me of Keith.

They snap the pics. "Hey, are you two dating?"

We laugh. "No," Polecki says, and we disengage, but casually, not in response to their question. "We've both got boyfriends."

Chapter 33 – Separation (Dev)

In the cab on the way back to my hotel, I take out my phone and prepare to go through the messages from Ogleby, my parents, friends, and so on. But first I call up Lee's message, the one from before the game. *All the other things aside, I still believe in you and you're a great football player. Wishing you the best of luck.*

It's the third or fifth or tenth time I've looked at it. Polecki's talk about boyfriends who know the life echoes in my head. Can Lee ever really know what I'm going through? He's not in the locker room, he doesn't play on the field, he doesn't have the gut reactions. But. But but but. He's a smart fox. And he knows how I feel, I think, about all of that. And where would I ever find a football player like him?

And then I think about his insistence on the meetings, the film spots, and I think, maybe he doesn't really understand what it's like. Or am I the one who isn't understanding, blinded by the glow of my career?

Some career. Outside the cab's window, Sabretooths flags spring up in my field of view. I almost become convinced that they aren't there when I'm not looking, and I swing my head around to try to catch them out. But the navy blue and gold flutters just about everywhere, and where they're not on car or window flags, they're on t-shirts and sweatshirts and athletic shorts, in the glow of streetlights and headlights.

And here I am in my red and gold, with nothing to show at the end of this season but a second-place finish. Oh, I'm sure they'll talk about the game for a while. One-point championships are pretty rare. But we'll always be the team that couldn't quite get it done. I don't begrudge Carson his souvenir ball, because he made a better play with it after my sack, but it means I don't even have that to hold on to.

For this I gave up Lee? I stare out the window. I don't know what to make of his last message to me, and I don't know what to make of my near-cheating on him. I mean, I didn't come or anything, but another guy had his paw—and tongue—on my cock. That's—that's not being faithful, even if I stopped it before it went further. Argonne called me a few choice names once it was clear there wasn't going to be a benefit to keeping his mouth closed, but I was beyond caring then, just thankful I recognized the smell before I did anything with the same guy Colin used.

'Used' is the right word. My fists clench. I don't know how he can justify sticking his cock in someone's mouth and not considering that cheating. Especially another fox—doing things with another species could just be experimentation, and when it's gay sex you're not going to get anyone pregnant. But to be with another fox, that'd be really bad if his wife found out about it.

So what was I doing with another fox? Well, he was the only one available, for starters. I'd be lying, though, if I tried to say he didn't remind me of Lee. Different, yes, and in the end I think it wouldn't have been very satisfying even if I'd gone through with it.

There's only one Lee, and the question is whether my life is better or worse with him in it. I close my eyes and rub my fingers against them. That isn't even a question, or it shouldn't be, except that he made it one.

His text message stares up at me from my phone, the words clear through the white cracks. I don't know what I can write to him that will say that I want him to come back, but only if he wants to come back, and if he doesn't then I understand, and if he does but he wants me to change then I don't know if I can do that, and all the other millions of things I want to say. Overwhelming all of it is just the physical need to hold him again, to feel him fit into my embrace the way I've grown used to, and, yeah, to feel myself slide into him in a more direct way.

Do I want him back just because I want to get laid? And if there's nobody else out there for me to sleep with, does it matter? I want to type, "I LOVE YOU, YOU FUCKING IDIOT," in all caps, just like that, but I start to type it and it looks stupid and then it looks desperate and I erase the letters and type them again three more times and then just stare at the phone. Then I put it down and stare out the cab's window again, and then look back at the phone.

I turn the caps lock off and type, finally, because I need to type something. *Hope you enjoyed the game. Polecki's a nice guy. You should meet him. See you soon.*

It says nothing, but I hope it says enough. I move on to Ogleby, who wants me to call all of my prospective sponsors right away in case Polecki tries to steal them from me.

"He's not going to do that," I say.

"He just came out because he saw the money you were making! He wants to get in on it. I know how these people work."

"Wait, what 'people'?"

"You know, the other guys, all those guys out there who want your money! Trust me, just leave it all to me and I'll take care of it. Nobody's going to steal your endorsements on my watch."

I exhale and try to keep myself calm. "Nobody's stealing anything, you jackass."

"That's what I'm trying to tell you! Don't worry about a thing."

"I just had coffee with him. We talked about doing a commercial together."

"You came out first. You should get the bigger fee. Just let me know what you're thinking about and we'll make it happen."

My head hurts. How crazy is it, I think, that I don't have Lee and I still have Ogleby. Yeah, he gave me my first break, and I've given him two years.

The words are out of my mouth before I realize I've said them. "You're fired."

The silence on the phone is longer than any I've ever had with him. After a moment, he says, "Hey, Dev, sweetie, the connection must've cut out for a minute there. I didn't catch what you said. If you didn't hear me, I just wanted to let you know that I'm going to make you a ton of money off this. Playing in a championship just rockets your stock to the top of the charts. You're going to be rich, and besides, next year we get to renegotiate your contract, and you can bet the Firebirds are going to pay top dollar, and if they won't, we'll find someone who—"

I hang up. I'll decide whether I want to send him an official letter of dismissal later. I've got a creeping feeling that I acted a little rashly. Right now I don't want to deal with it.

So once I get to the hotel, I call Mom from the room. "Oh, Devlin," she says, as Dad moves close to the phone to hear. "We're so proud of you. You did very well."

"Thanks," I say. "Not quite well enough."

Dad's deep bass comes through the line. "You did all you could be expected to. Good sack on McCrae."

I stand straighter. "Wish I could've gotten just one more."

"You have good, young team. Tell your teammates to stay together. You will win a championship."

Mom adds, "We're so excited to see you. Do you have time to have dinner tomorrow?"

"I fly back tomorrow morning," I say. "But I want to see you guys. How about a drink tonight?"

"That would be wonderful. How is Lee?" Mom asks.

He's somewhere else. "He's fine."

"Would he be coming with you?"

"Uh." I close my eyes. "No, he…he's got something else to do tonight."

"Oh. Maybe we can see him afterwards?"

"Maybe. I'll ask."

We get together in a small bar near the hotel they're staying in and sit around for about an hour. It starts with Dad going back through the play-offs, talking about the plays I made, and it sinks in that he's been watching and he's not focusing on my mistakes. Mom keeps asking about Lee for some reason, and that finally drives me to ask how my brother is doing.

They both pause when I ask. Then Mom says, brightly, "Oh, he's doing quite well! The firm is keeping him busy with—oh, something. He said it should bring in more business later on."

Dad says, "Free work is not the way to get business."

"He's working for free? A…" I can't remember the word for it.

"For a charity." Dad says the words slowly. Must really grate on him that Gregory isn't getting paid. "I believe."

"Can't imagine him being excited about charity work." It doesn't really sound like Gregory, with his insistence on a paycheck. I decide not to mention the million-dollar commercial again. I'll surprise them with a new plasma TV or something.

Mom looks at Dad and hesitates. They had an argument about it already, I bet. "Oh, I…he didn't really tell us the details, did he, Misha?"

"Whatever it is is not important. We did not pay for law school so he could work for free."

"Alexi is so smart for his age, they tell us…"

My dad and his practicality. I just listen to the familiar conversation rhythms, thinking about home. It's nice to know that I still have that, no matter what else happens. With Lee or without him, though my mother kept telling me to bring him by during the off-season. That was nice to know too, and woven as it was with Dad's talking about football, it felt like my parents were finally acknowledging both sides of my life together.

It's a little after eleven when I head back to the hotel. Thoughts run flying around my head, about myself and Lee and Polecki and Coach and Carson and my parents. What I want, of course, is not just anyone to talk to. Not Charm, not Polecki, not my parents. I want my fox. I haven't poured my heart out to anyone the way I have to him, and nobody has given back to me half the love that he has. I second-guess and third-guess my message to him, but resist the urge to take the phone out and type something else. It's easier to leave things in this unsettled state for now, to wait a little while before doing anything, to wait until I'm sure I'm not doing the wrong thing.

Because I also hate being reliant on him, and him alone. If nothing else, Polecki reminded me that I've done a lot. And I know now that I can keep on without Lee if I have to. Maybe that's the best thing he's done for me.

I snort. I don't want this to be one of those sappy movies where after teaching the hero the lesson, the best friend-slash-mentor-slash-gay boy-friend has to leave the hero to his own devices. But in the movies, the mentor is just a mentor. He doesn't have a life of his own outside the movie; he only exists to help the hero. Lee has a life, and goals and dreams, and if living with me isn't helping him reach those, well, then maybe he's better off on his own, too.

It feels like a very grown-up thought, and a very lonely one. I've been through four years of college and two in the "real world," or as real as professional sports can be. And Lee's the only guy I've met—the only person I've met—who even remotely feels like someone I'd want to spend the rest of my life with.

Sure, he's frustrating. But when I think about Fisher and how he's maybe played his last game, I think about what will happen to me when it's my turn to retire. Fisher has a wife and cubs. When retirement crosses my mind, it's a vague, formless dream. I can bring parts of it into focus: a house somewhere nice and quiet, a neighborhood where everyone knows each other. I don't know what I'd do. Maybe I could announce games on TV, or maybe I'd coach high school or even college. Or maybe I'd just relax and watch games and complain about the economy. But I can't squirm away, even in the dream, from Lee being there with me. Maybe he still works for a pro team, and we play video games in the evening and watch football and go to bed together every night.

Three months ago, I wouldn't even have considered that fantasy serious-ly enough to dismiss it as unrealistic. But damn if he didn't assault my fam-ily until they gave in, force the issue in the press, do all those things I was too scared to do and, impossibly, make them work. The problem is that he can't stop. I can't imagine him being in the dream with me and just relaxing.

But I can't imagine that life without him. Without him, the house grows to huge sizes and I wander from room to room, looking for something, looking for someone, looking for him.

Walking through the hotel lobby and up the stairs, because fuck the elevator, all the way to my room on the seventh floor, I force my thoughts away from the years-away retirement and the pangs that come with want-ing my fox. He'll respond to the message soon enough, and then we'll move forward, and whatever happens in the future will happen. I just hope that "see you soon" says enough to him.

Unfortunately, the only other thing my mind wants to obsess about is my play in the championship. I flop back on my bed, replaying every down, seeing my moves one step too slow, my reach inches too short. I wish I could go back and get a jump, anticipate just a little better, cut just a little quicker. There are so many things in life that you could change with small adjustments, and an inch here, a second there, any of those things could have changed the outcome.

I know that I need to focus on getting better, that I need to let it go, because I can't change the past. For tonight, though, I allow myself to review all the things I did wrong, what Lee would call self-flagellation and Dad would call being hard on yourself and Steez would call necessary. It's been held at bay by thinking about Polecki and Lee and my life, but when I have time to think, it all comes flooding in until I clench my fists, tail lashing in agitation, and I have to force myself to calm down. *You've lost games before*, I remind myself. *Everyone did the best they could. You didn't let down the team, or yourself. Or Lee.*

"Hey," Charm says, coming into the room, "you practicing meditation or something?"

I look up. "Just thinking about stuff. The past. The future."

"So, yeah." He drops his room key and wallet on the dresser, and taps the wallet. "Didn't lose it this time."

I can't help but smile. Fucking Charm. "Good. You need to hold on to that."

He plops down on his own bed and lies back. "I can't believe that fucking C.C. guy kicked better than I did."

"He didn't kick better," I say. "Just last."

"Ah, he…" He lifts a hand from the bed, waves it around, and turns his long head to face me. "Made the game-winning field goal."

"You kicked three to his one."

"He kicked three extra points. We got a good blocking team, too. Didn't faze him."

"You did everything you needed to."

"I thought so." He puts both hands behind his head and stretches. "I guess I should've gotten one more kick in there."

"I don't know what else you could have done." I glance at the clock. It's not even midnight. "You're back early."

"Yeah." He stares at the ceiling.

Slowly, it comes together. "Did you…meet anyone tonight?" He doesn't say anything. "You went out to a club, right?"

"Yeah."

"Didn't go well?"

"It was fine. These C.C. clubs, they're all stuck up, you know."

I try not to grin. "Did you even get in?"

He turns and glares at me. "I got in." Then he settles back and admits, "At the third club."

"Oh, jeez."

"None of the girls there were all that hot. And they weren't interested in me either."

"Whoa." I lean forward. "Hold the presses."

"Shut up," he says amiably.

"So you lost a championship game *and* you couldn't hook up after?"

"Shut up."

"Is this like the worst day of your life?" He throws a pillow at me, but his aim sucks and I don't even have to dodge. "I guess we're both dateless tonight."

I say it jokingly, but it brings my mood back down. He turns onto his side. "How are things going with you and Mrs. Gramps, anyway?"

I shrug and point to the phone. "He texted me before the game, and I just texted back. I guess we'll talk when I get back to Chevali."

"Good. I like him."

"Yeah. I do too."

We sit there for another few minutes, and then Charm sits up. "Well, fuck," he says. "I'm not gonna sit around here all night feeling sorry for myself. Let's go see if Brick and those guys are playing FBA '09."

I can't think of anything else to do, so I get up, too. We walk out and listen for the sounds of video basketball, and when we find it, Charm knocks on the door. It turns out it's not Brick; it's a bear and a sloth from the offensive line, plus Rodo and the backup running back, an elk. Apart from Rodo, I don't know any of the guys that well, but Charm gets us in and we sit with them and take our turns playing when a spot opens up.

We talk about the game, of course, with a little jawing back and forth from the offense guys to me, the lone representative of the defense, though Rodo takes my side for some of it. He was pretty quiet during the game, but did catch three balls for twenty-eight, which is okay. Better than nothing. And most of their jawing isn't at me, because I did get that one sack. It's more at the cornerbacks and how they couldn't keep the Sabretooths guys down when it counted.

The conversation is friendly until I jaw back at them and say, "We scored as many touchdowns as the offense did. You guys couldn't get anyone open but Strike."

"Fuck that guy," Rodo says. "Hope he's gone."

I turn. Rodo's rubbing the top of his head around the base of his antlers, which I'd guess are going to drop soon. It makes me think of the stags in the crowd, the ones whose antlers were gone already. I wonder what they thought of Polecki's coming out. I decide I don't give a fuck. "What, Strike? He's been great."

"You didn't hear?" I shake my head. "Oh, he talked to the media after and said we didn't get him the ball enough. Said if Ty had lateraled to him on that last kickoff, he thought he could've done something with it."

"Really?" I wonder if that's the comment I heard or if Strike kept talking in the same vein afterwards, because what I heard sounded a litle less provocative than that.

"Ty did a fucking awesome job," Charm calls from where he's playing against the elk.

"No shit." Rodo scowls. "We don't need some rainbow jackass telling us how to play."

"That asshole just do what he do," the sloth says, lounging back against the window. He's a big guy, and out of uniform, I can see that he keeps most of his fur trimmed, except for a mane around the back of his head and down his back (I assume from the way his wife-beater bulges out).

One of the bears joins in. "Yeah, where was he this game? When we needed him?"

I glance at Rodo, quiet amidst this exchange, because he should know how hard it is to shake coverage, but he just stays quiet, scratching at his antlers. Strike had a hundred-some yards and a touchdown. That's not "where was he when we needed him?" That's delivering.

The bear and sloth keep going back and forth. "If he gonna mouth off, he should back it up."

"Easy to talk a big game."

I look down at my paws, extend claws from the left to scratch the back of the right.

"Friend of mine from the Devils called after we traded for him," the elk says, without taking his attention from the game. "Laughed at me."

"I got a friend on the Manticores. I should tell them how awesome he is."

I've made fun of teammates before, but not in quite as mean-spirited a way. "Hey, you know, he did score us a few touchdowns in the playoffs."

Rodo raises an eyebrow at me. The elk doesn't pause the game, but turns his head slightly. "Sure," he says, "against those teams, it was easy."

"Really? So, like, C.C.'s and Hellentown's corners totally suck. That right, Rodo?"

"Don't drag me into this," he says.

"You don't need to defend him." The sloth taps two of his long claws against each other.

"I know I don't need to," I say, "but I thought we all bought into this 'team effort' thing."

"He didn't need to say that about Ty." Rodo speaks up then.

"He's an asshole," I say. "I'm not arguing that."

"You get along okay." The sloth eyes me from under shaggy eyebrows. "He like you."

"Yeah, fuck knows why."

"Maybe he don't like girls so much."

The room generally laughs; even Rodo smiles. Charm turns to look my way with one eye. "So what if he doesn't?" the stallion says.

The laughter quiets. Most of the guys glance at me and then look away, uncomfortable. "Hey," the sloth says. "Is not a big deal. But…"

"But he says he likes girls," the bear says. "So maybe he's hiding something."

The elk says, "We don't talk shit about you when you're not here."

"Good," I say. "I don't talk shit about you guys either." But the camaraderie that I felt walking in with Charm is dissipating.

"You don't shit on your teammates."

"I also don't score touchdowns that make people cream their pants," I say. "That guy helped us out, and yeah, he's an ass. I'm sorry it's harder for you to ignore him, but just close your eyes and think of him scoring and get the fuck over it."

"He didn't score, that's what we're saying."

I stare back at the bear. "Did you miss the part where he ran into the end zone? Because that looked like a score to me."

He shifts, grumbles. "Guy talks like him, he should score twice."

"Yeah, well." I stand up. "I didn't get to McCrae on the last play either. So maybe it's my fault."

"Hey now—"

"You got a sack—"

"—caused a fumble—"

"—got us a score off that—"

"Yeah," I say. "I guess I'm saying that we win or lose as a team, right? That's what Coach is always saying. Doesn't matter what asshole thing we do or don't say after. Doesn't matter if we like girls or not."

The room's silent. "Sorry," I say. "Charm, I'll see you back at the room."

"You don't have to go," the elk says.

"Thanks," I say, "but I don't want to piss on anyone's party. I'll see you guys on the plane."

Charm looks like he wants to leave with me, but he's in the middle of a game. I raise a paw to let him know I'm okay, and step out into the hall.

It's empty, and when I step away from the door, the noise of the video game fades into silence. I press my paws to my forehead and breathe in deeply.

Lee would tell me that standing up for Strike was the right thing, but I didn't even think about him while I was doing it. I just thought that after all this, after all I went through, I didn't want to stand around and be part of talking behind someone else's back. I just wish he wasn't such an asshole. It'd make him easier to defend.

But you don't do the right thing because it's the easy thing. You do the right thing because it's the right thing, and because you want to be able to stand up and walk out of a room knowing that you're the kind of person you can be proud of. And if you can be proud of yourself, then other people can be proud of you: parents, teammates. Boyfriends.

I don't feel like going back to my room right away, so I go down to the bar and order a drink. I recognize a group of my teammates sitting in a corner, low-key, but I don't seek them out. The bartender slides me across the martini I order with a grin. "Drowning your sorrows?" he says, and then, when I slide a ten across the bar, he shakes his head. "You guys played a hell of a game. On the house."

I push the ten toward him. "Then that's your tip," I say.

"Well, thanks." He shakes his head again. "Who are you?"

"Miski," I say. "Fifty-seven."

"Oh." He's an ocelot or a jungle cat of some sort; the light's dim and his scent is confused with all the alcohol and it's hard to tell. But his ears flick back and then forward. He stands up straighter and pushes the ten back at me. "Then it's my pleasure to serve you, sir."

I tilt my muzzle and raise my eyebrows. "Well," he says. "I'm a football fan. My boyfriend is too. So we were pretty inspired by you. And Polecki coming out now, too… seems like you had a lot to do with that. Did he tell you before?"

"No. I just met him for the first time. He seems like a good guy."

"Good." He beams and flicks an ear, and as he lifts a paw, I see a silver ring on one finger. "Good. I hope there's more. It's just…it's really inspiring to us."

I sip the martini. It's pretty good. "So you knew I was a Firebird," I say, "but you didn't recognize me? We've only got a few tigers on the roster."

"Sorry," he says, his ears going back again. "I know you guys are staying here, and when you walked up, I just saw a Firebird. I didn't connect that to the guy who came out 'til you said your name."

A smile grows on my muzzle. "Well," I say, "I am a Firebird." I raise my glass to him. "And you make a hell of a martini."

•

Strike isn't hanging around with the team anywhere, but he calls me, surprisingly enough, halfway through my second martini. "Hey," he says. "I'm sticking around C.C. for a bit, going to see Iva, blow off some tension, maybe get a movie deal lined up."

"Okay," I say, sipping the drink. "Cool."

"Figured I probably shouldn't come back around, but didn't wanna go without saying g'bye, you know? You're a good guy. Hope we end up on the same team again sometime."

"Yeah," I say, and I'm just buzzed enough to go on. "Why'd you have to say those things?"

"Huh?" He sounds genuinely puzzled.

"About people not getting you the ball, all that shit? I just—I just defended your sorry ass to a room full of people bitching about you. You didn't have to—" I take a breath. He doesn't interrupt. "Couldn't you just say, 'Good game, they played better'?"

"Sure." He chuckles. "Paper's full of players that said that, right? You see where my story was on ESPN? Right below the Polecki thing. That guy's a genius, I tell you. Made a big stage bigger."

"I don't think that's why—" Lion Christ, talking to Strike gives me a headache sometimes even when I'm sober. "I just mean, you could stay with a team, build up trust, be part of a…"

"A what? A family? That's sweet. And it's sweet you stuck up for me, but you didn't hafta, you know? Just pile on with the rest of 'em. I'll be okay. Make it to the playoffs with this team or another one next year, one of these days it'll hit big. Even if it doesn't, I got commercials, movies…don't you worry about Lightning Strike. He's gonna do just fine."

"What happens when you run out of teams?"

"Then I retire."

I take another drink. It is a really good martini. "All right. Well, look, I know I haven't been around as long as you, but...maybe try being a little more mellow next time, huh?"

"I got it all worked out. In a couple years I do the reformed bit, I'll get a few more years outta that. You take care, Devlin, and let me give you some advice, too."

Wow, I can't wait to hear this. "Okay."

"Don't leave anything in the locker room. Don't walk away thinking you could've done more. Do it."

I hang up and sit there nursing my martini. Damn. That was actually some good advice.

Chapter 34 – Families (Lee)

There's one more phone call before we leave Yerba. It's the following morning, and we're at breakfast at a Starbucks. You can't turn around without hitting one out here. But I hate it maybe a little less than I used to (and now I get a little grin when I go into the bathroom). The pastries are pretty good and I get an orange juice from the cooler, and we're eating outside on the patio when Pol calls. Hal takes it, and walks a little ways away.

It's a sunny morning, and even in January it's still almost sixty degrees at nine in the morning. Birds sing around us, and for a moment I just lean back in my chair and close my eyes, smelling the flowers and the atrocious coffee and the car fumes. I won't mind living up here, not one bit. But I can't quite shut out Hal's conversation, and flattening my ears is so associated with anger that even if I'm just trying to block out sound, it makes me tense, so I need to distract myself. I take out my own phone and pull up the calls, wondering if I should call Dev. I'm not even sure when he flies back to Chevali.

I see my father's number in the recent call list, and remember that I'd promised to call Mother. A glance tells me that Hal is likely to be occupied for at least another ten or fifteen minutes, and I don't want the call to be much longer than that anyway. "Sorry, we're leaving for the airport" will be a good excuse to cut it short.

So I call, and she answers. "Father told me to call you," I say.

"Yes. Well, I just have one thing to say, and your father thought it best that I say it to you directly, though I told him he could tell you, and quite honestly, I almost wish he would have."

"Okay."

She inhales. "This isn't because of you. Not entirely. But I'm withdrawing from the Families United work."

I raise my eyebrows, and then do a little fist pump, because she can't see me. But I keep my voice level. "So why?"

"A lot of reasons."

"The court case?"

"Not entirely. I don't believe that has any merit. It's grieving parents lashing out for someone to blame. It's the reaction in the group that disturbed me. I think...I think they may have lost sight of the fact that the people they are trying to change are people. When Celia said she would rather see her son dead…" Her voice falters and then returns, stronger. "Whatever you might think of me, I would never wish that of you. Never."

"Well, um. I appreciate that. Does that mean you won't be burning any more of my things?"

She inhales. "I am sorry about that. It seemed to make sense when Celia talked about it, and—no. I won't try to justify it to you. Or myself."

"I think under the circumstances I was justified in yelling," I say, though I can't quite get the appropriate chill in my voice. "But I didn't feel good about it. I'm—I'm sorry too."

It feels weak and not quite right to say. But it also feels better than I'd expected when I forced the words out.

"I still wish you could see that you would be much happier with a nice vixen, a family. But I don't wish you were…" Again, her voice falters.

As nice as it is to hear my mother tell me she doesn't wish me dead, I think once was enough. "Mother. I'm happy in my life. And I think I'm doing good."

"I know you think that." A little sharpness returns. "And I heard on the news that there's another football player now besides that tiger."

That tiger. I want to yell at her and I want to hug her and I can't do either of them, so I just clamp my muzzle shut and say through gritted teeth. "Yes. It's a really cool thing."

She makes an exasperated "tchah" noise. "However, I was pleased to see that one of the championship players did praise the Lord in his celebration, and several of them joined him in prayer. More than two, I think."

"So you're leaving F.U." I focus on the positive and not the religious claptrap. "Are you and Father…?"

"No. I don't think you should expect that. We are still separate people and still, I think, different. But…" She slows, becoming thoughtful in that way she used to do when she actually thought about things. "I don't know that I need Families United in the way I thought I did. I think…I think I was scared of being alone."

"Now that I can sympathize with," I say.

"You said you would know more after the game. About…how things stand."

She's still sharp. "Not quite this soon after. But thanks for remembering. I'm staying with a friend—a good friend." I reach out, tentatively, with another olive branch. "Do you have other friends?"

"Some friends, some family. I have your father to talk to, even though we don't talk as much or as deeply as we did once. And…"

The question hangs unspoken. I breathe in the flowers and the coffee and the dampness in the air that tells me that it rained overnight. The sky is clear but for a few clouds now, and the sun is bright on my fur. "You have me. As long as you don't push the religious sh—stuff."

Hal closes his phone and walks back over to the table. Mother says, "I'm not going to stop trying to make you live a better life."

"And I'm not going to stop trying to redefine what you consider 'a better life.'"

"Well." She sounds more relaxed. "I suppose we don't have to talk all that often."

Hal sits down, taking a sip of coffee and turning his ears courteously away. I feel good about this conversation, warmer than just the sunlight accounts for. "We don't have to." I look up at the clouds as she sighs. "But maybe we should."

"Maybe we should," she echoes.

I flick my ears even though Hal's telling me there's no hurry. "Sorry to cut this short. I have to get to the airport now."

She asks where I am and I tell her I'm in Yerba for a job interview. She wishes me well, and I thank her and tell her I got the job, and then say I'm glad I made her give up the religious wacko group. She starts to get angry, and then when I chuckle, she just says good-bye, with another one of those "tchah" noises.

"You have that grin you get when you've won an argument," Hal says as we walk to the rental car.

"It bothers me that you know me that well," I say.

He taps the side of his nose. "What happened? If you can talk about it."

"Oh, you know my mother was part of this fundamentalist group for a while…" I tell him briefly about Mother's changing views as we get into the rental car, warm and stuffy from the sun. We roll the windows down and the air rushes through my fur, into my face, cool and fresh.

Hal jokes that even when I'm not trying, I'm being an activist, and that just solidifies the feeling that was already growing. For the first time since walking out of our apartment—Dev's apartment—I feel like I have a direction, a purpose. I have a job, which I got with my own skills and took on my own terms, and I'm more pleased than I should be about Mother's change of heart. I think I played a big part in it, if not just by being her son, then at least by pointing her to the King case. But if she didn't do it just for me, then that's even better. Not everyone in the world has a gay son, so if I can convince her to leave that group, then maybe I can convince other people too.

And maybe I can do it without getting Dev's brother involved. Just write up the facts of the case, make Vince King a cause. His family might be interested in talking to me—probably not, but you never know. I'll have to tell Dev about it sometime, but not right now. It'll come in its own time, and he and I will figure things out as well. At this moment, the air smells sweet and fresh, and while the absence of Dev is a black cloud, the rest of my sky is clear and bright.

It's a pretty big black cloud, though, like one of those thunderheads that comes rolling through the sky in late spring back in Hilltown. I call up Dev's number on my phone and send him a text: *Miss you.* The words come easily and honestly, without any worry about how he's going to take it or whether it's the right thing to say. They sit for a moment as the message program sends them up to the satellites and on their way to my tiger, and then the program tells me they've been sent. I put my phone away and close my eyes, and lean out the window to feel the sun on my ears.

CHAPTER 35 – COMING HOME (DEV)

The plane the next morning is tense. It's earlier than we normally leave, which just reminds us that if we'd won, we'd be leaving at this time so we could get back for a full day of celebration in Chevali. Getting on, I end up three people behind Colin, and he keeps looking back at me. After he sits, I pass his seat and he pulls his tail in, staring away from me.

"You're not going to catch anything," I say loudly, staring down at him. Then, quieter, "Nothing you don't already have."

I move on past his seat, but he jumps up, ears back, and turns to grab my shirt. "You shut up," he says. "I was just stopping my tail from getting stepped on."

I yank my shirt away. "All I meant is you're already a prick. You're not going to catch that from touching me."

He glares, and I glare back, and we both know what he meant by pulling his tail in, and what I meant with what I said. "Just stay away from me," he says.

"Fine by me."

"Come on," Charm, behind me, pushes me forward. "Let's go find something over the wing."

I point back at Colin. "You better figure out your attitude pretty fast," I say.

He doesn't respond, just turns back to the front and slides down in his seat. Shit, I was hoping I'd be less fucking pissed at him, but I guess it's gonna take more than a day. Hopefully a few months is enough. Or he's right about one of us going to another team.

Looking back at his flattened ears, I think about him catching something from me and wish he could catch tolerance, and that leads me down a path of memory. I wasn't so different from him back when Lee found me. Only difference is, where Lee was a proud person, someone who forced me to see him as a person and returned any care and investment I made in him, Argonne is a "discreet" fag, who reinforces Colin's belief that gay sex is wrong by agreeing not to tell anyone about it, by giving blow jobs behind closed doors in secret.

So maybe this is how Lee goes down the road of exposing people's secrets in public. Strike's words come back to me: would I have wanted someone exposing my secret before I was ready? Not while I still held onto it, that's for sure. But knowing what I know now, having had a great quick chat with Polecki and having a great boyfriend, or at least having had one for a while and hopefully soon again…maybe I would. But I can't make that decision for anyone else.

Charm guides me to a pair of seats over the wing, just in front of where Ty is sitting staring out the window. Just to remind myself that there are good foxes on my team, I reach back over the seat. "Hey."

He looks up, takes my paw after a second. "Hey, Dev."

"Where'd you end up last night? I didn't see you."

He flicks his ears. "Wanted to be by myself."

"You doing okay?"

"Yeah." He manages a tight smile that just barely supports that response. "Tough loss. I'll get over it."

"You did great," I tell him.

"You too," he says, sort of automatically. "Great sack."

"I don't think anyone could've done better on that last play," I say. "Returns are half luck anyway, but you're the best return guy we've got. Bar none."

His smile gets a little wider, and it looks like I've got his full attention again. "Thanks," he says.

"We got a good team here, don't we?" Charm turns to take in the two of us.

"Fuck yeah," I say. "Hope we keep it together."

"That's fifty percent luck too," Ty says. "Least I know I'm not moving unless they trade me."

"Me neither. Rookie deals." Thinking about being traded is mildly depressing. We could be gone in a month through no choice of our own. The owner and GM don't care if we think we have a good team.

"Ha," Charm says. "My agent says I'm gonna get a good payday when he negotiates the new deal for me."

"Good luck." I grin at Ty. "I would say we're looking forward to seeing your numbers, but really, who gives a shit, kicker?"

"You wish you could get kicker money." He smacks my arm.

We settle into our seats and get our iPods out. Looking down the aisle, it's hard to see Colin's ears above the heads of the rest of the team, but I can just make out the black points.

I turn and stare past Charm to the window. Outside, they're preparing to take off, and the air is hazy with the C.C. smog. It almost feels like there's smog inside the plane as well. Usually when we're coming back, even after a loss, there's energy in the plane. We joke around, we mess with each other, we talk about next week. Now, of course, there is no next week, and we're probably all thinking about how tantalizingly close we came to winning a championship.

Flashes of the game still run through my head. I think they always will, at least until I get back. I can't change them, but I can work my damnedest to make sure that next time I get to a championship, I have no regrets when I walk off that field.

"Hey," Charm says, as I'm still staring across his chest to the window, "you wanna check out my pecs, do it in the shower like everyone else does."

"Don't need to," I say. "I just went to the Firebird Groupies web page. They got pics up all over."

He snorts. "I *wish* they had a page. I'd be on that thing every day."

I grin and lean back, closing my eyes as the plane taxis and takes off.

When we level off, Coach tries to give us a speech to get us excited for the future of the Firebirds, but it falls flat. Some of the guys are already listening to music, and while I appreciate the things he's saying with my mind—stuff like "this loss doesn't define us as a team" and "we'll be back here for sure"—it doesn't reach the place inside where I keep thinking about all those teams that only made it to one championship game, and lost.

I know the other guys are thinking about it, too, and that reminds me about Fisher, and how this might have been his last game, and then it occurs to me that I didn't see him on the plane. I push myself out of my seat and look around, and sure enough, there's only the other tiger from the second team, toward the back of the plane.

The defensive coordinator is sitting near me, talking to the line coach, and I wave to get his attention. "Hey, you know what happened to Fisher?"

He nods. "Went home with his family, I think. He told me he was going to miss the plane."

"Is he okay?"

"Okay enough to not have to go to the hospital, I guess." He shrugs. "He'll have plenty of time to heal up."

I sink back into my seat. I feel somewhat relieved. I guess I'll have to call Gena when I get back, too. Then I wonder if "plenty of time to heal up" means they're not bringing him back. I try to keep that out of my mind for the rest of the short flight home.

We land in bright sun that streams through the windows. In silence, we grab our bags and sunglasses and file off the plane—

—and into a small crowd of a hundred or so people dressed in red and gold, holding banners and signs and Firebirds pennants. I first notice them as a low cheering noise when the first guys step off the plane onto the tarmac, and then as I make my way down the stairs, sunglasses on to protect against the brightness of the entire world outside, the crowd comes into focus.

The signs read, "Go Firebirds," "You're Our Champions," and some signs for individual players. There isn't one for me, but I do get a cheer when I step out into the light. Maybe they think I'm Fisher. No, no, I hear my name in the cheers. It's comforting and flattering.

And as Charm steps off, they give him a big cheer too, and call his name. And the next guy gets a cheer, and the next guy, and Ty gets a big one, and they keep cheering for us as we walk toward the airport. Some people are holding out footballs and scraps of paper, so a few of us go over for autographs.

There are little groups of the same species: foxes, wolves, bears, coyotes. Brick goes over to the bears and signs there, with Pike and Kodi; Ty spends time with the foxes, next to Vonni and, a moment later, Colin. Aston signs for the wolves, although really he's in demand with everyone, and so is Jaws, even though there aren't any wolverines in the little group. I spot tigers standing with cougars, and since Fisher's not on the flight, I walk over and sign my name on season tickets, footballs, autograph books. One older tiger says, "It was just such a thrill to see the Firebirds in the championship again." A young female tiger says, "You were so close!"

"Thanks," I say over and over, "thanks for supporting the team." I shake paws and sign my name, and am about to move on when I notice a skinny kangaroo rat fidgeting, sandwiched between the bears and tigers. His ear is scarred near the base, and his Cläwz t-shirt is torn at the shoulder. But he's smiling, and he's looking at me, and he looks away when I look right at him, that way you do when you want to get someone's attention but you're afraid or self-conscious about it. So I take a step over to him while the big cats wave at Marais and he ambles over to them.

"Got something for me to sign?" I ask.

"Nah, I…" He keeps smiling, but stares down at the ground, tail curling around his legs. His voice is high and shaky. I'd put him at sixteen or seventeen, maybe. "I can't believe I'm talking to you."

I keep my professional smile on. "Thanks for coming out to support the team."

"Oh," he says, "I don't really like football. I mean, I didn't. I watched the game. I wish you'd have won."

"Yeah, me too." I feel like I should move on, but I'm curious now. "So if you're not a fan, why'd you watch the game?"

"I watched it with my dad." He gestures back to the back of the crowd, where an older kangaroo rat is standing with a banner. "He's a fan."

"Well, thank him for me," I say, and half-turn to go.

"Wait!"

I stop and smile, because obviously the kid has something to say and it's hard for him to get out. "The bus is waiting for me," I say.

"I know, I just wanted to say…thanks."

That can't be all, so I wait. He fidgets more and then drops his voice. "I came out 'cause of you."

My professional smile falters. "Uh. You did?" He nods quickly. "Well. That's great."

That encourages him. He looks up and smiles, showing a chipped tooth on the side where his ear is torn. "My dad loves football and he was going on about you and how it was a disgrace and I just couldn't take it, so I came out to him. It was rough…" The torn ear flicks. "I had to go live with a friend for a couple weeks. But then I moved back in and he said he's starting to understand it, and I feel, I feel so much better now, I mean, I can really be who I am. Like before I was in this shell and I thought I couldn't ever get out of it and I couldn't talk to anyone about it but you, you…" He gestures with skinny paws while I struggle to stay composed. "You gave me a way to get out, someone I could point to and tell my dad, 'I'm like him,' and it was *so hard* but it got easier…" He giggles nervously. "I'm sorry, I'm talking too much, I just, I wanted to say thanks. You saved my life."

I feel Lee at my side, and the annoying thing is I can hear him talking, see his brilliant smile as he says exactly the right thing to complete this kid's experience. But I can't hear the words, and all I'm left with is my own fucking tongue, which stutters a bit and then says, "I'm really glad. I mean, thank you. I'm glad it worked out for you."

Imaginary-Lee says, *Really, stud? He says you saved his life and you say 'I'm glad it worked out'?* I tell him to put a fucking sock in it, because the kid's smiling and wants to know if he can hug me. Maybe that'll make up for me not having any of the right words. So I wrap an arm around his shoulders and he clings to me and it's awkward and uncomfortable, but when I step back, he's bouncing, so I guess it was okay.

"Thanks! Thanks so much!" He bounces back to his dad. I meet the older rat's eyes for a moment, and he inclines his head. I raise a paw to wave. And for a moment, to my surprise, I feel pretty great.

The people around, mostly bears and tigers, give me big smiles, and Pike, standing a couple yards away, does too. Even Brick shoots me a thumbs-up in between autographs. In the bright light, eyes and smiles shine out from the crowd at me, but then, all of the fans here who came out to see us have shining eyes and smiles and more. They're not just here to get autographs; they're here to give back to us, to tell us that even though we came up one point short, they're still our fans, still proud of us.

Proud of us. I think back to the people who have said that to me recently, and whether I let it really sink in. A handwritten note flashes into my memory; I let it linger for a moment. It's probably still sitting on top of my trash. I feel bad about that. I resolve to take it out when I get home.

Then we're in the airport, out of the sun and in the cool building. On the wall of the arrival lounge, the airport personnel have put up a huge banner saying, "Welcome Back Firebirds," and all the employees have signed it with little messages.

Some of the guys stop and look, others just walk on by, already on their phones. I take a moment and read some of the messages. I can't help but smile. There's pressure in this job, but sometimes, even if you don't come out on top, the people will still love you. Even if you're a gay football player. I touch the spot on my ribs where I can still feel the kid's hug. Maybe especially if you're a gay football player.

It's hard to make myself walk on. After this banner, we'll all be going our separate ways, some of us on a bus back to where our trucks are parked, some of us getting picked up by spouses. It's like the end of school, except that vacation is a prelude now, not a goal. My ribs ache, my foot twinges, and the day-after soreness pervades my body, made worse by the plane flight. But there's no workout tomorrow, no stretching and camaraderie and film study. My playbook isn't in my bag; it's in the massive trunks the team shipped back separately with the equipment, our helmets and uniforms and all the things going into storage for a few months.

A paw lands on my shoulder. My whiskers twitch, and I turn to see Gerrard, Carson trailing behind him. "Take a week or so," he says, "then workouts at my place a few times a week?"

I grin. Of course Gerrard doesn't waste time starting workouts. "Can I bring, um…" I founder mid-sentence, realizing that I want to bring Lee, but I don't know if he'll want to come. Fortunately, Zillo walks by just then, so I grab his arm. "This guy?"

Zillo looks startled; Gerrard looks faintly disapproving. "If he really wants to work."

"What?" Zillo's ears flatten. He looks between the two of us.

"Off-season workouts," I say. "No argument. You're coming."

"Oh, um." He looks at Gerrard. "Yeah. Sure. I guess. You got my number, right?"

"I do," I say, turning on my phone to make sure.

When Zillo walks off, Gerrard fixes me with a look. "You make sure he comes," he says. "I'm not going to waste time running after him."

"I got it." I wonder what I let myself in for. But it's okay; Zillo's a good guy and maybe he'll pick up some work ethic.

Gerrard walks off, and I expect Carson to follow, but he doesn't. He sticks his paws in his pockets and sways his feline tail, watching the coyote go, and then he turns to me. "You can bring whoever you want," he says.

Just like that, like it's no big deal. "Uh. Thanks."

His muzzle twists, and it takes me a moment to process that he's smiling at me. "Shit builds up during the season. Off-season, relax and work it out."

"Yeah. Thanks," I repeat, and lift a paw to wave as he walks off.

My phone beeps. I take it out of my pocket and look at the text message, which might have been sent just now, or at any time while I was in the air. I read the two words once, twice, and then just stare at them, hearing them in his voice. They feel vastly meaningful and at the same time completely redundant. Just like that fox, to choose his words that way. I slide my thumb over them and put the phone back in my pocket. There's time to decide what the next step is.

Well, fuck. I *know* what the next step is. I just have to decide when to take it.

Epilogue (Lee)

Monday night. Hal's off on a date with Pol, practically ran right to her the moment we got off the plane. I'm rattling around the apartment that isn't mine, thinking too much in circles around my head. I need to write up the Vince King trial, and I want to write some stuff about Polecki coming out, in case anyone wants a football player's boyfriend's perspective (not ex-boyfriend; I refuse to believe that). Hanging around with Hal has rubbed off a reporter's lifestyle on me, I guess. And there's Gena; I want to call and ask her how Fisher's doing, whether I should get Hal together with him. The lack of information about his condition after the game makes me nervous, though it's hardly the biggest thing on my mind.

The TV and Internet are full of the championship game and Polecki's startling coming-out speech. A pair of analysts trying to be funny have rated his coming-out speech compared to Dev's. It's close, but Dev's wins because it was first. They talk about what it all means for the future of gay rights, for the UFL, for pro sports. They speculate on which sport will be next.

It's hard to watch. Mostly it reminds me that Dev hasn't answered my text. In Yerba, I could see the future; here in Chevali, I'm mired in the present uncertainty and loneliness, sweeping my tail across the carpet as I pace around, leaving more fur behind. I already vacuumed earlier today, already cleaned the dishes. The living room is as tidy as I can make it without disturbing Hal's things. I could look at apartments up in the Yerba area, but I don't want to take that step yet; I could (and probably should) look at the boards for the upcoming football draft.

I could just sit at the window and wonder why the dry air and the smell of the desert and cactus make me feel useless now.

It's a glorious evening outside, all purple night sky above and cool breezes below. A family of desert rats ambles down the street, the mother pushing a stroller, the father having an animated conversation with the daughter who barely comes up to his waist. Walking in the other direction, a cacomistle and coyote, both male, both about my age, converse animatedly over their Starbucks cups. They might be a couple.

I turn away from the window and draw my knees up on the couch. There's plenty of beer left in the fridge, Hal's generic light brand. Perfect feeling-sorry-for-myself refreshment.

Beer in paw, unsatisfying taste lingering on my tongue, I am feeling like a crappy country song when there's a knock at the door. I ignore it at first, and then it comes again, louder. I slam the bottle onto the end table hard, and stalk to the door to answer it.

"Hal's not home," I call through the door.

Then my nose catches up to my brain and I stop, throwing back the bolts on the door even before I hear the rumbled answer on the other side: "Good."

He's standing there in the hallway, all six-foot-two and gorgeous, in a neat suit with his Firebirds tie and a light saffron shirt that I bought for him. His gold eyes freeze me to the spot, icing my muzzle shut. He raises one eyebrow. "Wiley Farrel," he says in an approximation of my voice.

"Why…" I clear my suddenly-tight throat. "You didn't answer my…"

"Mm-hmm," he nods. "Was going to, but, uh. I think…I think we need to…" He coughs, clears his throat.

My ears perk up. "Talk?"

He shakes his head. His whiskers twitch in a smile. "Well, yeah. But I was gonna say 'fuck.'"

"Um." I inhale so hard I worry I might hyperventilate, just drinking in the scent and sight of him. "This is—uh—this is Hal's place…"

"Uh-huh." He grins. "He said it was okay as long as I take you and the sheets home after."

I flick my ears and try to hide the flush in them. I do shift my legs, as much to let him know that I still want that as to ease the awkward pressure rising in my groin. "Don't we want different things, still?"

"Yeah." He is trying hard not to lean in closer, inching forward and then pulling himself back. "But I dunno. I don't think we can't both be doing those things. And I think we can do them better together."

"So we should talk." My tail swishes behind me. I try to hold it still, but that pressure isn't any better. I let it go again.

Now he does take a step forward, inches from me. He drops his voice. "Yeah. But I think we should fuck first. Because I want you so bad right now that if we talk first, I'll agree to anything just to get you in bed again."

"Well, if that's what you want…" I can smell the answer to my question, loud and clear.

He lowers his head. His breath smells of something sweet and meaty, probably one of those burgers he loves so much. "I want it for the right reasons."

"So why should I let you in bed before we talk?" Like I have a choice.

I don't even see his paw come up under my chin. He lifts my muzzle gently with strong, warm fingers. "Because you want it for the right reasons, too."

My breath catches. I know right then I'll say anything that will bring him in the door, and I know how dangerous that is. "All right, doc," I say.

The smile lights up his muzzle then, and he gives me a short tiger laugh at the nickname. His paws reach around to pull me toward him as his body steps forward, muscle and force driving me back into the apartment. His arms are iron around me, the rise and fall of his chest a quickening steam engine. "C'mere," he murmurs into my ear, and kicks the door shut behind us. "Stud."

I'm hard as a rock already, and I want to just drag him back to the office and pull that suit off him. I know this isn't the time for talking, but words burst out of me before I can stop them. "I watched you," I say. "In the game. You were great. I watched every minute. I'm—"

He lowers his muzzle to mine, silences me in the very best way. "I know," he says in his velvet voice when he lifts his muzzle away, and his breath is so welcome on my nose and whiskers that I close my eyes, then open them again because I don't want to stop looking at him. "I felt you there. We can talk about it…" His paw reaches down to my rear. "After."

"Okay, but. But. This is just for us to talk." I pant, my ear flicking. My heart's racing and I feel giddy. I can't even try to stop my tail from its back-and-forth exultation. My paws lock together at the small of his back, resting above his tail. "It doesn't mean…doesn't mean everything's suddenly fine."

"Uh-huh." He scoops me up as easy as thought, my tail dangling free. "Which way to your bedroom?"

And I throw my arms around his neck and press my muzzle into his shoulder, and I show him.

Goddamn tigers.

Afterword

Dev and Lee, having finished the fourth book tied, will have to return in "Over Time" (January 2016), the fifth and final book in this series. But I have more stories of them and their friends in my mind, including a novel that takes place a few years down the line, so don't despair. The "Out of Position" series has always had a definite end in my mind; I just didn't expect it to take three quarters of a million words to reach.

Many, many thanks to those of you who have followed them for the better part of a decade now, from short stories posted on my website to this novel. Your support and excitement helps me make more books. Extra thanks to the people who have made and continue to make these books special: my writing colleagues Ryan Campbell, David Cowan, Malcolm Cross, Kevin Frane, and Watts Martin, who have provided inestimably helpful feedback; artists BlackTeagan and Kenket for their amazing illustrations; editor Jeff Eddy and Sofawolf Press for their unfailing support and professionalism; and my husband Kit Silver for his feedback on the story, his enthusiasm for it, and his love and support for me. I have said many times and will say many times again: if you love these stories, you owe him a thank-you, because they would not be possible without him.

See you all in a year and a half!

-Kyell, July 2014

CAST OF CHARACTERS

Chevali Firebirds (= starters)*

Gerrard Marvell	coyote	middle linebacker (Mike)*
Carson Omba	leopard	strong-side linebacker (Sam)*
Fisher Kingston	tiger	defensive end
"Brick"	black bear	defensive tackle*
Colin	fox	cornerback*
Lightning Strike	cheetah	wide receiver *
Ty Nakamura	fox	wide receiver/kick returner* (#88)
Aston	wolf	quarterback*
"Jaws"	wolverine	running back*
Norton	cheetah	cornerback*
Vonni DiCarlo	fox	cornerback*
Pace	jaguar	safety*
"Charm"	stallion	kicker*
Corey Mitchell	cougar	weak-side linebacker, started until injured, when his spot was taken by Dev
"Zillo"	coyote	linebacker (backup)
"Pike"	polar bear	defensive end (backup)*
Kodi	brown bear	defensive tackle (backup)
Jake	black bear	defensive tackle (practice squad)
Baki	cheetah	QB/WR (practice squad)
"Steez" Mikilios	cougar	linebackers coach
Vern Samuelson	wolf	head coach
John Corcoran	fox	Firebirds' owner
David Rodriguez	jackrabbit	general manager

Hellentown Pilots

Andy Buck	lion	quarterback
Kniss	wolf	linebacker
Price	wolf	linebacker
Aden	fox	wide receiver (#83)

Crystal City Sabretooths

McCrae	wolf	quarterback (#10)
Bridger	fox	wide receiver
Polecki	coyote	linebacker (#55)
Yates	coyote	linebacker (#52)

Family

Mikhail	tiger	Dev's father
Duscha	tiger	Dev's mother
Gregory	tiger	Dev's brother
Marta	tiger	Gregory's wife, Dev's sister-in-law
Brenly	fox	Lee's father
Eileen	fox	Lee's mother
Carolyn	fox	Lee's aunt
Angela Marvell	coyote	Gerrard's wife
Gena Kingston	tiger	Fisher's wife
Daria DiCarlo	fox	Vonni's wife
Jaren Marvell	coyote	Gerrard's son (older)
Mike Marvell	coyote	Gerrard's son (younger)
Bradley Kingston	tiger	Fisher's son (older)
Fisher Kingston, Jr.	tiger	Fisher's son (younger)

Other

Hal Kinnel	swift fox	reporter
Peter Emmanuel	fox	Yerba Whalers' GM

About the Author

Kyell Gold took up furry erotica writing after high school, making the team at his small liberal arts college as a walk-on. He was drafted late by Sofawolf and blossomed in the professional league, earning four Ursa Major awards in his first three years as a pro for his novels and short stories. He has since won eight more Ursa Major awards, including one for "In Between," the first Dev and Lee story, one for *Out of Position*, which also won two Rainbow Awards for gay fiction, and one for *Isolation Play*, the second Dev and Lee book.

His various online presences are linked from *www.kyellgold.com*, and you can follow him on Twitter at @KyellGold. In the off-season, he lives in California with his husband.

About the Artist

Blotch was one of the top-rated high school furry artist prospects of 2006 and starred in college before being made the #1 pick of Sofawolf. He's excelled in his first two years, garnering several convention GOH appearances. He has won the last three Ursa Major awards for Best Published Illustration (including a 2009 win for the cover of *Out of Position*), and in 2008, his full-color graphic novel *Dog's Days of Summer* won an Ursa Major for Best Other Literary Work. His next project is the Nordguard Adventure, a painted graphic novel to be released in three parts. *Across Thin Ice*, the first volume, has earned wide acclaim, and part two, *Under Dark Skies*, is forthcoming.

His all-ages gallery can be found at *www.blotchinc.com*. For more information on the Nordguard Adventure, please visit the official website at *www.nordguard.com*.

About Sofawolf Press

Sofawolf Press was founded in 1999 to provide a venue to showcase great writers of anthropomorphic fiction and to promote the genre to a wider audience.

Since the debut of its flagship publication, Anthrolations, a literary anthology of short stories, the Press has added to its lineup other magazine-length anthologies, novels, shared-world anthologies, and other novel-length collections, comics and graphic novels, artists' sketchbooks, and calendars. The Press continues to seek out new and creative ways of expanding its offerings of printed creations. Sofawolf's publications have won twenty Ursa Major awards, and in 2012, Ursula Vernon's *Digger* gave Sofawolf Press its first Hugo Award.

Please visit their website at *www.sofawolf.com* for a full list of titles available from Sofawolf Press. Thanks for reading!